Northern Light

by

Catherine Winchester

A sequel to North and South by Elizabeth Gaskell

Northern Light

by

Catherine Winchester

This is a work of fiction. Names, characters, places, and incidents, other than those clearly in the public domain, are the product of the author's imagination or are used fictitiously, and any resemblance to actual persons, living or dead, business establishments, events, or locales is entirely coincidental.

Acknowledgements

To my family and friends who supported this endeavour. Without your help and feedback this novel wouldn't be half as good as it is.

And of course, thanks must go to Elizabeth Gaskell, the author of North and South. Without her wonderful story I would never have been inspired to write this sequel.

Preface

I debated for a long time on how I should write this book. Should I stay faithful to Elizabeth Gaskell's style and try to imitate her? Or should I create something new and uniquely my own?

In the end, writing the book actually decided this for me and it came out as something of a hybrid. The language I use is very much my own, though perhaps more formal than I might use in conversation!

Also, while I researched the Victorian period extensively, I was very aware that I was writing for a 21st century audience and that the morals of the day just weren't going to cut it for a modern day audience. One example of this is that in North and South, Margaret and John never even share a kiss; not even after they have declared their love for each other! I have therefore attempted to acknowledge the standards of the day while still having my hero and heroine flout them on occasion.

In the end I knew that I would never please everyone with this story, no matter now I wrote it or how much time and trouble I took, however I do hope that the majority of you will find this book, it's characters and the story entertaining and faithful to the original.

After all, this story comes from my love of the original and my overwhelming desire to find out what happened next.

North and South: A Brief Recap

Due to a crisis of conscience, Mr Hale, the reverend of Helstone, resigned his post and moved his family north to Milton where, with the help of his friend Mr Bell, he began teaching the classics.

John Thornton was a Milton mill master who had been removed from school upon his fathers death at age 16, and had always regretted his lack of education. On the advice of the mills landlord, Mr Bell, he sought lessons in the classics from Mr Hale and over time they formed a friendship.

Mr Hale's daughter, Margaret, did not make such a favourable impression on Mr Thornton, for she had been educated by her rich Aunt in London and with her refined ways, he thought her haughty and that she looked down on him, a rough, northern manufacturer. However he could not help falling in love with her grace and elegance, not to mention her spirit!

Though in greatly reduced circumstances, Margaret tried to make the best of her new life in the north, making friends with the local mill workers and doing her best to stay happy, even though she found herself having to assist their servant, Dixon, with the household chores.

Following a lengthy strike there is a riot, during which Margaret tried to shield Mr Thornton from the rioters. After this he feels compelled to propose to her, not just because she had made a show of herself but also because he could not keep his feelings quiet any longer. Margaret, feeling insulted that he was proposing in an attempt to save her reputation and that he was not of her class, refused him.

Mr Thornton, though wounded by her rejection, is determined to prove himself a gentleman and continues to visit the house, to read with her father and send many kind gifts to her mother, who is unwell.

As her mother's condition worsens, Margaret writes to her brother, Frederick, who is living abroad for fear of being captured and court marshalled by the navy, asking him to return to see their mother one last time before she dies. Believing himself to be safe since they have moved north, away from their friends, he returns to England.

After their mother passes away, Dixon spots a sailor

named Leonards, whom she knows from Helstone and, fearing for his life, Frederick leaves immediately on the night train. Margaret hugs him goodbye at the station but they are seen by Mr Thornton. Not knowing that she has a brother, he believes the young man to be her lover. Leonards also sees them at the station and after an altercation, he falls and hits his head while Frederick escapes on the train.

The next day Leonards is found dead and Margaret questioned by the police. Fearing that Frederick has not left the country yet, she lies about being at the station. Mr Thornton, though he knows her words to be a lie, covers for her and the case is dropped.

Slowly Margaret begins to think that she has misjudged this manufacturer, but he in turn is hurt by her forward behaviour with this unknown man and claims to no longer have any feelings for her.

When her father dies soon afterwards, Margaret's aunt comes to remove her back to London. Both she and Mr Thornton believe they will never see each other again.

In London, Mr Bell comes to visit Margaret and as he had no children of his own, he tells her that he plans to make her his heir. Not many months later, he dies. Though she is of means now, Margaret still believes Mr Thornton is indifferent to her, and so stays with her aunt in London.

Because of financial troubles caused by the strike, Mr Thornton's mill is forced to close it's doors and lay off the workers. The only good news he hears is from one of his mill hands who had befriended Miss Hale. He informs Mr Thornton that the man at the station was her brother and even though she is lost to him, he takes comfort in that news.

As Miss hale is now his landlady and he has to end his tenancy of the mill, he journeys to London to make the arrangements. Margaret is upset that the mill has failed and comes up with a plan to loan him some £18,000 so that he might continue his enterprise.

Alone in the drawing room, Margaret explains her idea to him and John dares to hope that she might now share his feelings, which she admits she does and that she is ashamed of how she treated him in Milton.

The books ends with the following exchange.

"How shall I ever tell Aunt Shaw?" she whispered, after some time of delicious silence.

"Let me speak to her."

"Oh, no! I owe it to her, but what will she say?'

"I can guess. Her first exclamation will be, 'That man!'"

"Hush!" said Margaret, "or I shall try and show you your mother's indignant tones as she says, "'That woman!'"

Chapter One

John laughed at Margaret's teasing.

"Then let us run away," John suggested with a teasing smile. "We can be in Gretna Green by nightfall."

"Oh, if only that were possible." Margaret sounded rueful.

John had only been jesting but Margaret's words held more than a note of longing.

"Just say the word, Margaret, and it will be."

Margaret smiled and cupped his face with her hand, running her thumb over his cheek.

"I fear that is the coward's way out. No, people must be told."

"But there is nothing to say that they must be told today."

Margaret was about to argue when she realised he was right.

"Although," she cautioned, "The longer we wait, the longer it will be until we can be together."

"Nonsense." He smiled and Margaret's heart skipped a beat, for truly his was the most handsome smile she had ever seen. "If it is your wish, I shall return to Milton today and start making the arrangements."

Margaret frowned and John felt a brief sense of foreboding. "You do want to return to Milton?" he asked.

"Yes, of course." She removed her hand from his cheek and took hold of his hand, squeezing it firmly. "Actually I was just wondering how long it will be before I am allowed to return."

John felt his spirits soar once again at her words, pleased that she was eager to return to him. He reached out to gently push an escaped tendril of hair off her forehead and paused, for she was looking at him with such adoration in her eyes that it took his breath away for a moment. On impulse he leaned forward and kissed her lips gently.

At first he thought that Margaret would not respond, and why would she approve of such an indecent move? Not only was his behaviour inappropriate but they would be inviting censure, for someone could happen upon them at any moment. Margaret only hesitated for a moment though and as he was about to pull away, she returned the kiss.

John Thornton had not thought it possible to be any more in love with Margaret Hale than he already was, but these last few seconds had proved him wrong.

When he finally found the strength to pull away from her,

Margaret kept her eyes closed, not wanting the moment to end but when she finally looked at him, she saw the love that he clearly felt for her was written on his every feature. Indeed she had never seen him looking so relaxed and happy. Truly, he looked as if an unimaginable weight had been lifted from his shoulders.

"Margaret." Her name sounded like a sweet caress on his lips.

"John", she said, cupping his face in both her hands. "My John."

Never had two words filled him with such pleasure before. "My Margaret," he replied, gratified to see how his possessive words pleased her.

Drawing his face towards her, she kissed him again, marvelling at how right it felt.

"You must return to Milton," she said, when she finally released him, lowering her hands demurely into her lap, where they probably should have stayed.

"I don't want to leave you here alone. At least let me stay until you have told your aunt."

"No." She shook her head. "I have waited long enough for this and I am impatient to begin our life together. You have waited even longer; do you not feel the same?"

"Aye." John nodded, accepting her logic, though it still pained him to leave her. "I will write every day," he promised.

"And I."

John knew that he should probably leave now before the temptation became unbearable, but he couldn't bring himself to walk away. Once again he claimed another kiss from her, this one tinged with sadness though, for they both knew it would be probably be many days, though more likely weeks before they were reunited again.

"I'll miss you," John said, resting his forehead against hers.

"And I you," she replied. "Now, you must go before my will fails me and I make a dreadful scene as I beg you to stay."

And as it was her request, he found that he was suddenly able to stand and move away. He backed away to the door, unwilling to lose sight of her a second before he had to. He paused at the door and they stared at each other for a long while, then finally he reached behind himself, opened the door and exited.

The short journey from the parlour to the street seemed

suffocating and when he reached the outside, he gulped in great lungfuls of fresh air as he turned back to look at the house.

He stood there for longer than was reasonable, staring up at the house until finally reason made him turn away and head towards the station. The sooner he got back to Milton, the sooner they could begin their lives together.

Margaret stayed where she was for a few moments while she regained her composure. She gathered up the legal documents before her and took them with her to her room. She expected to be stopped and questioned on the way but she made it to her bedroom without encountering anyone. She went straight to the window, though she knew John would be long gone by now. To her surprise, she was in time to see him turn and leave. He had obviously found their parting as difficult as she.

Margaret watched until he was out of sight and tried to fight the longing she felt to go after him. She wanted nothing more than to follow him home to Milton and as she considered the idea, she realised that she looked forward to seeing Milton again.

She knew how impulsive her desire was but she also knew that these next few weeks would be interminable as she waited for the rest of her life to begin.

"So near and yet so far," she whispered, pressing her forehead to the cool glass.

She thought of going to speak with her aunt; she would have to be told at some point so it may as well be sooner rather than later, but she couldn't bring herself to taint the happiness she felt with her aunt's almost certain disdain for her losing her heart to a tradesman. She went to her writing desk, resolving to write to John immediately but as she picked up the pen, another thought occurred to her. With much haste she wrote a note and slipped it into an envelope.

Though it had been less than an hour since he had left Margaret, John's heart felt heavy from their separation. How cruel life was that they should discover their feelings for one another while living so very far apart.

He saw the train to Milton pull in and with a sigh, he left the waiting room and stepped onto the platform, staying near the edge until the departing passengers had exited the train. He walked along the concourse until he found an empty carriage, for he found that he was not in the mood for company but as he reached forward to open the door, a lady's hand rested on his arm.

"Margaret! What are you doing here?" he asked, confused that she should have followed him. His confusion deepened when she handed him her bag.

"I have come to join you." she stated.

"You're coming home with me?"

"Yes." She smiled.

"And what of your aunt?"

"I left her a note."

"A note!"

"Yes, explaining that I have returned to Milton and will write again as soon as I arrive."

"Why didn't you speak to her?"

"Because I am happy, and she will surely try to steal my pleasure from me."

John couldn't find fault with that logic. "But what will people say?"

"I am of age and I am self sufficient, so whilst I do not like being the subject of gossip, I find that I can bear the idea with equanimity. My heart is pure before God and that is what matters."

Realising that the train would be moving again very soon, Margaret reached out to open the door and stepped into the carriage, taking a seat by the window and looking to where John still stood in the doorway. After a moment's hesitation, he stepped in and closed the door behind himself; none too soon as the whistle sounded to signify the train was about to leave.

He stowed Margaret's bag in the rack above her head then looked from her seat to the opposite one. He knew where he should sit but when Margaret smiled at him, he ignored his better judgement and sat beside her, stealing another kiss.

When they separated he smirked. "Do you have any idea how many people you will have upset with this impulsive decision?"

"I do, but as long as you are not upset with me, I find that I am not too concerned."

"Margaret, how you continue to impress me with your strong and free spirit."

"I shall remind you of that one day when we are bickering like an old married couple."

"As long as we are together long enough to be called an old married couple, I shan't mind very much."

The journey passed in a pleasurable haze as they held hands, kissed and enjoyed the feeling of contentment that they both had now that they had finally found each other, but as the train drew closer to Milton, the relaxed atmosphere in their carriage began to disperse as reality threatened to encroach on their magical time together.

These last few hours had felt like a dream to them both and in the privacy of their carriage, they had been free to show their affection for one another, free from fear of censure.

As though he knew this might be one of the last kisses they were able to share for quite some time, John cupped Margaret's cheek with his hand and stared at her for a few moments as if committing her face to his memory, before he leaned in and gently kissed her.

When he pulled away, they both looked slightly forlorn.

"Will you come home with me?" he asked.

"There is nothing I would like more," Margaret smiled, "but I feel we both know that won't be possible until we are married."

John nodded, knowing that she could give no other answer.

"I could leave until our wedding day," he offered. "At least then I would know you were taken care of."

Margaret smiled sweetly at his consideration and reached out to cup his cheek, brushing her thumb over the stubble she found there.

"I fear that such an unusual arrangement would only incite gossip. Besides, I know how deeply your mother cares for you, I would not like to separate you from her prematurely. I feel she will value this time to adjust to our new situation. No, I shall stay at a hotel for now and try and find more permanent lodgings tomorrow."

"As you wish." John placed his hand over hers, savouring her touch.

"Do you..." Margaret was unsure how to word her fear.

Knowing she had something grave to ask, he took her hand from his face and clasped it between both of his.

"Yes?"

"Do you think she will accept me?" she asked hesitantly.

"How could she not?" he asked.

"I have done little to incite her warm feelings. Indeed, considering how dreadfully I have behaved towards you, I am still shocked that you feel anything other than disdain for me."

"Mother has only ever wanted what is best for me and your gesture of faith in me will be more than enough to convince her of your deep feeling. She may find it difficult at first but I'm certain that she will come to love you as I do."

Margaret couldn't help the sly smile that crept onto her lips.

"Not exactly as you do, I hope."

John laughed. He had been aware of Margaret's courage, integrity, sharp wit and strong mind but until now he had been unaware of her sense of humour. Now that she was showing this new side of herself to him, he found it a very pleasing addition to her character.

For her part, until now Margaret had never realised how little John smiled or laughed. She had seen quite a few examples of both since this morning and she found him all the more attractive for it.

"Will you allow me to escort you to the hotel, at least?" John asked when his laughter faded.

"I would like nothing more."

"And would you join mother and me for dinner this evening?"

"I probably shouldn't; I will have much to do this evening. I must first write to my aunt and cousin to explain properly what has happened, then I must write to Dixon and arrange for my things to be sent to me."

John nodded and looked out of the window. By his reckoning they had perhaps only ten minutes before they arrived in Milton.

"And you are sure about this?" he asked, turning back to her. "You would trust me with your investment."

"I can think of few people I would trust more."

"But there are some?" he asked.

Margaret looked up, fearing she had offended him but she was relieved when she saw the smile on his lips. He was teasing her.

She glanced out of the window then down at their joined hands.

"I cannot believe that we will soon be separated, unable to show the affection we have enjoyed these past few hours."

"We will soon be free to show our love," he assured her. "We shall be wed at the very first opportunity."

"I fear that will not come soon enough for my tastes," she confessed.

"It will be difficult," he agreed. "But the promise of what is to come will help us both endure."

"Yes," she smiled.

"Have you given much thought to a wedding?" he asked, knowing that Fannie's wedding had taken months to arrange because of her extravagant tastes.

"I would like something simple," she said. "I do not wish to attend any engagement balls or parties, though I am certain we will have to endure some. I simply wish to declare my love for you in front of God and our friends."

His heart swelled with pride.

"Even given your new found wealth?" he asked, still finding to hard to believe she didn't want something more extravagant.

"Even then. I love you, John." His name still sounded strange on her lips but she enjoyed saying it and was getting used to it. "I would much rather our resources were put towards our life together than spent on expensive lace and exotic flowers."

"People will say I am a gold digger," he warned her. "That I am simply marrying you to save my factory."

"Yes," she looked down, feeling guilty for the slight it might place on his character. "But we know the truth and that surely is all that counts." She risked looking up into his eyes, worried that he might be pained by the thought of the gossip that would follow him.

"I do not much care for the idle speculation of others," he assured her. "I care only for you, and I thank you for your faith in me. You don't know how much that means to me."

"I have had complete faith in you for a while now, I only wish I had been brave enough to tell you how I felt."

"I might still have denied my feelings," he said, honestly. His words might be hurtful but they were truthful and he wasn't in the habit of deceit. "I was so hurt, jealous even, I-"

"Yes," Margaret cut him off, knowing full well of what he spoke. "There is something I must share with you, about that night at the railway station and why I lied."

"Hush," he said. "He was your brother, I know that now. I

14

am sorry that I ever doubted you."

"You know?" She sounded surprised. "How?"

"Your old friend Higgins told me.

"But how did he-"

"His younger daughter, Mary, helped Dixon in the kitchen while he was over and shared what she picked up with her father. I don't know all the details because Higgins doesn't, but I know enough to understand that you were protecting him."

"I shall tell you everything," she assured him. "I know I can trust you to keep Frederick's secret."

"Is that his name?"

"Yes," she smiled as she thought of him. "He joined the Navy after school but he had not been in the service long when he was assigned to a new ship. His new captain was a tyrant, a monster, beating those weaker than himself to within an inch of their lives, including the children. Frederick and a few of the others felt they had no choice but to revolt and they set the captain and those loyal to him adrift in a row boat. The Navy called it a mutiny and until Mother fell ill, he had not set foot in this county since. "

"That was very brave of him," John observed.

"Or very foolish, though I confess, I do feel very proud of him. We write but even after all this time he is still in grave danger should the Navy ever find him. He lived in South America for a while but now lives in Spain, a town called Cadiz." She smiled wistfully. "We were very close as children and I only wish that he could meet you."

"Maybe, once the mill is up and running, we could take a delayed honeymoon there."

"Yes," she smiled. "I believe I would like that very much, though I wouldn't want to take you away from the mill if you felt you couldn't leave it."

"Mother is quite capable of managing it for a time in my absence."

"Well, let us see," she said. "There are many changes to come and I feel our attentions would be best focused elsewhere, for a while at least."

"How soon do you think we can be married?" he asked.

"I hope within the month. Now that I have found you, I find I do not wish to wait a moment longer than necessary." She smiled. "And what of the mill, how long will it take for you to resume operations?"

"Almost immediately," he assured her. "The mill closed without any debts left to settle and I still have some funds in reserve, plus we are still owed money from a few filled orders. I also have a few new orders in the pipeline that I may still be able to bid for."

"And what of ordering more cotton?"

"There is enough in the storage sheds to get things started, though I will have to order more immediately if we are not to face a shortage."

"Good." She smiled though it quickly faded as the next thought occurred to her. "I fear it might be bad form to ask Henry to continue as my financial advisor. Do you think Mr. Latimer might be willing to undertake the transfer of funds for me? He was, after all, Mr. Bell's banker."

"I'm sure he would be delighted," John assured her. He didn't want to ask the next question, fearing her answer, but he felt compelled to. "Margaret, I must ask you, was there ever anything between you and Mr. Lennox?"

"No," she assured him. "Though I must confess that he did ask for my hand once, just before we left Helstone."

"You refused him?" He felt a pang of jealousy as he realised someone else had asked for her hand.

"Yes. I have never viewed him as anything more than a friend."

John swallowed, pleased to realise that although Lennox had asked her, she had chosen him.

As the train began to slow he kissed her once more, knowing that their time together was nearly over. She responded fervently, realising, as he did, that propriety would keep them from displaying any affection in public until they were married. As the train slowed further they separated, and none too soon as the station buildings appeared through the carriage window.

"We're here," she said sadly as she looked out of the window.

John didn't reply.

"These past hours have felt like a dream," she continued, unable to turn and look at him yet. "I can't help thinking that reality will soon intrude and spoil things."

"We will not let it," John assured her. "Reality must be faced but I don't believe someone as strong as you would ever let a little thing like reality keep you from living your dreams."

"No." She turned to him and smiled. "Nor you, I believe."

"Never. You are mine now, Margaret, in all but name and I intend to rectify that as soon as is humanly possible."

With heavy hearts they exited the carriage and climbed into a waiting carriage outside the station. John dropped her at the Mitre Hotel and saw her to the reception desk. He wanted to accompany her to her room and make sure she was settled but he knew that would harm her reputation.

"Will you come to dinner tomorrow evening?" he asked her.

"I shall be glad to." She smiled. "I will speak with Mr. Latimer tomorrow and find out how quickly I can transfer the funds to you."

"Do you wish me to accompany you?"

"No, I'm sure the arrangements will be long winded and tedious. Your time is better spent getting the mill running again."

John took her hand and raised it to his lips, pressing a dry kiss to the back of it.

"I will send a carriage for you at seven. Until tomorrow."

The thought of being parted from him was almost unbearable and she wanted to throw her arms around him and demand that he stay with her, but Margaret was not a fool and she knew they had taken too many risks already. So instead, she smiled and bit her lip to stop herself from saying something quite indecent as she reluctantly stepped back.

"I look forward to it," she said, truthfully.

John backed away, unwilling to lose sight of her a moment sooner than absolutely necessary.

When he neared the entrance he hesitated, smiled, then finally turned and took his leave of her.

Margaret took a few moments to compose herself before turning to the reception desk.

Chapter Two

Hannah Thornton was darning one of John's shirts when he came in. She closed her eyes in relief as she heard the front door close and his familiar footfalls making their way towards her.

He was home safe.

She didn't look up as he came in, needing a minute to prepare herself for the despair she would surely see in his eyes, for not only did he have to give up his precious mill, he had to go begging to the woman he loved, asking to be released from his tenancy.

To her surprise he leaned over the back of her chair and kissed her cheek.

"Mother." His tone was warm rather than broken and, surprised, she turned to him. He looked relaxed, even happy.

"John?"

"We are saved, Mother," he said, taking the seat opposite her. He smiled to himself, his eyes focused on nothing. "We are saved," he repeated softly.

"John!" His unusual behaviour was disconcerting and she spoke more sharply that she might have wished. "Stop this nonsense and tell me what has happened."

He looked up at her. "She loves me, Mother, and she wishes to invest some of her fortune in the mill."

Mrs. Thornton was quite speechless for a moment as many thoughts occurred to her simultaneously. Finally she began to sort them into some kind of order.

"She has told you her feelings?" she asked. She hardly needed to ask who he was talking about.

"She has. If only I had not led her to believe that I no longer cared for her, we may have found each other a great deal sooner."

Mrs. Thornton frowned. "And the mill?" she prompted.

"She came to me, offering me some eighteen thousand pounds to invest on her behalf."

She inhaled sharply and swallowed before continuing.

"She has that much to spare?"

"Aye."

This was quite an unexpected turn of events and she really didn't know how to feel about it. On the one hand she still disliked Miss Hale greatly for the pain she had caused her son and Mrs. Thornton still felt her to be a proud

18

and disapproving young woman.

And yet she had both accepted her son and offered him a chance to restart the mill. Given the great sum of money involved, it surely showed the high regard in which Miss Hale now held her son.

Or perhaps she wasn't doing this for her son, perhaps this was for the hands, like Higgins. Then again, why would she agree to marry John if she did not care for him?

"And you have asked her to marry you?" She needed that point confirmed before she could order her thoughts any further.

"I have, and she has said yes."

Perhaps, she thought, it was Miss Hale's pride that finally allowed her to say yes. Now that she was of means, she may well feel as though she had more power than the last time he had asked for her hand in marriage. There would surely be gossip but it was her son who would be branded the fortune hunter this time.

Yes, she was certain that Miss Hale had always harboured feelings for her son. Her pride and the airs and graces she gave herself must have prevented her from acting on those feelings previously. Imagine, a lady accepting the hand and fortune of a Milton manufacturer! Now though, she was rescuing him, she was his saviour, how much better that must be for her inflated opinion of herself.

She put her sewing aside and reached out to take his hand.

"Are you certain this is what you want, John? There will be talk; people will say you are only marrying her because of her inheritance, they will belittle your hard work and undermine your good reputation."

John sat forward and looked into her eyes.

"As things stand, Mother, I have no need of my good reputation."

"That is hardly the point, we both know you will be great again one day."

"Perhaps." He leaned back in the chair. Mrs. Thornton would almost describe him as lounging. "But since when have we cared what others say? Even if I could find a way to get the mill running again, it would be a hollow victory without her at my side."

"And what of her indiscretions? She has ignited the gossip of the town twice already with her forward ways, and only one of those incidents involved you."

"The other gentleman was her brother. There was no impropriety on Margaret's part," John assured her.

"Then why didn't she tell us that?" Mrs. Thornton accused.

"She was protecting him. I don't know most of the details but he is on the run and only returned to this country because their mother was dying."

"So her brother is a criminal!" she sounded shocked.

"Only in name. She has told me of his supposed crime and I can't say I would have acted any differently given the circumstances."

"So you are determined, then?"

"I am."

Mrs. Thornton swallowed down her feelings and picked up her sewing again.

"So where is Miss Hale?"

"She's staying at a hotel overnight. Tomorrow she will try and find more permanent accommodation until we are married."

"She is here? In Milton?"

"She chose to return with me." He laughed, which Mrs. Thornton found very disconcerting. "I am sorry for laughing, Mother, but rest assured, I am not laughing at you. I know how you feel about Miss Hale but right now I feel as giddy as a school boy. I only hope that you will give her a chance, so that you might come to understand what it is that I love about her."

"I will give her a chance, John. She makes you happy and I only want what you want."

"Thank you, Mother. You will not regret it."

Mrs. Thornton could not agree, yet she couldn't not voice her opinion so she gave no reply.

Margaret was all nerves as she waited for the carriage the next evening. She tried to tell herself that she had met Mrs. Thornton many times before and this was no different, but she knew that wasn't true. Previously she had been just Miss Hale, now she was John's intended and it was imperative that she make a good impression.

Finally there was a knock at her door and she smoothed a hand over her hair, straightened her back and as calmly as she could manage, went to answer it.

"Mr. Thornton!"

"I thought we were past those formalities," he smiled.

"We are," she smiled. "You just caught me by surprise. Please, come in."

John stepped into her rooms and as soon as she had closed the door, he spun her around and captured her lips in a passionate kiss.

"My," Margaret exclaimed when he released her.

"I'm sorry. I had to collect you myself because I knew I wouldn't be able to go all evening without kissing you."

"Do not apologise, I rather enjoyed it," Margaret grinned.

"Still, we should head down to the carriage before tongues start to wag."

Though she agreed with him, Margaret smiled and reached up on her tip toes for one last kiss.

"There," she smiled impishly. "Now I believe we will be perfectly able to be the very picture of propriety for the rest of the evening."

John smiled and offered her his elbow as they headed down to the carriage. Though the driver was waiting, John helped her in himself before climbing in and sitting opposite her. The driver climbed up onto his perch and started the horses back to Marlborough Mill.

"I had a wonderful meeting with Mr. Latimer today," Margaret said. "He believes the funds can be in your account within a week, though he did try to insist we sign a contract beforehand."

"You don't want a contract?" he asked.

"I don't really see the point. Once we are married our assets will be joined, and I hardly see the point in wasting money on lawyers fees for a contract that will only be valid for a few weeks."

"You trust me that much?"

"I trust you completely."

John smiled. "I don't know what I have done to deserve such faith."

"It is not faith when you have given me ample proof of your integrity."

"You're too kind."

"I hardly think so. Considering how rude I was when we first met, I believe it is I who is undeserving of your good opinion."

John began laughing.

"What?" Margaret asked.

"I do believe we are now arguing about liking each other!"

"Yes." Margaret grinned. "Perhaps a change of topic is in order," she suggested.

"Indeed. I believe I may have found you a house," he said.

"Oh?"

"Yes. A business acquaintance of mine has retired and is travelling for a while so his house is vacant. Though far from fully staffed, there should be enough for your needs, if you can manage without a lady's maid. I have written to him explaining your circumstances and the temporary nature of your need. I expect his reply tomorrow."

"Tomorrow?" she asked, for surely it would take longer to write to someone who was abroad.

"Aye. He has only just left Milton and his first stop is to see his youngest son in London."

"And he would not mind a stranger staying in his home?"

"I don't believe so. He was saying before he left that his staff need someone to watch over them or they'll run riot."

"While the cat's away?"

"Exactly."

"Well, if he is agreeable, that would be a most satisfactory solution. And please assure him I will reimburse him for his trouble and any expenses."

"I doubt he will want anything," John assured her. "He remembers your father almost as fondly as I do."

The carriage slowed to a stop then and John got out and helped Margaret down. She stepped into the quiet courtyard and looked around.

"What?" John asked, noting her troubled expression.

"Oh, nothing, it's just... it feels wrong, being so silent I mean."

John nodded his understanding, he felt exactly the same.

"We'll make a manufacturer of you yet," he teased, taking her hand and placing it on his arm as he led her inside.

Mrs. Thornton was waiting for them in the front parlour and Margaret rushed forward to greet her.

"It is so good to see you again, Mrs. Thornton," Margaret said, shaking the other woman's hand.

"And you," she answered, though somewhat stiffly. "I hope you are settling back into life here without too many problems?"

"I'm settling in very well, thank you; it is almost as though I have never been away. Though I must confess, I do not much like living in a hotel."

"No?"

"I much prefer having my own things around me," she explained.

She had clearly said the wrong thing as Mrs. Thornton looked around the room, imagining the ways in which Margaret might want it changed.

Before the silence could become uncomfortable, one of the maids came in and announced that dinner was ready.

Although there were only three diners, the table had been set as though for one of their dinner parties. It was rather too lavish for Margaret's tastes but she complimented Mrs. Thornton nevertheless and it occurred to her that perhaps she was as nervous about this meeting as Margaret.

"I spoke to Higgins today," John opened the conversation once the first course had been served.

"Oh, how are he and the children?" Margaret asked.

"They're keeping well. He's looking forward to coming back to work."

"He must be relieved the mill is reopening, I can't see many other masters wanting to take him on."

"No, but they don't know what they're missing," John said with a wry smile.

"Oh? I take it he didn't cause you any trouble then?"

"Quite the contrary, in fact. He's responsible, reliable and he's come up with a few good ideas for the mill. In fact I'm rehiring him as the overseer."

"What happened to Williams?"

"I'm afraid his health has been failing for a few months now. The doctor does not expect him to live much longer."

"I'm sorry to hear that, but I'm pleased that you and Nicholas are getting along so well."

"He's a fair man." John observed.

"As are you," Mrs. Thornton entered the conversation.

"Indeed," Margaret added.

Their plates were cleared and the next course served.

"I was wondering," Margaret began, somewhat hesitantly. "Well, if now is not a bad time that is, I should very much like to learn a little about the business."

"About the mill?" John asked, sounding surprised.

"Of course," Mrs. Thornton sounded bitter. "You'll want to protect your investment, no doubt."

"Oh, no! I did not mean..." Margaret sighed and put her knife and fork down. "I have caused offence. I'm starting to think that I shall never get used to Milton ways. Please believe me, Mrs. Thornton, I have absolute faith in your son and it was not my intention to undermine him in any way."

John smiled encouragingly at her; he had not taken offence even if he didn't understand her reasons.

"Oh? Then I confess I am puzzled by such an unusual request," Mrs. Thornton continued. "Is it not unseemly for a lady to become involved in manufacturing?"

"Indeed, but the mill is important to John and he cares a great deal about it. As his future wife, what is important to him is important to me and I should like to understand it a little better. I have found the little that Mr Lennox has been teaching me fascinating and I believe the mill will be even more interesting."

"I would be glad to teach you everything," John said, his eyes bright with pleasure. He had known from the beginning that while she was a lady in the truest sense, there was more to her than that. She would never have been content to live Fanny's life of leisure for example; she needed challenges and although he wasn't quite sure how yet, perhaps like Higgins her involvement would be good for both the mill and its workers.

"Surely you will be busy getting things up and running again?" she asked, not wanting to inconvenience him.

"Your timing could not be better," he answered. "It will be a few weeks before the mill is up to speed so I should have all the time I need to teach you."

"Thank you."

"My pleasure. It may interest you to know that I tendered a bid for two contracts today to which I hope to receive a response soon."

"Do you have to wait for your bid to be accepted before starting work?"

"Ideally, but given the circumstances I'll start production in a limited fashion in the hopes of keeping the most valuable employees. It will also give us a head start on filling any future orders."

"So," Mrs. Thornton said. "When do you think you would

like to begin learning about the mill?"

"Oh, I hadn't actually given that much thought. I worried that things would be too hectic at the moment and I didn't want to be presumptuous."

"You'll need a day or two to unpack and settle in, I assume?" Mrs. Thornton asked.

"Oh, I do not have many possessions to bring with me," Margaret said. "Dixon will bring my clothes and the few sentimental items I have kept. I was wondering if I might store some things here at the mill? I..." she realised that she and Mrs. Thornton hadn't spoken about marriage yet, nor about her moving in here. "Well, I will not require them in the next few weeks and it would be unnecessary to unpack them until I have settled somewhere."

"I'm sure we'll find space," John assured her,

"You will be moving in here I assume, after the wedding?" Mrs. Thornton asked.

"We have not discussed it," Margaret admitted, "but I had assumed so."

"You won't find it too noisy for you?"

"Mrs. Thornton." Margaret smiled kindly. "I realise that I was horribly rude to you and your family when we first came here and I am very sorry for that. I did not mean to be unkind but your ways were very alien to me and I was not sure how to behave. I was also frightfully unhappy when we first came here, which I admit may have clouded my judgement. I am sure I shall still cause offence from time to time, however unintentional, but please believe me when I say that I now consider Milton to be my home."

Mrs. Thornton considered the young woman sitting in front of her for a moment. The girl seemed genuine and the affection she had for John was clear for all to see. She was willing to concede that perhaps she had misjudged Miss Hale and that maybe she would be a good wife to her son.

"I'm glad to hear it." She gave Margaret as warm a smile as she could manage.

Chapter Three

"Coming," Margaret called as she headed to her hotel room door. She was hoping it was a letter from London with news of when Dixon and her belongings would arrive.

"Dixon!" Margaret smiled warmly as she opened the door to see her lady's maid standing there.

"Miss Margaret."

"Well, come in," she stood back so that Dixon could enter the hotel room. "I must confess, I had not expected you so soon."

"Your aunt thought it best that I come as soon as possible. She believes you have taken leave of your senses."

Margaret smiled as she pictured the scene in Harley Street when her note had been found.

"And I suppose you are here to talk some sense into me?" Margaret guessed.

"Indeed I am. Quite aside from the shame you risk bringing down upon this family, this climate was not at all kind to your mother and I would hate for you to suffer the same fate."

"Sit down, Dixon. You must have had a long journey and will be grateful for a rest."

Dixon sat in one of the armchairs by the fireplace while Margaret went to the serving table. The tea that Margaret had ordered had been sent with two cups despite her insistence that one was plenty. Now she was glad of it as she poured a second cup for Dixon and handed it to her.

"Dear Dixon," she said once she had taken the seat beside her. "I know how much you dislike this town and it's climate but I find that I have come to think of it as home. All the while I was in London, I felt restless and out of sorts and now I understand why. Milton is where I belong, where I have a purpose."

Dixon's expression said she didn't believe it, but didn't feel it was her place to say so.

"I know this is hard for you to comprehend, and while I would very much like for you to stay with me for a few weeks while I get settled again, I completely understand if you would prefer to return to the south. I am sure Aunt Shaw would have a position for you, or perhaps you might prefer to retire. After all, you have looked after my family since before I was born; I believe you have earned the rest."

"Me retire!" Dixon turned her nose up. "What would I do

with all that time? The devil makes work for idle hands."

"Yes, he does," Margaret smiled. "But my point was that while I have chosen to remain in the north, you do not have to."

"Are you saying you no longer require my services, Miss Margaret?"

"Oh no, of course not! Dixon, you are like family to me and I would miss you dreadfully if you should go. At the same time however, I want what is best for you and if that is returning to the south, I want you to know that you have my blessing."

Dixon looked into her tea cup, unable to look in to Margaret's eyes.

"Miss Margaret, I have looked after this family for many years and I could no more think of abandoning you now than I could think of abandoning my own child."

That was the closest Dixon could come to saying she thought of Margaret as a daughter, and why shouldn't she? Dixon may started as Mrs. Hale's lady's maid but over the years she had taken on many different roles as required, from nanny to the young Margaret and Frederick to nurse when Mrs. Hale grew frail.

Margaret reached out and took Dixon's hand. "Then that is settled."

Dixon looked up and Margaret saw that her eyes were shining with tears. Knowing that Dixon was uncomfortable with too much affection, Margaret stood up and busied herself refilling their tea cups.

"Mr. Thornton is coming soon to take us to our new accommodations." Margaret told Dixon as she sat back down.

"We are not staying here then?"

"No. Mr. Thornton has a business acquaintance, a Mr. Maitland, who owns some drapers shops. Well he did; he is retired now and travelling with his wife while his eldest son looks after the shops. Mr. Thornton wrote asking if I might use his home while he is away and he received word this morning that we are more than welcome to stay there for as long as we wish."

"Well, your things are at the station, waiting to be collected."

"Thank you, Dixon. I confess I am not sure how much I will need but Mr. Thornton is happy for me to store some things at the mill."

"Miss Margaret." Dixon sat forward. "Are you certain about Mr. Thornton?"

"About marrying him, you mean?"

"Well, yes. Pardon me, but I never believed you cared much for him."

"It is true that when we first came to Milton I did not have a very high opinion of him, but the more I have come to know him, the more I have seen how good and moral he is. Indeed, I believe him to be one of the best men of my acquaintance."

"But he is a merchant and you are a lady."

"He is a gentleman, Dixon. Perhaps he does not have the right accent or the smooth manners of the south, but he is every inch a gentleman and I will not have you nor anyone else say otherwise!"

Dixon smiled, not because she had angered Margaret but because that show of anger revealed the depth of her affection for Mr. Thornton. Margaret would always rush to the defence of the weak but the fact that she was defending Mr. Thornton, who was more than capable of defending himself, showed that she truly cared for him and Dixon was sure now that this was no passing fad.

"Yes, Miss Margaret."

Margaret stepped down from the coach and onto the courtyard of Marlborough Mills.

"Margaret!"

She turned to see Nicholas striding towards her from the direction of the mill.

"Nicholas! Oh, how wonderful to see you again." She took his hand and leaned in to kiss his cheek. "I have missed you and the children."

"And us you. You're looking well."

"I am well, thank you. And you, how are you and the children keeping?"

"We're doing good. Better now the mill's to reopen."

"Isn't it wonderful?" she smiled.

"It's thanks to you, I hear."

"More thanks to Mr. Bell." She blushed.

"If you say so," Nicholas smiled. "So, ready for your first lesson?"

"Lesson?" she asked.

"You said you wanted to learn about the mill," John said as he came to join them from his office.

Nicholas noticed the warm glow that came over Margaret as she turned to the master.

"I did, I mean I do, but I confess I rather expected you to teach me."

"Nicholas has worked in mills most of his life whereas I have only run them. He is much more qualified than I to show you how we make cotton."

"But the mill is not yet running."

"All the better," Nicholas said. "You can hardly hear yourself think when all the machines are runnin'."

"And when you're finished, you're welcome to sit in on our meeting." John leaned down and kissed her cheek. "See you soon," he said with a warm smile.

Margaret blushed and turned away, suddenly at a loss for words. It really was appalling how he could reduce her, a grown woman, to a speechless wreck!

"Come on, lass, we'll start at the beginning, with the bales."

Over the next few hours Margaret listened intently as Nicholas explained how the cotton was cleaned, or picked, carded, drawn, spun and finally woven on mechanical looms into fabric. She asked a lot of questions and at times was appalled at the dangers some of the machinery clearly presented.

Nicholas did his best to assure her that Marlborough Mills had the best safety record in the town and that Mr. Thornton did everything he could to minimise the risks to his workers. His mill was one of the few that had installed a wheel in all the sheds, which helped to blow away the stray strands of cotton that filled the air. It was a concern that was close to Nicholas' heart since his own dear daughter, Bessy, had died from inhaling cotton fibres while working in a mill without adequate ventilation.

Knowing Nicholas's politics, his word on this meant much more to her than anyone else's might have, including John. She still didn't like how dangerous the machinery was but she accepted that as much as was possible had been done to reduce the risks.

Where he could, Nicholas operated the machinery so she could see it in action, and he told her stories of accidents and fires that he'd seen during his life in the mills.

Margaret began to see that while John looked every inch the stern and hard master, unlike many of the other local mill masters, he really seemed to care about his workers. Though she had formed her own opinions of what kind of man he was, it was nice to have evidence to confirm it.

"So that's it," Nicholas said as they exited the mill and walked over to the offices. "Think you can remember all that?"

"I believe so," she smiled. "You are a very engaging teacher."

"I can't rightly say that's something I've been called before." Nicholas smiled.

"There's a first time for everything," she teased. "So what are you and John- I mean Mr. Thornton meeting to discuss?"

"The men and when they're to come back to work. I've been to see most of the workers; a few have already found work elsewhere and are happy but most would like to return here."

"The men like working for Mr. Thornton then?"

"I wouldn't say they like it, but he's better than the rest and that's sayin' sommat."

"And what of the women employed here?"

"I've been around to them too. Same story."

"But everyone can't return at once, is that correct?"

"Not until we have orders to fill. We're to discuss who we want to keep most an' they'll start working again immediately. The rest will come back when we've got the work for 'em."

They headed up to John's office and Margaret listened intently as Nicholas and John discussed the employees. She learned that Nicholas had a very good idea of who earned their keep and was reliable and of who was perhaps less conscientious. She was also pleased to see that although they might not be among the top workers, John was willing for some of those who were in hardship to return to work early as well.

By the time they were finished Margaret had learned a lot from their conversation, specifically the ways the workers might be able to reduce the efficiency and safety of the mill. She bid Nicholas goodbye then and turned to John.

"So, how did you enjoy learning about the mill?" he asked.

"I must confess, I found it fascinating. The technology involved is quite ingenious."

"Yet you looked unhappy as you left the carding house."

"You were watching us?"

"I just happened to be looking out of the window as you left."

Margaret felt uncomfortable.

"Nicholas had been telling me of some of the dangers of the machinery. Some of his stories were a little graphic."

"It's dangerous work, I won't deny it. I do everything I can to keep them safe but accidents do still happen."

"Oh, I am not judging you. Nicholas told me you have the best safety record among the local mills."

"I like to think so. Still, it bothers you, doesn't it?"

"Yes," Margaret admitted. "I'm sorry."

"Don't be," he walked over to her, put his arms around her and drew her to him. "You wouldn't be the woman I love if you didn't have that big heart. Besides, I'd be lying if I said it didn't bother me too."

Margaret pulled away and looked up at him.

"I just wish there was something more we could do to keep them safe."

"And I am certain that if there is, you or Nicholas will find it."

"Yes, I suppose."

"So, have you had enough for one day or would you like to continue?" he asked.

"I would love to continue but I fear that if I try and take too much in at once, I shall not be able to recall everything."

"As you wish. How have you settled into Mr. Maitland's house?"

"Oh, very well. He sent a letter for his housekeeper to give to me, wishing me a happy stay and hoping that I felt at home there. He really is a very kind man."

"He is." John smiled.

"How do you know him?" she asked. "Does he buy from the factory?"

"He does, but I first met him when I left school. Remember I told you that I worked in a drapers shop?"

"It was his shop?" Margaret smiled, pleased by the warmth she saw in John's eyes.

"Aye."

"You must have liked working for him."

"Liked? Not so much. He was a hard task master but I respected him and he taught me many business principles that

31

have stood me in good stead since then."

"And now you are friends?"

"We are. He's been very good to me over the years, he gave me a lot of contacts when I was first starting out and I owe him a lot."

"I'm sure you have been good to him as well," Margaret observed. John was nothing if not loyal.

"Where I can," he admitted. "Now, will you join Mother and me for dinner again?"

"I fear I must prepare for my aunt's arrival," she said with a sigh. "Are you absolutely certain that Mr. Maitland doesn't mind my family staying there as well?"

"I am certain," he assured her. "In fact he has spoken of extending his trip by quite a few months so he might not be in need of the house for a good long while."

"Well, hopefully I will not be requiring it for too much longer."

John smiled, unable to contain his excitement at the thought that Margaret would soon be living under his roof.

"When does your aunt arrive?" he asked.

"Tomorrow at noon. I shall collect them from the station and we will join you for dinner in the evening."

"I look forward to it." He leaned down and kissed her forehead.

"You really shouldn't," Margaret warned. "If you thought that I gave myself airs when I arrived here, please believe me that while my cousin and her husband will most likely be interested though somewhat ignorant of our ways, in all probability my aunt will be completely insufferable."

"I like that." He smiled.

"That my aunt will be insufferable?"

"No, the way you said 'our ways'. You're one of us now."

"Indeed." She smiled. "I only wish we could just jump ahead a few months and find all this just a distant memory."

"It soon will be," he assured her. He took her hand as they walked out to the courtyard. "Will you come in for tea while your carriage is readied."

"I would like that." She smiled and they headed into the house.

They headed into the parlour and John rang the bell for tea.

"Your mother is not here?" Margaret asked, surprised.

"No, she is visiting Fanny this afternoon. My sister is in

quite a state at the thought of having dinner tomorrow with so many fine ladies from London."

"Oh dear, poor Mr. Watson."

"He is the one who asked for her hand," John reminded Margaret.

"True, but perhaps he finds her ways charming."

"That will wear off soon enough, I assure you."

"Don't be mean," she gently chided, unable to hide her own smile.

"You're right, I apologise," he said, though his own smile said that he was unrepentant.

"I like your smile," she said, suddenly. "You hardly ever used to smile."

"I didn't often have much to smile about."

"Well I shall now make it my business to make sure that you smile at least once a day," she said.

"Oh, is that so?"

"It is."

"And how do you intend to achieve this?"

"Oh, rest assured, I shall be very busy thinking of the many ways I might achieve this."

John laughed. "Sometimes you appear to be the perfect lady, poised and elegant but every now and then I get a glimpse of something else. Something wild and untamed."

Margaret tried to hide her smile but she was unsuccessful. He had fairly well just summed up her life. While her aunt had educated her and raised her to be a lady, underneath it all was still the wild child who loved nothing more than climbing trees in her beloved garden in Helstone. No amount of piano recitals or deportment lessons could ever totally rid her of her independent streak.

"Does that please you?" she asked.

"Very much. In fact I would go so far as to say it is the thing I love most about you. Ladies are ten a penny, they have been to finishing school and know exactly how to dress and behave. A creature like you is much more rare. You are as at home in the highest society as you are taking tea with paupers and though you appear delicate and fragile, underneath there is a ribbon of steel at your core that no one could ever hope to break."

"You flatter me," Margaret blushed.

"No, I speak only the truth, my love."

"Then I suggest you stop before we have to increase the size of these rooms to accommodate my inflated pride," she teased.

"I will stop only when I am good and ready."

"Then woe betide me for trying to stop you."

John reached over and cupped her cheek but a noise outside the door made him lower his hand.

"I cannot wait until I am free to show you my affection," he said.

"Mr. Thornton, please! Those are hardly the words of a gentleman."

John smiled, realising from her tone that she was only teasing him.

"Then I am no gentleman," he insisted, leaning forward to steal a quick kiss.

"And I suppose the fact that I rather enjoyed that means that I am no lady."

"Then at least we're in good company."

Margaret smiled but knew she had to leave before their teasing turned into something more serious. Though they were only jesting, there was an element of truth to her words. It was hard to explain because she had never felt like this before, but ever since they had admitted their true feelings for one another, the desire to touch him, to hold him, to kiss him almost overwhelmed her at times.

She was grateful to her father for instilling such a strong moral streak in her because without it, she feared she would not be able to resist her urges.

"I had better go," she said, standing.

John nodded, his own thoughts mirroring hers.

"Until tomorrow evening then." He took her hand and bent low to kiss the back of it.

The feel of his lips on her skin made her shiver and she smiled.

"Until tomorrow."

Chapter Four

Mrs Shaw had talked about little else but what bad choices Margaret was making ever since she had arrived and Margaret was finding it hard to keep her temper in check.

"You simply must stop this insanity, Margaret. You cannot live in this dirty, smoky town, I will not allow it!"

"I can and I will, Aunt. I realise that you do not like Milton or Mr. Thornton, though I cannot see why as you have never even met John, but I am not asking you to to like either. I simply ask that you respect my wishes and try to be happy for me."

"Happy? Happy that you are marrying a merchant!"

"Manufacturer."

"He is in trade, Margaret, that is all I need to know!"

Margaret stood up, her temper finally pushed to breaking point.

"No, all that you need to know is that I love him and I want to marry him. We all know that you married for money and not for love but I have no desire or necessity to marry for money. Mr. Thornton is a true gentleman, he is the kindest and best man of my acquaintance and the fact that he is in trade is of no consequence to me. I love him and I will marry him and if you are unable to support our union, I will thank you to return to London forthwith."

Margaret left the room before she said anything more damaging.

"Well I never," she heard Mrs. Shaw mutter as she left.

As Margaret entered the hall she saw Edith standing at the top of the stairs, trying hard to suppress a smile. Edith always took great pleasure in Margaret's outbursts.

"Are you quite finished?" she asked as Margaret climbed the stairs.

"For now." Margaret sighed sadly. "I am sorry. I know that she means well but I simply could not listen to another word."

"She will come around," Edith assured her. "I must confess that I had hoped you and Henry would form an attachment and I was shocked when I received your letter, but now that I am here I can see from your face that you are truly in love with this Thornton and you deserve to be loved, Margaret."

"Thank you," Margaret smiled. Though she was often selfish, Edith really could the sweetest person at times. Her smile faded as she prepared to ask her next question. "How is Henry?"

"He is keeping busy; so busy we have not seen much of him since you left London."

"I hope he is not too upset."

"He will be fine, Margaret."

"I do hope so."

"Come, we can't have you being this dour on the day of your engagement dinner. Come and play with Sholto for a while, that always cheers you."

"That's a wonderful idea."

Mrs. Thornton had gone all out for the engagement dinner and Margaret didn't know whether to be pleased or intimidated by her efforts.

Fanny was the first to greet Margaret and her party as they entered the parlour, almost running up to her and kissing her on the cheek.

"Oh, Miss Hale, how lovely to see you again! I was so thrilled when I heard your happy news."

"Thank you," Margaret said, thought she couldn't help but feel that her statement was untrue. "It is lovely to see you again as well."

Thankfully John came over to rescue her before Fanny could become too gushing.

Margaret introduced her Aunt Shaw, Edith and Captain Lenox to John, Mrs. Thornton and Mr. and Mrs. Watson.

It was a small gathering for an engagement party but Margaret had insisted on family only. Perhaps a larger party might be a good idea later but for now she wanted both families to get to know each other, even though her hopes of them getting along were rather low.

Mrs. Shaw was regaling a willing Fanny and a rather unwilling Mrs. Thornton with stories of London society while John and Watson were discussing the cotton trade with Captain Lennox. Edith and Margaret were watching from the sidelines.

"Margaret!" Mrs. Shaw called. "Margaret, Fanny tells me she has not heard you play, is this true?"

"We did not have a piano, Aunt. We sold it when we left Helstone."

"You told us you couldn't play the piano," Fanny said indignantly.

"I said I couldn't play well, and I cannot."

"Nonsense. There is a piano in the corner, Margaret," Mrs. Shaw gestured to the instrument. "Play that Spanish piece your brother sent to you a few years ago."

"Aunt, please." Margaret blushed. "I have not played in a very long time and I do not have the music with me."

"Then play something you do remember. Something jaunty."

Margaret could see that she wasn't going to get out of this. Fanny was looking incredibly put out while John was watching her with interest.

Slowly she made her way to the piano, sat at the stool and opened the lid. It was a very fine piano, very much like the one she had learned on in Harley Street.

She tried to think of a piece she knew by heart but her mind was blank until she remembered her mother frequently asking her to play Beethoven's Piano Sonata No. 14 in C minor, which had been her favourite piece of piano music. It wasn't jaunty and Margaret only knew the first movement by heart but that would have to do.

She stretched her fingers to give herself a little extra time to compose herself then when she could hesitate no longer, she gently bit her lower lip and began to play.

The music brought back memories of many evenings in Helstone, sitting with her mother and father after dinner and playing this beautiful tune on their upright piano. Her mother would sway slightly in time with the music while her father would tap his fingers on the arm of his chair, almost playing along with her.

Her playing was hesitant and faltering at times, then as she neared the end of the movement she hit the wrong key and panicked, losing her concentration.

"I'm sorry," she looked up at her audience. "It has been years since I've played that piece."

"That was... quite lovely," John said, stepping forward. Fanny looked sour and Mrs. Thornton's face was unreadable.

"You really should hear it played by a professional," Margaret said. "They do the music far more justice than I ever could."

"You play beautifully," he insisted.

"I wish that were true. I am rather more practised at that piece than most because it was a particular favourite of my mother's, but in all honesty I have neither the patience nor the inclination to become proficient."

"Play something else," Mrs. Shaw insisted.

"No, really, I have embarrassed myself quite enough for one night, Aunt. Fanny, you are a great music lover, are you not? I should very much enjoy hearing you play."

Fanny's sour expression formed into a smile and she got up, pleased to have the chance to entertain everyone.

John led Margaret over to the sofa and they sat down beside one another to watch Fanny play.

"I see you still have a few hidden talents that I have yet to discover," he said softly.

Margaret smiled and blushed.

"Well, brace yourself," he said, nodding towards Fanny. "You're in for an experience now."

Margaret wasn't sure what to make of Fanny's playing. While there was not a note wrong, it was rather staccato and not at all melodic. As for her singing voice, while equally flawless it had a sharp edge to it that was rather displeasing.

When she had finished, everyone clapped and smiled politely. Mrs. Thornton stood up before Fanny could begin a second piece.

"Thank you, Fanny, that was very nice. Now, if you will all make your way into the dining room, dinner will be served shortly."

John and Margaret shared a smile and then John nodded at his mother, thanking her for her intervention.

In general, the dinner went better than Margaret had expected. Captain Lennox had travelled widely and met with many different kinds of people so the customs of the north didn't faze him in the slightest. Indeed, though somewhat ignorant of their ways, he was very interested in local life and asked a lot of questions. Both he and Edith made a faux pas or two, usually an unintentional slight to the north though they truly didn't mean any offence. To Margaret's delight, Mrs. Thornton didn't seem to take offence either.

Mrs. Shaw, on the other hand made no bones about her feelings regarding life in the north, commenting on the noise, the smoke, the people, the weather, the buildings and generally letting everyone know that her niece was far too good for the town of Milton.

Margaret began to wish she were anywhere but here and

though she tried to intervene a time or two, she couldn't seem to divert her aunt onto another topic.

"And, of course, Margaret was always greatly in favour at the Balls. She was very much missed after her father moved the family up here. I can't tell you how many gentleman enquired after her when she left, quite devastated they were. Why even Charles Dickens's son asked me about her and when and if she will ever return."

Margaret looked over at John, her eyes silently asking him not to pay any attention, that he was worth far more to her than any of those London gentlemen, no matter how well connected they were. John smiled reassuringly at her.

"How very odd," Margaret said to her aunt. "I don't recall having met Charles Dickens, junior or senior."

"Well, he remembers you," Mrs. Shaw said firmly, though Margaret was in little doubt that this was a tall tale on the part of her aunt.

"Then I must consider myself even luckier than I had previously," John said to Mrs. Shaw. "Of course I have always known how special Margaret is, but I had no idea that she had picked me over so many more eligible suitors. I am indeed blessed that she chose me."

Since John's steely gaze was fixed on her aunt, Margaret caught Hannah Thornton's eye and smiled at her. She offered Margaret a nod and a sly smile in return.

"So, Fanny," Margaret took the opportunity during her aunt's indignant silence to redirect the conversation. "I understand that you have been redecorating some of the rooms in your home. I should very much like to see what you have done."

"Oh yes, indeed." And Fanny proceeded to monopolise the conversation with talk of wallpapers, curtains and furnishings until dessert was served, to Margaret's immense relief.

"So," Edith asked during a lull in conversation as they ate their plum pie. "Have you given any thought to the wedding yet?"

"Not much," Margaret confessed. "I have been to see Mrs. Thornton's dressmaker who is making my gown and we have booked the church for the fifteenth of next month."

"That's three weeks!" Mrs. Shaw cried. "You cannot get married in three weeks! It's impossible."

"Indeed it is not," Margaret assured her aunt. "The only

necessities for our union, namely the licence and church, are already in hand. All we need to do now is say the words before God and we shall be wed."

"But what about the flowers, the invitations, the wedding breakfast?"

"The invitations are being made and we are only having a small wedding, just close friends and family. The wedding breakfast will be here and it will also be a small, intimate affair."

"But-"

"I wish to get married to the man I love, Auntie, and I would really rather those present were moved by our declarations than by the flowers in the church or because my dress is the most expensive in London."

"But it's your wedding day!"

"Exactly. My wedding day. Well, mine and John's, and we wish to keep things simple. I know you don't understand it, but I truly hope you can accept our wishes and be happy for us."

"People will talk," Mrs. Shaw said. "They will say all kinds of nasty things about why you are marrying so quickly."

"Then let them talk," John said. "Margaret and I are not ones to pay much mind to idle gossip. We know the truth of the matter, that we are in love and don't want to wait any longer than we have to. The gossips will be proved wrong in time."

Mrs. Shaw sniffed, which Margaret knew from experience meant that she had no intention of backing down but needed a little time to regroup before pressing on.

John flashed Margaret a warm smile which she returned, though somewhat hesitantly. If her aunt kept this up, Margaret felt that she would surely be a nervous wreck by the day of her wedding.

"This pie is quite delicious," Edith said to Mrs. Thornton.

"Thank you. It's a family favourite."

"Delicious," Captain Lenox agreed.

Chapter Five

Margaret was seated at John's desk with her head resting against the back of the chair and her eyes closed.

She looked so peaceful and serene that John was loathe to disturb her, though they had work to do. He wondered what his mother would say if she knew he was shirking his responsibilities in order to watch a beautiful lady in repose. He smiled at the image that brought to his mind.

"Are you just going to stare at me all day?" Margaret asked, a smile forming on her lips before she finally opened her eyes and looked at him.

"You looked so peaceful," he said. "I couldn't bring myself to interrupt you."

"I'm afraid I have had no peace since my aunt arrived. The quiet here was such a luxury that I thought I would indulge myself for a few moments."

"Is she upsetting you?" John stepped into the office, looking worried.

"No, no more than she has whenever I have defied her. She is simply vocal, and unable to abide silences. Your taciturn northern ways do take a little getting used to but I have to say, overall I now believe I prefer them. One should only speak when they have something worth saying."

John smiled. "I wish someone had thought to tell Fanny that."

Margaret smiled, came around the desk and eagerly fell into his embrace. She breathed deeply, inhaling the scent of him.

"And I suppose we must get to work," she said with a sigh.

"Well, there is no one else around; the workers don't return until tomorrow so I believe we might be able to delay for a while without causing any great consternation."

Margaret looked up at him and smiled.

"I've missed you," she told him. The last two days had been monopolised by her aunt who had insisted on voicing her opinion with regards to the wedding arrangements. Margaret had allowed her to have her say and though she had held fast to the most important aspects of the occasion, she had also given her aunt some say in the wedding breakfast and she had allowed her free reign with Edith's bridesmaid dress.

"I've missed you too, my love." He leaned down and kissed her forehead.

"I suppose we should get some work done." She

sounded reluctant.

"We should." John sounded no more keen. "So do you want to start on the accounts or learn how to tender a bid?"

"Do you have many orders to bid on?"

"A few, and I have yet to hear about the tenders I put in last week."

"So how do you work out what to charge for an order?"

"I'll show you." John dropped his arms from around her and stepped away to get a second chair, which he placed next to his behind the desk. Margaret joined him and sat next to him. "First, we have to work out what filling the order will cost us and for that we need need to know the price of the raw cotton, the man hours needed to process it, the overhead of the mill and the delivery costs."

"Well I can see how you would know the price of the raw cotton, but how do you know how many man hours it will take to process the cotton?"

"Experience. This order, for example," he handed her a sheet with the details of the order. "I can say that it would take the whole mill around ten full days to complete, start to finish."

"It's a large order then?"

"Reasonably large, yes, but since they don't want the fabric all at once, we can stagger the production, allowing us to work on other orders at the same time."

"This all sounds very complex."

"It can be, but you just have to break it down to its most basic elements, then it's child's play."

"I doubt that," she smiled.

He took her hand and squeezed it reassuringly. He was certain that if anyone could grasp this, she could. She had probably been told her whole life that business wasn't something she needed to worry about and as such it might take her some time to pick things up, but her mind was sharp and once she was practised, he was sure she would be as competent as he or his mother, possibly even more so.

He worked out the bids on two different tenders and walked her through each stage of the calculations. He then showed her how to write the tender and what to include.

"And how long before you find out if your bid has been accepted?" she asked when they were finished.

"That depends. Generally speaking, the larger the order, the longer the wait because they ask more mills to bid."

"Fascinating," she smiled. "I really had no idea that business was so intricate."

"I'm pleased that you're enjoying learning about it." John smiled.

"Oh, I am indeed. I'm not so sure that I'm any good at it, but I am certainly enjoying myself."

"Something tells me that you're good at whatever you set your mind to."

"Well, I confess that I have become rather proficient at ironing since we came to Milton though in the beginning I thought I would never learn to remove all the creases."

"Ironing?" he asked. "Surely that's what you had Dixon for?"

"Dixon was my mothers lady's maid, not a household servant. Over the years she has done whatever is required of her but even she cannot run an entire household alone."

"So you washed and ironed?"

"Yes," she was puzzled by how strange he seemed to find this. "Why shouldn't I?"

"Well, it's just... you're a gentleman's daughter."

"A gentleman who was in reduced circumstances and could no longer afford more than one servant."

"I know that but somehow I can't see you washing and ironing."

"Do you remember the first time you came to tea and I was rather quiet?"

"Vividly," he said. He had fond memories of watching her bracelet fall onto her wrist and be pushed back up her arm, only to loosen and fall again a few moments later. He also had rather less pleasant memories of their later argument.

"I'm afraid I was rather exhausted that night because I had spent the day washing and ironing so that everything would be nice for your visit."

"So although you didn't like me back then, you performed manual labour all day so that I might feel comfortable in your home?"

"Is that so very hard to believe?" she asked. "I may be a gentleman's daughter and I may have been educated by a rich relative, but I assure you, John, I have never been frightened by the idea of hard work."

"No," he said softly. "I don't suppose you have." He leaned

over and kissed her cheek.

"What was that for?" she asked, smiling as she turned to him.

"For being you."

"Well, whilst you're in a good mood," her smile widened, "perhaps this is a good time to tell you that we are to have an engagement ball."

John frowned.

"I know, and I apologise but in the grand scheme of things it was better to lose this battle and win the more important ones."

"I'm sure I shall manage somehow," he assured her. "Where is this ball to be held?"

"I honestly have no idea. I am leaving all the arrangements to Aunt Shaw in the hopes that having a task will stop her from being so negative towards me."

"That's a very good idea," he smiled.

"So you say now. What you don't yet know is that she is visiting Fanny tomorrow to get her help."

"What does she need Fanny's help for?" he asked. "Mrs. Shaw has made it perfectly clear how little regard she has for Milton craftsmanship, surely she would not pay any mind to Fanny's taste?"

"I believe she is after Fanny's local knowledge of caterers, florists and the like."

"Oh. Well, at least with Fanny on board, Milton's economy will receive a nice boost."

"Indeed. And she is picking up the tab herself as a wedding gift to us."

"That is very kind of her, though completely unnecessary."

"She is happy, John. What is one evening out of our lives if it keeps her happy and out of our hair?"

"Very true." John kissed her then stood up to stretch his cramped muscles and went to look out of the window.

"It looks so wrong," Margaret said as she came up beside him.

"Aye, but not for much longer. The men start back tomorrow and I hope to have answers on some of my tenders by the end of the week. In a week or two I hope to have the mill back to full speed."

"I hope so too. It would be a nice wedding gift, would it not?"

John put his arm around her shoulder and looked down at her.

"Indeed." he leaned down and kissed her.

When he pulled away Margaret smiled.

"You had better not be so improper tomorrow when the workers return," she teased.

"Then I had best make the most of things while we are alone."

Margaret was counting the payroll at the end of the mills first week when she heard Thomas, the office clerk and Sarah, one of the household servants talking in the hallway outside. Since she seemed to have a head for figures and still knew very little in practical terms about the cotton trade itself, she had chosen to take an active hand in the bookkeeping, feeling that she could be of use here without needing to bother John too much.

She looked towards the door as Thomas asked Sarah where Mrs. Thornton was.

"She left earlier," she heard Sarah reply. "I think I heard her say something about her viewing a property."

Margaret frowned, puzzled by the idea of Mrs. Thornton viewing a house. She realised that she had lost count of the pay packet she was calculating and started again. Thomas entered the office a few moments later.

"You haven't seen Mrs. Thornton, have you Miss Hale?"

"No, Thomas, I haven't. Is it important?"

"It's just that I have some papers that she asked me for."

"I'm sure she'll be back soon," Margaret answered and returned to her counting. When she was finished she handed the payroll envelopes over to Thomas to check and then she headed over to the house. The door was answered by Jane.

"Do you know when Mrs. Thornton will be back?" Margaret asked the servant.

"Not too much longer now, Miss. Would you like to come in and wait?"

"Yes, thank you."

Jane showed her towards the parlour but Margaret put her hand on Jane's arm to stop her.

"Jane, would you happen to know where Mrs. Thornton has gone?"

"She is viewing houses, Miss."

"But why?"

"I believe she intends to move out once you and the master are wed."

"Thank you, Jane." Margaret had feared as much.

"Can I get you some tea while you wait? Or shall I call the master?"

"No, thank you. I believe I shall find Mr. Thornton myself." She left the house and crossed to the mill. She paused just inside and smiled, heartened by the industry going on inside, though she didn't have time to pause for too long. She went from room to room until she found John in the carding house. He smiled when he saw her and came over to her.

"Is something wrong?" he asked, raising his voice to be heard over the machinery.

"I'm not sure," she answered as honestly as she could.

They stepped to the side of the room to afford them some privacy, though they didn't need to worry too much about them being overheard thanks to the noise from the machines.

"Do you know anything about your mother viewing houses?" Margaret asked.

John frowned and she knew immediately that this was just as big a surprise to him as it had been to to her.

"I'll talk with her," he said. "But I suppose first we need to discuss what is to happen after we are married."

"John, I would no more ask your mother to leave than I would my own. We may not always get along or agree but I know how much you love her. And in any case, this house is more hers than it is mine so I wouldn't feel right if she left."

"You think you could live with her?"

"I believe so. I hope one day to love her as you do," Margaret smiled.

"I'll speak to her tonight."

"No, please, let me do it. I fear if you ask her to stay she will not believe that I want her here."

John almost bent down and kissed her but remembering that they had an audience, he just caught himself in time. Instead he smiled warmly and nodded.

"How is the payroll coming?" he asked as they began to walk through to the next room.

"Fine. Thomas is doing the second check and barring any problems, they should easily be ready to hand out by the end of the day."

"Good. And you and Thomas are getting on well?"

"He is a very helpful young man, though I fear that he is slightly uneasy around me."

"Uneasy?"

"I don't think he knows what to make of me; should he treat me as his boss, his underling or his friend."

"Do you want me to have a word with him?"

"No, thank you. We will find our own level naturally."

"You know," John smiled. "You really aren't fitting into my image of what a wife should be. I rather thought it was my job to look after you and rescue you but you seem quite capable of looking after yourself."

"Indeed I am but would you prefer a meek wife, someone who wanted to be sheltered and looked after?"

"No indeed, there is a reason I have not yet married, because I had never found anyone like you. You are my equal, Margaret, my partner, and not just in business."

Margaret smiled and then turned to the window as movement caught her eye.

"Your mother is home. I should go and speak with her."

"And can you join us for dinner again?"

"I fear not. Aunt Shaw wants to go over the plans for the engagement party with me."

"Then I shall wish you luck, because I am certain you will need it."

Margaret couldn't help but smile at his barbed comment, even though she knew she really shouldn't. John took her hand and raised it to his lips to kiss the back of it.

"You will find me before you leave for the day?"

"Of course," she assured him. She took her leave then, and headed across the courtyard and into the house, arriving just moments after Mrs. Thornton.

"Miss Hale," Hannah Thornton looked surprised as she turned to find Margaret in the hallway, behind her. "How are you finding the mill?"

Mrs. Thornton removed her shawl and bonnet and handed them to Jane.

"There are some things I am finding it difficult to master but overall I believe I am finding my way." Margaret smiled.

"I am pleased to hear it. Was there something you wanted?"

"Indeed, I should very much like to speak with you, if I may."

"Of course. Jane, perhaps you would bring us some tea."

"Yes Ma'am."

Jane scurried off to make the tea and Mrs. Thornton led Margaret into the parlour. They each took a seat and made small talk until Jane had returned and finished serving their tea.

"So, Miss Hale, what can I do for you?" Mrs. Thornton asked once they were alone.

"I do not mean to overstep my bounds, Mrs. Thornton, but it has come to my attention that you have not been to the mill all week. Then earlier today I overheard a conversation where it was said that you had gone to view a house."

"I do not wish to step on any toes, Miss Hale. I thought it prudent that I find myself alternate accommodation for after your wedding."

"I understand your reasoning and I thank you for your consideration, but I hope you will believe me when I say I have no wish to push you out of John's life or your home. You are very important to John and this home is more yours than mine. It is my hope that you will agree to live with us and continue to take an active role in the workings of the mill."

"And you believe we can both live and work together, do you?"

Margaret smiled kindly. "I know we have very different tastes and ideas, Mrs. Thornton, but this is a very large house and I see no reason why we cannot both be happy here. As for the mill, when I asked to know more about the business, I had no intention of actually working there. Now that I have duties, I find that I am enjoying them immensely, but we both know that in the future it will be impractical at times for me to continue to be so involved. At those times I am sure John will feel your loss even more keenly and I should hate for that to happen. While I am sure there will be difficulties along the way, I am also sure we can learn to both work and live alongside each other, if not together."

Mrs. Thornton considered the young woman before her for a long time. Finally she said, "You are a puzzle Miss Hale."

"How so?"

"I find you to be full of contradictions. When you first came here you gave yourself terrible airs and graces, and yet I truly believe you considered Bessie Higgins, a working class girl, to be your friend. Most of the time you behave like a lady with

48

very precise manners, yet you show flashes of courage and bravery that are at times very unladylike and even invite scorn and gossip. I feel as though I am naturally inclined to dislike you, and when you first came to Milton you did very little to improve my opinion, yet there is something about you that demands my respect, even though at times I also think you foolish."

"I am well aware of the frightful way I acted when I first came to Milton. I do hope we can move forward from there. I respect John greatly and I do not believe he would hold you in such high regard if there was not also something special about you. I do not know if you would ever be able to think of me as a daughter and I am not asking you to, but I hope for John's sake that at the very least you might one day come to be my friend."

"I believe that if we ever found some common ground, that might be possible." Mrs. Thornton conceded.

"I think we already have some common ground in that we both love and respect your son. Perhaps now that I am taking an interest in the mill we might also have something else in common."

"Perhaps." She smiled slightly. Despite herself she found she was coming to like this girl. "Very well, I shall remain in the house and begin helping out at the mill again, but I would ask something of you in return."

"Of course, anything I can do."

"I would like you to select a sitting room for yourself and decorate it as you see fit. Other larger changes can be dealt with a later time but if you have your own sitting room, you will always have somewhere you feel comfortable. I also presume that you will wish to redecorate the master bedroom."

"I honestly cannot say, I have never seen any of the bedrooms."

"Then perhaps a tour might be in order. You will, after all, be mistress of this house soon."

"Thank you, I believe I would like that."

"And perhaps... you might like to call me Hannah."

"I should like that very much," Margaret smiled, "if you would also agree to call me Margaret."

"Very well, Margaret. Shall we begin out tour?"

"Yes, I think that is a very good idea, Hannah."

***

When John entered the house that evening he wasn't sure what he would find. He certainly hadn't expected to hear laughter coming from his mothers sitting room. He opened the door a fraction and listened as his mother regaled Margaret with a story from his childhood.

"I believe," he said stepping into the room. "That I may be forgiven for that particular indiscretion. I was only seven at the time." Despite his words, his smile told them that he had not taken offence.

"Indeed," Margaret smiled at him. "From what your mother has told me, you sound like a most precocious little boy."

"In the nicest possible way," Hannah added.

"Of course," John conceded. He bent to kiss the cheek of first his mother, then his betrothed. "I did not expect to find you still here, Margaret. Did you not hear the whistle?"

"I confess I did. I am simply putting off the inevitable. Still, I suppose I should return home before Aunt Shaw sends a search party out for me."

She and Hannah stood up and Margaret clasped her hand.

"Thank you for a lovely afternoon, Hannah. I have enjoyed myself immensely."

Margaret leaned forward and kissed the older woman's cheek. Hannah looked slightly taken aback at the display of affection though not uncomfortable.

"And I," Hannah conceded.

"I'll show you out," John offered.

They paused at the front door and he helped her into her coat before they proceeded outside. The carriage driver was already waiting for her.

"Oh, I hope I have not kept you waiting long," Margaret said to the driver.

"Not at all, Miss."

"I really wish you and Aunt Shaw would let me walk here and back, John. It is not very far to Mr. Maitland's house and I am quite capable, you know."

"After seeing how you have turned my mother around, I would believe that you could walk on water right now."

Margaret smiled, reached up and kissed his cheek. "Good evening, John."

"Goodbye, my love. Take care."

"I shall."

John helped her into the carriage and waited until it had

driven out of the gate before returning to the house. He found his mother humming as she worked at her sewing.

"So," he said as he took a seat. "Would you like to tell me what happened here today? The last I heard you were thinking of leaving, now Margaret is calling you Hannah and you are sharing some of the more embarrassing incidents from my childhood with her."

"I am willing to admit that perhaps I have misjudged her." His mother smiled. "Underneath all those airs and graces is a heart of gold and it is clear that she cares deeply for you."

"I am not sure she will continue to if you keep telling her all my most humiliating stories," he teased.

"Nonsense. She will love you all the more for them, as I do."

"I most certainly hope so, because it doesn't look as if I have much say in the matter."

Chapter Six

John was walking through town when Mr. Latimer hailed him and they paused to talk.

"I've been hoping I might run into you," Mr. Latimer said once the greetings were out of the way. "I have finally made my way through Miss Hale's financial affairs and I was wondering if you would like to make an appointment so that I could explain everything to you."

"About her investment in the mill?" John asked. He was slightly confused since he had already received those funds.

"No, I mean about the rest of the assets."

"I thought you were already working with Miss Hale?"

"Oh, I am, yes. Truth be told there are not a lot of day to day decisions to be made. Most of Mr. Bell's assets are in property and those properties are already leased but considering that you are to be wed, I rather thought you would be taking over their management from Miss Hale."

"I see no reason to." John smiled, though it was slightly tight. "While legally her assets will become mine once we are married, morally they are still hers and I have no intention of taking them from her. I am grateful to her for her investment in the mill and the faith that investment shows in me but I know little of the property market and have no desire to learn. If she should ever ask for my advice on financial matters, I will happily give it, although I am sure she is quite capable of making her own decisions."

"Oh," Mr. Latimer looked surprised. "I must say, that is most... progressive of you."

"I am only doing what I believe to be right. Mr. Bell left those assets to his God-daughter, not to me. He had faith that she would know what to do with them, as do I."

"I see. So is it true that Miss Hale is working in your mill now?"

"Hardly in the mill, but she has taken an interest in the business side of things. She seems to have an aptitude for accounts, especially for getting overdue invoices paid. Providing she is willing, I thought I might ask her to take on the position of bookkeeper on a more permanent basis."

"Well, you must have enormous faith in her to entrust her with such an important task."

"I do indeed," he said simply. "There are few women as accomplished and tenacious as she, and I consider myself eternally grateful that she has chosen to spend her life with me."

Mr. Latimer wasn't quite sure what to make of this conversation. It wasn't that he thought women were incapable creatures, for his own wife was a stalwart in times of crisis, but the way Mr. Thornton was talking about Miss Hale was positively unheard of. Why he was almost implying that she was his equal in business matters! While he was willing to concede that Miss Hale had been a quick study while they were discussing her assets, it was well known that women had little interest in or aptitude for business. He could not see her wanting to continue to manage the assets once she had a family, for example.

Nevertheless, it wasn't his place to say anything.

"The wedding is next week, is it not?" Mr. Latimer said, opting to change the subject.

"It is. I hope you and your family will be there."

"Indeed we will. And this evening is the engagement ball, is it not?"

"Indeed," John said darkly. "You will forgive my reticence, but this ball is being given by Margaret's Aunt Shaw and I am quite certain its only purpose is to highlight the inadequacies of society in the north."

Mr. Latimer smiled at what he presumed to be a joke but John did not and Mr. Latimer's smile slowly faded.

"Still," John continued. "It will be an event not to miss, of that I am sure."

"Then I look forward to it," Mr. Latimer said politely.

"Until this evening." John flashed him a wry smile and tipped his hat. "Good day."

The engagement party was to be held in the ballroom of the McKinley Hotel, not Milton's best hotel but it's most expensive because of its fine location in the heart of the town. Clearly no expense had been spared.

Margaret had chosen one of her finer gowns to wear this evening; a dusky rose coloured silk dress with a fitted bodice and full flared skirt. The bodice was adorned with silk roses on the small sleeves and around the collar. Dixon had fixed her hair with dozens of tiny silk flowers in a similar shade and curled the front of her hair to frame her face.

"You look amazing, Miss," Dixon said when she was

finished, a tear shining in her eye.

"Thank you, Dixon. I only wish this evening were worthy of all your efforts to make me look so good."

"Mrs. Shaw means well, Miss Margaret."

"I am not so sure she does," Margaret said sadly. "I fear that this evening is simply a way for my aunt to show these 'backwards northerners' how much better we southerners are."

"Fear not, Miss, at least you will have the master there with you."

"Yes indeed," her face glowed with happiness at the thought. She reached out and took Dixon's hand. "I wish you could be there too," she said.

Margaret's parents had never been wealthy and as such, all celebrations had been in the home and although Dixon was there as a servant and not a guest, she was still present and welcomed as part of the family more than an employee. Aunt Shaw would never stand for having Dixon present, even as a servant.

Indeed Margaret had broached the subject of having Dixon go with her, only for Mrs. Shaw to almost shriek, '*A lady's maid at an engagement ball! Why I have never heard the like. She cannot attend as a guest and it would simply be insulting to ask her to join the waiting staff. What nonsense you do talk sometimes, Margaret.*'

"Never fear, Miss Margaret, I shall be there in spirit." Her smile was bright and Margaret was glad she didn't feel hurt by her aunt's snub.

Margaret smiled and squeezed Dixon's hand briefly before getting to her feet. She took a deep, calming breath.

"Well, I suppose I had better head downstairs. It is only one evening, is it not? I suppose I can endure anything for one evening."

She was talking to herself more than Dixon but she was relieved when Dixon agreed with her.

"Of course, Miss Margaret. Whenever you feel your temper rising, just look at the master and remind yourself that this is supposed to be a celebration of your union."

"You are right, of course ."

Dixon handed Margaret her shawl and Margaret kissed her quickly on the cheek.

"Good night, Dixon."

"Good night, Miss Margaret."

Margaret pulled her shoulders back, stiffened her spine and walked out of her room and down the stairs with as much pride as she could muster. She was pleased when she saw her aunt's eyes widen in admiration as she descended the stairs.

Margaret thought it rather silly that she wasn't allowed to attend her own engagement party with her betrothed but she waited patiently for John and his mother to arrive.

The ballroom looked beautiful and, Margaret admitted, looked much more tasteful than most northerners would have chosen.

People in the north, especially those in business, needed to show off their success by displaying their wealth. In the south lavish displays of money were distasteful and to be avoided at all costs. At Fanny's engagement party for example, the flowers were everywhere and in large, almost overwhelming arrangements. Here, her Aunt Shaw had opted for smaller, tasteful arrangements of expensive orchids on each table. Clearly her aunt had spent more on the flowers than Fanny had but only a trained eye would spot that.

Margaret understood how things worked in the north however and she no longer judged them for their displays of wealth, even if it wasn't to her personal taste. Were she to host a party she would know that John needed to display his wealth in order to encourage confidence in him and his business. She had tried to explain this to her aunt but Mrs. Shaw wouldn't have any of it and had ignored every suggestion Margaret had made.

As people began arriving, her aunt started as she meant to continue, telling anyone who would listen of the horrendous time she'd had organising the party. How everything from the food to the flowers to the band was big, garish and crass. How she had had to oversee each small detail to ensure that everything was simple, elegant and top quality.

Margaret tried to intervene a time or two since her aunt was clearly offending some of the guests, but eventually she stopped trying. This was Aunt Shaw's party and if she was determined to show these uncouth northerners how it was done, so be it. Margaret only hoped that those who knew her would not judge her based on her aunt's behaviour.

John arrived early and Margaret found her aunt much more tolerable after that. She was also surprised to see that John was handling the barbed comments and criticisms with remarkable equanimity.

Mrs. Thornton was her usual steely self, giving as good as she got. She only stayed for an hour before leaving, saying that she had a terrible headache. Margaret didn't believe Hannah Thornton had ever suffered from a headache in her life, but she understood her desire to leave early.

As soon as they were able, Margaret and John slipped away from Mrs. Shaw and began making their rounds of the guests. Margaret was careful to apologise to those whom her aunt had offended.

John talked shop with a few of the mill owners and Margaret listened with interest, until another voice she recognised caught her ear.

"Yes, it is very unusual indeed. I heard she even accompanied John back here alone, without a chaperone! I mean, of course the damage is already done so it hardly matters that she is chaperoned any more but such wanton behaviour is hardly becoming, is it? I don't care how rich she is."

That was the voice of John's sister, Fanny.

"John seems very smitten with her." That was Mrs Slickson's voice.

"Oh, he is. He spent far too long with his head in the mill to learn what he needs to about women and I'm afraid she has taken advantage of his good nature. You know, it wouldn't surprise me if the baby wasn't even his, given her outrageous behaviour at Outwood Station with that young man last year. Dreadful business."

"You are sure she is with child?" Mrs. Slickson asked.

"Can there be any doubt with such a sudden wedding, not to mention their unorthodox behaviour."

"Well, it is possible they are getting married for love."

"Aye, but not likely."

Both women giggled and at that point, Margaret took the opportunity to turn round and face them. Their laughter stopped immediately.

"Fanny," she smiled and held out her hand. "I'm so pleased you could come this evening. And Mrs Slickson, so good to see you again. I thank you for your concern about my condition and your clear worry about my moral standing, but I can assure you that I am not with child, not John's and certainly not my brothers."

"Your brother?" Fanny gasped.

"Yes, the gentleman I was seen with at Outwood Station is my brother, Frederick."

"Well, I wasn't aware you had a brother."

"No," Margaret smiled. "But then that is the trouble with gossip isn't it? Rather than ask what the truth of a situation is, you prefer to fill the gaps with the most salacious slander you can imagine. Which is much more entertaining, I will grant you but when you are maligning someone's character, hardly honourable behaviour."

She caught John turning to look at her from the corner of her eye, she hoped he hadn't heard what Fanny had been saying.

"Now, please enjoy yourselves and try to keep the gossip to subjects which actually have a foundation in truth. Good evening."

She turned away and walked the few paces to John's side, linking her arm through his and smiling up at him. He smiled back, his expression full of love. Margaret had no idea if the women saw, but if they did, she was certain that their husbands didn't look at them the same way John looked at her. While she didn't condemn ladies who married for money rather than love, she did pity them, for while they surely had the financial security they wished for from the marriage, they had no idea of what had been sacrificed for that security.

"Are you all right?" John asked. "You looked a little upset."

"I am fine, thank you."

John was about to speak to Mr Henderson again when one of the hotel porters came up to him with a note.

"There has been an accident at the mill," John told Margaret as he read it. "Higgins is hurt."

As a snub to John's business, Mrs. Shaw had organised the party for a Friday night, despite Margaret telling her many times that the mill would be open until eight o'clock and that John really needed to be there. It said a lot about his love for her that he had left early to come to a party that he had little interest in.

"We have to go," Margaret said. Without a second thought she made her excuses to her aunt and she and John rushed outside to hail a cab to take them to the mill.

"I hope he is not seriously injured," Margaret said. "It is

almost nine o'clock, what was he doing at the mill so late?" she wondered aloud. "Unless he has been injured for over an hour and we are only just finding out now."

John didn't offer any explanation and if she was honest, she was slightly angry that he seemed so calm. She knew that he had a lot of respect for Nicholas so his attitude was puzzling.

"Do not fret, my love," he tried to reassure her. "We will be there soon."

The cab pulled into the mill courtyard and Margaret immediately jumped out and since it was the only building with the lights on and the door open, she ran to the house.

She came to a screeching halt as she entered the parlour because not only was Nicholas fine; standing in front of her and smiling, in point of fact, there was also a whole crowd of people behind him, dressed in their Sunday best and smiling warmly at her.

Margaret found herself speechless as she tried to figure out what was happening. John came in behind her and put his hand on her shoulder.

"You must excuse our ruse," John said. "But we all knew how much you were dreading tonight and we wanted to give you the engagement party you deserve."

Happiness began to break through the shock and Margaret smiled.

All her friends were here, including Dixon, Nicholas, Mary and the Boucher children, Sally and a few of the other workers she had made friends with.

Margaret was surprised that Hannah Thornton had invited the mill hands into her home but she seemed happy enough, in her own stern way.

James and Peter were providing the music; James playing the fiddle and Peter the piano. They didn't play particularly well and clearly hadn't practised together but no one seemed to care. The food looked home made and Margaret wondered if everyone had brought a dish. Mrs. Thornton seemed to have provided the large bowl of punch since it was served in one of her large Waterford crystal bowls.

Only a few minutes after her arrival the music was playing, laughter filled the room and a few of the children were dancing. Margaret was in heaven.

"You seem very happy," Hannah said as she approached Margaret whilst she was talking with Nicholas.

"I am indeed," she smiled. "In fact this reminds me very much of the harvest festivals we used to have in Helstone. The village wasn't particularly large or rich but after the harvest every year we would throw a party for the whole village in the church hall. Everyone contributed to provide the food, decorations and entertainment. Nothing was particularly grand and no one stood on ceremony but I have some very fond memories of those gatherings."

Hannah smiled. "I thought John had taken leave of his senses when he asked me to organise this, but I can see now that he knew you better than I."

"Well, I thank you for organising this for me." She pulled Hannah into a hug and after a brief hesitation, Hannah somewhat stiffly put her arms around Margaret. "This is so much nicer than anything Aunt Shaw has done for me."

"You must thank Nicholas also," Hannah said as they separated. "It is he who invited your friends."

"Thank you Nicholas," she kissed his cheek. "This is quite the nicest party I have been to since I first came to Milton."

John joined them at that moment with glasses of punch for everyone. The food was consumed and as the level of the punch bowl gradually lowered, the laughter grew louder. Margaret attempted a dance or two with the children and though their dances were unfamiliar to her, she had fun trying. Though she initially protested, even Dixon was talked into a quick dance with Nicholas. Margaret took a very quick turn on the piano and taught Sally how to to play Chopsticks.

Eventually the children began to grow tired and slowly the guests took their leave and headed for home. Margaret found her spirits lowering as she realised she would soon have to return to her aunt.

"What's wrong, my love?" John asked her.

"Until this moment I had not realised how stifled I have felt by my aunt's presence. I am afraid I am not looking forward to returning home this evening."

"Then it is a good thing that I have sent word that you won't be returning tonight," John smiled.

"Excuse me?"

"Mother has prepared the guest room for you and you will stay here this evening. I have sent a note to your aunt saying that Higgins is gravely ill and that you wish to remain with him and nurse him."

"But you know how gossip spreads," Margaret said. "She will soon learn the truth and then she will be terribly vexed with me."

"She is not local, no one up here will tell her the truth at the expense of one of their own."

"But I am not one of their own."

"You are now," he assured her. "Please, you have been looking so stressed lately that I just wanted to give you a small respite. Take the guest room tonight. Tomorrow you are working here in the office so you might as well stay. Besides, you deserve some time to yourself."

Margaret smiled. "Very well, thank you." She let out a long breath. "I do feel as though a weight has been lifted."

"If you would like a bath or tea or reading material, anything that you want, just ask me or ring the bell for one of the servants."

"To be honest, John, I think I should just like a good night's sleep."

"Then you shall have it. Dixon is staying in the room next to yours and she has already taken care of an outfit for tomorrow."

"You have thought of everything," she smiled.

"When it comes to you, I try." John leaned down and kissed her forehead. "Come, let me show you to your room."

"Thank you, John. And thank you for a delightful evening."

He left her at the door and she entered to see Dixon already waiting for her.

"Oh, Dixon, you do not need to see to me this evening. We have had a lovely time, just go to bed and I shall take care of myself."

"Nonsense, Miss Margaret. I enjoy seeing to you."

So Margaret sat at the dressing table and patiently waited while Dixon took all the clips and roses from her hair, then helped her into a nightgown. Margaret climbed into the bed and sighed with happiness. Soon she would be spending every night in this house, and with that happy thought on her mind, she drifted off into a peaceful sleep.

The next morning Dixon helped Margaret dress before returning to Mr. Maitland's house. She assured Margaret that Mrs. Shaw would be none the wiser as to what had really happened the night before and that Margaret was only to return when she had finished work for the day.

Margaret thanked her again for her part in last night's party and then headed down to breakfast. As she approached the dining room she heard John and his mother talking.

"I was pleasantly surprised at how well they behaved. I only hope they do not become too informal with you at work."

"You needn't worry, I am quite capable of putting them in their place should they overstep the mark, not that I expect them to."

"Well, I hope you're right. It really is quite odd, a woman of Margaret's station mixing with the working classes."

"Not given her upbringing. Her father ministered to all sorts of people in his parish and as his daughter, it is only natural she made friends from all classes."

"I suppose. And I must admit that she does genuinely seem to care for them."

"See, did I not tell you that you would like her, if only you gave her a chance."

"Aye, you did and I must say, while she is not at all what I had pictured for you, I believe she will make you a fine wife."

"Thank you, Mother. Coming from you that is high praise indeed."

Margaret had paused in the hallway, unwilling to disturb them but now she felt uncomfortable, as though she was eavesdropping on them. She walked into the dining room and smiled brightly.

"Good morning. No, please don't get up," she said to John as he made to stand.

"How did you sleep?" John asked after she was seated.

"Very well, thank you. And thank you both for last night. Truly, it was a wonderful surprise."

"I'm glad you enjoyed yourself." Hannah smiled.

Jane came in to serve Margaret's breakfast and pour her a cup of tea from the pot.

"Thank you, Jane." Margaret then turned to John. "I was speaking to Sally at one point last night and she mentioned how her mother is always trying to put a little aside for special occasions but that her father always finds the money and spends it in the tavern."

"What of it?" John asked. Unfortunately that was a tale he had heard many times before.

"I was thinking that perhaps we could offer to run a savings book for the workers where they can pay in as much or as little

61

as they would like every week and only they can withdraw the money again. That would allow them to save a little for special occasions or to pay for medical bills or simply give them a little put aside if they should fall on hard times."

"What if they use it to save for a strike?" Hannah asked.

"I had thought of that myself," Margaret admitted. "And I admit I haven't found a way to prevent them from doing that."

"We can simply refuse to pay out if there is talk of a strike," John suggested. "We can make it clear this is to be used for personal reasons and not for union reasons. Not that they should need to save for a strike if they work here; I haven't prevented any of my workers from paying into their union."

"That sounds reasonable," Margaret agreed. "Should I suggest it to Nicholas?"

"Why not," John agreed. "He has also been making noises about getting together a school and nursery. Some kind of formal arrangement to look after young children so that their parents can work and a way to educate the older children who cannot afford proper schooling."

"That sounds like a wonderful idea," Margaret agreed. "Though a lot more complicated than a savings book or the canteen."

"Thanks to his children, Higgins hasn't had the time to investigate it himself. I was wondering if perhaps you could look into it," John suggested. "Find a location and work out costs, things like that."

"And the workers would be paying for this, yes?"

"Yes, though there are a few out-houses in the back that might be of use once cleared, which would save on the cost of renting somewhere."

"Are you sure this is wise," Hannah asked her son. "We are their employers, not a charity."

"And they will pay for the services, just as they now pay to eat in the canteen. As I see it, everybody wins. The workers are free to work without worrying about who is caring for their children and happy workers are more productive and less likely to strike."

Hannah conceded the point with a shrug, though it was clear that her views on employee relations were rather less progressive.

"What are your plans for today?" John asked Margaret.

"I have a few letters to write, chasing up outstanding

invoices and then I must count the wage packets. Did you have an opportunity to go to the bank yesterday?"

"Aye, the money's waiting for you in the safe," he confirmed.

"Thank you. I also have a fitting for my wedding dress later but though the day is busy, I hope I can find time to have a word with Nicholas."

"And don't forget, you and your aunt's family are joining us for dinner this evening," John reminded her.

"Are you sure you want to see them after the dreadful way my aunt behaved yesterday?"

"I'm sure I can put up with her for a while longer, though after we are married I may speak to my fellow magistrates and see if we can't have her banned from the town of Milton altogether." John teased.

"Don't be bad," Margaret laughed and even Hannah managed a smile.

"That woman," Hannah shook her head. "How she ever raised such a pleasant daughter I'll never know."

"You like Edith then?" Margaret sounded surprised.

"She is a little delicate for my tastes but she is certainly affable enough and she seems to care a great deal for her husband."

"She does. Much like the rest of us, she has her faults; she is inclined to be a little selfish at times and when we were children, she could be a monster when vexed, but her heart is pure and her love is strong. I shall miss her and Sholto so when they return to London. Even the Captain is most agreeable company."

"Perhaps she and her husband might visit on their own," John suggested.

"It is possible, I suppose. Since returning from Corfu they haven't travelled much because of the baby, but he is growing up quickly and they might be much more inclined to travel now."

"Then they are always welcome here," John told her. "Just so long as she leaves her mother at home."

Margaret couldn't completely stifle the laugh that escaped her.

Chapter Seven

The next few days flew by in a haze of work, socialising and bickering with her aunt and before Margaret knew it, her wedding day was here. She looked in the mirror but it felt as if there was someone else looking back at her.

"Miss Margaret?"

"Yes, Dixon?"

"You looked miles away there, Miss."

"Yes, I was. I feel very odd.

"It's only natural to be nervous," Dixon assured her. "It's a big day."

"Oh no, I am not at all nervous," she raised her hand to stop Dixon from fixing her hair. "The truth is I am a little sad."

Dixon put down the clip she was holding and sat on the stool, beside Margaret.

"I think that is only natural as well," she said kindly. "Your mother and father would have loved to be here today and it's not surprising that you would feel their loss more keenly today, of all days."

"Thank you, Dixon," Margaret smiled. "You are far more loyal than our family has any right to, you know."

"Nonsense."

"No, Dixon, it's true. You are the closest thing I have left to family now and the only person who knows my parents as well as I did. I only wish it were possible for you to give me away today."

"I will be there with you for as long as I can be," Dixon assured her. "And I will watch the ceremony from the back of the church."

"I know you will." She smiled warmly. "And I love you for it."

"Don't talk such nonsense," Dixon chided, though the tilt of her chin as she stood up said that she was both pleased and proud that Margaret thought so highly of her. "Now, sit still and let me finish your hair or this wedding will never happen."

Margaret did as she was told and sat patiently as Dixon brushed, combed, curled and pinned her hair atop her head, then placed the veil onto her creation so Margaret could see how it looked.

"You have surpassed yourself, Dixon. I feel that I look quite handsome." Margaret smiled at herself in the mirror. It always amazed her how Dixon managed to tame her thick mane of hair, for it was a task beyond her own talents.

"You look very handsome, Miss Margaret."

Dixon had tears shining in her eyes as she looked at her charge. Margaret reached behind her and squeezed Dixon's hand.

Once at the church, Margaret told Edith and the Captain that she needed to see the Reverend and excused herself to go and find John. She slipped into the side chamber, where the bridegrooms had often waited when her father had conducted weddings, and found John sitting with his head in his hands.

"You're not having second thoughts, I hope," she teased.

He looked up in surprise and a warm smile spread over his features as he drank her image in.

"You look..." He couldn't find the words. Her dress was a cream shade in a simple style with a fitted bodice, pinched waist and full skirt. Her veil, which was pushed back at the moment, was a delicate cream lace, held in place by a dozen tiny flowers on the crown of her head. She looked to him like an angel with a floral halo.

"Thank you."

Margaret also couldn't help but admire him. He cut a very fine figure indeed in his morning suit and Margaret felt a fluttering in her stomach as she observed him.

"Isn't it bad luck for the groom to see the bride before the wedding?" he asked as he came over to her.

"I don't believe in superstitions like that," she said firmly. "And I needed to see you before the ceremony."

"Oh?"

"I just... I wanted to say that if my father could have been here, he would have been so happy, John. You were his favourite pupil and I know he thought very highly of you. I only hope that wherever he is now, that he can see us and know how happy we are together."

John smiled and kissed her lips very gently, as though he was afraid he would spoil her beauty if he were too rough.

"Words can't do justice to how I feel about you," he told her, his voice husky with desire. "I thank the Lord every day for my good fortune and I hope to spend the rest of my life showing you how much I love you."

Margaret reached a hand up and cupped his cheek.

"And I love you, my darling. I thank the Lord every day

that you gave me a second chance."

"I would have given you a thousand chances," he assured her.

Margaret felt the sting of tears and tried to blink them back.

"Oh dear. You must not make me cry," she chided him, smiling through her tears. "What will people think?"

"Who cares what they think." He wrapped his arms around her waist and pulled her to him. "Soon you will be mine and the rest of the world can go hang for all I care."

"That is a little drastic, but I confess, I do share your sentiments."

A knock came at the door and they separated as John called for them to come in. Margaret dabbed at her eyes to dry her remaining tears.

"Oh, here you are," Father Byron said to Margaret. "Mrs. Shaw is looking for you."

"I'm sure she is." Margaret smiled. "Are we ready to start?"

"Whenever you two are. Would you like a few more minutes?"

John and Margaret looked at each other. "No," they said in unison and smiled.

"Right, then let's get the proceedings under way, shall we?"

The church was one of Milton's smaller ones, chosen because they did not want a grand ceremony. As it was, their guests filled most of the pews without the church being too cramped.

As Margaret entered the church on Captain Lennox's arm, she saw Nicholas and the other workers she was friendly with seated towards the rear of the church. She smiled warmly at them, glad that they had decided to attend when they might easily have felt out of place.

As she neared the altar, John turned to look at her, his expression warm and welcoming. He stepped towards her to take her from the Captain then escorted her the rest of the way himself.

The service flew by and later Margaret would be left with few memories other than the look on John's face as he placed her ring on her finger. Before she knew it, John was lifting her veil and they were signing the register. She grinned, for while her over excited mind was currently unable to remember saying 'I do', this was a sure sign that they were now man and wife.

While she thought no one was looking, she kissed him quickly on the cheek and he smiled warmly at her impudence. She was Mrs. John Thornton now and as soon as they were alone she intended to give in to all the urges that had been plaguing her for the past four weeks, morals be damned.

They walked back down the isle, arm in arm, and Margaret glanced up at her husband and wondered what she had done to be this lucky.

As they left the church, the guests threw rice and the couple were inundated with well wishes.

John had closed the mill today in honour of their wedding and although some workers from the mill had attended the church, they weren't invited to the wedding breakfast. Margaret understood that they couldn't attend, though she was sorry for it and took the time before they left the church to thank them all personally for coming.

The breakfast was relatively easy since Mrs. Shaw now seemed to have accepted the inevitable and rather than pointing out the inadequacy of the north, she chose to pout in silence instead.

Margaret didn't care. They ate their food, listened to the speeches and as soon as was acceptable, saw their guests off and headed up to John's bed chamber.

Margaret closed the door behind them, leaned back against it and let out a long sigh, seeming to deflate with it.

"Surely you are not unhappy?" John asked as he untied his cravat.

"I believe relieved is the word," she smiled at him. "We are finally man and wife. We have endured the gossip and scorn and are free to be alone together without inviting censure."

She pushed away from the door and walked up to him, wrapping her arms around his neck.

"So, Mr. Thornton, kiss me as I know you have longed to ever since that day in London."

John smirked and lowered his lips to hers. He started off gently, kissing her softly and with the reverence he felt she deserved. He was unable to keep that up for long though and as her lips parted beneath his, he deepened the kiss.

Margaret whimpered as she felt his passion and desire and found those same emotions reflected within herself. When he pulled away she felt slightly light-headed, as though she had forgotten to breathe.

"My," she whispered.

John cupped her cheek with his hand but his smile slowly faded.

"John? What is it?"

"Margaret, we have never spoken about what happens between a man and wife. Usually a bride's mother would explain everything before the wedding but..." He didn't know how to finish that sentence without reminding her of the loss.

Margaret smiled reassuringly, though it was tinged with sadness.

"While I may look innocent, and indeed I am sure that I am naive in many aspects of marital relations, I am aware of the... mechanics."

"You are?"

"Indeed. A combination of reading and helping with a few births has given me a fairly clear understanding of the theory."

"You were present at births?" he sounded surprised.

"Only two. Helstone was rather remote and it wasn't uncommon for us to be snowed in on occasion over the winter. As the vicar's wife my mother was often called upon to help with medical matters during these times and as as I grew older I would assist her."

"Somehow I can't see your mother acting as a midwife," John admitted.

"In all honesty she mainly held their hands, Dixon was the one who did most of the work."

"But you are comfortable with what we are about to do?"

"I find I am eager, though I confess I am also slightly apprehensive."

John leaned down and kissed her softly.

"You have nothing to fear from me, my love. I will be as gentle as I can be and take things slowly. You can ask me any questions you wish and I will answer them as honestly as I am able."

"I...." Margaret bit her lip. "I have heard it said that it is painful."

"The first time can be, but I will do everything I can to make it as pleasurable as possible."

"I'm sure. I trust you implicitly, my darling."

"I want to see you," John said as he smiled and reached behind her for the buttons on her dress.

Margaret blushed and dipped her head but she made no

move to stop him. Though she had little idea of what to do, instinct served her well and desiring to touch his flesh, she slipped her hands beneath his jacket and tugged his shirt loose so that she could run her hands over the planes of his back.

Margaret stretched languorously and sighed. She felt throughly sated and tired in the most appealing way.

"Good morning, my love."

She felt lips brushing the top of her head and mumbled an unintelligible response. She felt her head bobbing up and down slightly as John chuckled, causing his chest to rise and fall.

"I wasn't aware I had worn you out so throughly," he said as he began to play with a strand of her hair, running it through his fingers as though it were the finest spun silk.

Margaret snuggled in closer, unwilling to reach full consciousness quite yet.

John seemed content to simply lie there and when she was finally ready to face the day, he smiled warmly at her as she raised her head off his chest and looked up at him.

"Sleep well?" he asked.

"Mmm," she smiled lazily.

"I do believe I have rendered you incapable of speech!" he teased. "Wonders will never cease."

Margaret's only reply was to place a kiss on his chest.

"Not too sore?" he asked her.

"A little," she finally spoke. "But in a rather pleasant way."

John smiled and reached over with his free hand to brush a strand of her long dark hair off her forehead.

She smiled and rested her head back on his chest.

"I wish we could stay here all day," she said.

"We can if we wish."

"What would the servants say?" she teased.

"Let them talk, they're only jealous anyway."

"Well, I suppose as today is the only honeymoon we will be getting, we should make the most of it."

"We really should," he agreed. "But I think that having skipped dinner last night, first we must replenish our reserves with a hearty breakfast."

"But for that we will have to get dressed," she complained. "And I really have no desire to waste my energy on such a mundane task, especially not now that I know there are so many more appealing activities we could be engaged in."

John laughed. "Margaret Thornton, you really are a wicked woman, do you know that? You put such impure thoughts into my head that you must surely be the devil himself in disguise."

Margaret raised her head, resting her chin on his chest. She looked the very picture of innocence.

"And what's your excuse?" she asked. "For you made me feel things last night that were so good that they might well be considered a sin."

John smiled at the compliment. "Well, I suppose if we are to be damned to hell, at least we shall go there together."

They lay there for another half an hour making small talk about nothing in particular, until finally Margaret felt ready to face the day.

"Well, I suppose we should at least show our faces downstairs," Margaret said with a long suffering sigh. "Though I think I should like a wash first."

"I will have a bath drawn for you," John said, kissing the top of her head before he slipped out of the bed.

Margaret rested her head on her hand and watched him as he pulled on a robe. She felt strange. She was a woman now, no longer an innocent girl but it was more than that. She felt whole, complete, as though she had been missing something her whole life and was only now realising it.

"Are you just going to lie there and watch me?" he asked.

"It is a very nice view," she observed.

"Wicked, wanton woman," he chastised with a laugh. "I will send Dixon up to you once your bath has been drawn." He left then and Margaret reluctantly got out of bed and pulled her robe on before the servants walked in to find her naked!

Chapter Eight

It was nearly noon before Margaret was bathed, dressed and made her way downstairs. She found John and Hannah in the drawing room.

"What sort of time do you call this?" Hannah asked, though there was a mischievous twinkle in her eye.

Margaret blushed. "I'm afraid the excitement of yesterday must have taken its toll on me," she lied.

"Indeed," Hannah's tone said she didn't believe a word of it.

"Mother," John's tone was warning. While Margaret had been happy to be teased by him, being teased by his mother was a different matter altogether and he worried that Margaret would be offended.

"Very well," Hannah told her son before turning back to Margaret. "There is a very serious matter we need to discuss."

"Oh?" Margaret paled at the thought that she had disappointed her mother in law on only her second day as John's wife.

"Yes. When we discussed my staying here you promised me that you would turn one of our rooms into your personal sitting room and as yet you haven't even chosen a room, let alone redecorated it."

Margaret smiled with relief.

"Yes, indeed I did promise you that but I find I have been enjoying my time at the mill to such a degree that I have been rather lax in fulfilling my side of the bargain. I believe the room beside our bedroom would make a very nice room for us and I am rather partial to the wallpapers in there so very little would need to be altered."

"Then I shall see to it that the furniture is moved out tomorrow so you can begin to furnish it at your leisure." Hannah smiled warmly at her new daughter. "Now, if you will excuse me, I am spending the rest of the day with Fanny. Apparently she has a new cabinet she wishes to show me."

Her dislike of Fanny's love of possessions was clear and Margaret appreciated her attempt to give the new couple some privacy.

"Thank you, Hannah. I do hope your time with Fanny will not be too taxing."

"She is my daughter; somehow I shall manage, I'm sure." She went over to John and kissed his cheek. "Don't wait up for me, dearest, I may be late back." She went over to Margaret

71

and to her surprise, also bent to kiss her cheek. "Enjoy your day," she encouraged.

Margaret smiled at John.

"So, my love, what do you feel like doing?" he asked her.

"How about a quick lunch then a stroll around the town. Now that I am your wife, I feel the need to show you off a little."

"That sounds like a grand idea."

They had a simple lunch of sandwiches then set out, arm in arm, for their stroll. Being a Sunday the factories were quiet, the air was reasonably clear and the streets were less busy than usual, with children and families out for a walk rather than being engaged in the usual hustle and bustle of work.

They saw a few people they knew, nodded in greeting to them and they walked in companionable silence until John asked "What are you thinking?"

"Nothing in particular," Margaret smiled up at him. "I'm thinking how nice this is, walking with you, and how lucky I am to have found you. I'm thinking how pretty that little girl over there is, by the bakers shop. I'm thinking that it can't be long now before summer returns and how much I long to feel the sun on my skin."

John smiled. "You seem perfectly relaxed," he stated.

"I am. Aren't you?"

"Indeed, though I am sorry that I cannot give you the honeymoon you deserve."

Margaret tightened her grip on his arm and rested her head on his shoulder.

"Do not worry on my account. After everything that has happened, I believe a few weeks doing nothing would most likely come as a terrible shock to my system. Besides, I would much rather forgo a honeymoon now in the hope that one day in the not to distant future we might take a trip to Spain. I do so long for you to meet Frederick."

"And I should like to meet him. You have told him of our marriage, I presume?"

"Oh yes, and I received his reply a few days ago. He was thrilled for me, though sorry that he was unable to be here. He is married himself now to a lady called Dolores. And, would you believe it, also working in trade! Oh, how my aunt must despair of my mother's side of the family, dragging her good name down."

"Indeed," he smiled. "So tell me something of Spain, what is it like?"

"Surely your sister must have told you, since the Alhambra is one of the places she longs to visit?"

"I am sure she has, though I confess I have little patience for Fanny's ramblings and have developed the art of drowning them out when it suits me."

"Well, Cadiz, where Frederic lives, is quite a distance from Alhambra, and a few hundred miles further south. Frederick says that is it almost always sunny and warm, sometimes too warm. He says that the winds off the Atlantic can be harsh at times and the rainy season frequently causes flooding, though thankfully it is usually of very short duration. It is one of Spain's largest trading ports and according to Frederick, it is one of the oldest cities in the whole of Europe."

"And what of the people?"

"Very friendly. In one of his letters Frederick wrote that once you have been introduced to a Spaniard, he will forevermore greet you with the warmth one might reserve for a long lost son. They are a very family orientated society; children are very important to them and it is not uncommon to find many generations of a family living under one roof, by choice rather than necessity."

"Have you given much thought to starting a family?" he asked.

"I have," she turned and smiled up at him. "Though I confess I would like a few months to enjoy married life before having children, but I suppose that decision is out of our hands."

"There are steps we can take to reduce the risk," he said.

"There are?" she sounded surprised.

"Indeed, though they are not foolproof. And I suppose it would probably have been prudent to have had this discussion before last night."

"Quite," she smiled. "Although if I am already with child, I shall not be unhappy."

John stopped walking and turned to her. He gazed at her for a long while until she blushed and looked away.

"Do not be self-conscious," he said, putting his finger under her chin and gently tilting her head up. "You are remarkably handsome and you must get used to my staring, for I have no intention of ever stopping."

Margaret smiled and met his gaze.

"Your expression is unusual," she said.

"It is?"

"Yes. It is hard to explain but you look content and yet also slightly wild and possessive. It is a look that makes my stomach flutter, though I am not sure why."

"Perhaps because you can read my true thoughts and that excites you."

"What are your thoughts?" she asked.

His smile widened. "I'm afraid they are not fit to repeat in public."

"Then perhaps we should return home. I believe I have had quite enough fresh air for one day."

"What a very good idea," he said.

Chapter Nine

Margaret was at her desk, writing letters to chase up outstanding invoices when there came a knock at the door.

"Come in," she called, setting her pen down and looking up. "Nicholas! What can I do for you?" her shock at his unexpected appearance caused her to use his first name when she usually called him Mr. Higgins while at work.

"I was looking for the master."

"He is in town at the moment. Can I help you?"

Nicholas looked unsure so Margaret stood up and made her way around the desk.

"Thomas, when Mr. Thornton returns, please ask him to come to the house." She turned to Nicholas. "Come with me."

She led him across the forecourt and into the house. Jane greeted them, though neither had a coat for her to take. Jane was clearly curious as to why the overseer was in the main house, though she tried to hide her curiosity.

"Jane, bring some tea to the study, would you?" she asked the young maid before guiding Nicholas into the spacious study. She took a seat by the fireplace, though it was unlit. "So, what is troubling you, Nicholas?" she asked.

Nicholas looked almost guilty. "It's the Union," he admitted after a moment.

"The Union?" she was surprised to hear this since she and John had done everything possible to help their workers. Not only was the canteen providing the workers with a square meal every day at a fraction of the usual cost, they were now running a savings book, which most of the hands had chosen to pay into. And, although it was taking some time to find a suitable teacher, they had managed to set up a school room where the children could be looked after by other mothers whilst their parents worked. Margaret even taught the older children for two afternoons a week, until a proper teacher could be found for them.

"Aye," Nicholas confirmed. "They don't tell me much now that I'm an overseer, but I still hear things. Turns out that Hamper is up to his old tricks. He promised the men a wheel in the carding 'ouses again, and it's fallen through again."

"Oh no," Margaret sighed. In her opinion the wheels were a necessity not a luxury, because they helped to clear the air of the cotton fibres that clogged up the workers lungs.

"This time he says the price of cotton has shot up and

he can't afford to install it."

"So is the Union talking about another strike?" Margaret asked.

"I believe so, until wheels are installed in all the mills."

"And will they strike as one, like they did before?" That hardly struck her as fair, since John had installed wheels in all his sheds years ago, long before she even came to Milton.

"I couldn't tell you, Miss Margaret. Like I said, I'm management now, as bad as the master in some peoples eyes."

"This is troubling," Margaret said. Just then Jane arrived with the tea. "Just leave the tray, Jane, I will pour."

Margaret poured two cups as she thought over the implications of a strike.

"I'm sorry," Higgins said.

Margaret looked up, shocked.

"Whatever for?"

"For the Unions. If it wasn't for me we wouldn't have had that last strike. I feel as if this is my fault."

Margaret reached out and touched his arm.

"You must not blame yourself. You truly believed what you were doing was right and no one can fault you for that. Now that you know the reality, you have come to us in the hopes we can smooth things over. Believe me, Nicholas, none of this is your fault."

Just then Margaret heard the door and Jane telling the master they were in the study. John came in seconds later looking puzzled.

"We have some disturbing news," Margaret told him. She and Nicholas then explained as much as they knew.

"Hamper will never learn, the fool." John shook his head in frustration.

"What should we do?" Margaret asked.

"I will have a word with Hamper, find out the truth of the matter but... well if the Union is intent on striking, all I can do is appeal to my workforce. If they choose to go out on strike with the others, I'll have no option but to dismiss them."

"Isn't there another way?" Margaret asked.

"I can't make Hamper install a wheel any more than I can stop Slickson playing games with his workers or Dickinson pressing extortionate fines out of his workers wages. All I can control is my own mill. The last strike drove me to the brink of ruin; I can't risk that happening again because of someone else's business practices."

Nicholas was surprised to realise that he sided with Thornton on this. As much as he still believed that standing together gave the Union power, he could also now see how unfair it was that all masters were punished for the transgressions of the few. It was an uncomfortable position to find himself in and he wasn't sure which side he should support.

"I'd best get back to the mill," Nicholas said, getting to his feet.

"Yes," John agreed. "Thank you for telling us. You will keep me informed if you hear anything else, won't you?"

"Aye, master, you can count on it."

When he had left, John took the chair that he had vacated.

"If the worst happens, what are we to do?" Margaret asked.

"I don't know," John sighed. "I can import hands from Ireland again but they need training and much of their work is flawed in the beginning. We will almost certainly still be late in filling our orders and have to pay fines on them."

"But we will not go under again," Margaret tried to reassure him. "We still have plenty of assets."

"That is hardly the point," John said. "If the mill cannot support itself, I may as well close it now."

"But the workers?"

"We are not a charity, Margaret," he said kindly. "And if we cannot balance the books then we don't have a business."

Margaret knew he spoke the truth.

"After the hardship of the last strike, do you really suppose they will want to strike again so soon?" she asked.

"It was well over a year ago and memories are short, especially when they feel wronged." He sighed. "I will speak to Hamper at the dinner this week. If we all pressure him, maybe this can be averted."

"I do hope so." Margaret reached out and squeezed his hand.

Usually after dinner Margaret would retreat to her own sitting room, next to her and John's bedroom. Not so much because she disliked Mrs. Thornton but more so that both women could have their own space and wouldn't get on each other's nerves.

Tonight though, Margaret decided to join Hannah in the

drawing room as they both waited for John to return. Dinner had been a largely silent affair and though there was no ill-feeling between the two of them, a tense atmosphere hung in the air.

Margaret finally put her book down since she was able to remember almost nothing that she read, and walked to the window to look down into the yard. *'Hannah has the right idea,'* she thought. *'Her embroidery doesn't require too much concentration.'*

"He won't be much longer now," Hannah assured her daughter in law.

Margaret turned around and smiled, then resumed her seat.

"You really are very worried," Hannah observed. "I confess I thought your interest in the mill would be a passing fad, not something you would truly care about."

"How can I not care?" Margaret asked. "Not only is it important to both John and you, literally hundreds of lives depend on the mill. To take it lightly would be frivolous in the extreme."

"And if a strike does happen, will you still be able to see both sides then?"

"I will," she assured Hannah. "Whilst I believe that our mill is as good to its workers as it is possible to be, I realise that other mills are not. The workers have no power as individuals and if they have any hope of improving conditions, they must stand together. Of course to do so at the expense of the few well-run mills is rather self-defeating but as I have come to realise, there are rarely any simple answers in these matters."

"And what would your suggestion be?"

"Talk to the workers and Union leaders. Unfortunately in this case, Hamper is the problem and I can no more force him to sit down and talk to his men than I can make a canary bark."

Hannah actually laughed at the analogy which helped to break the tension in the room.

"Well, let us hope that John brings good news," Hannah said.

As though on cue they heard the sound of hooves trotting into the yard.

"He's home," Margaret said as she turned back to the window. She seated herself and tried to look as calm as possible when he entered the room.

78

"Both Mrs. Thorntons in the same room after supper? You should be careful or people might think you are friends," he teased as he bent down to kiss Margaret's cheek.

"Come now, John, anyone would think we didn't like each other," Hannah said, deadpan.

Margaret smiled as John bent to kiss his mothers cheek, then went to pour himself a drink.

"How was the dinner?" Margaret asked.

John loosened his cravat as he came and sat beside Margaret on the sofa. He reached out and took her hand, caressing the back of it with his thumb as though he found it relaxing.

"Good and bad," he answered. "There have been two nasty accidents recently that have got peoples' blood boiling. One boy lost a finger in the machines and a girl was scalped a few days later. The boy had only worked at Hamper's for two days and wasn't properly trained. The hands are getting restless and they seem to have focused on the accident and Hamper's refusal to install a wheel as a sign that he doesn't care about his workers."

"Who did the girl work for?" Margaret asked.

"For Watson. Fanny has been heard by her servants making some unsympathetic comments, which hasn't helped matters any."

"So what is to happen?" Hannah asked.

"If the workforce is all agreed, and that's every single one of them, then Hamper has agreed to install the wheels."

"But surely they will agree?" Margaret said.

"Hard to say. Rumours fly about the wheels, some say that are good, some believe they are an unnecessary expense that could stop them getting a pay rise."

"Surely we can educate them?" Margaret suggested.

"I doubt they'll listen to a master, any master, but I was thinking along similar lines. Higgins has told me that most of my workers are opposed to striking. I'm thinking of having a meeting before work, speaking to all the workers and telling them what I will have to do do if there is a strike. As overseers go, Higgins is popular with them, I'll ask him to talk to those who have influence and see if they can't talk some sense into the union leaders."

Margaret leaned into John and he put his arm around her shoulders.

"I suppose that is all we can do," Hannah agreed.

"It's just a matter of waiting now," John agreed.

And so for the next month, while they implemented the few ideas they had, mostly they stayed focused on their work and tried to be patient, until finally the next masters dinner arrived.

Margaret was sitting at her dressing table, brushing her long hair through when John entered the bed chamber. She smiled at him in the mirror.

"I began to think you would never come to bed," she said.

He walked over to her and rested his hands on her shoulders as he bent to kiss the top of her head. She was wearing a white silk nightgown that was revealing since it skimmed her curves, yet was still considered acceptable nightwear for a young wife.

"You did not have to wait up."

"Of course I did," he chided him. "How was the dinner?"

It had been John's turn to host the monthly meeting of masters and though she had wanted to listen in on their discussions, she had somehow found the strength not to eavesdrop on them.

"Our scheme seems to have worked and Hamper has agreed to install the wheels."

"Thank God," Margaret said, viably relaxing. "Though I suppose we have yet to hear how the Union will react."

"We do, but at last we have reason to hope things can be resolved amicably."

Margaret stood up and stepped into his arms. John inhaled deeply, breathing in her scent of lavender and roses. Somehow, no matter how much time she spent in the mill, he could always detect the delicate scent of her soap.

"I don't know why you continue to attend these dinners," she said. "You are always rather grumpy afterwards."

John smiled slightly. She knew full well why he had to attend the dinners but she was putting her parts on, as his mother might have said. Even so, he found it adorable.

"Then perhaps tomorrow we shall have dinner together," he suggested. "We could dine out for a change. It would give you an opportunity to show off some of those fine gowns you brought back from London."

Margaret looked up at him. "I would really rather we dined alone in our rooms," she said coquettishly.

"You are a wicked woman," John smirked slightly, though it was a pale imitation of his usual smiles.

"But you love me for it."

"I do." he leaned down and kissed her deeply.

"You can't kiss a woman like that and then leave her wanting," she admonished. After these dinners he was rarely in the mood to be intimate with her and tonight she intended to change that. That was why her hair was already down, since John enjoyed seeing it loose, and why she had chosen this nightgown.

"Then what would you suggest I do?" he asked.

"Well, for a start I think this should go," she said, tugging on his cravat.

"Really? And then what?"

"Then, I think you should have a bath."

"At this time of night?" he almost laughed at the idea.

"I have already had Jane draw it and I have used Dixon's special bath salts which are supposed to aid relaxation."

"Still."

"And, if you are a very good boy and don't argue with me, I might just agree to scrub your back for you."

John smiled. Actually the thought of a nice hot bath was rather appealing.

"Very well, you win again, my love."

He allowed her to lead him to their bath chamber and stood still as she undressed him. He had to say though, if relaxation was her aim, she was failing miserably since her ministrations were only serving to excite him. Still, he stood passively and allowed her to undress him, though he was sure that she was intentionally taking her time to tease him.

Finally he was naked and to his surprise, she then pulled her own nightgown off and stepped into the bath. She held her hand out towards him and he accepted her invitation and stepped in with her. She sat at the rear of the tub and settled him between her legs as she began washing him with the sponge. He gave himself over to her attentions.

She washed him firmly and throughly and slowly he felt the tension draining out of him. As she washed his hair and massaged her fingers into his scalp, he couldn't help moaning with pleasure. He was almost literally putty in her hands right now and when she rose and dried him off, he found that he was more than ready to do his duty in the marital bed.

As they lay sated in each others arms afterwards, Margaret tracing patterns on his chest with her fingers, he once again thanked the Lord for his good fortune in finding this woman.

"John?" she finally broke the easy silence that had formed between them.

"Mmm?"

"Why do these meetings upset you so?"

John sighed deeply but he didn't answer.

"Is it because of me?" she asked.

"What makes you say that?"

"I choose to ignore the gossip but that doesn't mean that I am unaware of it."

"Then you can guess what they say."

She could. They would probably say, like others in Milton, that he was a gold-digger, that he married her for her money; that he was a fool to allow his wife to work in his mill and that she worked there only because she did not trust him.

"Tell me honestly, John, is there any way I can make things better for you?"

"What do you mean?" he asked.

"Well, if I stopped helping with the accounts, would that help matters?"

John tightened the arm that was around her shoulders.

"I love working with you," he answered honestly. "I love that I can talk to you about the mill and know that you are not only interested but that your answers and suggestions are practical and informed. I love that you smile sometimes when you tell me about what you have done at work that day and I have never found a bookkeeper who has been able to rival your ability to get overdue invoices paid. You are my wife, my partner and my equal; I would gladly be ridiculed every single day than give up any part of our relationship."

Margaret raised her head to look into his eyes and smiled at him. She found herself choked with emotion.

"Do you mean that? You are not just humouring me?"

"I respect you too much to ever humour you, my love. Yes, it irritates me when others tell me how you should behave and cast aspersions on your character and our relationship, but only because they do not understand what we have together. The very idea that you should behave more like Fanny is an offence of the highest order."

"Really, John, you shouldn't talk of your sister in that way," she gently chastised him.

"But I must. Do you think she would ever have done what

you just have for her husband because he was troubled? She is far too selfish to put her husband's needs before her own. Besides, she is no admirer of yours so I don't know why you are constantly defending her."

"I know she does not like me and I'm sure that is at least partially my fault, but I think that she means well."

"Do you know why she doesn't like you? Because you are everything she would like to be. Even when you had little money, you were a true lady; refined, elegant and educated. You have an air of nobility about you, a dignity and majesty that no amount of money can buy. That is something Fanny will never have no matter how hard she tries."

"Don't you think that is a little unfair?"

"No I don't. She is mean and spiteful when it suits her and she looks down her nose at everyone who is not of means. Did you know that she even taunted me for not speculating when I closed the mill? Never mind that my father's speculation was the reason we lost everything when Fanny was a girl. Watson has also told me what she thinks of you working at the mill and it doesn't bear repeating. I know that she is my sister and that I must shoulder some of the blame for how she has turned out, but that doesn't mean I have to like her or her small-minded opinions."

"She taunted you?" Margaret sat up looking very indignant. "Why that..." she didn't finish her sentence because she had been raised not to speak such words aloud.

"Oh dear, now you are upset and the bathwater will have cooled. How am I to calm you down?"

"Do not tease me, John. She can say what she likes about me but she is your sister; it is unforgivable that she should be so mean spirited towards her own family, especially since you have been so good to her."

John sat up and took her hands in his. He smiled warmly at her.

"You are the most loving and loyal creature I know," he said. "And I love you for it but you must try not to let a small mind like my sister's get to you."

Margaret took a deep calming breath, though clearly she was still perturbed by his sister's actions.

"Come on, love, it is late and we must try top get some sleep or we shall be in no fit state for work tomorrow."

"You are right, of course." Margaret sighed and allowed

83

John to pull her with him as he lay back down. She curled into him and although she felt that she would never calm down enough to asleep, she soon found the rhythmic rise and fall of his chest lulled her into a deep slumber. But as soon as she awoke, her grievances returned to her, full force.

"Hold still, Miss Margaret," Dixon chided as she tried to braid Margaret's hair.

Though Margaret was no longer a Miss, she never corrected Dixon. She rather liked when Dixon called her 'Miss Margaret' since it felt like a term of endearment.

"I'm sorry, Dixon. I am rather upset this morning and it is making me restless."

"What troubles you so?" Dixon asked.

Since she and Margaret had moved into the house at Marlborough Mills, Dixon's duties had been cut back to what they should be. She was only Miss Margaret's lady's maid now and the housework fell to the other servants. She was much happier because not only was she doing what she had been trained to do but the work was also easier on her ageing joints.

"It's John's sister, Fanny Watson," Margaret confessed. "I learned something rather disturbing last night, Dixon, and I am unsure what to do about it."

"Can I ask what you discovered?" Dixon asked, aware that though it was not her place to pry, Mrs. Hale had often chosen to confide in her and it was possible that Miss Margaret would want to do the same.

"She has been rather disloyal to her brother," Margaret confided, though she was unwilling to go into detail. "I knew that she was no great admirer of mine but to hear her speak ill of her brother... Well, let's just say that it troubles me a great deal."

"Not all families are as close as yours, Miss Margaret. It would be lovely if everyone showed the same loyalty you do, but the sad truth is that few people were raised with your parents love and kindness."

"I know you are right, Dixon, yet still I am finding it hard to forgive her."

"I never said you should forgive her," Dixon corrected. "Only understand her a little better. Loyalty is a rare quality in this world and it should be prized wherever it is found. You are one of the most loyal people I know and you should never apologise for being protective of those you care about."

Margaret smiled at Dixon in the mirror. "Indeed it is rare," she said. "And I do cherish it when I find it, Dixon."

Dixon blushed at the compliment. Unsure how to respond, she continued without acknowledging the remark.

"Mrs. Watson is not part of this family any more so I wouldn't let her gossip concern you, Miss Margaret."

"That is good advice," she said, though not quite so easy to put into practice, she lamented silently. She decided to move the conversation on. "So how are you settling in here?"

"Very well. Indeed I find I hardly notice the noise from the mill these days."

"Good."

"There," Dixon pronounced as she slipped a final pin into Margaret's hair. "All finished."

She helped Margaret into her clothes, though she still tried to insist that she could dress herself.

"Oh, Dixon, would you remind the kitchen that I won't be here for dinner this evening."

"You are visiting that Higgins again, I assume?" she asked.

"Yes," Margaret smiled at Dixon's insistence of calling him 'that Higgins'.

While she did enjoy spending time with him and his family, she also liked to give John and his mother one night alone every week. Hannah had been very good about accepting Margaret into their lives and, knowing how much Hannah loved her son, she tried not to take John away from her completely.

"I thought I heard the cook say something about the master dining out this evening."

"Oh, I thought he was joking. He knows I go to see Mary and Nicholas on Wednesdays. Well, he will just have to take his mother to dinner in my place. I'm sure she'll enjoy that."

Margaret headed downstairs and entered the study. Wednesday mornings were set aside for her to manage her own business matters. Although there wasn't an awful lot of work required, she felt it was best to keep on top of things.

She picked up her post and began opening it. The first letter was from the bank, confirming the rent payments and she carefully entered the details into her accounting ledger.

The next letter was regarding another of Mr. Bell's speculations. It seemed to Margaret that Mr. Bell seemed to speculate a lot. She supposed he could afford to lose the money, as indeed he had done on two of the ventures since she'd become his heir. This letter detailed the third speculation to make money, and quite a substantial sum it was.

She felt a little guilty as Mr. Bell's investments piled up in her bank account but she really didn't know what to do with the money. Speculation wasn't in her nature since it was really just glorified gambling and the mill wasn't in need of any additional finance. Indeed now that the necessity to pay rent was gone, which Margaret had insisted upon once they were married, John had finally been free to raise the wages to what they were five years ago. Ideally Margaret would like to have given them a larger rise but John was right, if the mill couldn't support itself, they might as well give up.

Margaret had considered starting some sort of charitable venture with the money, but the people of Milton were proud and unlikely to want charity in any form.

Margaret put those thoughts aside for now and continued going through her business post.

John came in mid-morning to join her for tea. Usually he did not indulge in such luxuries but on a Wednesday Margaret liked to discuss her own business dealings with him. She was reasonably confident of her management skills now but she still liked the reassurance of discussing things with her husband. She had offered to turn over her property and business dealings to him in their entirety but he had refused, insisting that whilst he was happy to help and advise her, this was her money. They had compromised with John joining her so that she could talk over anything she was unsure about.

She told him of her latest windfall with a little dismay and he listened, equally shocked by Mr. Bell's frequent good fortune. Though if he himself had been at all tempted by this success to try speculating, the recent misfortune of local businessman Mr. Reynolds was enough to caution him. Much like John's father, Reynolds had lost everything and he and his wife were now living on the kindness of his sister and her husband.

"You are becoming quite the heiress," John smiled.

"Should we not do something with this money though? Perhaps buy more property or invest in other businesses."

"What property, what businesses?" he asked. "Most new ventures are as risky, if not more so than speculating. And as for property, it would require some investigation on both our parts before we had an idea of what gave the best returns."

"You are right, of course," she agreed. "I just feel as though... As though there is something I ought to be using it for, but I have no idea what I mean by that."

John reached out and took her hand. "There is no hurry. When the time is right, or more importantly, when the deal is right, you will know it. You have proven that you have good instincts; listen to them."

Margaret smiled. "Well, I am finished here so when we are done with our tea I will join you at the mill. Oh, and before I forget, Dixon said that you have told the kitchen that we were dining out tonight. You must have forgotten that I am having dinner with Nicholas and the children this evening."

"I had, I apologise."

"I am sure your mother will be happy to accompany you."

"I believe she has plans this evening," he said

"Really?" Margaret had never known Hannah to willingly socialise with many people at all.

"Indeed, she is dining with Mr. Whitaker and his sister."

"Daniel Whitaker, the printer?"

"That's him."

"I wasn't aware that they were friends."

"She has been rather circumspect about the friendship." John agreed.

"You don't think that... well, that perhaps there might be a romance blossoming between them?"

"I wouldn't like to speculate, but Whitaker has been a widow for nearly five years now."

"Well, it is hardly a pairing I would have envisaged but if it makes her happy, then I wish them well."

"They are more alike that it might seem on the surface. Whitaker comes from humble stock, the son of a sailor. He made his money in the merchant navy, which is hard and dangerous work. He saved enough to quit when he was 25 and invested in a printing press, one of Milton's first. He upgraded to the rotary press when it came in and has never looked back since."

"He seems like such a genteel fellow to have had such a harsh past."

"He has worked hard to better himself and the fortunes of his children." John smiled.

"Then indeed they do have much in common. I believe

there is little your mother wouldn't do for her son."

"I am blessed," he smiled, letting her know he counted her among his blessings. "If mother could find a little happiness of her own though, I'd not begrudge her."

Margaret smiled. Both mother and son possessed a fierce loyalty to and love for each other that was truly admirable.

"And what of Mr. Whitaker's sister? Is she single?" Margaret asked.

"Her name is Mary Bristow, and she is widowed. Unluckily her husband died in an accident not five years after they were married. Her brother has taken care of her ever since and raised her sons as his own."

"He truly does sound like a man of good character. If your mother does have feelings for him, I only hope that he reciprocates."

John frowned, remembering how harsh unrequited love was. Margaret saw the pain that flashed across his face and sought to distract him from the memory.

"Perhaps you would like to join me this evening," Margaret suggested. "I'm sure Nicholas will not object."

"Aye, I might just do that. I have something I'd like to discuss with him."

Chapter Ten

Nicholas looked from Margaret and John to Thomas, one of his adopted children.

"The teacher says he's a bright spark," he smiled with pride. "I'm glad you found someone so good."

"Miss Tate is a very capable and caring woman," Margaret agreed. "I have heard many fine reports since she started."

"What about the other children?" John asked.

"Miss Tate says that Kelly and William have an aptitude for maths but Scotty's not so fast as his brothers and sister. Alice, Sarah and the twins are too young for schooling yet but Mary's been trying to teach 'em to read a bit at home."

John looked at the children as they ate their simple supper thinking what a shame it was that even though some seemed exceptionally bright, all would no doubt end up in working in the mill as soon as they turned eleven. He remembered how bitterly he had hated leaving school, and he had been sixteen at the time. Though better educated that most, he had always felt that he lacked something, hence why he had sought lessons with Mr. Hale in the first place. His mother had never understood it but John had a thirst for knowledge that industry alone just couldn't sate.

"So," Nicholas asked John. "Not that you're not welcome, but what brings you here tonight? Not been stood up I hope?"

It said a lot about their relationship and the mutual respect that had formed between them that Nicholas felt able to tease his master.

"As a matter of fact I was," John smiled, showing that no offence was taken. "But the main reason I wanted to come was to ask you about your position as overseer. I know it's lost you some friends but I just wanted to make sure you were settling to the task without too many hiccups."

"A few don't want to call me friend any more but most seem reasonable. Only those that don't do their work have anything to fear from me, and I'm happy to say they're few and far between."

"Good," John sat back in his chair. "Because I was wondering how you'd feel looking after the factory for a few weeks."

"On me own?" Nicholas sounded shocked.

"Mother would look after the office work but you'd have sole charge of the factory. Would you be willing?"

"I don't know, Master. I hadn't rightly given it any thought. Is there something wrong?"

"Not at all. As you know, Margaret never got a honeymoon and at some point I'd like to take her to Spain to see her brother."

Margaret watched the exchange between the two men with interest. Nicholas had always been a proud man, and rightly so since he had a lot to be proud of. She didn't know of many people (and even fewer who were as hard up at times as Higgins had been in the past) who would have taken in eight children who weren't his own. Still, these days he seemed to have lost some of his anger, which pleased Margaret immensely.

"I'm sure the lass would like that." Nicholas smiled at Margaret.

"Indeed I shall," Margaret agreed.

"Well, I don't see any reason why I couldn't manage on my own for a few weeks. I might need your mother to sign for deliveries and such like, but I'm sure we can work sommat out. When were you thinking of goin'?"

"Not for a few months at least. I want to make sure this talk of a strike has completely died down before we go."

"Well whenever you go, I hope you'll enjoy yourselves."

"To be perfectly honest," Margaret smiled. "In over sixteen years John has never had more than three days away from work. I'm a little worried that he will go slightly insane being forced to take so much time off."

"I always said you'd be the death of me," John said, reaching out to take her hand.

Higgins observed the couple as they smiled at each other. Ever since Thornton had taken him on, Higgins' respect for the man had grown. In recent months though, since Margaret had accepted him, he had come out of his shell and Nicholas had observed sides of him he would have sworn didn't exist before.

He was so much more relaxed nowadays. He was still firm with his business and its workers, but the tension that had seemed to radiate from him before was gone. Outside of work or away from the observations of the other employees, he was also willing to banter with his overseer and more than ready to smile when pleased.

The humanitarian in him had also grown. Nicholas was sure the softening of his stance with regards to his workers was the result of Margaret's influence, even before they were betrothed, but since they had been together Thornton genuinely seemed to care about the people in his employ now. Just two months ago he paid out of his own pocket for the doctor to attend one of his hands when the man fell ill. The poor fellow had died, too weak to fight off the infection but Thornton's gesture hadn't gone unnoticed by Nicholas or the other workers.

"So, Kelly," John tuned to the oldest of the Boucher girls. "What is Miss Tate teaching you in school?"

"We practised the times tables today," she answered. "I find them hard to remember sometimes but it's gettin' easier."

"Practice makes perfect," John said, smiling at her. "Why don't you practice with us?"

Kelly looked startled at the idea of reciting her times tables in front of these two fine people, but like Nicholas, she wasn't one to be easily cowed. She stood up from her chair, as Miss Tate made them do, and began reciting her two times table with as strong a voice as she could muster.

Chapter Eleven

Margaret was full of nervous energy as she ran around their bedroom, thinking of a dozen or more things that she hadn't packed.

"Oh, what about John's cufflinks?"

"I've packed them, Miss Margaret," Dixon repeated for perhaps the hundredth time.

"And my green dress?"

"You already asked me," Dixon reminded her.

"Yes, of course." Margaret took a deep breath and sat on the bed. "I'm sorry, Dixon, I'm just so excited to be seeing Frederick, even though I know it will take us days to arrive there. And at the same time I feel guilty about leaving the mill. What if something should happen while we're away?"

"Nothing will happen that Mother and Higgins can't handle," John assured her as he entered the bedroom.

"I know," Margaret answered. She felt out of control and it wasn't a very pleasant sensation.

"Come on, love. The cases are being loaded onto the carriage and we will be in Liverpool within a few hours. You'll feel easier once we're on our way."

"I do hope so," she said as they walked out of the room.

By the time they got outside, the cases had been loaded and secured to the top of the carriage and Hannah was waiting in the courtyard to bid them farewell.

"Be safe," she said, cupping John's face in a rare show of affection.

"I will, Mother. Call Watson if you have any problems you can't handle."

"There's nothing I can't handle better than that buffoon," she assured him.

"Right you are." He smiled.

"I will be fine, John. You've no need to worry about me or the mill."

"I can't help it, Mother." He kissed her cheek and stepped away.

Hannah stepped up to Margaret.

"Look after him," she implored.

"I will," Margaret assured her before pulling her into a tight hug. Hannah looked uncomfortable at the gesture but put her arms around her daughter-in-law anyway.

"Take care," Margaret said as she pulled away.

"I will," Hannah assured her, patting her hand. "Try to enjoy yourself and don't fret about us too much."

"I'll try," Margaret smiled and reluctantly stepped away and into the carriage with John and Dixon.

It was silly but though she was pleased to be seeing her brother again, she felt slightly upset at the thought of leaving Hannah and the mill for a month.

John was right though and by the time they arrived in Liverpool she felt much easier. They were staying at an inn overnight and would set sail from the port the next morning.

"How long do you think it will take?" Margaret asked as they lay in bed that evening.

"If the wind is in our favour, three days, perhaps a little less."

"And if not?"

"Four, perhaps five but clippers are very fast, Margaret. We should make good time."

"I do hope so." She raised her head and looked up at her husband. "I doubt I shall get any sleep tonight."

John smiled. Though they had been married for the best part of a year now, he was still seeing new sides to his wife. This aspect of her personality reminded him of a child on Christmas eve.

"Well, there will be little else to do on the ship so you can catch up on your sleep then."

"You are too good to me, you know." Margaret smiled.

"I give you your honeymoon more than six months late and I am too good to you?" he sounded incredulous.

"Yes. I know you must find it even harder than I to leave the mill and yet you haven't said a word of complaint. You continue to indulge my erratic moods without any reproach when I am sure I would have driven many a man half mad by now. I know for a fact that I have severely tried Dixon's nerves."

"Only because she is as excited as you at seeing Frederick again."

Margaret stretched forward and kissed him.

"What did I do to deserve you," she asked rhetorically.

"Well," John smirked. "I believe most people can be bought for eighteen thousand pounds."

Margaret gasped and lightly punched his chest.

"Mr. Thornton, how dare you be so impertinent! I've a good

mind to deny you my affection until we return home."

"You could not be that cruel."

"Indeed I could."

"Perhaps, but I don't believe that even you have the willpower to resist me for a whole month."

"You think very highly of yourself for a tradesman." Margaret couldn't stop a smile from tugging at the corners of her lips.

"And you think very highly of yourself for a tradesman's wife."

"I thought I had bought you, which makes you my slave, not my husband."

"Well in that case, I am at your service, madam."

Margaret could contain her laughter no longer.

"You are too bad, John."

"It's your fault," he said. He suddenly grabbed her and turned them so she was lying on her back and he was hovering above her. "You bring out the devil in me."

Margaret recognised the desire in his eyes and was sure it was reflected in her own.

"So I am to blame for your base instincts now, am I?" she asked, barely suppressing a gasp as he began kissing her neck.

"Oh yes. Your every move seems designed to incite my passion."

"It is not conscious, I assure you." Her hand began caressing the firm lines of his back.

"Which only makes you all the more enticing." He began tracing a line of kisses over her collar bone.

"Then it seems I cannot win."

"Oh no," he assured her.

"Then I suppose I had better submit with good grace," she said, with a long suffering sigh.

John looked up at her, then taking him quite by surprise, Margaret knocked his arm out from under him and pushed him over, so she was on top again.

"What happened to giving in with good grace?" he asked, not at all displeased by her display of dominance.

"I decided this was more fun." She leaned down and kissed him passionately. "Besides, I have a lot of nervous energy to work off, so just lie back and think of England, darling. There's a good boy."

John lay back and closed his eyes, preparing to enjoy

the night ahead.

He frequently wondered why his peers often chose women of inferior intellect and with little spirit. They were handsome, to be sure, but they were little more than ornaments adorning their husband's arm. He was certain that none of those women or ladies would ever show the same passion that Margaret brought to the marital bed.

In the past his mother had sometimes seemed to be pushing meek and malleable young ladies into his path, people that she believed would make him a good wife, not that's she had ever pressed her cause though. He sometimes wondered what would have happened if he had chosen one of those ladies. Would they have stood by him when the mill closed down? Somehow he couldn't see them enduring hard times like his mother had when he was a boy.

Margaret on the other hand, Margaret would be with him through thick and thin, and not only with him, she would be fighting right alongside him. She was a rare treasure indeed and he still did not feel worthy of her love. That didn't mean he was foolish enough to look a gift horse in the mouth, however. No, he would love her for as long as she would have him and if he was good to her and very very lucky, that might just be for the rest of his life.

"Frederick!"

Throwing caution and decorum to the wind, Margaret ran down the gangplank and straight into Frederick's waiting arms. He scooped her into a bear hug and spun her around, his grin just as broad as hers.

They were still hugging tightly when John and Dixon reached them.

"Oh Margaret, my little goose! I began to think this day would never come."

John smiled politely at the lady who had clearly accompanied Frederick, but he wouldn't chastise him for the lack of introduction. The joy on Margaret's face was enough for him to forgive them both any indiscretions right now.

"Don't be silly, Fred." Finally she pulled away and looked at him, cupping his cheek in her hand.

"You look radiant, Margaret."

"After three days at sea, believe me I do not feel it. You though, you look perhaps the most content I have ever seen you."

"I am. Did you get my last letter?"

"About the baby, yes. I cannot wait to see him."

"And you shall."

Seeming to realise that there were other people who needed greeting, they finally stepped apart and Margaret took John's hand as Fred greeted Dixon and hugged her tightly.

"Dear Dixon, how I have missed you."

"It's so good to see you again, Master Frederick."

John leaned down close to Margaret's ear.

"Little goose?" he asked.

"Fred's pet name for me," she smiled for a moment at the memories from her childhood the name evoked, before stepping forward with John. "Fred, I would like you to meet my husband, John Thornton."

They shook hands.

"Margaret told me how kind you have been to the family, especially to my parents. I am sorry I didn't get the chance to thank you while I was in England, though I hope I can rectify that now."

"It was my honour. Your parents were wonderful people."

"Thank you." Fred reached out for the woman who had been standing quietly beside him. "And this is my beloved wife, Dolores."

John and Dixon shook her hand but Margaret opted for a hug. When she pulled away Margaret looked embarrassed.

"Oh, do forgive me. It's just that Fred had told me so much about you that I feel I know you already."

"It is no problem, Margaret. I too have heard much of you and very much look forward to knowing you." Her English was good though heavily accented. She tended to drop her H's and say her J's as an H. She also pronounced Margaret as Mar-gar-eta.

"Come," Fred said. "I have two carriages waiting to take us home. We should just have time for a drink on the terrace before dinner."

The cases were loaded and John offered to travel with Dolores and Dixon so that Frederick and Margaret could share a carriage. No one seemed to object, so the siblings rode together.

"I am sorry about Father," Fred said. "I wish I could have been there for you."

Margaret smiled sadly. "It could not be helped. Besides, it is a much greater comfort to me to know that you are safe."

"I am safe, Margaret, and happy. Dolores and her family have been so good to me and though I still miss you all every day, they have adopted me as their own."

"I'm glad of it," Margaret said, taking his hand. "And how is..."

"Enrique? You say it like Henry but without the H and add a 'kay' at the end. En-re-kay."

"Enrique," she repeated, sounding it out on her tongue.

"He is very well," Frederick smiled. "Dolores dotes on him and he is quite the most handsome baby you have ever seen."

"I can believe it," Margaret smiled. "And work?"

"Work is splendid and busy, though Dolores's father has been very good about letting me spend time at home with Dolores and the baby."

"Do you have a nanny?"

"After a fashion. The Spanish like to be very involved with their children but there is a what we might call a mothers help. She doesn't just look after the baby but helps Dolores with anything she might need. She is watching him for us now."

"That sounds very practical."

"What about you? Haven't you and John thought of starting a family."

"We have discussed it but we would rather wait a while before having children."

"Ah," Frederick said knowingly. As siblings he felt able to be more free with her than he might with others. "Dolores' faith prohibits us from practising any form of birth control."

"Do you mind that?"

"Not especially, though I confess that the idea of having a dozen or more children is a little daunting."

"Yes," Margaret smiled. "I can see what you mean."

The carriages pulled into the Plaza de Mina and stopped in front of one of the large houses that surrounded the square.

"This is home," Frederick said as he climbed down from the carriage and helped Margaret out.

The house was a large neoclassical mansion that was rather intimidating for both its size and grandeur. As the drivers unloaded the luggage, Frederick showed Margaret and John inside and gave them a quick tour before showing them to their bedrooms.

The house was occupied by Frederick and Dolores, her parents, Anthony and Conchita and her younger, unmarried brother, Christobal.

"You and John will be in here, Margaret," he said, opening the door to one of the most beautiful rooms Margaret had ever set eyes on, though she conceded that it might be because it was so very different from anything she had ever seen before. The floor was a light marble and had been shined so that it gleamed. The furnishings were white or very light in colour and the windows were covered with the finest netting Margaret had ever seen. In the middle of the room stood a large four poster bed, with more of the fine netting tied back to each post.

"That door there leads to the dressing room and over on the right, that door leads to Dixon's room." Fred explained. "You'll probably want to leave the windows open overnight as it gets very warm, so let the netting down around the bed; it stops the insects from attacking you. I'm sure you want to freshen up so I'll send a servant up with some warm water. When you're ready, come and join us for a drink on the back terrace. Dolores' parents have gone to the theatre this evening and Christobal has gone out with some friends to give us a chance to catch up."

"That was very thoughtful of them," John said.

"They are lovely people. I'm certain that you will like them."

"Indeed," Margaret smiled and kissed Frederick on the cheek. "Thank you for making us feel so welcome."

Fred smiled and excused himself. Margaret looked around the room and made her way to the window. She looked out to the gardens behind the house and saw plants that she had never seen before; cacti, palm trees and a grass so thick and lush that it could almost be called reeds.

"Everything is so exotic," she said, quite awed by the experience. Although she had read much about Spain in the hope of knowing a little more about where her brother lived, it hadn't prepared her for the reality of its sun-kissed beauty.

"I believe it is warmer here than the factory," John said. "Though far less humid. This climate would never do for cotton spinning."

Margaret turned and smiled.

"Is that all you have to say?" she teased. "I bring you to this wonderful, warm, exotic country, introduce you to my only brother and all you can do is think about work."

"I'm sorry, my love," John laughed. "I will do better."

Just then a servant knocked and entered with a large jug of warm water which she emptied into the basin. Dixon set about unpacking their belongings while John and Margaret had a quick wash.

"I believe I shall try wearing something light," Margaret said. "It might make the heat a little more bearable."

When they had dressed, they headed down to the back terrace to find Dolores and Fred sitting at the table out there and cooing over their baby.

"Oh!" gasped Margaret as she glimpsed the boy. "He is quite lovely."

"You would like to hold him?" Dolores asked.

Margaret grinned and nodded so Dolores placed the child into her arms.

"Oh, he is adorable, isn't he John?" she said, quite captivated with Enrique's cherubic face. John came up behind her and looked over her shoulder at the child.

"Indeed," he said, unable to stop himself from imagining Margaret holding his child in her arms.

Frederick poured them both a glass of a dark red punch that he called sangria, while Margaret asked Dolores how old the baby was and how well he was developing.

As the ladies doted over the child, John and Fred got to know each other a little better. John was very interested in Fred's work as a junior partner for the family firm, Barbour and Co. They both imported and exported goods, mainly between Spain and the Americas.

When dinner was served on the terrace, Enrique was placed into a bassinet while they ate rather than being taken away. Fred explained that children were welcome at the dinner table in Spain unlike middle and upper class families in England.

They drank red wine with the meal, which Margaret found a little heavy but John seemed to enjoy. They were both a little taken aback at the cold tomato soup that was served, called gazpacho. Fred explained that it was a local delicacy in the south of Spain. The main course was seafood paella, a rice dish served with muscles, prawns and cuttlefish.

The tastes were unusual but they were not unpleasant, though Margaret did wonder how Dixon would fair on such dishes.

The sun began to set as they finished the main course and Fred lit a series of oil lamps that surrounded the terrace.

"What's that smell?" John asked.

"Citronella oil mixed with the lamp oil," Fred answered. "It helps repel the insects."

"It smells lovely," Margaret commented.

Dessert was then brought out and of all the possible dishes, it was rice pudding!

"I thought it would make you feel at home," Fred said with an impish smile. "It's quite popular in these parts, though it's rarely served warm like back home."

"Thank you," Margaret smiled at his thoughtfulness.

Keen to show off his adopted country, Fred explained the plans he had for them while they were visiting. It was quite a list and included everything from the opera to the Torre Tavira or Tavira Tower, which had something called a camera obscura that projected an image of the whole town onto a screen. Although Fred tried to explain it, Margaret couldn't quite understand but she hoped the mechanism would become clear when she saw it for herself.

When he had finished detailing his plans for their visit, his list of places he wanted to show them was so long, Margaret doubted that the three weeks they had would be enough!

Conversation naturally led to the history of the region and Fred and Dolores happily explained it, along with local idioms and customs.

Fred was just regaling them with descriptions of the many festivals, or fiestas in Cadiz when Dolores' parents returned and Frederick introduced them.

Anthony and Conchita welcomed them with a hug and a kiss on either cheek, which surprised both Margaret and John. They knew, however, that the customs were different here so neither took offence. Margaret had rarely received such a warm welcome even from her own family and she found that she rather liked it. She remembered Fred once saying that once you had met a Spaniard he would thereafter always greet you like a long lost child. Margaret finally thought she had an idea of what he had meant.

Dolores parents joined them on the terrace and conversation flowed freely. Baby Enrique spent much of the evening being passed from person to person and aside form a brief cry when he became hungry and was taken inside to be fed, he was perfectly well behaved.

John was hesitant with the child at first, never having been around many babies before but he soon got the hang of it. When he saw Margaret smiling at him as he cradled the child, he couldn't help but wonder again what their child would be like.

Finally Enrique began to grizzle and Dolores decided it was time to put him to bed. After their long journey and the difficulty getting a good nights sleep on a boat, John and Margaret decided to retire also.

Chapter Twelve

The next day Fred went into the office early while Margaret and John had a leisurely breakfast with Dolores and her mother. Having married an Englishman, Conchita's English was almost as good as her daughters, though she had learned the language much later in life.

When Fred returned mid-morning to take them sightseeing, John surprised him by asking to see the docks. Margaret had no objection, though Dolores thought it best not to take the baby down there and stayed at home.

The docks were constantly thronged with boats, people and cargo and put ports like Liverpool to shame. John had gotten a glimpse of the industry around them when they disembarked here and had been interested to learn more. Fred happily explained what was happening around them, then he pointed out which ships belonged to his family's business and when he was done, he took them to a building not far away and showed them around the offices of Barbour & Co.

Fred constantly worried that he was boring his sister but although she did not think to ask nearly so many questions as John, she too was interested in the busy port and the business being transacted there.

As Frederick once again begged for her forgiveness she smiled.

"You forget, Fred, not only am I a manufacturers wife, I work in his mill and run my own, albeit tiny, property empire. I find all this fascinating."

"Does Aunt Shaw know all this?" Fred sounded scandalised, though his smile showed that he was teasing.

"Very little," Margaret confessed with a sly smile. "And what little she does know is enough to turn her grey."

"How she must despair of the pair of us, Margaret. We must surely be the black sheep of the family."

"Considering that she spends half her life complaining and the other half sitting in judgement, I can live with that as long as we both are able to remain this happy."

Lunch time was fast approaching and Fred took them to a local tavern and introduced them to tapas, which was a large selection of small dishes, each only a few mouthfuls in size. Fred drank wine with his lunch and although it was almost unheard of to drink at this time of day among the manufacturing classes of England, Margaret and John joined him, though they both added water to their glasses.

Once they had eaten, Fred began to quiz John about his cotton mill. John was happy to talk about his business and his pride in it was evident.

They headed back to the house after lunch for a siesta. Margaret had no desire to sleep in the afternoon but she could see that everything was closed or closing as they returned to the house and there was little point in staying out. Fred retired to his room and Margaret and John did the same.

"This makes me feel like a child," Margaret said. "Being ordered to take an afternoon nap."

"But we're not children any longer." John smiled wolfishly and Margaret recognised the desire in his eyes.

"Did you have a better idea?" she asked, innocently.

John stepped in front of her then reached behind her and pulled the clips out of her hair so that it cascaded down her back. He then put his hands on her hips and pulled her to him as his lips found their way to her throat.

Margaret closed her eyes and sighed deeply.

"I believe I could get used to these siestas," she remarked a few moments later as her gown fell to the floor.

Two nights later Fred and Margaret were walking home from the opera, arm in arm. A few paces behind them John and Dolores were chatting happily.

"So you really do work in the business then?" Fred asked her.

"Didn't you believe my letters?"

"Honestly? No. I mean I thought you helped out but not that you took an active role."

"I take it Dolores doesn't help in the family business."

"She did before she was married but she is a Roman Catholic and it would be very unseemly for her to work now that she is married."

"I believe it is very unseemly in England also, but I find it hard to care since I enjoy it so much."

Fred smiled at his sister. They had always been good friends as children because although she was a girl, there was something about Margaret that refused to back down from a challenge. Indeed back then he often thought her courage meant that she should have been born a boy. Seeing her now though, fully grown and lovely, he no longer wished for a brother, though he still admired her courage.

"Are you still having trouble with workers?" Fred asked.

Margaret had told him about the possibility of another strike in her letters.

"I believe the crisis has been averted but considering how harsh the work is, even at a good mill like ours, I think it is only a matter of time until the workers strike again."

"So they would stop working for your mill, even if it isn't you they're upset with?" he asked.

"Indeed. I can see their point; only if they are united will their complaints be heard, though at the same time I feel it is unfair for those who are happy with our working conditions to be forced into a strike."

"But how can they be forced into a strike?" he asked.

"Those who go against the Union face tough sanctions, for those who live and work around them will no longer speak to them, help them, nor even look at them in many cases. They are outcasts to the rest of the community and should they ever face hardship, they will be left to suffer alone, as they abandoned the Union when it needed them."

"That is indeed a punishment few could bear," Fred said with a sigh. "It's a shame you can't up sticks to somewhere that doesn't have any other mills. Maybe set up shop in Helstone, for example," he teased, trying to lighten the sombre mood that had fallen over them

Margaret laughed. "As tempting an idea as that is, I fear that those in the south would not have the temperament for cotton mill work."

"Then move the mill here. I assure you, the Spanish are a hardy breed."

"Oh, truly I would love it if that were possible. I do miss you so."

"And I you."

"Have you heard any more news from Mr. Lennox?" she enquired.

"No, not for a while. I fear it is a hopeless case."

"Don't say that."

"But it is true. And even if I could return home, there is no saying that Dolores would want to. I have a good life here, Margaret."

"I can see that, and I can see that you are truly happy with Dolores."

"Indeed, she is wonderful," he turned to glance back at his wife. "Though she seems rather too enamoured of your Mr. Thornton for my taste."

"Don't tease me, Fred. It is clear for all to see that she only has eyes for you."

"And John for you. I must admit I wasn't sure what to expect. Judging by your letters, I rather thought him a stern, brooding sort of man."

"Indeed he does have that side to him, but thankfully he has little to brood upon these days. Even less so since arriving here." She gave a wistful sigh. "I do so miss the sun sometimes. Whilst even Helstone did not have such glorious sunshine as here, Milton seems so very dull in comparison. Sometimes I am not even sure if it is cloud or smoke blocking the sunlight out."

"That climate is bad for you, Margaret. You were born to run outside. Indeed I don't believe you were ever happier than in our garden at Helstone."

"That is not true," she smiled warmly at Fred then glanced back at John. "I have found a pleasure that outshines even Helstone in my affections."

"Then it is true love indeed."

Margaret nodded.

"Well, as long as you are happy."

"I am. Please don't think of me as I was when you visited Mother. That was a time of great sorrow and I am infinitely happier in Milton now."

"If only the sun would shine." Fred added.

"Then my life would almost certainly be too perfect to be real." Margaret laughed.

They arrived back at the house and paused for John and Dolores to catch them up.

"Would you care for a nightcap on the terrace?" Fred asked as they went inside.

"It's late," John hesitated.

"Life runs later here," Fred explained. "That's why we sleep in the afternoon, so that we might enjoy the cool evenings for longer. You really must try to take advantage of it."

"Yes," Margaret said, unable to stop the blush that coloured her cheeks as she remembered how she and John had spent the afternoon. "Unfortunately we were unable to sleep this afternoon, perhaps tomorrow evening instead."

"One of these days I will hold you to that, Margaret." Frederick kissed her good night and she and John headed upstairs.

"Margaret?" John called as he climbed the stairs to their room.

"In here," she called and he opened the door to see her standing at the window with Enrique in her arms. She turned and smiled as he entered. "Say hello to John, sweetheart," she told the boy.

Enrique just stared at him for a moment then looked up to Margaret and reached a chubby hand out to her cheek. Margaret smiled at the boy.

"Why, Mrs. Thornton, I do believe you have fallen in love with another man," he teased as he joined her, resting his hand on her shoulder and offering the baby a big, toothy grin.

"Indeed, I fear that I have. Can you ever forgive me, my darling?"

John kissed her cheek, which caused Enrique to gurgle.

"I believe he is feeling left out," she said, holding the boy closer to John so that he might also kiss the baby's cheek. Enrique laughed after John had kissed him and waved his arms in glee.

"He is such a lovely boy, isn't he?" Margaret asked rhetorically.

"Indeed," John agreed. "Are you perhaps thinking of starting our own family?"

"I confess I am feeling rather broody, but I do not want to make such a decision in haste. Do you believe it is the right time for us to start a family?"

"To be honest, I hadn't given it much thought before now. Whilst I should dearly love to see you holding our child in your arms, I find myself feeling rather jealous of the attention you would lavish on them."

"That *we* would lavish on them," she corrected gently. "And I find myself feeling slightly resentful of the idea that a child would take me away from the mill. The thought that I would have little more to occupy my days than Fanny fills me with dread."

"You will never be as idle as Fanny," he assured her. "And we can always employ nannies and such to enable you to work at the mill and so that we still find time to be alone together."

"Yes," Margaret looked down to the baby clasped in her arms. "Though I should hate for our baby to have the childhood I did with Aunt Shaw. Edith and I hardly ever saw her. Indeed if I hadn't returned to Helstone a few times a year, I believe I would have had little idea of what a loving family is."

"I confess that while it seems a little extreme, overall I find the Spanish attitude to children much nicer than our English ways."

"And I," Margaret agreed.

"So where does that leave us?" John asked.

"We must take some time to each think it over. If we are both still of the same mind when we return to England, then perhaps we can start trying. We will then have at least nine months to work out the details."

John kissed her cheek and Margaret handed the baby to him. He lifted the boy's vest and, holding him high, blew raspberries on his stomach while Enrique kicked his legs and gurgled with delight.

The rest of the holiday passed in a flash and before she knew it, Margaret was once again standing on the docks, only this time she was wishing Fred a tearful goodbye.

"I'm sorry," she said as she wiped her eyes with a handkerchief.

"Don't be, just promise to visit us again."

"I promise." She had no idea when that would be, more likely years than months away, but she would visit him again, come hell or high water.

John said his goodbyes to Dolores then Frederick and, with one arm around Margaret's shoulders, he led her onto the boat.

Dixon was equally upset at the parting but aside from dabbing her eyes a time or two, she tried not to show it.

Margaret waited on the deck and watched the shore until it was out of sight.

"Come inside," John urged gently.

Margaret nodded and allowed herself to be led to their cabin.

"I cannot believe I was sad at the idea of leaving Milton and now I am sad at the thought of returning."

"Surely you are sad because you are leaving your brother, not returning to Milton." John still worried that one day she would wake up and choose to leave the life she had built with him.

"No, you are right. I am actually looking forward to seeing our friends and the mill again. I do hope everything has gone smoothly in our absence."

"Mother is more than capable and I'm certain that nothing is wrong."

The next day John found Margaret up on deck again, gazing out to sea.

"Are you all right, love?" he asked, worried that her parting from Frederick had been harder than he had originally thought.

"Hm?" she turned to him, sounding distracted. "Oh, yes, perfectly all right, I was just thinking."

"What about?"

"It is probably a foolish idea."

"I cannot say if you won't tell me."

Margaret took a deep breath and prepared to pitch her latest idea to him.

"Fred said something when we were talking about the strikes, how it would be lovely if we could move away from the other mills so that we would not be affected by what the other masters do."

John listened intently as they walked over to a bench and sat down.

"He was only jesting, suggesting we set up a factory in Helstone, but I have been unable to put the idea out of my head."

"How so?"

"Well, I was wondering if it would be possible to build a factory just outside of Milton, close enough to the trade routes but far enough away that we could form our own community. We could build the workers decent housing, a proper school for their children, medical facilities, shops; our own village, if you like, based around the mill."

"And where is the money to come from to pay for this?"

"Mr. Bells property portfolio and the money from his speculations. I have no idea yet if it would be enough but if it was, think of it, John. You could expand, build a much larger mill and take on many more orders that we are able to now. And the workers could live somewhere where the air was not constantly filled with factory smoke and they would no longer be part of a Milton union so there would only be any trouble if they were upset with us. Everyone would win."

John was frowning but Margaret now knew it was a sign of him thinking, not of disapproval necessarily.

"It sounds very nice, but it would be a great risk."

"Would it? Would it really? John, you know the cotton industry like few others, you have an excellent reputation and I know you are offered many more orders that you are able to bid on."

"And how are we to recoup the funds from this venture?"

"Well aside from the profits from the mill, we will of course charge the workers rent for their houses, businesses will rent shops from us and the workers would have to cover the costs to send their children to the school, though we might consider subsidising it to make it more affordable. We won't profiteer off of our workers but we should be able to charge them a fair rent."

John didn't speak for a long time. After a while he got up and went to stand by the railing, where he had first found Margaret. When she could stand the silence no longer she joined him and put her hand on his arm.

"Please say something, even if it is only that you believe I have gone insane."

"I don't think you've lost your mind," he said, smiling at her. "I have heard of similar ventures but this is a huge undertaking, and one I'm not sure that even you can afford."

"But you think it possible?"

"I have no idea. Until we know what it would cost I cannot even guess if it would be possible."

"But as well as the property, I have a large amount in the bank from Mr. Bell's speculations. It is my understanding that there are a further two speculations that have not come to fruition yet. Those could add to our funds."

"Or they may not," he cautioned. "The money in the bank would surely buy the land and probably pay for a good part of the mill to be built, but as to the cost of building a whole village, I simply cannot say."

"You are right, of course. When we get back I shall ask Mr. Lattimer to enquire about the total value of Mr. Bell's assets and engage a firm of architects to give us a quote for the work."

Though they resolved not to talk any further on the subject until they had some definitive information, John found his mind frequently returning to the slums of Milton. He didn't visit there often but he had seen enough.

Whole families crammed into one or two rooms with no decent sanitation or wash facilities. Disease and illness were rife. He did not usually like to dwell on his hands living conditions because there was nothing he could do to change things but Margaret's idea was starting to take hold in his mind.

He had heard of the cotton mill village in Scotland called New Lanark, originally built some 50 years ago by David Dale, who had been appalled by the living conditions of his workers. John had never considered that an option for himself as he didn't have the resources but if Margaret did, then they could surely make a real difference to their workers lives.

Though he cautioned himself not to get his hopes up, he found himself wishing that somehow they could make Margaret's dream a reality.

Chapter Thirteen

The first week back at the mill was so busy that neither John nor Margaret found the time to talk, or even to think much about building a new mill or starting a family.

The mill had run quite smoothly in their absence, and although of course there had been a few problems, Hannah Thornton and Higgins had managed them with relative ease.

Most of Margaret's time was spent updating the accounting ledgers while John was bringing himself back up to speed on the orders and preparing the tenders that had built up in his absence.

Margaret found herself looking forward to Sunday with more excitement than usual. She believed they would have caught up with their work by then and the idea of not having to rise so early as well as spending some quality time with John was most appealing.

When she awoke on Sunday morning, John's chest was pressed against her back and his arm draped around her waist. She had woken at the usual time since her body had trained itself to, but she smiled as she realised that she could spend a little longer in John's embrace.

John murmured a plea for her to go back to sleep as she snuggled further down under the covers and sighed with contentment, deciding that was a very good idea indeed.

The next time she opened her eyes, John was clearly awake since his hand was gently stroking her flank.

"Why don't you wake me like this every morning?" she complained.

John propped his head up on his hand and leaned forward to kiss her shoulder.

"Because you are always awake before me."

"Then perhaps I shall have to feign sleep in future." She turned onto her back and John leaned down again, this time planting a soft kiss on her lips.

"How did you sleep?" he asked.

"Like a baby."

"Good."

"Speaking of," Margaret began, somewhat hesitantly. Perhaps first thing in the morning wasn't the best time for this conversation but they had to finish it at some time so why not now? "I have been thinking about us having a child and, I must say that my feelings haven't changed. I know that if we are able to build the new site for the mill, it couldn't be a worse time, yet I find that I don't care about the extra work, I would still like a child."

She looked up at him, her expression questioning and slightly apprehensive but he smiled reassuringly.

"I was prepared to wait in case you did not want to start a family but I am in total agreement. Nothing would please me more than sealing our love with a bairn."

Margaret smiled at his use of the local colloquialism.

"Then perhaps now would be a good time to start trying," she suggested.

John's smile turned slightly predatory. "What an excellent idea."

"What sort of time do you call this?" Hannah asked, trying to suppress her smile as John joined her in the parlour. "You've missed breakfast."

"Sorry Mother," he leaned over and kissed her cheek. "Margaret and I decided to take advantage of the day of rest-"

"Hush," she chided. "I was young and in love once too." Her smile broke through her stern countenance and John found himself in the unusual position of blushing as he realised that his mother had guessed how he and Margaret had spent their time.

"Will you be attending church?"

"The noon services," he answered. "Margaret is just finishing dressing and then we will be off."

Hannah got up to ring the bell for the servant. "I will ask the kitchen for some bread and jam. We can't have you running about town on an empty stomach."

"That's very thoughtful of you."

Hannah reached out and took her son's hand. While he and Margaret had been away, she found that her fondness for both grew considerably and though she was on her own for the first time in her life, save the occasional afternoon with Fanny and dinner with Mr. Whitaker, she was not resentful of Margaret. Indeed, whenever she wondered what they might be getting up to while they were away, she found herself smiling, knowing that while in each others company they would surely be having a grand time.

She looked down at her hand as it clasped her son's and wondered just what it was that she wanted to say. Perhaps more to the point, she wasn't sure if she even knew how to say what she wanted to. She swallowed and looked up into John's eyes.

"You and Margaret take your time."

John smiled and patted his mothers hand. He knew her well enough to know how much she was trying to say with that simple sentence.

"Thank you, Mother," he said. His voice was warm and full of love for this strong woman, who was surely just as responsible as he for the man he was today. He bent down and kissed her cheek.

"Oh," she tried to shrug the gesture off as though he was some silly schoolboy being overly enthusiastic. "Be off with you."

"Yes, Mother, of course, Mother, as you wish, Mother."

Hanna couldn't help but smile at his impudence, though she tried her best to hide it.

John and Margaret had been walking on eggshells around each other all week. They were both aware that she was 'late' but both were equally unwilling to mention it lest they somehow jinx themselves. Margaret felt rather foolish for believing in such superstitions but she couldn't help feeling the way she did.

"So, did Mr. Lattimer get back to you?" John asked as they ate breakfast.

"Not yet, though I have not yet checked this morning's post."

"It's been over a month already; how long does it take to value some properties?" Hannah asked, shaking her head in consternation.

Though a stern woman, when she had heard of Margaret's idea and how strongly John supported it, she had been proud of them both. Not only because this was the right thing to do but because creating a model village would surely put her son's name on the map, not just as a manufacturer but also as a humanitarian and philanthropist.

"He wants to be certain and he is having some trouble getting accurate valuations for some of the properties. He has been given three different estimates, all vastly different from each other and he wants to be sure before saying anything definitive," Margaret explained.

113

Armstrong and Sons had already been retained as the architects, though everything was very much still in the costing stage. Last week they had finally estimated the cost for each phase of the building work. Though they couldn't be definitive until the land was purchased and actual plans drawn up, the figure seemed to be quite reasonable for such a large project. Now Margaret could only hope that they would have the necessary resources to fund the project.

Should they fall short of their target, they had discussed the possibility of looking for outside partners but both felt it better to do this alone if they could, lest someone else's vision overshadow their own ideas.

"Well, there's no use pouting about it, we will know when we know," John said. "We'd best be getting to the mill."

Margaret nodded and quickly finished her toast.

It was mid-morning when John saw her dash past his open office door, heading to the lavatory. He got up to follow her and heard her retching through the door.

"Is Miss Margaret all right?" Thomas asked hesitantly. Clearly her quick flight from their office had worried him.

"She is fine," John assured him. "Probably something she ate at breakfast disagreed with her. Go back to work, I'll take care of her."

Thomas turned and headed back to the accounts office. Moments later Margaret emerged looking pale and drawn. Neither of them said anything as John led her to his office, which was closer and more private than hers, then went to fetch her some water.

"How are you feeling?" he asked her, handing her the glass.

"A little queasy," she confessed.

"You know what this means, don't you?" John finally found the courage to broach the unmentionable subject.

"Yes, I believe I do." Margaret couldn't help the smile that formed on her lips.

John broke out in a wide grin.

"You are with child?" he asked to be certain.

"Yes. Yes I believe I am."

Much as a jack-in-the-box once released springs up and into life, John jumped to his feet and almost roughly, hauled his wife out of her chair and into his arms. Margaret laughed at his glee as he spun her around in his arms. Despite her slight feeling of sickness, she was as pleased by this news as her husband.

"Oh, no." John's mood suddenly altered and he put Margaret down. "I haven't hurt you, have I?"

"John, I am with child, not suddenly made of glass. I'm fine, I assure you."

Relieved, and unable to help himself, his grin returned and he hugged her tightly again.

"Oh, Margaret, you've made me the happiest man in Milton."

Margaret pulled away and cupped his face in her hands. She was surprised though not upset to see tears shining in his eyes.

"John Thornton, you are quite possibly the most adorable man I have ever known."

"Is that a good thing?"

Margaret laughed and threw her arms about him.

"It is a very good thing," she assured him.

Chapter Fourteen

A month later John and Margaret were in the study looking over blueprints from Armstrong and Sons. They had already been over the plans with the architect a couple of times and made alterations where necessary. Now the plans had been perfected and they either had to give the go ahead to buy the land and start building work or scrap the project and lose only the architect's fees.

"So?" John asked.

Margaret took a deep breath. While she had every confidence in the scheme and she knew that they had the money to cover the cost, it was still a great undertaking. Indeed whilst the mill could be built within a year, the first stage of the housing would take longer to complete and the other houses and town buildings, such as the school and hospital would take probably years, possibly even a decade. And when all was said and done, this was still a risk, which is why she hesitated.

Finally she looked into his eyes and, unable to say the words, she nodded. John smiled and, dipping his pen into the ink well, handed it to her so she could sign the deeds for the purchase of the land and when she handed it back, he signed the contract for the architects.

Margaret let out a breath that she had been unaware she was holding.

"It's done," he said. "Now, how shall we celebrate?"

Margaret felt her face flush.

"I believe a walk would be beneficial. I feel rather flustered."

John felt the same, though he was more skilled at hiding his fears.

"Then let's take a stroll to the Mitre Hotel and take afternoon tea there."

"In the middle of a work day?" Margaret sounded scandalised.

John smiled. Though the mill was still of utmost importance to him, he now knew that there were more important things than work and that it was possible to enjoy both his work life and his home life.

"I believe I can be spared for an hour or two. Besides, my wife is in a delicate condition and must be treated with the utmost care. Who knows what might happen if I were not to indulge her every whim."

Margaret narrowed her eyes and wagged her finger at him, as though he was a child being told off.

"Do not tease me, Mr. Thornton. I am indeed in a delicate condition and it is quite possible I may become homicidal if provoked."

"I wouldn't dream of it," John laughed, offering her his arm.

The days were growing shorter and winter was nearing, so they paused in the hallway to put their coats on before leaving through the courtyard and heading out to the street.

"Do you not need to speak with Nicholas before we go?" Margaret asked.

"I already did," John assured her.

"So pandering to my whims is just an excuse and you had always intended to swing the lead this afternoon?"

"Caught!" he shook his head in mock defeat. "I will take my punishment like a man, madam, but do not be too hard on me, I beg of you. What man in his right mind would not leave work behind for the chance of spending time with Milton's most handsome lady?"

Margaret glanced at him from the corner of her eye and John's heart skipped a beat. He knew that wicked look and suddenly he was eager for the day to be over and to find himself alone with his wife.

"I am not convinced that you deserve mercy, Mr. Thornton," she said, raising her chin in her most haughty manner. "But I am open to persuasion."

John laughed out loud, causing a few pedestrians to turn and look at the couple.

"Oh dear, laughing in public," Margaret teased. "What would your workers think if they saw their master behaving in such an outrageous manner?"

"They would see me for the lovesick fool that I am," he said, unable to resist leaning down and stealing a quick kiss.

Margaret blushed as she saw passersby looking away from them, embarrassed by such a public display of affection. Margaret found that she did not much care for their censure and smiled at her husband.

They arrived at the hotel a few minutes later and entered the restaurant, only for Margaret to grab John's arm and pull him back from the doorway.

"What is it?" he asked, puzzled by her behaviour.

117

"I believe I saw your mother in there, taking tea with Mr. Whitaker," she whispered.

John ducked his head back into the restaurant and confirmed her suspicions.

"Did you know she was coming here?" he asked.

"No. She said she was going visiting this afternoon and I assumed she meant to your sister. What should we do?"

"Clearly she does not want us to know of her relationship with Mr. Whitaker yet."

They caught each other's eye and began giggling, though they tried to stifle it as best they could.

"Come on," he took Margaret's hand and led her from the hotel. "Until she decides to trust us, we had best find somewhere else to celebrate."

Margaret looked out over the land and to the hills in the distance, somehow unable to believe that in a year or so this site would be home to a mill and a village. She and John walked forward, in the direction of the railway that bisected the land, which was one of the reasons that they had purchased this particular parcel of land. An extension to the canal would also have to be built, but right now it was hard to imagine this place as anything other than a beautiful landscape.

Once this had been a farm but the owners went out of business almost fifty years ago. Part of it had been purchased by the railway but the rest had fallen fallow and few signs of the industry that once occurred here remained.

"I wonder where the ruins are?" Margaret said, for they had been told that the farm house, stables and a few out houses were still divisible from the landscape.

"Perhaps over one of those rises," John suggested. "Or through those trees. Why? You are not proposing we find them, are you?"

"Not today, but someday I should like to explore the site more."

"And someday we shall," he promised.

"Are we ready?" called the photographer.

John and Margaret turned to him. Though the ambrotype plates this photographer was using were a somewhat time-consuming preparation, it was a cheaper, easier and faster process than it's predecessor, the daguerreotype, John also preferred the glass finish of the ambrotype to the metallic finish of the daguerreotype plates. It had been Margaret's suggestion to document the mill being built and today they were here to capture breaking the ground.

The architect, Mr. Anderson and his sons joined them with a spade, as well as two other employees who had worked on the plans and the site foreman, who would oversee the building work.

Mr. Anderson handed John the spade as they grouped together in front of the camera and John handed it to Margaret.

"Me?" she asked.

"This was your idea," John said. "It seems only fitting that you break the ground for us."

Margaret wasn't sure it was such a good idea given the long and voluminous skirt she wore, but the prospect did excite her. It took her a few moments to arrange her skirt so that she could stand on the spade without compromising her modesty but finally she was ready and as the spade sank into the earth, she paused and the photographer opened the shutter and took the photograph.

Margaret's pregnancy had progressed with relative ease until now. Her morning sickness had lasted a few weeks but it was not too severe and since then things had been rather effortless.

Now though, nearing her eighth month she was beginning to find that moving was becoming much more laborious. She would have quite happily settled in a chair and been perfectly content not to move for the rest of the day, but unfortunately she also required frequent trips to the bathroom.

Indeed she had never been more grateful for a lady's maid because without Dixon, she was sure she would not even be able to tie her own shoes.

Her breasts were also swollen and sore and although she didn't feel as though she was eating much (or anything) more than usual, she seemed to have gained a lot of weight, so much so that she had removed her wedding band because it was uncomfortable. She had also suffered a few nose bleeds, which meant that she needed to return home to change; an added inconvenience that she didn't need right now. Indeed, she was ready for this baby to be born now because she feared that she would be unable to keep her equanimity for another month.

As the bell sounded for the end of the work day she looked

out of the window to see the workers all heading home for the evening. Alas her day was not over yet. Her head had ached all day and she found that she had difficulty concentrating. Indeed she was of half a mind to just leave the work undone and crawl into bed.

Five minutes later she decided that she was getting nowhere fast and that it was probably best to return to the work tomorrow, when she would hopefully be refreshed and clear headed.

Just then John opened the door and came in to her office. Clearly his day had also been wearing because he was already tugging his cravat loose as he came in.

"Are you ready to go, my love?"

"I am." She smiled wearily. "Today seems to have lasted for a week."

"You look pale, are you sure you're all right?"

"I'm fine, I just have a slight headache, that's all."

John offered her his elbow and they headed across the courtyard to the house but as Margaret climbed the few steps to the house she began to feel dizzy. Her vision began to darken at the edges and before she knew what had happened, she had collapsed, only saved from a nasty fall by John's quick reflexes.

Chapter Fifteen

"Mother!" John called as he carried Margaret into the house.

"John?" She ran to him, knowing from his tone that something was seriously wrong. She followed him into the parlour and watched as he laid Margaret out on the sofa.

"What happened?" she asked.

"She fainted. She complained earlier of a headache but said it was nothing. I must go for the doctor."

Hannah nodded and went to Margaret as John ran out. She undid some of the buttons on her dress in case her swelling stomach had perhaps been too tightly confined, although her clothes had been specially made to accommodate her pregnancy so it was unlikely.

She wondered how long it would take for John to fetch the doctor and was relieved when she heard horses hooves canter out of the yard since he would surely be much faster on horseback than on foot.

"Mrs. Thornton?"

She looked up to see Jane standing hesitantly in the doorway.

"Get me some cold water and a cloth," she instructed the girl. When Jane returned she dampened the cloth and placed it on Margaret's forehead, hoping the cool water would sooth her.

"Is there anything else?" Jane asked.

Hannah knew that Jane only stayed so that she might hear some gossip to share with the other staff but Hannah had no intention of indulging that pastime.

"Just leave us. Dr. Donaldson will be here soon." Jane left and Hannah took her daughter in law's hand. "Hold on, my girl, the doctor is on his way."

It seemed to take an eternity but it was probably not more than fifteen minutes until John returned with the doctor. They strode into the room like a hurricane and John rushed to Margaret's side. Hannah stood back so as not to get in the way.

Dr. Donaldson examined Margaret for a few minutes then stood back.

"Will she be all right?" John asked.

"The baby is putting a strain on her body," the doctor pronounced.

"What does that mean?" John snapped. He was worried and

his temper was beginning to show.

"I cannot say," Dr. Donaldson answered truthfully. "She is essentially supporting two people and that is putting tremendous strain on her. She may give birth to a healthy child or the strain could prove too much and both mother and child could... well." He left the sentence hanging.

"What can we do?" Hannah asked, stepping forward.

"She must have complete bed rest, she is not to exert herself in any way. I recommend a simple, bland diet of foods that she can easily digest and plenty of water. Then we will just have to wait and see if she is strong enough to come through this."

"Is there nothing else?" John asked.

"I'm afraid not. It is possible that if her condition worsens, that she may begin to have seizures. If that happens you must call for me at once. "

John felt awful. He had encouraged her to have children, he had impregnated her and now his child was killing her.

"If it helps at all, once the child is born, the symptoms disappear almost immediately and it is rare to hear of it happening with a second pregnancy."

"So this happens often?" John asked.

"Not often but it is not unheard of."

John looked down at Margaret's unconscious body and it struck him that he might already have lost her. He knelt down beside her and was relieved to see the slight rise and fall of her chest. He tucked his head into her side and prayed that she would be fine.

"We should get her into bed," Dr. Donaldson suggested when John hadn't moved for a few minutes.

John raised his head and nodded. Fool that he was, he had never even considered moving her but of course she would probably be uncomfortable here. He picked her up in his arms and carried her upstairs to their bedroom.

"I will stay until she awakes," the doctor said as John laid Margaret out on the bed.

"Will that be long?" John asked.

"I hope not." Dr. Donaldson looked slightly uncomfortable. "Mr. Thornton, I do not know your arrangements during this time in your wife's life, but from now on you must sleep separately until the child is born."

"Yes, of course," John said absently as it suddenly occurred to him that perhaps their continued love making had brought this on.

He had always known he was not worthy of her affection but now he had proof. His baser urges had brought all this about, from impregnating her to continuing to make love to her while she was with child.

He truly didn't deserve her and now he might have killed her.

Suddenly Margaret groaned and opened her eyes. She smiled as she saw John hovering above her.

"What happened?" she asked, her smile turning to a frown as she realised that she was awaking from no normal sleep.

"You fainted," he told her.

"Oh, how embarrassing," she smiled, struggling to sit up.

"No, lay still, love." John placed a hand on her shoulder. "You need to rest."

"Don't be absurd. It was a simple fainting spell, nothing serious. Perhaps I forgot to eat lunch today."

Her expression turned worried when she noticed that John paled at her words.

"Doctor?" she turned to look at him.

"You are very ill, Mrs. Thornton."

"But I don't feel unwell."

"Your heartbeat is fast, your hands and feet are swollen and your husband informs me that you have suffered a few nose bleeds in recent weeks. In short, Mrs. Thornton, your body is struggling to support the new life you are carrying. You must have total bedrest until the child is born. I will visit you daily to make sure that you are keeping well."

"But I cannot stay in bed for a whole month!" Margaret said. "I will surely be driven insane."

"Perhaps you might be permitted to move to a chair during the day time but I must insist that you do not venture out of this room and if you should have any more headaches, you must lie down immediately."

"May I not even go to my sitting room next door?"

"Well, that might be permitted but no further. You are a very ill young woman and must take care of yourself."

Though his words struck fear into her heart, she couldn't help but feel he was exaggerating the danger. Women had been giving birth for centuries; it surely could not be such a dangerous condition as the doctor was making out.

"Thank you, Doctor," John said.

"I will come by and see you tomorrow, Mrs. Thornton," The doctor said as he prepared to leave.

Margaret nodded.

"I'll send Dixon in to help you disrobe," John told Margaret as he followed the Doctor out of the room.

Dr. Donaldson wrote a list of acceptable foods including plenty of fruit, porridge oats and water, white bread, steamed chicken and other very simple and easily digestible foods.

The Doctor left, promising to send the bill to Marlborough Mill and John filled his mother in on what else had been said, asking her to inform the kitchen of Margaret's dietary needs and to have a spare room made up for him. Then he returned to Margaret's side and sat with her for the rest of the evening, insisting that she rest. As the hour latened he kissed her on the cheek and got up to leave.

"Where are you going?" she asked.

"I will sleep in one of the spare bed chambers until you are recovered."

"Surely that is not necessary." She sounded incredulous.

"The doctor said we are to sleep apart, my love."

"I am certain he was speaking of not having marital relations, not of sharing the same bed."

"Margaret-"

"No! John, I have not slept alone since we were married and I am certain that being left alone will only cause me to fret more, not less. I also know that you are of a strong enough character that we might share a bed without you having to give in to your carnal instincts. In fact I am certain of it as we have on quite a number occasions now, slept side by side and not engaged in any activity other than sleeping."

John hung his head, realising that she was right. Of course he wanted her, he always wanted her, but he would never take her knowing that she either did not want him or that he could harm her.

"You are right, of course. I'm sorry."

"You have no need to apologise, simply desist from treating us both as though we were mindless animals who are little more than slaves to our natures."

John disrobed and pulled on a night shirt, though he had not been in the habit of wearing one for some months now. Margaret didn't question it and decided that perhaps it was best

124

if she didn't remove the nightgown that Dixon had helped her change into earlier.

As John climbed into bed beside her, Margaret turned onto her side, which was the only position she was comfortable sleeping in with her stomach so swollen. To her immense relief, after a few moments John shifted closer and pulled her back against his chest.

Chapter Sixteen

"John, please! For two weeks now I have done everything asked of me. Or perhaps I should say I have not done anything of consequence at all. I haven't gotten dressed, I have been nowhere but my bedroom and this sitting room, I allow Dixon to accompany me everywhere I go, I eat all the bland food that is placed in front of me and I have done nothing at all to help in the mill. But, John, please! If I am forced to live this... this half life for much longer I shall be driven mad!"

"Margaret, my love, please listen to reason!" John dashed a hand through his hair as he paced in front of his wife.

"Reason? How can I listen to reason when I am little more than a prisoner in my own home? I have not seen anyone other than you and Dixon for the past week. Why even your mother has not visited me despite my asking her to."

"I told her to stay away," John admitted. "Knowing the adversarial relationship you two have had in the past, I thought it best if you did not see each other until the child is born."

"But I am slowly losing my mind!" She knew that she was getting worked up, a state the Doctor had warned her against, but she simply couldn't help it. Leading such a small existence was taking its toll on her and she no longer had any control over her anger.

"I would rather you were driven insane than dead!" he yelled.

"I am pregnant, John, not dying."

He took a moment to calm himself before continuing. "I did not want to tell you in case it made you anxious, but Dr. Donaldson says there is a very real danger that your condition could worsen and both you and the baby will die."

Margaret paled at those words.

"Margaret, please. I do not know how I would go on living, knowing that I had caused your death."

"Don't be so ridiculous, John, how on earth could you possibly have caused my condition?"

"That is my child in there," he pointed to her stomach. "My child that is killing you."

Margaret's anger faded slightly as she realised both how much danger she was in and that he was blaming himself for this.

"Darling," she reached her hand out to him. To her relief he clasped it after only the briefest hesitation, and settled at her feet on the floor. "You really are the most caring man I know but you cannot possibly blame yourself for this. It is my child in here too, so I am just as responsible."

"But you are not... You..."

Suddenly she realised what he meant.

"The strain this child is putting on me has nothing to do with my being a gentleman's daughter and you being a tradesman. You are every inch a gentleman I assure you, and my body is not rejecting your child because it believes him or her to have come from a different social class."

"But-"

"No," she said firmly. "I have even asked the doctor about the cause of my condition and he assured me there is no known cause. He has treated the finest ladies and the lowest of the working classes who were married to their own kind. This is not your fault, my darling. If anyone is to blame for this, it is me."

John wished he could believe that but no matter how logical her argument, he would always feel that this was his fault. He rested his head against her leg and looked into the fire.

Margaret gently ran her fingers through his hair, soothing his troubled spirit as best she could.

"I feel a headache coming on, I must lie down," Margaret said after a few moments. While she did want something to occupy her mind, for she genuinely didn't see how completing the accounting ledger from the quiet of her writing desk in her sitting room could be at all dangerous, she wasn't taking her situation lightly and had followed the doctors orders as best she could.

John was on his feet in seconds and carried her through to their bed. He placed her gently upon the covers, as though she were the finest porcelain doll, then he sat beside her and took her hand.

"You're right," he said. "I was seeking to protect you but all I have succeeded in doing is isolating you."

Margaret smiled and reached up with her free hand to cup his cheek.

"But I do not want you working on the mill, even from the house. For all we know it is the hours you have put in there that has weakened you and caused this problem and you only became involved because the mill is important to me."

"Darling John, you seem determined to make this your fault

but you do not seem to listen when I tell you that I shan't break. I know my mother is a lady and my father a gentleman, but I am not a delicate flower that must be protected. Yes, I am unwell at the moment, but it can no more be blamed on working at the mill than catching a fever could be."

"I hardly need remind you that this climate killed your mother," he said kindly.

"If that is true, then surely the air in Oxford is responsible for my father's death, in which case I find myself with something of a quandary, for if the air in the north killed my mother and the air in the south killed my father, where am I to live? The north pole perhaps?"

Despite his fears, John smiled slightly at her reasoning.

"I made my own choices, John, so if indeed there is blame to be apportioned it must be laid firmly at my door. After this baby is born, I fully intend to continue to make my own choices and take full responsibility for them. I love working at the mill not only because it is important to you but because it has become important to me."

John raised the hand he held to his lips and pressed a gentle kiss upon the back of it. Perhaps she was right, or perhaps he was. Regardless, he would not argue with her any more.

He heard the whistle blow to signify the end of the lunch break and looked over to the window.

"I must get back to work" he said, his regret at leaving her evident in his tone. "Try to sleep; that always helps your headaches and rest assured, things will be different from now on."

Margaret smiled, hoping that what he said was true. Dixon came in and sat with her when John left but though she felt like a child needing a minder, Margaret was in too much pain now to argue. She closed her eyes and eventually dozed off.

She awoke a little while later and was pleased to find that her headache was gone. Dixon hovered around her as she pulled her dressing gown on and slowly made her way into the sitting room. She was surprised then when Dixon left her but she didn't question it. Instead she picked her book up and prepared to spent the rest of the day following the adventures of Jane Eyre.

She was shocked when not twenty minutes after Dixon left, there came a knock at her sitting room door and Nicholas and Mary entered. Nicholas looked very uncomfortable since

Margaret wasn't dressed properly and he kept his eyes focused on the ground.

"Sorry to disturb you, lass. Master said you was wanting some company and suggested Mary and me come see you. I didn't realise you'd be... well-"

"Don't be silly, Nicholas, Mary, you are both more than welcome. Please, just think of my night clothes as a hospital gown. They don't seem to want me to get dressed each day. Perhaps they think I would abscond if I were properly attired," she joked. "Come and sit down. I am desperately in need of some different company."

They entered, though they seemed somewhat hesitant, and sat on the small sofa opposite her.

"We were right sorry to 'ear you were poorly, Miss Margaret," Mary said.

"Thank you."

"How are you feelin'?" Nicholas asked and Margaret realised that they had probably been told nothing of what was actually wrong with her.

"Mostly I feel fine but the Doctor insists that I do next to nothing. He says my body cannot support two lives."

"Is it dangerous?" Mary asked.

"So the doctor says."

"Well," Nicholas said. "Better safe than sorry."

"Of course, but the sooner this child comes, the better." Because she was tired of constantly being asked how she was, she opted to move the conversation forward. "Now, what of the children? How are they fairing in school?"

"Doing nicely." Nicholas smiled, his pride in them evident. He and Mary then continued to regale Margaret with tales of the children and their various antics. Jane came when Mary rang the bell and brought the tea that Margaret asked for.

After a while Margaret began to worry that Nicholas and Mary needed to get back to work but he assured her that Mary had finished in the kitchen for the day and that the master had told him he was free to stay until Margaret grew tired of him.

"You will not lose any wages because of it, I hope."

"No, master said not to worry."

Mary left soon afterwards to take the children home but Nicholas stayed until after the bell rang and only left when John returned home.

"How are you feeling?" John asked.

"Very well," she smiled at him. "Thank you for asking Nicholas and Mary to come and visit me, it was wonderful to see them again."

"I'm glad you enjoyed it." John smiled. "Are you ready for dinner?"

Margaret gave a long suffering sigh at the thought of steamed chicken and white rice followed by a dessert of fresh fruit. She had eaten the same thing for the past two weeks and it was getting a little tiring now.

"I suppose so. I know I must keep my strength up."

She expected John to ring the bell for Jane or Dixon. Instead he walked over to her and scooped her into his arms.

"John!" She thought he was about to take her back to bed and was indignant at the idea. When he bypassed her bedroom door and headed down the stairs she was surprised. "Where are we going? I thought I wasn't allowed to leave my rooms?"

"You are not allowed to exert yourself," he clarified. "But in this case, I am the one exerting myself."

He carried her into the dining room where Hannah was already waiting. She smiled warmly at Margaret as John set her back on her feet beside the table.

"I see you finally managed to talk some sense into my son," Hannah said. "I told him that he was holding on too tightly but he wouldn't listen to me."

"Well, it took me two weeks," Margaret said with a smile as she sat down.

The dinner was served and if Margaret was expecting to share the delightful cooking they usually ate, she was sadly disappointed. Instead, they shared her basic meal so that she didn't feel alone.

"Perhaps next you might see if you can be allowed some more leeway with your diet," Hannah suggested. "One week of this would be enough to put anyone off eating."

"I will try," Margaret assured her. "However I fear that is beyond even my powers of persuasion."

John watched them, taking no offence at their words but taking immense pleasure that his wife's smile seemed natural and free, as opposed to the reassuring yet slightly false ones she had been giving him for the past few weeks.

The rest of the meal passed without incident until their dessert plates were removed. Suddenly Margaret groaned and leaned forward, one hand going to her stomach. In a second

John was at her side, clutching her hand.

"What is it, love? Shall I call the doctor?"

Margaret seemed to be holding her breath and she looked to be in considerable pain. After a few more moments she finally relaxed and looked up.

"Yes, I think that would be a very good idea," she said as calmly as she could.

"What's wrong?" he asked, wanting to give the doctor her symptoms as best he could.

"I believe the baby is coming."

Chapter Seventeen

"But it's too early!" If possible John sounded even more alarmed than Margaret.

"Only two weeks," his mother said sternly, lest he become too agitated. "You were early too and it didn't do you any harm. Now carry Margaret to her bed then go for the doctor. I will look after her."

Seemingly pleased to have been giving something to do, John happily obeyed her orders. As he climbed the stairs he heard her barking orders to the servants, asking for warm water, clean towels and a jug of cool drinking water.

John deposited Margaret in their bed and looked down at her, unwilling to leave her side even to fetch the doctor. His mother strode into the room moments later.

"What are you still doing here? Go and fetch the doctor!"

John bent to give his wife a quick kiss then disappeared. Hannah sat on the bed beside her daughter in law and took her hand.

"Now that he's gone I have some unpleasant truths to tell you," Hannah said as kindly as she could. "I don't care how natural it is or how long women have been giving birth for, it is not easy and it will likely be the hardest and certainly the most embarrassing thing you will ever have to do."

Margaret wasn't as innocent as Hannah seemed to believe. She had been present at births before yet somehow, until now she had managed to forget all the screams that she had heard. How had those women managed it, she wondered, all that pain, all that exertion, sometimes for hours!

Suddenly Hannah's expression softened.

"And try to remember that no matter how bad it feels now, it will all be worth it when you hold that child in your arms."

Margaret smiled tightly and nodded. Yes, she had to 'keep her eye on the prize' as she had once heard Higgins say.

"Don't leave me," Margaret implored.

"I won't."

She gripped Hannah's hand tightly as Dixon entered with the towels and hot water.

"Now, Miss Margaret, don't you fret over anything. The doctor and I will take care of you," Dixon announced.

In the event, the birth was comparatively easy. Because of her condition, Dr. Donaldson had suggested a chloroform birth, so Margaret had been anaesthetised and the baby removed using forceps. Given her frailty, the Doctor was careful to only put her out for few minutes at a time and anaesthetise her again when she showed signs of regaining consciousness.

When she finally awoke she could hear crying and tried to crane her neck to see the baby.

"Stay still," Hannah said gently. "They'll bring her to you when she's been cleaned."

"She? It's a girl?" Margaret smiled.

"Aye, a beautiful baby girl." Hannah smiled.

Moments later John approached the bed, his arms so filled with blankets that Margaret couldn't see the baby until he kneeled down beside the bed.

Margaret was entranced by her. The baby's big blue eyes seemed to look all around her, as though taking in her surroundings. Margaret held her arms out and John placed the baby into them.

"Hello sweetheart," she cooed.

Though loathe to leave them, John went to speak to Dr. Donaldson.

"Will Margaret be all right now?" he asked softly.

"In my experience she should recover very quickly but I would advise her to take things easy for the next few days, just to be safe."

"And the baby?"

"Whilst I don't recommend she has full care of the infant yet, she should be allowed to feed it and bond with it. You don't have a wet nurse, I assume?" In his experience, few northern women did.

"No," John confirmed. "Dixon insisted on taking on the duties of a Nanny but I had intended to find help for her. For the moment one of the household servants can assist her."

"A good idea. The baby will probably be hungry soon but I'm sure your mother can assist Margaret with that so I shall take my leave. I don't expect you to have any difficulties now but if anything untoward should occur with your wife or the baby, do not hesitate to fetch me back, day or night."

"Thank you, Doctor."

"My pleasure." He looked over to where Margaret was cuddling the baby and smiled before turning to leave.

John headed back to his wife but as her side of the bed was crowded with his mother and Dixon, he got onto the other side of the bed and sat beside his wife.

Margaret offered him a bright smile and leaned against him. He put his arm around her shoulders and looked from mother to daughter. He was so happy at the moment and he felt as though he might burst with pleasure. Silently he said a prayer that both mother and daughter wouldn't suffer any further misfortunes.

The baby began to cry then, her chubby little face screwing up as piercing cries issued from her tiny mouth.

"Now master," Dixon said. "I believe young Miss Thornton is feeling hungry so it might be advisable for you to leave for a few moments."

Though he really didn't want to, he knew that morals dictated that he wasn't present for the feeding. He thought that was ridiculous since he had spent many hours over the past year kissing Margaret's breasts, but for fear of embarrassing her he chose to leave. Besides, he needed to check that the nursery had been made ready for its new resident.

He entered the nursery and looked around. The room was painted in bright, airy colours and he leaned into the crib and picked out a small rag doll, dressed in suit and with top hat made of felt. This was a toy he had been given when he was a child. He had no memory of the toy but his mother said it had been a favourite of his and that he had slept with it until he was four years old.

Although not given to large displays of emotion, his mother did have a sentimental streak and she had kept many keepsakes from his and Fanny's childhoods. She had happily handed this toy back to him though, in the hopes that his son might gain as much pleasure from it as he had when he was a boy.

Well, now he had a daughter rather than a son but hopefully she would still love the toy as he once had.

John wasn't a man who was particularly given to introspection, more because he didn't have the time for it rather than because he lacked insight but as he looked around the nursery, he couldn't help but wonder how he had been so lucky.

When he had first seen Margaret Hale he had thought her haughty and condescending. When he had next seen her at her father's house he had been attracted to her, though even then he could never have guessed how big a part of his life she would become or just how deeply he would grow to love her.

Their journey to finding each other had been rocky and fraught with prejudice and misunderstanding but, by the grace of God, somehow they had found their way to each other.

He was still standing in the nursery when his mother came to stand beside him.

"You're a grandmother," he said.

Hannah didn't answer so he looked over to her and saw that her eyes were shining with unshed tears. He put his arms around her and drew her to him.

"Come now, it's not that terrible an event, is it?" he teased.

Hannah pulled away, smiling slightly as she wiped her tears.

"No," she agreed. "It's just... there were times over the years when I wondered if the rest of our lives would be a struggle and even when the mill was successful, you didn't look happy. I began to fear that you might never find the time to have a family of your own."

John smiled warmly at his mother and put his arm around her shoulders, drawing her to him.

"I would have been nothing without you," he told her.

"Oh hush." Clearly uncomfortable with the sentimentality she was displaying, she stiffened her back.

"You know, nothing would please me more than if you could find someone."

"Me! I'm far too old for such nonsense. Once was enough."

"But he didn't love you as he should have," John said. "You deserve someone who appreciates and respects you and it's my dearest wish that you might find that someone."

Hannah smiled and nodded.

"Margaret should be finished by now, why don't you go and see her."

"Aye, I think that I will." He knew he couldn't push things any further.

When he went back into the bedroom, he saw that Margaret, who had changed into a fresh nightgown, was seated in one of the chairs by the fire as Dixon and Jane set about changing the bed linen. As he knelt down beside her chair he saw that the baby was asleep in her arms.

"Isn't she perfect?" Margaret said softly.

"Aye," he agreed. "We must choose a name for her soon."

"I was thinking, perhaps Elizabeth," Margaret suggested.

"Or Bessy for short."

"I think that's a grand name." He kissed her cheek. "Elizabeth."

"Now Miss Margaret," Dixon said when she had finished making up the bed. "You'd best hand that baby over and get yourself some sleep. You too, master. It's gone dawn and neither of you has had a wink of sleep."

Margaret couldn't agree more with the sleep suggestion, but she was loathe to part with her baby.

"Nor have you," Margaret argued.

"No but I've spoken to cook and young Jenny, the scullery maid, will be helping me for a few days." Dixon had taken a shine to the young girl ever since she had started working at the house a few months ago. "She might be young but she's the oldest of eight, so she's quite used to caring for babies."

Margaret looked down at her sleeping child but finally her desire to sleep became paramount and she handed her over to Dixon.

"She'll be just down the hall, Miss Margaret, so don't you worry about a thing."

"I trust you, Dixon."

Dixon smiled, pleased by such praise.

"Now, get some sleep, the pair of you."

She left and Margaret took John's hand. He was still kneeling beside her chair.

"I have to check on the mill," he said.

"Dixon is right, John, you haven't slept either. You need sleep just as much as I do and if ever there was a day to take off work, it's the day your first child is born."

"I know, and I won't be long, love, but I must let Higgins know what's happened so that he can take over for the day."

Margaret nodded, knowing that he was right.

"Then go now so that you can return to me sooner."

"Do you need help getting to bed."

"I will be fine," she assured him.

He smiled, kissed her gently on the lips then left. Since she was still quite sore, Margaret was slow getting to her feet but instead of going to the bed, she made her way to the window and pulled the curtains back slightly.

The sun was risen now and the courtyard was buzzing with activity as the workers arrived for the day. She saw John heading across the yard to the offices and smiled at the surprised expressions he was receiving, for he looked far from the stiff and formal master they were all used to. He had dark circles under his eyes, his chin bore a days stubble growth, his cravat was missing and his shirt was wrinkled and undone at the collar. To complete the worn and ravaged look, he had no jacket or waistcoat.

Margaret smiled, remembering how worried he had been all night.

As he entered the offices she let the curtains close again and made her way over to the bed. Climbing in she fully intended to wait for John before she went to sleep but moments after her head rested against the pillow, she had fallen into a deep slumber.

Chapter Eighteen

Margaret awoke to a sound she had not heard before. John was talking to the baby but his voice was soft, gentle and slightly higher than she'd ever heard him speak before. It was actually very sweet.

"You are the most handsome baby in all of Milton, aren't you, huh? No? You're the most handsome baby in Darkshire? Oh, well I stand corrected. Yes I do."

John was holding Elizabeth and gently swaying her in his arms as he spoke nonsense to her. Margaret smiled at them as the baby began to grizzle slightly.

"Are you getting hungry? I'll bet you are. You're a growing girl, aren't you? But mummy's very tired at the moment and she needs her rest. Do you think you can wait for just a little while longer? Daddy will pull lots more funny faces for you if you can."

"That I have to see," Margaret said.

John turned to her and grinned. "Look who's up! Say 'hello, Mummy'. 'Hello, Mummy'."

"I think she might be a bit young for that," Margaret teased.

"She's a prodigy," John proclaimed. "She's already smiled at me."

Bessy grizzled again.

"I think that means 'that's all very well, Daddy, but I'm still rather hungry," Margaret translated.

John handed the baby over, though somewhat reluctantly and Margaret began to feed her.

"My, someone is hungry," she said to Bessy.

"Dixon and Jenny gave her pap earlier to tide her over while you slept but there's nothing like mother's milk." John came and sat beside her on the bed.

"What time is it?" Margaret asked John since she seemed unable to look away from her daughter.

"Nearly four," he said.

"Have you been to the mill?" she asked, noticing that he was fully dressed. "Daddy's just a tiny bit obsessed with his mill," she told Bessy. "But that's one of the many reasons we love him."

"Briefly," he confirmed with a smile. "Just to make certain that Higgins had no problems. I'm all yours for the rest of the day."

Margaret finally tore her gaze away from Bessy and

smiled at John.

"You still have to show me those faces, don't forget," she teased.

"Oh no. As much as I love you, I only do that for Bessy because she's still too young to tell tales on me."

Margaret laughed.

"How do you feel?" John asked her.

"Sore but all right. I think I'd commit murder for a hot bath right now, though."

"Your wish is my command. I'll have some food brought up too; you haven't eaten since last night."

As though his reminder had prompted it, Margaret's stomach rumbled.

"Perhaps that would be a good idea," she agreed.

John rang the bell and in short order arranged for a bath to be filled and a tray brought to Margaret while that was being done. Margaret handed Elizabeth over to John while she ate and, unwilling to be separated for long, convinced him to accompany her to the bathroom with the baby.

Margaret sank down into the hot water with a long sigh.

"Too hot?" he asked, worried.

"Oh no, it's wonderful," she said, relaxing as she got used to the heat. Dixon had added healing salts to the water which stung slightly but Margaret knew from experience how well they worked.

"That's Mummy's contented face," John told Bessy. "We like that face."

Margaret sank low in the water, leaned her head back and closed her eyes as she listened to father and daughter bonding. He was right, she was content. She joined in with their conversation from time to time but overall she was happy to lie back and let the water sooth her aches and pains.

When the water finally became too cool, she got out and dried herself off. As Margaret's lady's maid, Dixon should have been called to help but Margaret wasn't in the mood to be cosseted at the moment. She donned a simple cotton night gown and brushed her damp hair through before it could tangle.

When she was finished, Margaret and John lay on their bed playing with a variety of the baby's toys as they talked while Elizabeth lay in between them. John told Margaret what the doctor had said about her condition improving now the baby was born and Margaret confirmed that she had suffered no symptoms today. He told her how many good wishes and congratulations he had received for her from the hands and how many letters and gifts had been arriving for her all day. Mary had also brought the finest bunch of wild flowers he'd ever seen, which she'd picked and arranged herself and the school children had made a card for her in class this morning, which they had all helped decorate.

Margaret opted not to open her cards and gifts yet though, tomorrow the rest of the world could intrude but tonight was just for her family.

"I'm so proud of you," John said, reaching over Bessy to cup Margaret's cheek. "She's perfect."

"You aren't sorry we didn't have a son?" she asked, because surely every man wanted a son.

"She's healthy and she's ours; that's all I care about." He leaned over and kissed her gently.

Hannah came in to see how they were doing but she didn't stay long. Dixon came in frequently to check on them and see if they needed anything but they wanted for very little. After two more feedings Margaret grew tired again and Dixon came to remove the baby for the night. Margaret realised that if she was to continue to be involved in the mill in even the smallest capacity, she would need to trust others with the care of her daughter, but it wasn't easy to let her go.

Bessy went to Dixon without any fuss and though she felt the loss, Margaret knew beyond a shadow of a doubt that Dixon would love Elizabeth as her own.

Although Margaret had agreed to take things easy for the week, the next day after John had left for the mill, she got dressed with Dixon's help. It had been so long since she had worn anything other than a nightgown that she immediately felt better to be wearing proper clothes.

Though he left the house later than usual and came back to the house regularly to check on Margaret, John needed to return to the mill. Margaret didn't mind because she knew that her absence was causing him additional work and after Dr. Donaldson's visit, she used the time to bond with her child. After her second feed of the day (and by golly, could that girl eat!) Margaret introduced the baby to the house and it's staff taking her on a tour from the kitchen to the servants rooms at the top. It took quite a while as every servant she encountered wanted to talk to the baby.

Though this would be quite unheard of in most houses, because the Thorntons had few pretensions they were a little more relaxed with their staff than many families. Plus, Margaret knew that Elizabeth was hard to resist so who was she to deny them a cuddle.

Truth be told, taking her cue from Frederick and Dolores, Margaret also wanted her daughter to be much more involved in her and John's life than many children from upper class families were.

When the tour was finally over, Margaret ate lunch with Hannah, John and the baby. Although Hannah though it odd for Margaret to want the child present at meal times, she personally had no objections and they took it in turns to care for the baby while the others ate.

After lunch Margaret knew that she had many letters of thanks to write and so Hannah offered to take care of Elizabeth while she worked. Margaret opened the cards and letters first and realised that most local people had obviously already heard about the birth. There were also a few gifts, which Margaret thought was very kind of people.

As well as their flowers, Nicholas, Mary and the children had sent the baby a knitted doll and a card which all of them had signed. Most of the other presents were also toys for the baby, such as rattles and children's books, though Mr. Maitland's wife, whose house she had stayed in when she first returned to Milton, had sent a book for Bessy and a collection of healing, relaxing, invigorating and energising bath salts for Margaret.

Margaret was touched by the gesture, first of all because the lady had thought of Margaret as well as the baby, but mainly because Margaret had not met either Mr. or Mrs. Maitland yet. After extending their trip time after time, they had only returned to Milton a few weeks ago, while Margaret was under house arrest at the Doctor's orders.

First she set about writing to Mrs. Maitland, thanking her for the kind gift, asking about their time abroad and hoping that she would come and visit when Margaret was able to receive visitors again.

Next she wrote letters to Frederick, Edith and Aunt Shaw about her happy news, though she kept them short and to the point. She would write them longer letters over the coming week but right now she had many other people she needed to correspond with as well. Next she began the letters thanking those who had sent a letter, card or gift for their kind wishes.

By the time the last whistle of the day sounded at the mill and John returned home, Margaret still wasn't finished, but she had all week to catch up so she wasn't too perturbed.

The next day Margaret was feeling much better. Her soreness was fading and her hands had shrunk back to their normal size so she was able to wear her wedding ring again. After Dixon had done her hair and she had dressed, she felt just as full of life and energy as she had before she fell pregnant. Still, she knew that she had promised John that she would take things easy, so although she insisted on eating proper food finally, she did keep to the house and used the time to finish her thank you letters.

By the fourth day Margaret was raring to get out, so leaving Bessy with Dixon, Margaret called a carriage and ventured into town to buy a perambulator for the baby. Those who saw her seemed surprised that she was out and about so quickly but Margaret assured them that she was fine. Somehow she managed to cross the courtyard without John noticing or being informed. She hoped he wasn't too upset with her.

John was surprised to see the large contraption filling the hallway that evening and though he was concerned for her, he had come to expect nothing less from Margaret. He could picture her walking the hills and parks of Milton, pushing the baby in her perambulator, and since she seemed to have come to no harm during her trip, he decided not to let his temper get the better of him.

The next day, knowing that she shouldn't yet take a walk on her own with the perambulator, Margaret opted to show Elizabeth around the mill instead. She avoided the machinery since the noise in there would surely terrify the baby but she showed her around the warehouses, the school, the canteen and and offices. Again she was frequently stopped by people offering their best wishes and wanting to see the baby.

She had expected John to be upset that she was walking through the factory, but instead his face lit up when she came into his office.

"Training her up already?" he teased. "Well, she's a little young but we can always use the help."

John took the baby from her and seemed quite unperturbed as Bessy proceeded to tug at his cravat.

"I think she's telling you to relax a little more," Margaret said. John wasn't the only one who could tease.

"Five days old and already she's trying to tell me what to do. Should I be worried?"

"Most definitely," Margaret said. "Something tells me that Miss Elizabeth Thornton will be able to wrap her daddy around her little finger."

The next day was Sunday and after church, John and Margaret took the baby for a walk in the perambulator. They stopped at Nicholas's house and spent some time with him and the Boucher children. Higgins's wife had been up and about within hours of their childrens' births but he had been surprised to see Margaret about so quickly, given that she was a lady. He was beginning to think that all this talk of ladies having a delicate constitution was poppycock.

Baby Bessy was handed about from her parents to Nicholas, then Mary and even Tom had a quick hold while supervised by Nicholas. The baby's calm nature amazed Nicholas but Margaret assured him that he hadn't heard her screaming for her dinner yet. Still, he was right, she was a remarkably calm child. Margaret wondered if that was because of her nature of if perhaps taking her around and keeping her interested in new things was occupying or distracting her.

That evening, after Dixon had removed Bessy for the night, Margaret went into the bathroom to get changed into her night clothes, as had been her habit recently.

As she disrobed she looked down at her body and wondered if she would ever feel attractive again. She felt fine with her clothes on but without the help of a good tailor, she could see the damage that pregnancy had wrought on her body, even after the swelling in her hands and feet had gone down. She wondered if John would still like her. He had been as sweet as sweet could be since Bessy had been born but he had not shown any kind of passion for her at all.

She felt well enough again to resume marital relations, in fact she was rather looking forward to it, though she was also feeling quite apprehensive of John's reaction. She had chosen one of the night gowns from her wedding trousseau, made from cream silk. It was reasonably loose and she hoped it would hide a multitude of sins.

John was already in bed when she came out and she saw his eyes widen as he saw her. Immediately she felt self conscious and looked down. She climbed into her side of the bed and scooted over to him. As had been his habit in recent weeks, he was also in a nightgown, so as she rested her head on his chest, she ran her hand over the cotton fabric.

"Margaret," he caught her hand to stop her.

Hurt, Margaret turned away and curled her knees up to her chest. As her tears fell silently on to her pillow, she cursed how emotional she felt these days.

"Margaret." John put his hand on her shoulder but she shrugged him off, unwilling for him to discover how his rejection had hurt her. "Don't be like this, please."

Margaret couldn't answer him without letting him know that she was crying.

"Darling?"

Margaret was unable to completely stifle the shuddering sob that escaped her. Worried, John leaned over and saw her tears for himself. Immediately he felt awful. What had he done to her now?

Knowing that she had been discovered, Margaret sat up and wiped at her eyes.

"I'm sorry, I've been very over-emotional since Bessy was born."

"Margaret, please, don't do this."

"Do what?" she feigned ignorance.

"I've known you for years and seen you during the best of times and the worst. This is more than you just being over-emotional."

Margaret looked into his eyes, knowing that she had been caught in a lie. But she couldn't maintain eye contact and turned away from him.

"You don't..."

"Margaret, please." Though she was facing away from him, he put his arms around her and pulled her back against him. "You can tell me anything."

"Do you no longer find me appealing?" she finally asked. She disliked how weak she sounded but she couldn't help it.

John began laughing which immediately dampened her self pity and ignited her anger. She ripped herself out of his embrace as she got off the bed and turned back to face him.

"Don't you dare laugh at me, John Thornton! I may have

144

gained weight carrying your child but I am still your wife and I deserve your respect."

John's mirth immediately died as he realised he had once again hurt her.

"My darling, I only laugh because your notion that I no longer find you attractive is quite frankly ludicrous. These last few weeks, lying with you but unable to have you have been torment beyond belief and it is only because I respect and love you so much that I have been able to control myself."

"Then why refuse my advances this evening?"

"You gave birth less than a week ago. Whilst there is nothing I would like more than to resume our previous relationship, I could never do so knowing that I might cause you pain."

Margaret narrowed her eyes at him, unsure if she believed him or if he was just placating her.

He crawled to the edge of the bed and kneeled up. He pulled his night gown off and threw it aside so she could see for herself the effect she had on him.

"Do you need any more proof of my ardour?" he asked.

Now Margaret felt embarrassed at her outburst, which only brought more tears. John went to her and this time when he wrapped her in an embrace, she didn't pull away.

"I'm sorry," she said, hiding her face in his chest.

"You have nothing to be sorry for, my love. You have been through a lot, it's no wonder you are taking a while to find your equilibrium again. In fact I'm amazed at how quickly you are recovering."

"You make it sound like I had major surgery," she said.

"Worse." He was serious. "You could have died, Margaret, and the thought of doing anything that might harm you or worsen your condition has occupied my thoughts day and night."

Margaret looked up at him. No wonder he had been so gentle with her.

John reached up and tenderly wiped her tears away.

"Now tell me honestly, do you really feel up to resuming our marital relations or did you just fear that I had stopped wanting you?"

"Both. I truly do feel healed now and also I..." She lowered her face as she blushed. "Well, I have missed you too."

John hugged her to him and picked her up off the ground.

Margaret shrieked in surprise then smiled.

"John, release me this instant!"

"Never!" he turned and placed her down on the bed. "You are mine and I will never let you go, you silly woman. Never!"

"I love you too, in case you were wondering." She smiled.

"Good, because we have a problem."

"Oh?" Her spirits sank at that statement.

"Yes. I'm afraid, my love, that you are wearing far too many clothes."

Margaret found that idea laughable since she only wore a thin nightdress. Still, if he wanted to see her, she wouldn't deny him. She sat up and closed her eyes as she pulled the gown over her head and off. She kept her eyes downcast or closed for fear of his reaction.

John stood beside the bed for a few moments, drinking in the beautiful sight that lay before him.

"Margaret? Margaret, look at me." His tone was firm, almost commanding though not unkind.

Slowly Margaret raised her gaze to meet his. The passion she saw in his eyes, the desire written in his every feature, left her in no doubt that he still found her more than appealing. She smiled shyly and though still slightly self conscious at her altered appearance, she finally believed him.

Chapter Nineteen

Margaret arose on the Monday feeling happy, sated and loved, though her pleasurable feelings soon dissipated as she remembered that, according to custom, she would be receiving visitors this week.

Though she very much wished to return to the mill, she knew that she must remain in the house each morning to receive any callers. She was certain that Fanny would be among them and was most apprehensive about her visit. Poor Fanny had been trying for a child ever since her marriage to Watson but she was still unsuccessful. As much as Margaret's feelings for her had darkened when she learned how she had treated John when the mill closed, she had no wish to hurt Fanny.

Fanny had kept a low profile for most of Margaret's pregnancy, coming to the house on only two occasions after they had announced their happy news. The first was to congratulate her on the news, and it had been clear that underneath her snippy exterior, she was hurt by the fact that her attempts to have a child had been unsuccessful.

The second occasion was to attend Hannah's yearly dinner party. Margaret had been six months pregnant at the time so she had chosen the dress that best hid her baby bump and asked Hannah to seat her clear up the other end of the table from Fanny, less her swelling stomach remind the girl of her own misfortune.

Hannah continued to visit Fanny but she too had chosen to steer clear from talking about Margaret's pregnancy with her daughter.

Unfortunately, etiquette said that now Fanny must call on her sister in law, and Margaret was not looking forward to it one bit.

In the afternoons she hoped to work at the mill for a few hours while Dixon watched Elizabeth and, so as not to lose time with her daughter, she opted to keep the baby with her when the visitors called, though she would ask Dixon to take her away when Fanny came to call.

Mrs. Latimer and her daughter were the first people to call. They brought with them a beautiful flower arrangement and a box of rather indulgent Belgian chocolates. Margaret thanked them and told them how well Bessy was doing. Mrs. Latimer did most of the talking, telling her own stories of child rearing, while her daughter sat demurely beside her. Margaret had often tried to engage the girl in conversation but though she was unfailingly polite and very sweet, it was hard to get her to start a discourse.

Margaret sometimes wondered if it was because her mother spoke so very much that Miss Latimer had learned to say so little. She had heard from John, who had been told by Mr. Latimer, that Miss Latimer was engaged to a businessman named Cartwright and Margaret congratulated her on the union.

Both ladies asked to hold the baby and Margaret freely consented, happy to let her daughter experience as many different people as was possible. As a child, Margaret vividly remembered all of the rules when she had lived with her Aunt Shaw in London. Every aspect of her life was dictated to her, who she could see, what she could do and where she was allowed to go, each moment of the day. She had hated every second and longed to return to Helstone where, on the whole, her parents trusted her to look after herself. She wanted Bessy to have a childhood like hers in Helstone, not Harley Street.

Once the Latimers had taken their leave, it was not five and ten minutes later that her next caller came. Margaret had retreated upstairs to feed Elizabeth so when Dixon came in informing her that Mrs. Watson was here, Margaret asked that one of the servants be sent to fetch the elder Mrs. Thornton back from the mill. Hannah was much more experienced at handling her daughter and though Margaret didn't need her help, she would very much appreciate it.

She left Bessy in Dixon's care, lest the sight of her upset Fanny, and headed down to greet her visitor.

"Oh, Margaret, what a pleasure it is to see you," Fanny gushed. "You did have us all so worried for a time there but I am pleased to see that you are looking quite healthy again. Indeed one might almost think you had never been unwell."

Margaret ignored the implications of that last line and poured them both some tea.

"I am feeling much better, and thank you for your kind wishes, I was so pleased to receive your card."

"Oh, think nothing of it."

Indeed Margaret didn't. She knew Fanny's handwriting well enough now to realise that she hadn't even written the card herself.

"I must say, you seem in good spirits today."

"Oh, indeed I am," Fanny smiled, clearly not intending to continue but rather leave Margaret wondering.

Hannah came in seconds later and Fanny's mood dampened slightly, knowing that her mother would not put up with her antics quite so easily as Margaret.

"Mother, how lovely to see you."

"I'm glad you could join us," Margaret smiled at her mother in law and poured her a cup of tea.

Hannah nodded, accepting the sentiment and letting Margaret know that she understood her desire to have her here.

"You're looking well," Hannah told Fanny.

"Indeed I am, Mother, very well."

"Oh?" Hannah didn't need to say more, that one syllable both asked why and let Fanny know that she wasn't in the mood to play guessing games.

"Mother," Fanny grinned. "I have the most wonderful news. I am with child."

"Oh, Fanny, this is indeed wonderful news," Margaret said, genuinely meaning it. Finally Fanny was having her own family and hopefully that would help to lessen her resentment towards Margaret. "I am so pleased for you."

"Yes, congratulations," Hannah said, smiling. "I know how much you have longed for this."

"And the timing couldn't be better if I had planned it. I shall be at my largest over the winter months when the air is cool. I should so hate to be pregnant and give birth during the summer months. It is very warm out today, is it not? Why I had to get my fan out on the way over here, it was so hot."

"Indeed," Margaret smiled tightly. Of course Fanny's pregnancy would be better than Margaret's, just as her child would surely be more intelligent, more handsome and in every way possible, better than Bessy.

"Of course I shall sleep alone until the baby arrives. I am so very delicate that I should hate for the child to be harmed in any way."

"Of course," Margaret agreed, though she wondered if perhaps Fanny wasn't as enamoured of her husband as she would have others believe.

Fanny continued to expound on the wonders of pregnancy for the remainder of her visit and it wasn't until she left that

Margaret realised she had not even asked the name of Margaret's baby.

"Thank you for staying with me," Margaret told Hannah.

"Fanny may be my flesh and blood, Margaret but believe me, I am under no illusions about her character." She smiled and Margaret returned it.

The lunch bell rang soon afterwards and John joined them as they ate. Elizabeth sat quietly in her bassinet until John had finished eating, when he plucked her from the basket for a cuddle.

Playing with a child at the dining table was the height of bad manners but neither woman seemed to care. In fact the look of adoration on John's face caused both of them to share a smile or two.

When the whistle rang to signify the end of the break, Margaret handed Bessy over to Dixon and Jenny. Although Jenny wasn't a trained nanny, she had proved herself competent and capable over the past week and Dixon had asked if she might be retained as a permanent helper for Dixon when she looked after the baby.

Margaret knew her to be a sensible girl and she had seen how much Jenny loved the baby. In her mind that was a lot more important than the title of nanny and had agreed to Dixon's request. It also didn't escape her notice that while Dixon would have no power over a proper nanny, she could still order Jenny around. Not that she abused that power, of course, but Dixon did like things done a certain way.

Margaret kissed Bessy goodbye and with a few hesitations, accompanied John over to his office.

"Are you sure you want to return so soon?" he asked.

"I am certain," she assured him. "While part of me would dearly love to stay with her, I find that I am also eager to catch up on what I have missed."

"Mother and Thomas have been doing a grand job in your absence," he assured her. "Though you have been missed. We have a stack of outstanding invoices that seems to grow daily."

"Then I shall set to it as soon as we are done here." Margaret smiled.

They went into John's office and he explained everything that had happened since she became ill; the new orders they had undertaken and how they were progressing, the problems John was experiencing sourcing cotton and the results of the latest survey that parliament had commissioned into working practices in the mills.

"And the new mill?" Margaret asked when he had finished. "How does that fair?"

While she was ill, John had been forced to take over the management of her properties so that he might keep the finance for the new mill flowing.

"The house on Pond Street has been sold, finally, along with the shops on Windsor Terrace. They all fetched a good price and the mill is approximately three months away from completion. The first lot of housing is progressing well, so that the hands will be spared the daily walk from Milton as soon as possible. Phase one of the village should be completed in six months, then phase two will begin, which will house the the additional staff we hope to take on after the first expansion."

"You seem to have everything well in hand," she observed.

"I would be happy for you to take over once again."

"The mill is the most important aspect of this project so it is only right that you oversee everything associated with it."

"If you insist, but I will keep you informed of all developments and ask for your opinions."

"Thank you," she smiled.

"I am going out to the site in three weeks to check on progress for myself. Would you like to accompany me?"

"Very much," she smiled. In fact she was eager to see the progress. The last time she had been to the site, the builders had only just begun the work. "Now, I think I had better get to work or I will get nothing done today."

"As you wish." he came around the desk, took her in his arms and kissed her gently. "Don't work too hard," he said, a note of pleading in his voice.

Margaret understood that he was worried about her and knowing how deeply he cared for her, she admired him for letting her to return to work at all. Many husbands would not have allowed it.

"I will be very careful not to over-exert myself," she assured him. "You have my word."

That was good enough for John, he kissed her once more then stepped away, allowing her to leave.

The next morning, Margaret dressed and prepared to face more callers, but her mood was lighter now that she had seen

Fanny. To her surprise, her first callers were Mr. and Mrs. Maitland, accompanied by John, who introduced Margaret to them.

"It is so lovely to finally meet you both," she said with feeling.

Though Mr. Maitland was showing signs of ageing there was something in his countenance that said he'd give any youth a run for their money in the energy stakes. His dark hair, greying at the temples, was swept straight back from his face, which was itself slightly darkened from his travels.

Mrs. Maitland was tall and poised. She was dressed in an unusual style, that she explained came from Milan. Her hair was swept back into the latest fashion, though the few tendrils escaping at the sides and back hinted that perhaps she was not as stiff as one might assume at first glance.

As John chatted with Edward Maitland, Margaret got to know Eleanor a little better. Despite the age difference they had much in common, having both been raised in the south and both chosen to marry northern tradesmen. Eleanor was currently cradling baby Elizabeth in her arms and looking completely smitten by her.

"Oh, I do so long for a grandchild," she confided. "Though none of my children seem inclined to indulge me. Were I not so long in the tooth, I would seriously consider having another myself." She grinned at Margaret. "Can you imagine the scandal!"

Margaret was soon proven correct in her assumption since, though she was a southern lady and very well groomed, she was quick to laugh and her humour was never far from the surface. Margaret was inclined to like her very much.

"Mama was frightfully shocked when I chose Edward," Eleanor confided later in the conversation. "In fact she took one of her turns and was confined to her bed for the rest of the week."

"Oh, nothing serious, I hope?" Margaret asked.

"Nothing a little backbone wouldn't have cured," she said with a sly smile. "Actually it was perfect as far as I was concerned. My father was always more open minded and once he had convinced himself that Edward was a solid sort of fellow, he was quite happy to see us wed."

"Did your mother ever come around?" Margaret asked.

"On our tenth anniversary she told me that while she had

hoped I would find myself a gentleman, perhaps even a lord, she could see that I was happy and, rather grudgingly I must say, told me she was sorry."

"Well, I suppose all is well that ends well."

"Perhaps. Unfortunately she never would venture north to come and see me or the children, we always had to go and visit her. Edward couldn't often take much time off work so frequently I went alone with the children, which I think that is what mother hoped would happen. What about your parents, how did they take the news that you were betrothed to John?"

"I'm afraid they both died before that happy event." Margaret looked away, the pain of her loss momentarily cutting her to the quick.

"Oh, my dear, I am so sorry." Eleanor reached out and took Margaret's hand. Unlike with other women, this was no rehearsed pleasantry, this was heartfelt compassion. Margaret smiled at her kindness.

"Thank you. I think they would have been happy for me. I know my father thought a great deal of John, so he would have been pleased. My mother would probably have been most unhappy that I was to spend the rest of my life in Milton, she never liked the climate here, but she only ever wanted what was best for me, so I am sure I would have had her blessing also."

"How wonderful."

"My aunt Shaw on the other hand..." Margaret cringed with embarrassment at the memory as she began to tell Eleanor all about her Aunt's awful behaviour.

Chapter Twenty

John and Margaret stood and observed the new mill, Bessy cradled in Margaret's arms.

"Oh my," Margaret said in awe, for she hadn't see the site since the day they had broken ground. "Look, Bessy, isn't it wonderful?"

It was much larger in reality than she imagined it would be from the plans. When fully staffed it would house almost three thousand workers, though John estimated that it would be many years before they were able to expand to full capacity.

John stood behind his wife and daughter, his hand on Margaret's shoulder as he took in the sight before him.

A few moments later Mr. Armstrong, the architect, joined them and proceeded to explain what was happening, what was still to be done and when it was likely to be finished. He then showed them around the mill so they could see how the work was progressing for themselves.

Everything had been streamlined, from the canal that brought the raw cotton in at one end of the mill, to the railway platform that took the finished product to various destinations throughout the country at the other end. The whole process as now as efficient as it could possibly be.

Next Mr. Armstrong took them to the first residential phase. Five rows of houses looked complete, but there were a further five streets that looked almost complete and another five that had not long been started. Each house had a small yard at the rear with plumbing (where the lavatory facilities would be) and where a family might hang out their washing. Each street had a wash house and it's own well and there was a small road between the houses, more than wide enough for a carriage should one need to pass.

Areas had been left on every fourth street that would be turned into parks where children might play or families might walk. Margaret was pleased to see that these areas had been left with some fairly large trees intact, making the parks look greener and providing something for the children to play on. Margaret smiled as she remembered the many times she had skinned her knees while climbing trees as a child in Helstone.

They looked around one of the nearly finished houses and saw that the lower floor was two rooms, a kitchen at the rear and a living area at the front. The upper floor had been divided into three, two small bedrooms for the children and one larger for the parents.

Not all the houses would be the same, Mr. Armstrong explained, some were slightly larger for larger families and some of the dwellings in the next stage of houses would be grander, for employees such as the overseers, teachers, shop keepers and their families.

As part of phase one of the homes, a community hall cum school room and a few shops were also being built. The shops were on the end of some of the rows of houses, while the community hall was being built at the edge of the development so that when the next phase of housing was built, it would be in the centre and within easy reach of everyone.

Other community buildings would be built as the population of the village grew, such as a proper school building and a small hospital.

Margaret and John were very impressed, though Bessy was less so, grizzling her way through the last ten minutes of the tour. Knowing that she was probably tired, Margaret returned to the small gig John had driven here and laid her in her bassinet. By the time John joined her, Bessy was fast asleep.

"This is amazing," she smiled at John. "I really think this is going to work."

John smiled. He was a realist and whilst he knew that many things could go wrong with this project, he was still hopeful.

"We'll make it work," he assured her.

They climbed into the gig and John picked up the reins and they began the journey home, except that part way down the dirt track they had rode in on, John turned off down a small tributary lane.

"Where are we going?" she asked.

"You'll see."

Margaret could see from his self-satisfied smile that he was up to something. The horse walked on for another few minutes, through a small wooded patch from which they emerged into a meadow. In the corner of which was a farm house, though it had clearly seen better days. Most of the window frames were rotting and missing their glass and the roof was long gone. The front of the house had a small, badly overgrown garden surrounded by a wall, with a path leading to the house, though both the gate and front door were missing.

"What is this?" she asked as John stopped the gig outside. She got out and looked up at the house, John followed suit, picking up the handles of the bassinet and carrying it with him. Over the door was a badly weather-beaten, wooden sign but the name 'Rose Farm' could still just about be read. Margaret immediately decided to call the house Rose Cottage.

The house was in a bad condition, to be sure, but even in its dilapidated state, it had a certain kind of charm.

"Remember we were told this land used to be a farm? Well this was the farm house," John explained.

"When they said it was a ruin, I assumed it was just rubble."

They walked through the property and Margaret could see from the rear windows that there was a walled garden out there, though it was very overgrown.

"Well, it's far from habitable," John said, "but I was thinking that we could restore it and make it our home."

Margaret turned to look at him, her face lit up with pleasure.

"You think we can do that?"

"Why not?" he asked. "I've had Mr. Armstrong look it over and he says the structure is sound, we just need to replace the window frames, put a new roof on and replace some of the timber."

"It's beautiful," Margaret said, turning back to the garden. "It reminds me a little of Helstone," she said softly. "I'd love for Bessy to grow up somewhere like this."

"Then I'll tell Armstrong to start work tomorrow."

"Can we afford to do it now?" she asked. "Shouldn't we wait?"

"We can afford it," he assured her. "I'm covering the cost of the house with the profits from the mill; it isn't coming from your property."

"Mr. Bell's property," she corrected. Suddenly her smile faded. "Is it big enough? I mean for us, Bessy, your mother and the servants."

"Well it's got five bedrooms for us and we're going to put three rooms in the attic when the new roof goes on. There's also a two story stable block on the other side of the garden wall and we can convert the top floor into accommodations."

Quite uncharacteristically for her, Margaret ran at John. He just had the time and foresight to place the bassinet on the floor before catching her.

"This is amazing, John, I love it." She grabbed his face and landed a heavy kiss on his lips.

"I had hoped that you might," he said when she released his face.

"You know me too well."

"I hope not. I had rather hoped to spend the rest of my life being surprised by you."

Margaret smiled and threw her arms around his shoulders. John was still holding her feet off the ground.

"Oh, I can just imagine living here. It's so warm and cosy, a real home. Does that make sense."

"I think anywhere you are is a home, so yes, it makes perfect sense." He laughed, enjoying her glee. "If I had known an old ruin would go over this well with you, I'd have bought you one years ago." John finally released Margaret and set her feet back on solid ground.

"Ah, but not any old ruin will do," she cautioned. "It has to be chosen with love."

John picked up the bassinet and took hold of Margaret's hand as they continued to explore the lower level of the cottage and its garden.

Summer gave way to autumn and as the leaves began to turn from green to vibrant shades of yellow and red, the Mill was finished.

Situated two miles out of town, it would be a long walk for the workers but nothing too exceptional. John had shown Nicholas around the new mill a month before it was finished and asked his opinion on whether to open the new mill as soon as it was finished or whether to wait until the first phase of housing was ready, which would be another four months.

Nicholas was impressed by how light and airy the factory was and the safety procedures John had implemented. The wheels for example, were built directly into the walls and able to be much larger that those they currently had and as well as internal staircases, each floor also had doors leading to an external iron staircase, for use in the event of a fire.

Nicholas assured John that the workers were fit and the walk would be worth it to them so John arranged for Marlborough Mill to be closed from Saturday to Monday while the machines were transported and installed in the new mill. The workers had grumbled about the walk adding to the length of their day but most were placated by Higgins. Those that weren't were assured that they were free to leave with a good letter of reference. In the end, no one opted to leave.

The builders who had finished on the mill moved over to the housing phase and as such it was finished a month early.

Margaret was especially pleased by this development because it meant that the workers could be in residence by Christmas. She had initially feared that they would have to move during January or February, which were normally the coldest months of the year.

The workers were again given an extra day off on the Saturday to help them move, though they were asked the make the time up during the next week. Most were happy to.

The houses, though small were well finished, keeping the damp and draughts out and the heat from the fires in. Each house had a fireplace in the middle of the house so the heat warmed all the rooms through the chimney.

John already ordered a lot of coal to power the mill's beam engine that ran the machines. Now he more than doubled that order so that he could sell the remainder to his workers at cost price, allowing them to keep their houses warm even in the coldest months.

He made deals with many local tradesmen that they would bring their wares by cart to the village, though he hoped that if business was brisk enough for them, they would consider opening shops eventually.

Though the mill was named Thornton Mill, the village didn't have a name and most people called it Thornton's village.

John was slightly bemused that the village bore his name and suggested changing it. He even offered the hands the chance to vote on a name but not being very imaginative, Thornton village won the vote. After a few months it was shortened to Thornton and when recorded in the county records it began to be called the Village of Thornton.

Though the farmhouse was finished soon after the mill, Margaret declined to move in until both the workers houses were finished and the servants quarters in the stable block had been completed. She didn't want them to think that they were thinking of themselves to the detriment of their workers.

She used the intervening time to choose decorations and even helped to decorate Bessy's room herself. She left the front parlour and dining room to Hannah, knowing that those rooms would be used for entertaining and trusting her judgement of Milton taste better than her own.

Though everything about the house, aside from the stonework, now looked brand new, it still felt warm, as if it had a long and rich history. Margaret hoped that in time, the Thorntons would contribute their fair share to that history.

In honour of Dixon's long service to her family, Margaret opted to give Dixon her own suite of rooms over the stables, so that she might have a place to call her own and a little privacy. The youngest servants took the attic rooms and since most of the others servants were married, they opted to rent houses in the village.

Something John hadn't considered was that he'd have to hire a gardener for the cottage, but there was plenty of room left above the stables to make quarters for both the gardener cum grounds keeper and his young assistant, who doubled as the stable lad and carriage driver.

Fanny had been invited to come and see the house but she declined every invitation, claiming that her pregnancy was troubled. Worried for his sister, John had enquired about her health to Dr. Donaldson, who had assured him that Fanny was one of the healthiest mothers he had come across. Sure that Fanny would not make up such a callous lie, he questioned the doctor further, to which he confessed that Fanny's biggest problem was that she suffered from a little heartburn at times.

John knew her to be vain and shallow, but he did not realise she was also a hypochondriac. Presumably because Margaret's pregnancy had been difficult, she thought hers must be too, or perhaps she just envied Margaret the worry and attention she had been afforded. Either way, to snub Margaret's and his mother's invitations with the excuse that she was unwell was unforgivable.

Margaret told him to pay her no mind and if she had just snubbed him, he would have but she had snubbed two of the three women he loved most in the world, and he was certain that had Bessy been old enough, Fanny would have found a way to be mean to her as well.

It was strange to think that once Fanny was among those people whom he defended, yet now she was one of his antagonists, though she was more an annoyance than a genuine threat.

As they were lying in bed one evening, two weeks after

159

having moved in, John was once again tense. Having written to his sister asking her to come and visit when she had the time, she had written back saying she was still too poorly. Her baby wasn't due for another two months, mid February at the earliest. Did she really intend to spend three whole months without ever leaving the house?

"If it troubles you that much, John, invite Watson over for dinner. He will surely bring Fanny with him."

"If she does not want to come, Fanny will only throw one of her fainting spells to get out of it."

"Then we are better off not having her here at all. I want the people who come here to feel welcome, not resentful."

John let out a long sigh. "Aye, perhaps you are right."

Margaret smiled and laid her head on his chest, wrapping her arm around his waist. She knew how much it pained him to be at odds with his sister, but there was little she could do besides offer him some comfort.

Chapter Twenty One

Malcolm Watson was born at 3pm on February the 19th. Margaret was delighted to hear the news and immediately dispatched a blanket embroidered with ponies, which she had spied months ago in Milton and purchased for just this occasion.

John spoke to Watson, hoping that they could visit with Fanny before the week was up. Watson assured them they could come by at any time and Fanny would be happy to receive them, even if she was poorly.

Fanny was indeed pleased to welcome John, Margaret and Hannah, though they had opted to leave Bessy with Dixon, lest one child start the other crying.

"Isn't he marvellous, Margaret? Such a handsome boy," Fanny gushed over her new son.

"Indeed he is." Margaret agreed as she looked down at the baby in her arms, for Fanny was right, he was quite adorable.

"And I am so glad we had a boy," Fanny continued. "Watson was so longing for a son, as all men do, and of course he needs an heir to his business empire."

John felt his anger rising but Margaret placed a soothing hand on his arm.

"Of course," Margaret smiled tightly.

"So," Hannah decided to redirect the conversation. "I hope the birth was not too troublesome."

"Oh it was. Terribly painful and so... well, it would not do to talk about such things but I have never worked so hard before in my life. No one ever told me it was supposed to be that difficult, did they you, Margaret?"

"I have attended the births of women in Helstone so I knew how hard it could be. Luckily for me, because of the risks involved, I was anaesthetised and the baby was removed with forceps."

Of course there were hours of labour pains to get to that point, but Margaret chose to leave that part out.

"Anaesthetised?" Fanny asked.

"Sent to sleep."

"Well I never! Why didn't anyone tell me that was an option! In my weakened state, anything might have happened. Oh my Lord, it frightens me to think of what damage might have been done. If only Dr. Donaldson had thought to put me to sleep then-"

161

"Dr. Donaldson is an excellent physician," Hannah interrupted her daughters rant. "If you had needed sedating, I assure you he would have done so."

Fanny harrumphed and John suppressed a smile.

Baby Malcolm had already been held by John then passed to Margaret, then on to Hannah. Not long after meeting his grandmother though, he decided to start crying.

"Oh dear, it must be time for his feed," Fanny said. "John be a dear and ring the bell for the nanny."

John did as he was bid and moments later, the nanny arrived to take the baby and Margaret stood up.

"Perhaps we should leave you in peace to feed Malcolm," she said, fearing Fanny might be embarrassed by the mere thought that they would know she was breastfeeding her baby.

"Me feed Malcolm? My dear Margaret, that is what wet nurses are for. I shall never regain my figure if I... well, you know."

"No," Margaret said stiffly, sitting back down. "Though she is eating solids now, I am still feeding Elizabeth. Indeed I find it one of my more pleasurable pastimes, an opportunity to bond with her."

"And Margaret regained her figure within a month, if I recall." John smiled at her. "Though I must confess, I did like her with a few extra pounds as well. It was all in the right places and only accentuated her figure."

Margaret blushed as she remembered how he would stare at her. Considering how low she had felt after she had gained weight, it had taken her a long while to truly believe that he still found her attractive, only by that time her body was well on it's way to finding it's rightful balance again and the excess weight was almost gone.

Fanny's mouth hung open with indignation. John didn't know if it was because he had spoken out of turn or because Margaret dared to breastfeed their baby, but whatever the reason, he took an undeniable pleasure in having vexed her.

"And what of Malcolm's father, how is he coping?" Hannah asked.

"Oh, he loves the little tyke. Of course he works long hours so does not get to see as much of him as he would like, but I am certain that he will find more time to spend with us when things at the mill are less hectic."

As far as John knew, things at Watson's mill were just fine.

In fact at the last masters dinner Watson had regaled the other masters with tales of his and others' antics at the local tavern, so perhaps overwork was not the issue.

Shortly after that, they made their excuses and headed back home.

Although she could easily walk the distance to the mill, Margaret drove the gig today since she needed to pop into Milton later. Elizabeth was with Jenny today as Dixon needed to sort through Margaret's winter wardrobe and bring out her summer clothes. Margaret didn't much mind which of them looked after Bessy since she trusted both completely. She was glad of it too, for without that trust she would never have felt happy returning to work.

As Margaret walked in to her office, Thomas greeted her with a smile.

"Morning Mrs. Thornton."

"Good morning, Thomas. Have we received the plans from the architects today?"

"Aye, got 'em this morning. They're in the masters office, but he's in the mill right now. Do you want me to fetch him?"

"No no, just so long as they arrived safely. We can look over them tonight."

Margaret sat down at her desk and began sorting through the receipts. John never kept them in date order, which tended to irk her somewhat at times.

She had been working for about half an hour when there was a knock at the door and Davey Cooper stood there. Cooper was John's assistant in the office, he fetched and carried, wrote letters and did general administration.

"Mr. Dawlish is here," he said. "I put him in the masters office but I don't know where the master is."

"Check the mill, he's sure to be there," she said to Davey. "I'll see to Mr. Dawlish."

She entered John's office with a large smile on her face and shook hands with him.

"Mr. Dawlish, I'm so pleased you could come. I'm afraid my husband has been detained in the mill but I am certain he will be here shortly. May I offer you some tea while we wait?"

"No, I'm quite all right, thank you Mrs. Thornton."

Margaret sat down at John's desk.

"I understand that you are considering opening a shop in

our little village."

"Aye, that's the plan, providing I like what I see."

"I am almost certain that you will." She smiled. "What is it that you sell?"

"I'm a grocer but out here, I might carry a few other items too, if I think they'd be popular."

"You will certainly be a welcome addition. We have a grocery cart come to the village every other day, is that yours?"

"Aye, that's Mark, my shop boy. He visits the outlying areas of the town mostly, where we haven't got shops yet."

"I've met Mark a few times now; he's a very friendly boy. And I must say, using a cart is a very good idea. I take it trade out here is brisk, if you are considering taking a shop."

"Aye, it's not too bad."

"Well, if you have any questions I would be happy to answer them. I know almost as much about this place as my husband."

Mr. Dawlish looked slightly uncomfortable.

"Though I have heard of your unusual marriage, I had not realised you were so involved in matters of the business."

"My husband likes me to be his equal and since I know all about the mill, he can discuss anything with me, even things me might not wish to confide in others."

"Still..."

"I work because I enjoy it," she assured him. "And John allows it because he knows how much pleasure I get from it."

Dawlish narrowed his eyes slightly, as though sizing her up. "Very well," he decided to test her. "How many people work here?"

"At the mill, currently three hundred and fifty two, but over the next few years it is our hope to expand that to over three thousand. As for the village itself, including spouses and children who aren't employed at the mill, there are five hundred and twenty people living here, give or take a few."

"Give or take?" he asked.

"Why yes. I believe some residents are away at the moment, visiting family."

"And what do they earn?"

"It varies depending on the job. The piecers for example earn 6 shillings 10 pence while an overseer earns 27 shillings 4 pence, though the average wage is around 18 shillings a week."

"And the rent on their properties?"

"Again it varies according to size but the average is 3 to 4 shillings a week."

"So they've a fair disposable income then," he said.

"Reasonable, especially the households where both adults work. Of course they do have other costs besides rent such as food, heating, school fees, though we do subsidise the school. Then there's clothing and other occasional goods but on the whole, our workers have much more disposable income than the mill workers in Milton."

"How come?"

"Because we do everything we can to help them." Margaret smiled. "The mill for example has a cafeteria where the hands can have a hot meal, they can even buy their family's evening meal there and take it home with them, which many do since the food is bought wholesale and works out cheaper than buying it for themselves. We do something similar with coal and they buy it off us at cost price."

"And you can afford this?"

"I assure you, Mr. Dawlish, we do not run a charity. Our workers pay for the goods and services they receive and though not as high as Milton rents, we make a healthy profit on the houses."

"And what rent would you seek to charge me?"

"That depends, will you want just the shop or the accommodation above also?"

"Just the shop for now."

"Then 2 shillings a week to begin with to help you settle in and build the business up. At six months that will rise to 3 and the end of the first year 4 shillings."

"I can understand what Thornton sees in you." Dawlish gave her a smile as he realised that he couldn't trip her up. "Your mind really is very sharp."

"As is my tongue, on occasion," she shared his smile.

"I'm sure," he chuckled.

They were interrupted by John as he came rushing in and offered his hand to Dawlish.

"So sorry I'm late, I was held up in the mill, one of the looms broke down."

"Never fear, Mr. Thornton, your charming wife had been keeping me occupied."

165

"So, would you like to go and see the shop?"

"Indeed." Dawlish stood up. "Will you be joining us, Mrs. Thornton?"

"I fear that I cannot today," she smiled. "But if you should choose to become part of the community, I hope to see you much more often." She excused herself and left them alone.

"What an unusual creature," Dawlish said.

John smiled. He enjoyed seeing his wife through other peoples' eyes since it always served to remind him how captivated he had been by her in those early days. Not that he wasn't still passionate about Margaret, but familiarity made it easy to take those qualities he so admired for granted.

"She is one of a kind," he agreed.

Margaret returned to her office and finished her work for the day, then she drove the gig into town and stopped at the stationers for office supplies. She then made her way to the Princeton district, leaving the horse and gig with a local boy to look after, with the promise of 6 pence when she returned.

She made her way through the small streets and alleyways to Mrs. Parish's house. Sam Parish worked at the mill and had moved into one of the houses in the village. Recently though, his mother had fallen ill and been forced to give up work. With his father long dead and Sam unable to visit her regularly, he and his wife wanted her to come and live with them.

Sam had come into the accounts office on Saturday afternoon but rather than paying money into his savings book, for the first time he wanted to draw some out.

"For a special occasion?" Margaret asked, just to make conversation.

"No, Mrs. Thornton. My mother is coming to live with us but she can't manage the walk out here."

Margaret looked up, shocked. "So this money is for a carriage?"

"Yes, Ma'am."

"Don't be ridiculous," Margaret said, putting the cash away again.

"But you don't understand." He sounded a little desperate as she put the money back in the safe. "My mother is poorly, and it's at least six miles from her home in Milton to here. She can't manage that kind of walk anymore, even with help."

"I understand perfectly, Sam, which is why I will collect

166

your mother for you. John or I venture into Milton at least twice a week, often more. I can easily stop by and collect your mother for you. Save your money, Sam, one day you might be glad of it."

Sam looked both shocked and slightly awed. "You'd really do that?" he asked.

"Of course I would. It's no trouble at all."

When Margaret got to the tiny house, Mrs. Parish was packed and waiting for her, Margaret took her bag and helped her walk the short distance back to the gig. She paid the boy his sixpence for a job well done and to his credit, the boy insisted on putting the cases on the gig and helping Mrs. Parish in, even though he'd been paid. Margaret gave him an extra penny for his trouble.

Mrs. Parish seemed slightly intimidated by Margaret, only speaking when spoken to so Margaret asked a lot of questions to try and draw her out a little.

By the time they arrived back at the village she had discovered that Mrs. Parish was suffering from some kind of lung complaint, like a cold only much worse. Margaret had heard the cough for herself and seen her shortness of breath over just the short walk from her home to the gig. She also discovered that no doctor had seen her because the family couldn't afford the fees.

Lack of affordable medical care was an issue that had plagued Margaret ever since she had met Nicholas's daughter, Bessy. While they planned to build a small hospital in the village at some point, they as yet had no idea how they would staff it. Once the building work was finished and the mill running at full capacity, she hoped that she and John might be able to afford to retain the services of a doctor, even if only part time, but that was years in the future. Right now there was neither the population to warrant it nor the necessary funds to pay for a doctor.

She saw Mrs. Parish safely into her new home then returned to finish her work at the mill. This evening she would speak to John about doing something to get medical help for villagers who needed it.

John was still out of the office with Mr. Dawlish, so she checked that Thomas hadn't had any problems in her absence and returned home to spend a few hours with her baby.

Hannah was busy darning John's shirts so Margaret tucked

Bessy and a few supplies into the perambulator and set off for a stroll through the fields around the house. It really was quite beautiful out here at times. As she neared the top of a hill between the house and the mill, she had two spectacular views. On one side she had the mill, the village and the new houses that were part built and on the other she had the rolling hills of Darkshire.

She picked Bessy up and showed her the views, explaining that one side showed the ingenuity of man while the other showed the grace of God. Bessy seemed interested and gurgled 'ba'. It was the only word she could say and though it could be found in no dictionary, Margaret had discovered that the word meant everything from 'I'm hungry' to 'that's nice', depending on the tone of voice Bessy used. Both John and Margaret were adamant that this was her first attempt at speech.

When Bessy grew bored of the scenery, which was after only a minute or two, Margaret withdrew a book from the perambulator and sat down on the grass to read it to her daughter.

Bessy loved books, though in all fairness it was probably the illustrations which attracted her. She showed little interest in the newspaper and had only wanted to chew on Margaret's copy of Jane Eyre.

When she grew hungry, Margaret withdrew the sandwich she had brought with her and began to eat. She turned her head sharply to the left as she thought she spied movement in the bushes beside her but she could see no one there. She decided it was a trick of the light until a few moments later she turned again, this time spying two dark eyes in the bushes. She recognised them as canine immediately.

Having grown up in a small village, Margaret had come into contact with all sorts of animals, from sheep dogs to bullocks so she wasn't afraid of the animal. She tried talking gently to it to coax it out but the animal remained hidden until she finally threw the second half of her sandwich towards the bush. Cautiously it emerged from the bush to eat and she realised from its skinny build that the dog must be stray.

It was large and shaggy, with dark, soulful brown eyes and a slightly wiry black coat. Margaret was enamoured with it, more for it's timidity that it's looks. Bessy also seemed fascinated by the creature and told it 'ba' several times.

When it had finished eating, Margaret expected the creature to run off again but although it didn't venture any closer, it didn't move away either.

"There's no more," she told the dog, regretfully. "If you come back to the house, I can get you more though. Would you like that?"

Needless to say, the dog didn't answer so Margaret placed the book and Bessy back in the perambulator and headed back to the house. She glanced back from time to time to see that the dog was following them, albeit at a safe distance.

Once home Margaret handed Bessy over to Jenny, then headed to the kitchen to find the dog some food. As she came outside again she thought briefly that the dog was gone but (probably smelling the plate of ham she was carrying) he soon made himself known again. This time Margaret didn't throw the food at him but held each piece of ham out towards him.

The dog seemed to consider her offer for a while, cocking it's head to one side as though confused by the gesture. Eventually though, the dog walked slowly forward and took the ham from Margaret's hand. She continued to feed it pieces while talking softly and when the food was gone, Margaret slowly reached out with an empty hand to pet the animal. Though slightly jumpy, the dog sniffed the hand for a moment, then looked away, as though indifferent but as she scratched behind it's ears, the dog began to pant with pleasure.

Margaret was captivated that the dog trusted her enough to do this. She wanted to look after it but she couldn't allow an unknown dog into her home. Plus, she wasn't sure the dog would trust her enough to go inside with her. In the end she opted to see if she could tempt it into one of the empty stalls in the stable block. She went back into the kitchen and got a little more ham and a bowl of water, but when she came outside again, the dog was gone.

She called it and coaxed it but it didn't return, so Margaret left the food and water in the empty stall in the stable. Maybe the dog would return, maybe it wouldn't. She hoped it did.

That night John listened with interest to Margaret's pleas for a Doctor but he just couldn't justify the expense right now. Cotton prices were once again on the rise and if he didn't keep his eye on the bottom line, he'd have to end up cutting wages again, which Margaret agreed wasn't something she wanted.

Hannah listened to their conversation with interest and tried to remember something Daniel Whitaker had said to her about one of his friends or acquaintances, though the conversation had been many months ago.

She thought his friend was not only a doctor but also very liberal in his thinking. Perhaps he would have a suggestion for helping the hands get medical help when they needed it.

Though she didn't say anything now for fear of getting Margaret's hopes up, she vowed to ask Daniel more about this fellow the next time she saw him.

She smiled slightly at the thought of seeing Daniel again. He really was the sweetest man, though nothing like John's father had been. Whitaker was far more relaxed than she and even at times had a devil may care attitude which, while Hannah thought it slightly unbecoming, did interest her. She had never been spontaneous, was never given to sudden bouts of gaiety or laughter and almost every move she made was planned out, either by her or when John grew older, by him.

The idea of going for an impromptu picnic instead of taking tea at the Mitre as planned had at first shocked Hannah, but Whitaker had talked her into the picnic and she had enjoyed herself. Now she found herself questioning her life.

The past couldn't be changed and she knew that her meticulous planning and organisation had been necessary but now, as she neared old age and possibly retirement soon, she wondered if the reins needed loosening a little.

Hadn't she earned a little fun? And she was sure that Daniel was just the man to teach her how.

She still kept the relationship mostly hidden from John, not because she feared his disapproval but more because admitting her feelings for Daniel was, in her mind at least, akin to a commitment, and even after all this time Hannah still wasn't sure she was ready for that.

Chapter Twenty Two

Edmund Wallace was a man of means, far beyond even the wealthiest men in Milton. His grandparents had emigrated to America when they were young and made their fortune in oil. Money they had in spades, social standing however, they did not. As such their daughter, Edmund's mother, Christine, had been brought back to England by her mother with the intention of finding a titled husband.

She had met and married Richard Wallace, the Earl of Darkshire and, although it was a loveless marriage, she had borne him two sons, Harry, the eldest and Edmund.

When Edmund was 12 his grandmother had died, leaving both of her grandsons a sizeable inheritance.

Since Harry was to inherit their father's lands and title, Edmund could easily have become a feckless sort of fellow, whiling away his days with superficial pursuits, and indeed he was heading that way until one day, when he was aged 15, one of his school friends was involved in a bad accident, breaking his leg so badly that the teachers thought it would have to be amputated.

Edmund had stayed with the boy as he was brought back to the school and had later held his hand as the doctor examined him. Instead of removing the leg though, the doctor believed it could be saved. He cleaned and sewed up the wound, set the bone using a splint (all of which caused his friend, Jack, a great deal of pain) and then taught Edmund how to change the dressings and clean the wound every day.

To everyone's surprise, three months later Jack was as good as new. In fact had it not been for the scars on the leg, one might believe that nothing had ever happened.

Edmund was captivated by the whole event and his mother was delighted when he announced his intentions to train as a physician.

While Edmund enjoyed his training, he was slightly disturbed by the fact that so many doctors believed that the poor were undeserving of help. Many professed that they believed it was God's way of culling the weak, some said that the poor had only themselves to blame for their predicament and others just didn't seem to care.

As a boy, his mother had often told him tales of her homeland and to young Edmund's ears, it sounded like a paradise. There were no classes in America, she would explain, and everyone had an equal chance to make something of their lives. Though he knew nothing of poverty or hard work, he understood the inherent unfairness of the British class system thanks to primogeniture. By sheer accident of being the first born son, his brother would inherit all his father's land and his title, while Edmund would receive nothing.

As he grew older, Edmund began to realise that the English way of handing money and titles down a family line was wrong. He knew of many a nobleman who was stupid, incompetent or just lazy. They did not deserve their titles or lands and it was unfair that they received this wealth and position when there were so many who were more deserving.

Then, a few years ago while visiting London, he had met a German fellow named Karl Marx, whose ideas on workers' rights, government and capitalism were truly revolutionary.

Edmund had no need of money for he had inherited more than enough for three lifetimes and when he returned to his home of Hanton in Darkshire, he vowed to treat anyone who needed him, not just the rich who could afford his services.

Edmund had heard talk of John Thornton and his model village and though still inclined to see capitalists as the enemy, he was impressed by Thornton's ideas and the ways he was trying to help his workers. When his friend, Mr. Whitaker asked if he would be willing to meet with Mr. Thornton and discuss the possibility of treating the mill hands, he readily agreed as he was both eager to help the working classes and to learn more about this Thornton.

Upon arriving at the mill, Edmund's first surprise was in the woman who greeted him. She emerged from one of the offices and from the way the other workers treated her, she obviously worked there, yet everything about her, from her posture to her wardrobe, clearly showed her to be a Lady. Though her accent was southern, she shook his hand firmly, something many ladies like her found most distasteful.

She introduced herself as Mrs. Thornton and Edmund recognised her from the stories he had been told. She was the rich wife that John Thornton had married only for her wealth. Knowing how little his own father cared for his mother, he was inclined to dislike this Thornton already, for his wife was the most handsome and charming woman he had seen in a long while.

"I am so sorry but my husband is held up in town," Margaret explained. "We are having some difficulties with our cotton supplier and he is having to find an alternate source. He sends his apologies that he could not be here to meet you himself but if you will stay for lunch, he hopes to have his business sorted by then and be able to join us."

"It is no problem," Edmund assured her. "Perhaps you could tell me what your husband plans are, if he has shared them with you?"

"I should be glad to," she said. "Shall we start with a tour so that you can see for yourself what we are trying to achieve here?"

"Lead on, Madam."

Margaret started in the mill, explaining all the safety procedures that had been put in place, such as installing a fire bell, adequate exits and running fire drills once a year, then she explained what illnesses the workers were prone to and what they were doing to stop them, as with the danger from breathing in cotton dust and the wheels which ventilated the work space.

Next she showed him the canteen and introduced him to Mary Higgins who was still preparing today's meal.

From there she took him into the village and showed him the housing that had been built.

"The slums in Milton are awful, cold, damn, cramped. Here we are hoping that everyone can afford a decent home that is warm, dry and if not exactly roomy for the larger families, then at least less cramped than they had before."

They met Sally Lacey in the street, who Margaret greeted warmly. She asked if Dr. Wallace might see around her house and Sally readily agreed, seemingly pleased as punch at the chance to show off her fine home.

Edmund was impressed. He didn't spend a lot of time in the slums but he had seen enough to realise that this was more than just a step up for these workers; these homes were castles by comparison.

Next Margaret showed him Mr. Dawlish's grocery shop, and explained their hopes for attracting other businesses to the village.

"How many people do you expect to live here eventually?" Edmund asked.

"Right now the mill is running at a little over one sixth of

173

its full capacity. As we build more housing we hope to have the funds to buy more machines and barring any great catastrophes, within a few years the mill will employ three thousand and the village will house something like three to four thousand people."

"Such grand plans," he said. "It is very adventurous of you."

"Or foolish," she grinned.

She showed him to the community centre which was made up of one large room and two smaller ones.

"In the day time the large room is a school, run my Miss Tate. Those too young for school are looked after in the smaller rooms. In the evenings events are sometimes organised here, like dances. The town meetings are held here and on Wednesday evenings and Sundays it also becomes our church. The Reverend Hall from Milton comes over to give sermons. If you agree to help us, this is also where you would hold your surgery."

"That's a lot to cram into one small building," Edmund commented.

"Everything has to pay for itself, Mr. Wallace. We hope to be able to afford to build a proper school, church and small hospital one day but at the moment, every penny counts. If we are wasteful now we might be unable to complete the project, and that would be dreadful shame."

"Indeed," he said as they left the community hall and headed back towards the mill. "And you do not mind your husband frittering away your fortune?"

Margaret stopped and turned to face him.

"First of all, it is not my fortune. That money was my Godfather's and while I thank him for remembering me in his will, I did nothing to earn that money and would gladly give back every penny if it meant I could have Mr. Bell back. As for my husband, John Thornton is the most honourable man I know and if you think him some sort of fortune hunter who is 'frittering' away my money, then you clearly don't understand either of us or what we are trying to accomplish here."

"I am sorry, Mrs. Thornton, I didn't mean to cause offence."

"Yes you did, Mr. Wallace. You intentionally used inflammatory language to see how I would react, but I am not some toy you can play games with! My husband loves me and I know for a fact that he would have married me when I had not a penny to my name, but I was too young and foolish to see him for the good and kind man that he is. I thank God every single day that John loved me enough to give me a second chance. I know what ignorant people say about us but I had thought you were brighter than most, and I had been led to believe that perhaps you might share some of our ideology. I hope I was not misled."

"Indeed you were not," Edmund said sincerely. "You are right, I was testing you and I am truly sorry for that. I should have realised that you were not the kind of woman who would ever engage in a marriage of convenience and from the bottom of my heart, I apologise."

Margaret considered the man before her for a few moments before nodding. "Apology accepted."

They continued on their journey back to the mill but Edmund couldn't help but steal the occasional sidelong glance at Margaret. She was quite extraordinary and if he felt himself to be in danger of falling for her before, now he knew that it was inevitable.

He told himself that she was a good, God-fearing lady, not a wench; she would never consider breaking her marriage vows and yet some small part of him still hoped that perhaps she might love him with the same passion that she clearly had for her husband.

He was to be severely disappointed in this hope, but as yet he had not the slightest idea of just how much pain his unrequited love would cause him.

John arrived home to find a stranger holding his baby. He stopped dead in the doorway and watched as the man bounced his daughter up and down on his knee. Neither man nor child had noticed him and as he felt a pang of jealousy distort his features, he was glad that he went unnoticed. He rearranged his expression to one more congenial and stepped into the room.

"I don't believe I've had the pleasure," he said, holding his hand out. "John Thornton."

"Doctor Edmund Wallace," the man replied, shaking his hand firmly. "So good to finally meet you. Your young wife has been telling me of your plans for the village and I must say, I am most impressed."

"With the plans or the wife?" he asked, unable to keep a

tinge of malice from entering his voice. He didn't know why but something about this man got his hackles up.

"Both, if I am honest. And your daughter here is quite lovely as well. You are a lucky man, Mr. Thornton."

Though it almost gave him physical pain, John forced himself to be polite. "Call me John, please."

"Then you must call me Edmund."

"John." He turned to see his wife coming into the room, a warm smile on her face. Instantly he regretted feeling jealous because no matter how well Edmund thought of his wife, Margaret only had eyes for him. She kissed him on the cheek, sparing no thought for etiquette.

"Lunch is nearly ready," she said, taking the baby from Edmund. "Why don't you boys go through and I'll take Bessy up to Dixon." As free as they were with Bessy at mealtimes, they knew that business could not easily be discussed with a child in the room.

"Good idea." John said. He bent down slightly and kissed both Margaret and Bessy.

Margaret smiled, wondering what had brought on this display of affection, but enjoying it none the less. As she left, John led Edmund through to the dining room.

They made small talk until both Hannah and Margaret had joined them, then as the meal progressed, Edmund laid out his questions and concerns for them to rebut. They answered as best they could and after lunch, Hannah went to supervise the mill as the others adjourned to the study to continue their discussions.

By the time the clock chimed four, between them they had hashed out a deal. Edmund would hold his surgery in the village one morning a week initially, using one of the rooms in the community hall. It would be a squeeze but Margaret was sure the younger children could be looked after somewhere else for one day. Perhaps they could go to the park on surgery days.

John had agreed that his employees could take time off to attend the surgery but if they didn't want their pay docked, they had to produce a note from Edmund stating that they had valid reasons for wishing to see him.

As the village increased, Edmund offered to increase the amount of time he spent there as necessary, up to one or possiblry two days if there was the demand.

John offered to pay for any medicines as well as to provide Edmund with accommodation overnight should he need it and in turn Edmund agreed to reduce his fees to a donation from those who could afford it. The donations were for Hanton Hospital in his home town, which treated paupers and those from workhouses.

The only point of contention was the fact that Edmund wanted an assistant or nurse to help him and Margaret had offered her services until someone better qualified could be found. She was far from a nurse but she she had often tended to the ill and infirm in Helstone when she was younger.

John was totally and irrationally against the idea. He claimed she was needed at the mill, but she didn't work there full time anyway. Still, not wanting to argue in front of anyone, she simply assured Edmund that someone would be found to assist him.

Margaret showed Edmund to the door where his driver was waiting with the carriage, then she returned to her husband, her expression asking him to explain himself.

"What?" he acted innocent.

"You know perfectly well 'what', John Thornton."

"Must be serious if you're using my full name," he teased.

"Don't try and distract me, tell me why you were acting like a possessive Neanderthal back there."

"I don't trust him," John admitted.

"Why on earth not? He was a perfect gentleman and he's offered to treat the mill workers basically for free."

"Only because of you," he snapped.

"What? John, I have had almost nothing to do with this. Your mother set this meeting up, you were running late for it so I stepped in. Edmund has agreed to help us, I thought this was what we wanted?" She sounded both hurt and confused.

John looked at her. She truly didn't see the way Edmund looked at her, she couldn't feel his hungry eyes roaming over her body when he thought no one was looking, she hadn't spotted the light in his eyes when she smiled at him. She thought he was just being a possessive old fool. And maybe he was.

He let out a big sigh and shook his head as though to clear it.

"I'm sorry, my love. I... You're right, this is what we wanted and his offer of help was very generous."

177

"And you'll let me help him until someone more suitable can be found?"

"Of course." He considered saying something more, warning her to be on her guard but he knew she wouldn't be satisfied with such a vague statement and for some reason, he didn't want her to know that he was jealous. He almost felt as though, if he gave voice to his fears, that they would become reality. He knew that it was superstitious nonsense, but nonetheless he still found himself unable to speak up.

Chapter Twenty Three

When Bessy was nine months old, Margaret and John had her christened by Reverend Hall in the community centre, after the Sunday church service that he regularly held there.

Edward and Eleanor Maitland were the Godparents and other than a few workers and staff, they were the only ones invited.

Margaret had delayed having the christening because she only wanted those who really cared about Bessy to be present, which included people like Dixon, Jenny and Nicholas. She knew that she could not invite them if she turned this into a 'society occasion', so after seemingly endless dithering, she finally chose not to tell most people about it until after the christening.

Bessy was dressed in the christening gown that John and Fanny had worn. Margaret would have loved to dress Bessy in her own christening gown since her mother had made it herself but somewhere in all the moves it had been lost. The gown Bessy wore now, while not made by John's mother, had been in the family for two generations, worn by Hannah, her children and now, her grandchild. It had history, which was almost as meaningful as a hand made gown.

After the ceremony, the Maitland's came back to the cottage to enjoy Sunday lunch with them and stayed until quite late. John and Edward stayed in the parlour while they discussed a number of topics, though Margaret, Hannah and Eleanor decamped to the back sitting room (which was far more cosy than the parlour) and discussed topics ranging from literature to fashion to the Crimean War.

Bessy spent most of her time with the ladies, doing her utmost to chew the ear off of one of her dolls.

Though Margaret had been leaving food out for the dog every day, it was another two weeks until she saw it again.

She walked into the stable block to see if her horse had been set to the gig yet, when she saw the dog lying in the straw of the empty stall where she had been leaving it's food. It had raised it's head as she came in and stared at her.

Margaret entered the stall, bolted the lower half of the door behind her and slowly approached the dog. It's eyes widened in fear as she grew close but he didn't stand up or move away. Margaret began to wonder if the dog feared a beating, but if so, there was obviously something about her that the dog trusted.

Deciding the dog would be happier if she were on its level, she sat down in the hay (a rather laborious task with all her long skirt and petticoats) and reached her hand out to it again, reaching behind it's head to scratch behind the ears. The dog seemed to smile at her and half closed its eyes, enjoying the sensation. After a few minutes of scratching, the dog laid on its side and raised its top legs, exposing its belly.

"Well, now I know you're a she, at least," Margaret said, rubbing the dogs belly. "You are such a dear sweet thing, it's such a shame you don't have a home to go to."

Just then Jimmy, the stable boy cum gardeners assistant cum carriage driver came in, calling for her, probably wondering where she was since her horse had been ready to go for a while now. The dog was on it's feet in a second, standing protectively between Margaret and the stable door. She didn't growl but it was clear that she was on the defensive, protecting Margaret.

"You got a new dog, Mrs. T?" he asked.

"No, Jimmy, he's just a stray I found, but I think I might like to keep him. I always wanted a dog when I was young but I spent too much time in London to care for one."

"You ought to get him checked out first. Strays can carry all kinds of nasty things."

"Of course, I am just not sure where to find a good veterinarian near Milton."

"I know the stable lad at the Miller farm, do you want me to ask 'im who looks after their animals?"

"Would you? I'll arrange for him to come and check the dog over before I decide whether to keep her or not."

"No problem, Mrs. T. Oh, and your horse is ready for you. She's in the yard."

"Thank you, Jimmy." Margaret made her way around the dog, opened the door only as wide as she had to in order to get out then bolted it again. "Would you give her a water bucket while I'm out, please? I'll see to her food this evening."

"O' course, Mrs. T. Anything for you."

That evening Margaret took Bessy into the stable with her as she brought the food out for the dog. When Bessy saw the dog, her eyes lit up and she pointed at the animal.

"Beel," she said. "Beel beel."

"What's that sweetheart, ba?"

"Beel, beel." Bessy began wriggling with excitement.

"Bill? But she's a girl, darling, we should give her a girls name."

"Beel!"

Margaret laughed. Of course Bessy wasn't really saying Bill, but it was close enough for Margaret and girl or not, the dog was now called Bill.

"She's very friendly, darling, but you can't pet her yet. The vet is coming soon and after he's seen Bill, maybe you can pet her."

"Ba, beel. Ba ba."

"That's right, darling." Margaret put the bowl of food just inside the stable door then locked it again. "Now, let's go inside and get ready for Daddy, shall we? He's going off to speak with those nasty masters tonight, so we need to be extra nice to him."

"Ba!"

"Absolutely," Margaret agreed with a smile. "I couldn't have put it better myself."

The first surgery at the community hall went very well. Only three people came to see Dr. Wallace and Margaret felt bad for him but he assured her this was normal.

"I'm not local so they don't trust me and they can't yet believe I'm not going to charge them in some way. In a few weeks word will spread from the few I do see and people will start to come."

"I do hope so. It would be such a waste of your generosity were it to always be this quiet."

Mrs. Parish was one of the three people he saw and he diagnosed consumption and recommended laudanum to treat her symptoms.

Hesitantly, Mrs. Parish asked the question she feared most.

"Is it... bad, Doctor?"

Edmund's grave expression was enough to answer her question.

"Usually. I'm very sorry, Mrs. Parish, but I am not hopeful. The laudanum will help with the pain and reduce your cough reflex, but it won't cure you."

"How long 'ave I got?"

"It's hard to be specific since everyone is different, but I would say four to six months."

"Right," She nodded, her northern stoicism taking over. "Well, that's that then. Thank you for bein' 'onest wi' me, Doctor."

"I'm only sorry it couldn't be better news." Edmund gave her a regretful smile.

"Well, we've all got to go sometime."

Margaret was upset by the news but at least Mrs. Parish had medicine to treat her condition now, even if a cure was impossible.

When all the patients had been seen, Edmund began teaching Margaret what the equipment he had in his bag was, how to dress and bandage wounds (for which they practiced on each other) and how to assess the patients' needs so that the sickest were seen by him first.

Margaret enjoyed her morning immensely and asked Edmund to have lunch with them again. John was in Liverpool trying to source more reliable cotton but Hannah was there and they talked among themselves. Most of the talk was Edmund's tales of the many places he had visited from London to as far away as India when he was ten years old.

Margaret was captivated but Hannah, though she found the stories interesting, wasn't quite so enamoured of their guest. She couldn't put her finger on what troubled her but something did.

Chapter Twenty Four

The next evening, John returned home from the mill to find a troubling sight in the rear sitting room.

"Margaret?" John called to his wife who came into the room as she heard his call.

"Yes?"

"What is *that*?" he asked pointing to a large, black, shaggy dog who was curled up in John's chair.

"Oh, that's Bill."

"Bill?"

"Bill," she confirmed.

"All right, so perhaps you might like to tell me what *Bill* is doing in my sitting room?"

"Our sitting room," she corrected.

"I don't care whose room it is, I want to know why a flea bitten, mangy old mongrel is sitting in my chair!"

As John's voice rose, Bill lifted her head to observe him.

"She does not have fleas or mange!" Margaret assured him.

"She?"

"And she's in here because your daughter and I have both fallen in love with her."

"But... but you can't keep her."

"Don't be so heartless, why on earth not?"

"Look at him! Her! Whatever. It looks like cross between a bear and a goat!"

"I think she's part wolfhound and maybe some collie. It's hard to say for certain."

"She's a mongrel."

"Why yes, John, she is. Very observant of you."

"Don't take that tone with me! I've been at work all day and I don't expect to come home to find strange dogs sitting in my chair!"

"Don't pull the work card on me; in case you've forgotten I not only work in the mill, I also raise your daughter, act as nurse in the doctors surgery and find the time to manage this house. Plus, I had to endure a visit from your sister and her precious baby Malcolm today, who as you know is ten times better than Bessy at everything so if you really want to go into who's got it worse, I win because when I married you, I got lumbered with your sister!"

John watched while her back straightened and her face became flushed as her argument gained momentum. She looked so beautiful that he couldn't sustain his anger. And she did have a point, no one deserved to be subjected to Fanny for a whole morning.

He began laughing.

"Don't you dare laugh at me, John Thornton!"

"I'm not laughing at you, I'm laughing because you're so lovely that even when I'm angry, I can't seem to manage to stay that way. You have me well and truly under your spell, Mrs. Thornton."

"Does that mean we can keep the dog?" Margaret smiled sweetly.

"I suppose so, as long as she stays off my chair."

Margaret went up and wrapped her arms around his waist.

"Thank you."

"And that's assuming she really is disease free, of course."

"The vet has already checked her over," Margaret reassured him.

"How on earth did you manage to get him out here so quickly?"

"Ah, well, you see... Bill's kind of been coming here for a while now."

"A while! Why didn't I know?"

"Because I kept her in one of the stalls in the stable block."

"You crafty little minx," he said, though he sounded pleased with her.

"Well I wasn't going to let her in the house without having her throughly checked over. Who knows what diseases she could give Bessy. Anyway, yesterday we took her to the Miller farm and put her in their sheep dip, just to be sure, then we gave her a nice bath and today the vet came and gave her the all clear."

"So I'm called heartless when you're the one who dropped that poor animal in a sheep dip?" he teased.

"Bill didn't seem to mind." Margaret shrugged.

"Now, about the name, it doesn't exactly say friendly family pet to me. Or bitch, if I'm being honest."

"Your daughter chose it, take it up with her."

"But she can only say 'ba' and 'no'," he observed.

"Well when she saw her, Bessy definitely said Bill."

John pulled Margaret to him and kissed her forehead. He could hardly remember a time without her now, without the levity and joy she brought to his life. When he did try and think back to those times, they seemed awfully bleak and mirthless by comparison.

"So, what does Mother think of Bill?"

"She likes her actually, said she reminded her of a dog one of her neighbours had when she was a girl. And don't tell anyone, but I'm fairly certain I caught her sneaking chicken out to Bill when she was being kept in the stable block."

"Mother? Sneaking a stray dog food?"

"Yes, I swear," she smiled but it quickly faded. "Actually, the neighbour she told me about was a good friend of hers and though I don't know exactly what happened, I think he died."

John's smile faded too as he thought of his mother losing her childhood friend. No wonder she liked the dog if it reminded her of her friend.

"I've got to go into town tomorrow so I'll buy her a collar and lead while I'm there."

Margaret leaned up on her tip toes and kissed his cheek. "Thank you."

Chapter Twenty Five

By the time she was almost two years old, Elizabeth Thornton had already amassed quite a vocabulary, though in all honesty some of her words bore very little resemblance to the actual word. Skirts for example, were called 'sowens', in Bessy's mind at least, but somehow both the adults and the child had learned enough of the other's language to communicate in rudimentary ways.

Unfortunately 'no' was quickly becoming Bessy's favourite word!

It was a Sunday afternoon and Margaret was just putting the finishing touches on the garden furniture while Bessy was banging two brightly coloured wooden bricks together on the grass beside her mother.

John came up behind her, wrapped his hands around her waist and planted a kiss in the crook of her neck. Margaret smiled and leaned back against him.

"Are you sure this is a good idea?" John asked her.

"I know how much you like our Sundays together but we must socialise a little. At least with a garden party we get to see everyone at once and we can keep Bessy with us."

"What if it rains?"

Margaret looked to the sky. Though currently blue she knew that could change quickly. Unfortunately there was just no way of accurately predicting the weather.

"Then we'll move inside. Anyway, if it does rain our guests will probably just go home early."

"Then I shall pray for rain," he said, holding her tighter and planting a series of kisses on her long neck.

"Dada, Dada!" With the bricks forgotten for now, Bessy held her hands out to her father, looking quite desperate for a cuddle. "Dada!"

Though he had fully intended to pick Bessy up when he was done with his wife, clearly it wasn't quickly enough for his daughter, and she hauled herself to her feet and slowly made her way over to them, reaching up to tug on her father's coat.

"Dada!"

"Oh dear, someone's feeling left out," Margaret said.

Reluctantly letting his wife go, John bent down and picked Bessy up. Margaret turned around, putting one hand around her husband's waist and the other around Bessy's back.

"Cheeky Madam," she told her daughter.

Bessy placed a chubby hand on her cheek and Margaret snapped playfully at the hand with her teeth, causing Bessy to pull her hand away and shriek with laughter. John had never thought himself to be a very paternal man but Bessy had changed his mind in a heartbeat. As he watched mother and daughter playing, he wondered if there was any sweeter sound than a child's laughter.

Margaret and Bessy continued the game until Dixon joined them.

"The guests will be here in in thirty minutes, Miss Margaret, and I need to get Miss Elizabeth dressed."

Margaret thought that Bessy looked fine in her play clothes but she knew they wouldn't do for a social event. John passed Bessy to Dixon and the child happily went away with her, wrapping her arms around Dixon's neck. Margaret leaned her head against John's shoulder as they both watched until they were out of sight.

"Sometimes I swear she likes Dixon more than us," she said.

"Give her time," John replied, placing a kiss on the top of her hair. "As soon as Dixon starts to try and tame that mane of beautiful hair, she'll grumble just as much as you do about Dixon."

Margaret smiled. It was odd that she didn't feel more jealous of Dixon, and Jenny for that matter. Instead she considered herself lucky to have two people who loved and cared for her daughter almost as much as she did.

Putting those thoughts out of her mind, she turned to the tables again, making sure that everything was perfect.

The trestle tables had been erected in a long line and covered with white tablecloths. Small vases of flowers were evenly spaced along the middle of the tables to stabilise the cloths in case there was a wind, and chairs lined each side. Each place setting had been prepared as though for a dinner party, complete with crystal glasses, which Margaret thought was a little too formal for a garden party but Hannah had been insistent. Since they were entertaining Milton society, which Hannah was much more familiar with, Margaret had happily deferred to her opinion.

On one side of the garden was another, sightly lower table where the children and their nannies would eat and near the house was a third table where the drinks could be prepared, since the kitchen was rather a long way from the garden.

Extra waiting staff had been hired to make certain that everything went smoothly and a string quartet was inside tuning up, though again Margaret thought both to be rather extravagant.

Back in Helstone her parents had thrown a garden party every summer and everything about it was kept simple and done for convenience to make the day as enjoyable as possible. The food was served cold and laid out alongside the drinks for people to help themselves to. The children played on the grass as the adults talked and laughed. Margaret hoped that despite the formality of this party, she might once again achieve the happiness of those times in Helstone.

The walled garden looked amazing. Though so overgrown that it had almost had to be stripped back to nothing, the gardener had worked his magic on it, reviving and taming many of the rose bushes that had been smothered by weeds. The flower beds had been properly shaped and defined and somehow he had managed to turn the central patch of weeds into a luscious green lawn with not a single weed in sight. He had also managed the somewhat miraculous feat of making the garden look wild and untamed while still being neat and tidy. Currently adding to this wild look was Bill the dog, whose scruffy self was sprawled on the lawn, basking in the sunshine.

Almost everyone who had been invited was coming and among them were the local mill owners and their wives, as well as Mr. and Mrs. Maitland, Daniel Whitaker and his sister, Mary Bristow, Doctor Wallace, the mill's architect Mr. Anderson and his wife and, unusually for a Milton society event, children were also welcome, as were their nannies where necessary. Margaret was in no doubt that Milton's next generation would arrive buffed, tucked and dressed to perfection. Margaret understood that people liked to have their offspring admired, though personally she would prefer it if Bessy was admired for her sweet temperament and her intelligence rather than because of her wardrobe and hair style.

Nevertheless, this garden party had been her idea and she intended to be the best hostess possible. As the guests arrived, Margaret greeted them warmly and they chose a glass of either white wine, sangria or apple juice from the waiters who were lined up by the garden door. When everyone had arrived, she mingled with her guests, making sure everyone was having a good time and that their glasses stayed topped up.

Bill opted to head inside when the children arrived. She didn't so much mind Bessy climbing on her and pulling her around, but she drew the line at other children. Bessy was part of her pack, after all, but these other children weren't.

Margaret checked in on the children a few times as they played on the lawn but she soon saw that Dixon had things well in hand. Even the older children seemed unwilling to disobey Dixon and were playing happily with the younger ones.

As lunch was served, Margaret thought that the one good thing about the formality of this garden party was that she had been required to make a seating plan rather than just letting people sit where they liked. As such she was able to seat herself and John next to the Maitlands on one side and the Andersons on the other and though it was perhaps slightly mean spirited of her, Fanny was seated as far away as possible.

Margaret hadn't seen a lot of Fanny since they had moved out of Milton. In fact she had only seen her on three occasions, one was Bessy's first birthday party and the second was the day Margaret had first allowed Bill into the house. On that occasion Fanny had been shocked that such a scruffy animal was to be allowed into their home and became quite indignant about it. The final time was a chance encounter in Milton. She had been unsure what to expect from Fanny's son, Malcolm, today and given Fanny's bragging about him, she half expected that he would be an overindulged tearaway who would spend the afternoon raising hell.

Instead he was as meek and mild a boy as Margaret had ever seen. While they ate, Margaret couldn't help her gaze repeatedly drifting over to the children's table and watching as his stern nanny helped him to eat his dinner. The few times the boy did show signs of animation, the nanny quickly quelled it with a harsh look and Margaret found herself feeling immensely sorry for the boy. While she had spoken with Fanny and her husband earlier, not once had either of them mentioned Malcolm, except to boast about him. Margaret found herself doubting that the boy even saw his mother very often.

That was not unusual, of course. When Margaret had lived with her aunt in Harley Street, she had mostly been raised by the help, seeing her aunt for only a few minutes each day, if that. Only when the girls were older and on special occasions did Mrs. Shaw have them dressed up and allow them to attend dinner with the rest of the family. Even then, they were expected to remain silent unless spoken to.

Her thoughts were interrupted when Watson burst out laughing.

"I know," Watson said to Slickson. "So I says to them, *'What do you think I am? Santa Claus?'* I mean they already get a week's holiday in the summer while we service the machinery, now they want two days at Christmas!"

All the mill owners were highly amused at this point.

"What do you think, Thornton?" Hamper called out to him.

"My workers have had two days off at Christmas for the past three years, and they get a bonus in their pay the week before."

The mill owners stopped laughing.

"You aren't serious?" Dickinson asked.

"When have you ever known me to joke about my mill?" John asked. "My workers are good to me, they stay past their time when they need to and don't even ask to be paid for it. I don't see any reason I shouldn't repay that generosity."

"How the 'ell do you get 'em to stay past their time?" Watson asked, ignoring Fanny's indignation at his use of profanity.

"I never asked them to. The difference is I respect my workers and they respect me. Maybe if you tried to understand their plight a little better rather than breaking their will, you might have a more willing workforce."

The mill owners and their wives were looking as John as though he had just spoken in tongues.

"Our firm takes two days at Christmas," Mr. Armstrong said, trying to ease a little of the tension. "Though I confess it is more because I enjoy spending the time with my family than out of any charitable motives for my workers."

"There's that too," John said, catching Margaret's eye and smiling warmly at her.

"I think you're mad to lose a whole day's work," Hamper said. "If you aren't careful, this mill and it's workers will ruin you."

John didn't bother to answer that. He knew his way was right and that if anyone was in danger of going out of

190

business, it was the others, but he also knew that it was pointless to argue with them. They were set in their ways and nothing short of a miracle was going to change their minds.

"Anyway, I know you won't be interested, Thornton," Watson said dismissively. "But there's a new speculation I'm getting in on."

"Oh," Hamper leaned forward.

"The Lewis and Western Railroad company in America. They're expanding pretty quickly and are looking for outside investment."

"What's the risk?" Mr. Whitaker enquired.

"Risk? Investments in American Railroads have done nothing but rise since their inception twenty years ago. I've never come across a more sure thing in my life."

John and Margaret shared a look. John wondering if Watson would ever see how risky speculation was and Margaret fearing what might happen to Fanny should one of his gambles fail spectacularly, as she had seen so many others do.

Chapter Twenty Six

When Bessy had turned one year old, Margaret had held a birthday party for her. Though the party had been a resounding success, both she and John had been miserable that day, first getting everything arranged, then making sure the guests were happy and then organising the clear up. In the end they only got to spend one uninterrupted hour with their daughter before she fell asleep.

Margaret had learned from her mistake though and this year, despite many enquiries from friends, there was to be no party. Instead John had taken a rare holiday from work and they were taking Elizabeth to Blackpool for four nights.

Because of the problems sourcing a regular supply of cotton, John had been working long hours lately. Added to the original supply problems, two ships carrying substantial orders of raw cotton had recently gone down in the Atlantic, forcing prices even higher. John had managed to build up quite a store of cotton so that if a shortage did occur, the mill could continue working for a while but it had cost him both time and money to do so.

The second stage of housing had been finished and John had ordered the new machinery for the first expansion of the mill, however given the recent problems he was unwilling to risk expansion at the moment in case he just expounded on the problems he already had.

Eventually Margaret had talked him into taking Friday, Saturday and Monday off from work and getting away to 'clear his head' as she phrased it. As he settled into the hotel room and walked to the window to look out on the town of Blackpool, he couldn't help but think how right she had been. Already he could feel the tension beginning to drain out of him and he walked out onto the small balcony, closed his eyes and turned his face to the sun, letting the warm rays relax him even further.

Suddenly a gentle cough from behind him interrupted his reverie and he turned around to see Margaret laid out across the bed, her modesty protected only by a well placed bed sheet that she had draped over herself. John smiled.

"Why, Mrs. Thornton, are you trying to seduce me?"

"I would never dream of it, darling. I was simply feeling a little warm."

"And you decided that disrobing would be the

quickest way to cool down."

"Exactly."

"And where is our daughter while her mother is having this hot flash?"

"She was rather tired from the journey, so she's taking a little nap in Dixon's room."

"So in other words," he said, walking towards the bed. "We will be uninterrupted for an hour or so."

"Oh, at least," Margaret agreed.

John grabbed the bed sheet and pulled, savouring the image of his wife as she lay there waiting for him.

"And here I thought Bessy would be the only one opening presents this weekend." He smiled as he climbed onto the bed and leaned down to kiss Margaret as his hands began exploring her soft curves.

After they had made love, Margaret had pulled a robe on and now stood in the window, looking out over the seafront and off to the horizon. John watched her from the bed, one arm behind his head as he drank in her figure with his eyes.

"Come back to bed," he told her.

Margaret turned around and smiled.

"Is that all you think about?" she teased.

John pretended to think for a moment. "Well, there was five minutes last month where I was thinking about local government, but basically, yes."

Margaret laughed and came and sat next to him.

"Later, I promise, but Bessy will be awake any moment now and calling for her Dada."

"And Mama," he said.

"You know you are her favourite," Margaret said without a hint of jealousy.

"Only because I see her less," he assured her.

"So, now that you are relaxed and happy, tell me why you don't want to expand the mill?" Margaret said, reaching out to take John's hand.

She had of course heard his reasoning before but while he was working, he seemed so involved in problems that he often couldn't see the solutions. John explained once again about the cotton shortages, the lost shipments, the rising prices and how much more difficult it would be to source twice as much cotton if the mill doubled to 700 workers.

Though she had been trying to talk him into expanding previously, now that she too was away from the mill, she began to see things clearly as well. This wasn't just a question of having the finances to expand, they had that, what they couldn't be sure of was having the cotton to process.

"How much longer do you think it will take you to find a reliable supplier again?" she asked.

John shrugged.

"No way to tell, could be weeks, could be months. Next week the market could be flooded with cheap cotton again, as it was a few years ago and those that are currently pressing for maximum dollar would be forced to sell at a fair price, but there's no way to tell if or when that will happen."

"What about getting cotton from somewhere else, like Egypt, India or the Caribbean?"

"It's not as good as American cotton but Indian is pretty close. And some buyers prefer cotton that comes from the Empire."

"I'm sure Captain Lenox once mentioned something about having family in India," Margaret said absently. "I'm almost certain I remember him saying something about them being out there on business, employed by the British East India Company if I'm not mistaken. Perhaps if I wrote to him, he might enquire on your behalf."

"I suppose it's worth asking." John agreed.

"But until then I think you are right. We cannot expand the mill, nor continue the with the next phase of the housing project until we have a regular supply again."

John sat up, leaned over and kissed her.

"Now, why don't you get dressed," he suggested. "Then I'll take us all for a walk on the promenade and we'll have dinner in the hotel restaurant downstairs."

Margaret found time the next day to write to Captain Lenox and enquire if his relatives could help John to source a reliable supply of cotton from India. She hoped he might get back to her within a week or so but she knew that was probably very optimistic.

Over the weekend they talked the situation over a few more times as Margaret or John had a new idea, but each time they came back to the same conclusion. Margaret hated to think of the machines just standing there idle, possibly for months but she could see little alternative.

On their second day, Bessy's birthday, they gathered in the hotel suite to open her gifts. She looked utterly enthralled by the cuddly toys but didn't have an awful lot of time for the other, more grown up gifts. Margaret thought that perhaps they were a little too old for her and hoped that she might grow to like them as she got older.

When that was finished, Dixon was given the rest of the day off so that she might have a rest or explore the town. John played with Bessy on the bed while Margaret set about writing thank you cards to everyone who had sent Bessy a gift.

They ordered room service for dinner that night, knowing that Bessy wouldn't be welcomed in the restaurant. Though still officially off duty, Dixon came to check if they needed anything when she got back from her afternoon outing and Margaret invited her to join them for dinner. Though Dixon tried to shrug the idea off, Margaret went down to order a third meal for Dixon. When it came she could choose to eat with them or alone in her room, but Margaret hoped that she would stay.

In the event, she did join them and they took turns to amuse Bessy as the others ate.

Dixon had initially been horrified by the lax attitude Margaret and John showed to bringing up their daughter. She had never heard of a baby being present at the dinner table and she wasn't inclined to approve. Over the past two years though, she had been forced to admit that the love these two had for their child was something special and well worth breaking a few rules of etiquette for.

The next day all four of them went to church then walked around the town until they found somewhere to eat lunch. They returned to the hotel mid afternoon so that Bessy could have her nap and John and Margaret went out alone that evening while Dixon looked after Bessy.

It was a warm evening as they strolled arm in arm back to the hotel and Margaret sighed with contentment.

"Do you suppose there will ever come a time where all we have to do every day is eat, play with our children and make love?" she asked.

"You would go as insane as I if you had nothing more to fill your days," he said. "We've only enjoyed this break so much because it's a rarity. Were we to live your cousin Edith's life of

195

leisure this kind of activity would be commonplace and cease to have any pleasure."

"You're right, I know," she said, resting her head against his arm. "Sometimes though, I wish we had more time together. Sometimes I think that if I didn't work at the mill, I would only see you for two hours a day."

"Things are difficult right now but they will get better again," he said. "I promise."

Margaret smiled up at him.

"Don't listen to me," she said. "I'm just becoming old and grumpy."

"If you're old, what does that make me?"

"Antique," she teased.

John smiled and playfully shoved her away from him.

"Oh, strike a woman, would you," she tried to sound indignant but failed miserably. "Well I'll teach you!"

She ran at him and rather than be caught, John took off over the sand with Margaret hot on his heels. She was fast for a woman, he thought. Eventually he allowed her to catch him and after falling to the ground, she began tickling him.

John might be deeply in love with Margaret but he wasn't about to let her have everything her own way and after a few minutes he turned the tables on her, causing her to shriek with laughter that was heard for quite a distance and would spawn many tales about what happened on the beach that night. Sadly, none of those stories ever came very close to the reality.

Chapter Twenty Seven

It took two weeks for Margaret to receive a reply from Captain Lenox but the news was good. Though he had relocated to London, his cousin, Bernard Lenox, was indeed employed by the British East India Company and would be happy to deal with Mr. Thornton. Bernard was expecting to hear from Mr. Thornton as his earliest convenience to discuss the specifics and the Captain had enclosed the address for his cousin's office.

Margaret immediately took the letter through to John, urging him to write today, then she returned to her own office and, despite being on 'company time' she replied to the Captain and Edith, thanking them for their help and the prompt reply.

Margaret did so long to see Edith sometimes, for although they had little in common nowadays, they had grown up together and shared many experiences.

She wondered if perhaps she might be able to visit during Wakes Week, while the mill was closed for the machinery to be repaired and serviced. John would probably want to stay and oversee the work but then he wasn't that keen on London in any case, although surely he would not mind her leaving for a few days.

In the event, a deal was quickly worked out with Bernard Lenox and it was decided to use the Wakes Week to interview new staff for the expansion. Margaret didn't mind too much because she was as excited about expanding the mill as John.

As he did every year, John made the second week in September Wakes Week, which gave him two months to be sure of the new cotton supply source before he took on new staff. Nicholas had agreed to work through that week and take his annual holiday at another time.

The week before, John advertised in the Milton Times for experienced hands, telling them to arrive between 8am and noon from Monday to Wednesday for interviews. Given that the mill was two miles out of the town and easily five miles from the Princeton district where most mill workers lived, he had expected a trickle of people throughout the week. So it was safe to say that he was a little shocked when on the Monday morning, the queue from the mill office could be seen from their bedroom window.

"It's not even seven yet," he said to Margaret as they both

197

looked down in shock at the men and women lining the road that led up to the mill.

"We can't let them stand out in this heat all day," she said. "They'll collapse."

"How are we to see so many people in one day?" he asked.

They discussed it over breakfast and by the time they headed to the mill, they had a plan in place.

John headed straight into the office to speak to the office staff while Margaret (followed by Bill) and a few of her household servants headed to the community centre.

Ever since Margaret had returned from Blackpool, Bill had been her constant companion. Jenny had told her how upset Bill had been at her absence and it seemed that Bill wasn't about to give her new mistress another chance to abandon her. She had to sleep by the Aga in the kitchen overnight but other than that, she followed Margaret around faithfully and today was no different.

Thankfully the school was also closed this week since many workers chose to go away in Wakes Week, either on holiday or to visit with family, meaning that the community centre was empty. The queuing workers were directed there, where their names were taken and where fresh water had been drawn from the well so that they might have a drink after their long walk.

John and Higgins had planned to interview the men while Margaret and Hannah interviewed the women, though it was decided in the end that if they each saw people on their own, they would get through the queue twice as quickly.

Hannah and Margaret set up shop in the two small rooms at the community centre to interview the women, while the men were directed back to the mill offices where John and Higgins were using offices to see people.

It took until gone five o'clock that evening but eventually everyone was seen.

Over the previous weeks they had devised a list of questions, not just about the work and their experience but also about their lives, their plans, their reasons for wanting to work here and whether or not they planned on moving to the village.

Those with over two years' experience went to the top of the list which was the majority. Next, those with wives and children who also wanted employment at the mill were given priority. Finally, those who intended to make use of the villages services, for example by sending their children to school, were also given an advantage.

At the end of day one though, that still left two hundred and fifty suitable candidates. Higgins took a final look through the names. Having been a union man he knew most people in Princeton and if there were any known layabouts or trouble makers, he weeded them out.

Tuesday was just as busy, though thankfully Wednesday slightly less so.

"I had no idea there were so many mill workers in Milton," Margaret said as she handed the interview sheets over to John.

"Well, there are ten mills in Milton, love." John said.

"I know, but I didn't expect those already employed to take time off and try to get a job with us."

"You're getting a good reputation," Nicholas explained. "Most o' workers at the other mills get paid less, have bad housing and no hope of ever sending their bairns to school."

Margaret couldn't argue. Were she in their position, she would try and improve her family's lot in life too.

"Well, I think we've done enough for one day," John said, rising to his feet. Interviewing wasn't something he was used to and he found himself much more tired mentally than usual. "You get off home, Higgins. We'll go through these final candidates tomorrow and we can inform them of our decision on Friday."

"Right you are, master. You gettin' off too?"

"Soon, I must just check how servicing the machinery is coming along, make sure there's no problems and such like."

"Then let me come with you. I know these machines better than you do, and we'll be faster with two of us."

"Aye," John smiled. "All right then."

He kissed Margaret softly. Higgins turned away out of respect for them, not disgust. He was well used to their affectionate ways by now and in fact, it pleased him to see a couple so in love.

"You get off home, I'll be back in half an hour."

"I'll hold you to that," she said, though lethargy was making her less playful than usual.

Bill, who had been sleeping beside Margaret's desk, also got up and stretched, preparing to accompany her mistress home.

John made the rounds of the mill and spoke to the chief

mechanic who was overseeing the work. Everything seemed to be progressing on schedule and so John left them to it. He would need to return later and lock up, but right now he just wanted to sit down and close his eyes for a moment.

When he got home, he discovered that Margaret had come up with a much better idea, and was waiting in a steaming hot bath for him to join her. He did, and let the warm water and soothing bath salts ease his tired mind.

By the time the water had cooled and they had dried and dressed, it was nearly eight o'clock and John returned to the mill to lock the gates.

Usually, although he wasn't on holiday like the hands were, this was a light week for him, work wise. A time when he could catch up on those jobs that he never got around to or that he kept putting off because he didn't much like them. That meant that the next two days would be busier than usual and as he strolled back to the house, he found himself wishing, much like Margaret had in Blackpool, that there would come a time when nothing could separate him from her; not work, not family, nothing.

It was a pipe dream, of course, but nevertheless it was an exceedingly enjoyable dream.

On Friday morning Higgins made his way into Milton with lists of the mill's new employees. He posted copies on notice boards, in the taverns and anywhere he thought people might congregate. There were some who couldn't read, but Higgins knew that someone local would read it for them.

Due to the sheer number of applicants, most people were disappointed that their name and address didn't appear, but he assured all those who asked him that the mill would be expanding again in the future and suggested that they reapply. That seemed to satisfy most.

At the bottom of the list were the details for moving into the village. That could be done at any time but to save the long walk, John was laying on horses and carts on Sunday afternoon that would go back and forth from Milton to the village, helping to carry as many of their possessions as they could manage in that time.

He knew that Margaret was allocating the housing today and would be ready to hand the keys out to each family as they arrived on Sunday.

Most of the mill workers, even those who had gone away for Wakes Week, would be around on Sunday, ready to get back to work next day, and Higgins knew that many of them would help the newcomers fetch and carry their belongings.

Higgins was also moving this weekend now that the slightly grander overseers' houses were ready. He was a little loathe to leave his neighbours but given that he had nine children and himself to fit into four small bedrooms, he was glad of it also. The new house was more expensive but it had a small garden for the children to play in and though they couldn't have a room each, Mary had her own room and the others would only have to double up.

Higgins spent most of the morning in the Princeton district, going from list to list and making himself available to those who had questions.

As John popped his head into Margaret's office on Friday night, he felt ashamed as he saw her slumped over her desk, sleeping. Though she insisted she liked working, she was too good to work herself into the ground like this. She deserved better.

Bill raised her head as John came into the office, keeping watch over her mistress as she usually did.

"Good dog," he said softly as he approached Margaret and gently shook her shoulder. "Margaret," he called.

She sat up, slightly bleary eyed and it took her a moment to realise where she was.

"Sorry," she apologised as she began sorting through the papers on her desk. "I must have nodded off."

"Don't apologise. I'm the one who should be sorry, working you into the ground like this."

"Oh, John don't get maudlin on me, I'm fine. It's just been a long week and my poor female brain can't handle it."

"I think your 'poor female brain' can handle more than mine," he said, gently tugging at her arm. "But come on, leave that now. Let's get you home and fed, this will still be here tomorrow."

"But I have the-"

"But nothing." He placed a finger over her lips. "I shouldn't have given Thomas the week off, which is why you're so overworked. I'll hire another office clerk to help you if I have to, but I won't have you overworking yourself anymore than you would let me."

Margaret nodded. She was awfully weary so she allowed him to stand her up and lead her home. She ate her dinner, though she didn't seem to taste it and afterwards she went straight to bed, sleeping for nine hours straight.

The next morning she felt refreshed and raring to go. The only problem was that John wasn't beside her and this was the first time in perhaps two years that she had woken up alone.

She leaned over to see his night stand and, sure enough, there was a note resting there with her name written on it. The note said that he was sorry for leaving her but he had gone to the mill early so that he could get a head start and shoulder some of her workload.

Margaret rolled her eyes. That insufferable man!

Though Bessy was at breakfast as usual, Margaret asked Jenny to feed her this morning as she wanted to get to the mill as quickly as she could. She rushed through breakfast with Hannah, who could guess what Margaret was thinking and when Margaret left to walk to the mill, Hannah shook her head and picked Bessy up out of her chair.

"When is your Daddy going to learn that Mummy won't break?" she asked the baby.

"Sawbees!" Bessy presented Hannah with her slice of strawberry jam covered toast.

"Thank you, sweetheart, but I could tell that from your mouth. You're a mucky little pup, aren't you!"

Bessy giggled.

Chapter Twenty Eight

Margaret was quite a sight to see as she strode up the road towards the mill looking ready for a fight. The large black dog at her heel did nothing to dispel this image and as Nicholas saw her approach, he thanked his lucky stars that he wasn't the master.

Margaret opened the door to John's office but found it empty, so she headed to her office to find that John was sitting at her desk, doing her work. She stood in the doorway, waiting for him to look up, her expression asking him what he thought he was playing at.

"I just... I finished the housing allocation chart for..." His words trailed off. "Don't be angry, Margaret, I was trying to do something nice for you."

"I can't help it. I know your intentions were good, John, but everyone works harder than usual from time to time. I need you to realise that a little hard work won't kill me."

"I know that, I do, but you've put in more hours this week than you usually would in two."

"Because we've been busy. John, I don't work part time because I can't handle a full week's work, I would love to spend more time here with you but I choose to leave early so that our daughter at least knows one of us. I don't want her growing up knowing her nanny better than she knows her parents but one week of long hours won't do her or me any harm, darling."

"Why haven't you ever told me this before?"

"Because I thought you understood. I know you need to work long hours and I don't begrudge you that. I wish I could feel happy working the same hours also, but with Bessy at home... Well." she swallowed. "What I'm trying to say is that you don't need to protect me. This week has been tougher than usual for me, but that's okay and I don't need you to ride to my rescue just because I'm a little tired one night."

"I wasn't trying to rescue you, I was trying to help you."

Margaret sighed and let go of the rest of her anger.

"I know, darling, but some kinds of help are just insulting, as though you're saying I'm not good enough."

John finally understood why she was angry.

"I'm sorry. You know that I would never think that. Margaret, you... you're perfect, in every way and I would never want you to think otherwise."

"I know." Margaret smiled. "And, I guess that since you finished my work, that means I now have to help you with yours," she looked smug, knowing that there was no way he could refute her logic.

The rest of the day was surprisingly easy for both of them. Aside from almost tripping over Bill a few times, he found that he liked working with Margaret again. It reminded him of the early days, when they were engaged and he was still showing her the ropes. She hadn't needed his supervision for a long time now and they worked from separate offices so as to keep things professional, but he began to wonder if he could manage things so that they were able to spend a little more time together.

That Sunday was busy as Margaret handed out keys to the new workers and John pitched in to help them move their belongings. In the end he had laid on twelve horses and carts to help the workers move and after a few dozen trips, the carts piled high with cases, trunks and possessions, they finally seemed to be winning the battle.

Once the keys were handed out, Margaret organised water to be brought out regularly to quench the men's thirst. She smiled on the occasions when she spotted John because he looked so happy. She had often noticed that he enjoyed manual labour, when he could use his hands and get involved in the work himself. Right now he was very far from the master most of the workers expected him to be, laughing and joking with the workers as they manoeuvred another heavy trunk into a house.

She walked over with her cup of cool water from the well at the end of the street and as he took it from her, she found herself captivated by a bead of sweat that was running over his collar bone, threatening to dip below his loosened collar.

Seeing that her attention was diverted, John grabbed her around the waist, causing the water to fly everywhere and Margaret to squeal as the cold water splashed her hair and back. John held fast as she tried to wriggle away though and eventually she calmed down.

He claimed her lips in a kiss that would, make most upstanding citizens blush. Things were more relaxed among the working classes though and the mood was so happy among those present that no one seemed to mind their public display of affection.

When John finally released her, Margaret felt breathless.

"Don't think that makes up for getting me wet, John Thornton," she said, though her harsh words were belied by the twinkle in her eyes.

"No?"

"Oh no. I'll get you back."

"I can't wait," he told her, releasing her after one final kiss.

As she headed back to the well, Margaret was glad that she'd worn one of her old dresses today because things were about to get ugly.

She continued filling jugs with water and handing mugs out to the workers, aided by some of the local women, and when John walked past half an hour later, ready to get to work on the next street over, he was more than a little shocked to find himself drenched with a jug of cold water.

After that it devolved into a war, men against women with all sorts of receptacles being used to hurl water over the opposition. Other streets became involved as the men hijacked their water pumps to fire back and pretty soon most of the village was engaged in a giant water fight. By the time it broke up about an hour later, Margaret was soaking, her hair hanging lank around her shoulders but her smile was bright as she fell into John's arms, giggling.

John, deciding that he couldn't trust her, picked her up in his arms to carry her back to the house. Bill, who was also decidedly wet, ran around the couple, barking for her mistress to be released.

Margaret protested, hitting his shoulders and calling to be set down immediately but John paid her cries no heed and her shrieks and laughter could still be heard long after they had vanished from sight.

Some of those who were new to the village felt slightly uneasy about the display they had witnessed, as they wondered just what kind of man they were working for. Those who had lived in the village a while smiled at each other, knowing full well how much the master cared for his wife and how playful they could be with each other.

The story of The Great Thornton Village Water Fight would go down in local legend and though at times the truth was embellished, the story was retold in some fashion for generations.

Chapter Twenty Nine

By mid-Novenber, thanks in part to the locals trusting him more and in part to the increasing population, Dr. Wallace's weekly half-day surgery was full and he was talking about extending his hours to a full day soon.

He would arrive on Tuesday evening and stay overnight at Rose Cottage then after his surgery he would take lunch with the Thorntons before heading back into Milton and catching a train home. Putting in longer hours wouldn't be difficult for him, though he cautioned Margaret that he may sometimes need to stay overnight on the Wednesday as well if he was held back too long.

Margaret assured Edmund that it was no trouble but both of them had noticed how frequently John needed to work late on a Tuesday, often skipping dinner all together. Margaret had asked him about it but he assured her time and again that it was just a coincidence. She still didn't believe him.

Margaret still acted as Edmund's nurse and longer hours would take more time away from her baby, but she enjoyed helping him and would be loathe to give it up. She was also able to document any medicines he gave out and reimburse him for the cost before he left, something that would become much more complicated were someone else to take over as his nurse.

She decided just to see how things went for the time being.

When Edmund arrived at Rose Cottage the following Tuesday, he was surprised to see John was there, especially since he had arrived early. John shook hands with Edmund, even though every fibre of his being said that this man wasn't to be trusted.

"I'm sorry I can't join you this evening, I have a prior dinner engagement in town."

"Oh, not a problem," Edmund assured him. "I'm sure your wife will look after me wonderfully, as always."

John scowled, kissed Margaret on the cheek and left, telling her not to wait up if he was late.

"He really doesn't like me, does he," Edmund said as Margaret took his coat.

"Oh, don't be silly."

"Please, to be attending a dinner engagement without his wife he must dislike one of us very much, and I'm sure it isn't you."

Margaret smiled, even though she suspected Edmund was right.

"Tonight is the monthly dinner for the local mill owners. They take it in turns to host each month and I'm afraid that as a woman and a doctor, neither of us would be particularly welcome."

"Does John have to go? Surely everything he's doing here must make the other owners a little angry. Why I heard that in September, this mill stole the others mill's workforce."

Margaret laughed. "Hardly. We did take on another three hundred and fifty, as you well know, but that hardly emptied out our competing mills, most of which were bigger than us to begin with."

Margaret led Edmund through to the parlour and out of habit poured him a brandy, his usual tipple. Bill raised her head from where she slept in front of the fireplace but soon realised that Edmund was no one interesting and went back to sleep.

"Oh, it's a little early, my dear," he said as she handed him the glass, though he took it none the less.

Margaret looked at the clock. "Oh, I hadn't realised you were early. Do excuse me, can I get you something else?"

"Don't worry, starting early won't hurt me just this once. Come, sit," he patted the seat beside him. "Tell me all about your lovely daughter. Where is she, by the way?"

"Oh, she's in town with Hannah being fitted for some new dresses. For some unknown reason, and I honestly believe it was a moment of insanity on my part, I agreed that we would spend Christmas with my aunt and cousin in London. Given the heinous way Aunt Shaw behaved when John and I married, all of us must look our absolute best so that she doesn't have any additional ammunition to use against John."

"Oh come now, surely she can't be that bad."

So Margaret proceeded to tell him some of Aunt Shaw's comments and antics while she was last in Milton.

"Hm, I must say I am inclined to agree, she sounds like a frightful woman."

"Oh, but I am being too harsh again. Truly I am grateful to her, she almost raised me and without her my education would have been a fraction of what it is. I just wish that she could get past her prejudice and see what wonderful spirit the people in the north have."

"It sounds more like her objection was to the person, not the place. Perhaps if you had chosen someone from northern nobility, like say, my brother or me, she would not have been half so put out by your marriage."

Margaret ignored the feeling of disquiet that those comments gave her. She was getting used to them since Edmund often walked the line between what was appropriate and what wasn't, but still they made her slightly uncomfortable.

"Oh, believe me, she is equally appalled by the place as the man. John put her in her place a time or two, though."

"I'll bet. So, she raised you?"

Edmund often asked about her life, which Margaret found sweet if slightly odd. People in the south were not usually so inquisitive. Still, she had no secrets so she was happy to talk about herself if her audience was interested enough.

They chatted happily until Hannah and Elizabeth got back from town. Sitting on Edmund's knee, Bessy told them all about her visit to the drapers and the pretty dresses she would be getting.

Dinner was served shortly after and, because Edmund was now used to their relaxed ways, Bessy ate with them, sitting in a specially constructed chair so she was at table height, though her table manners still left a little to be desired!

After dinner Hannah picked up her embroidery while Edmund and Margaret chatted. Margaret found that she very much enjoyed Edmund's company. He was educated, intelligent and, like John, he listened to her and her ideas and didn't simply dismiss them because she was a woman.

After kissing everyone goodnight, Bessy was eventually taken off to bed by Dixon.

Having started drinking so early, Edmund was getting a little the worse for wear by ten o'clock, when Hannah retired for the night. Margaret was tempted to head to her bed as well but it would be rude to leave Edmund on his own since he was a guest, and besides, she always waited up for John, whether he liked it or not.

Edmund began to regale Margaret with tales of the upper classes and the antics he had seen over the years. Often large amounts of alcohol seemed to be involved, at least Margaret assumed so, for how else did one find oneself half naked in a lake at 3 o'clock in the morning?

Still, his tales were fun and they laughed merrily until Margaret thought she heard a cry from Bessy and went to check on her. She returned a few minutes later.

"All quiet, I must have imagined it," she said, going to the window and looking out. John would be back soon and then hopefully Edmund would want to get some sleep.

She was surprised when Edmund came to join her at the window and turned to him.

"Margaret." He said her name softly, almost as though it was a caress.

Margaret suddenly felt very uncomfortable. "Edmund," she said, her voice holding a note of warning, though Edmund paid it no heed.

"Margaret, you must know how I feel about you."

"Please don't."

"I cannot keep it to myself any longer."

"Edmund, please stop, I do not want to hear this."

"You have to, Margaret."

"No. I am a married woman and I love my husband."

She turned away but Edmund grabbed her arm and tugged her back, seizing her other arm and holding her to him. He kissed her. Margaret kept her jaw locked shut and struggled to get free. When that didn't work she went still, hoping that he would get the message.

Bill was growling while her mistress struggled, then she began barking and snarling.

Suddenly Edmund stopped and released Margaret, only to receive a hard slap around his face.

"Edmund, you forget yourself! You are a guest in this house and if you cannot respect me or my wishes, I would ask you to leave at once."

Margaret backed away and Bill placed herself between her and Edmund. She reached down to stroke the dogs head, finding her presence oddly soothing. She couldn't be sure but she thought the only reason Edmund released her was because Bill had bitten him.

Edmund cradled his reddened cheek with his hand. He looked contrite.

"I'm sorry, Margaret, please forgive me. I... I don't know what I was thinking."

Margaret knew that he had imbibed too much alcohol and she blamed that for his unexpected behaviour and as offended (not to mention hurt) as she was by his actions, she knew he offered a vital service to this community that the mill workers couldn't afford to do without.

"Very well," that was as close as she could come to a accepting his apology. "We will talk in the morning when you are thinking clearly again. Good night, Edmund."

She left the room and headed upstairs. Bill followed, as she usually tried to do and for once Margaret didn't chastise her to go to her basket by the Aga.

The fire in the bedroom was roaring and warm and Margaret felt as if she needed it as she pulled one of the armchairs closer to it, though the chill she felt couldn't be attributed to the temperature.

Bill curled up beside the chair and Margaret let her remain there.

Finally she felt warm enough to undress and pulled on a nightdress and her warm winter robe but she didn't feel comfortable getting into bed without John here. She looked out of the window for a few moments but she couldn't see him coming so she let the curtains fall closed again. She began to grow concerned as it was nearing midnight and he was never this late.

She returned to the fire and not ten minutes later she heard him come in. She breathed an audible sigh of relief that he was home at last. He took his time making his way to the bedroom and when he came in he looked ashen.

"John! Whatever has happened to you?" she asked, her own problems long forgotten as she rushed to him. His hands were icy cold. "Come, sit by the fire," she said, almost dragging him over to the chair she had just vacated. "What happened?" she asked, kneeling beside him as he sat down. She wondered if perhaps there had been an accident or fault with his carriage and he had been forced to walk back here. That would account for his lateness and how chilled he was.

He still didn't speak but instead reached one hand out and cupped her cheek. Margaret thought she saw tears in his eyes which sent a shiver of terror through her.

"Is everyone all right? Is it Fanny? Is she hurt?"

"No one is injured," he said, his voice choked with emotion. He looked into the flames of the fire.

"John, you're scaring me. Please, tell me what's wrong. You are so cold that it feels like you must have walked

210

back here from Milton."

"Nothing is wrong," he assured her. "I always knew this day would come and yet I find myself oddly unprepared for it."

"What day?" Margaret was beginning to think she might have to call Edmund in to see him, perhaps the cold had affected his mind in some way that made him talk in these riddles.

He looked at her again, then down to where she was clutching one of his hands.

"You don't have to pretend any longer, my love. I know."

"Know what!" she was growing impatient with her worry.

"I saw you, tonight," he said, as though that explained everything.

"Yes, you saw me before you left and here I am again."

"No... No, I saw you with him. I always knew you would wake up one day and realise the mistake you had made in marrying me, I just always hoped that-"

Margaret cut him off by slapping him across the face. She rose to her feet and stared down at him.

"John Thornton, how dare you imply such a thing! There is so much wrong with what you just said that I hardly know where to begin!"

Shocked out of his self pity by her anger, not to mention the slap she had delivered, he stared at her in confusion, daring to believe that somehow, perhaps, there was the slightest chance he had misread the situation.

"First of all, I love you and only you, which I tell you on an almost daily basis and one would hope that you would believe me by now. Secondly, even supposing I had done wrong, what does it say about your feelings for me that you would just let me go? Do I mean so very little to you, John?"

"No-"

"And finally," she cut him off. "What you witnessed was in no way consensual and he received the very same blow you just did for his efforts, though I dare say his was slightly harder. Why do you think I have allowed Bill in our bedroom if not because I felt uneasy without you here."

John looked down at the dog and finally registered Margaret's meaning. His expression had turned first from one of hurt to one of confusion and now to one of anger. He stood up and headed towards the door but

Margaret blocked his path.

"You will sit right back down and stay there until I have finished with you, sir."

John was torn. He knew that his lack of faith in her had hurt her deeply, but he also knew that Edmund had hurt her and he couldn't let a slight like that pass. Still, he was the one in the wrong in this instance so he reined his anger in and sat back down.

"Good. Now, explain yourself."

"You're too good for me," he said. "I have always known it and a part of me has always expected you to realise it one day. When you first rejected me all those years ago, I didn't blame you. I couldn't. It only made me love you more and still, even now, somewhere inside me I keep expecting to wake up and find that this has all been a dream."

Margaret sat back down on the floor beside him as her anger abated slightly.

"I have always known how Edmund feels about you, from day one I could see it in his eyes."

"That's why you have never liked him?"

John nodded.

"You enjoyed his company so much, it only seemed logical to me that he was the better choice for you. He is a gentleman, he has the same upbringing as you, he is well educated, closer to your age and he has no need of your money, as I did."

Margaret reached out and took his hand.

"You are a fool, John Thornton," she said as she raised herself up to her knees and kissed him lightly. "But you are my fool, and I will never let you go."

He looked into her eyes for a long while, as though trying to gauge the truth of her statement.

"Do you believe me?" she asked.

Finally John nodded.

"Good. Now stay there while I get you a drink to help warm you up." She looked back as she reached the bedroom door but John showed no sign of moving so Margaret headed downstairs to fetch John a whisky. Bill, her ever present shadow, followed her. John was still in the chair when she returned, though his hands were tightly curled upon the arms causing his knuckles to turn white.

Margaret handed him the glass. "Drink," she ordered.

John did as she asked and when the glass was empty she

212

took it from him, then took his hand and pulled him to his feet.

"Let's get some sleep," she said. "It's been a long day."

John nodded and began undressing. Margaret pulled her robe off and draped it over the chair beside her bed. Though she and John usually slept without night clothes, she felt a little odd about removing her night gown tonight but chided herself that she was being silly. She took the garment off and climbed under the covers, looking to John who appeared frozen as he stared at her, seemingly in anger.

"What is it?" she asked.

John gave no reply but instead turned on his heel and stormed out of the room.

Confused, Margaret clambered out of bed and snatched up her night gown. Only as she went to raise the garment over her head did she notice the dark purple bruising on her upper arms where Edmund had gripped her.

She heard a shout and crash, followed by barking which spurred her to action once again. She threw the gown over her head and pulled her dressing gown on as quickly as she could. Still, by the time she reached Edmund's room the servants, Jenny and Jane as well as the elder Mrs. Thornton were crowding the doorway.

"Let me through," she cried, pushing past them.

John had Edmund pinned up against the wall, shouting insults at him between each blow he delivered. Bill barked furiously at the pair of them while Edmund just stood there and did nothing to defend himself.

"John, stop!" She grabbed his fist as he drew his arm back to take another swing and he turned to look at her. "Stop," she repeated quietly.

John looked torn.

"Please, he's not worth it. Come to bed."

Finally John released Edmund, who slumped to the floor, and allowed Margaret to lead him back to their room, though a few times he stiffened and she thought that he might pull away from her again.

"What was that all about?" Hannah asked as they passed her.

"Get back to bed," Margaret told the servants. She gestured for Hannah to follow them and as soon as the bedroom door was closed behind Bill, Hannah demanded answers.

"Will someone tell me what is going on?"

"Edmund was very... inappropriate earlier this evening and John is rather upset," Margaret said softly, in case the servants were still in the hallway listening.

"I feared something like this would happen," Hannah said with a long sigh.

"You knew he had feelings for me?" Margaret asked.

"It was plain for all the world to see."

"Except me, apparently," she said, more to herself than the others. "I mean I knew he liked me but I am married. It never occurred to me that he would... well."

"It's not your fault," John said. "I'm sure you did nothing to encourage him."

"I certainly didn't mean to," Margaret said.

Hannah looked sceptical.

"If you had seen the ugly bruises he left on her arms, Mother, you would agree with me."

At once Hannah was both chastened by his comment and angered by it. Margaret was one of 'hers' now, and how dare some little upstart hurt her!

"Leave it, Mother," John cautioned, now suddenly the voice of reason. "Things are already in enough of a mess."

"If I had known," she said, shaking her head. "If I'd had any idea, I would never have asked Daniel for an introduction."

"Please," Margaret said. "There is no lasting damage done and no one is to blame. Edmund just had a little too much to drink and forgot himself. I would really rather we just forgot the whole thing and continued as though nothing has happened."

Though she had seen some harsh sights since she had lived in the Milton, John knew that Margaret was unaccustomed to violence and he understood her desire to forget what had happened this evening, even while he knew that it would not be possible.

John put his arm around her shoulders and drew her to him, kissing the top of her head.

"I'm sorry," he said.

"What do you have to be sorry for?" Hannah asked.

"Mother, please, we'll discuss this in the morning. Right now Margaret needs her rest. She's been through an ordeal and I haven't helped matters."

"No, John, really I'm fine, just a little tired, that's all," Margaret assured him.

Hannah tutted but bid them goodnight and left.

"Come on," he said. "Let's get some sleep."

Margaret disrobed again and climbed back into bed. John joined her moments later and Margaret scooted closer to him and kissed him on the lips, but John was stiff and unresponsive.

"John, please. What else can I do to make you believe that you are the only man for me?"

"Nothing," he said, cupping her cheek with one hand. "But you have been through an ordeal."

"I have been kissed by someone I did not want to, that is hardly an ordeal."

"You are hurt," he said, his hands going to the bruises on her arms and lightly caressing them.

"I am bruised, that is all. I have had many worse injuries, John. The only thing that really pains me is the idea that I have disappointed you in some way and hurt you."

"You have not hurt me," he said. "You could not."

"We both know that is untrue," Margaret said, her eyes downcast with shame. "But I need you to realise that I was just a silly young girl then, John, and my thoughts were clouded by unhappiness and prejudice. I am no longer young, nor I hope, silly. I know my own mind now and I know what I want. I want you and only you."

John smiled, wondering for the millionth time what he had ever done to deserve this angel.

"And now I would like to show you how much I love you," she said, her eyes asking him to understand.

"Are you certain I will not hurt you?"

"Yes," she assured him, leaning down to kiss him once again. This time he responded.

Bill sat in front of the fire, watching the proceedings but when her mistress finally kissed her master, she knew that the trouble had passed for now so she laid her head down on her paws and went to sleep.

Chapter Thirty

When Margaret awoke the next morning, it took her a few moments to remember the events of the night before. She wondered why she had awoken naturally since she was so late getting to sleep. She reached for the pocket watch that she kept on the nightstand but found only a wet nose instead. Remembering how Bill had helped her last night, she scratched her behind the ears for a moment.

"It's gone nine," she heard John say. She turned over to face him, confused.

"Why aren't you at the mill? And why didn't you wake me?"

"To be honest, I wasn't sure what I would do if I was faced with Wallace this morning. I asked Jane to give the keys to Higgins to open up."

"And Edmund?"

"Has gone to the community centre. Dixon offered to help him today."

"John, I am fine, really."

"You wanted to assist him?"

"No, I mean that you did not have to stay home with me."

John pushed a strand of hair back from her face.

"Perhaps I have been a little slow to realise the depth of your affection, my love, but I think that you overestimate my affection for the mill compared to you. All you would have to do is say the word, Margaret, and I would gladly sell up and leave tomorrow."

Margaret smiled. Knowing just how much the mill did mean to him, that was quite a statement. She felt the sting of tears in her eyes.

"I'm sorry," she said. "I feel as if this is all my fault."

"None of it is your fault. If anyone is to blame, it's me. I knew how he felt about you, yet I repeatedly left you alone with him, giving him chance after chance to-"

Margaret put a finger over his lips.

"Hush. We have spoken quite enough about blame when really the only fault lies with Edmund. I would rather we talk about what is to happen now than rehash last nights events again."

"What would you like to happen?" he asked.

"I would like to forget what happened last night, to go on as though he had not..." She sighed. "But I know

216

that is not possible."

"Would you like him to keep working here?"

Margaret wasn't sure how to answer that.

"I would like for the workers not to lose their doctor because of what happened, but whether that service is provided by him or another doctor, that should not bother me very much."

"Then we will find someone else," John assured her.

"If only it were that easy," Margaret lamented. "Where are we to find another doctor who is willing to help our workers for fees that will not send them to the poor house?"

"Perhaps we might have to subsidise the service for a while but somehow we will find a way," he assured her.

Margaret nodded, though she was far from certain it was as easy as he said. Regardless of how often he reassured her, she would always believe that this was her fault. If only she had considered that Edmund might feel something for her and further realised that he might act on those feelings, she could have prevented this.

"Are you hungry?" John asked.

"I think we have missed breakfast," she smiled.

"Not at all. I told the kitchen we would eat in bed today and they will prepare the food when I ring down."

"How very decadent," Margaret smiled.

Because she had received such a shock, despite her protests that she was fine, John decided to take the day off to stay with her and make certain that she suffered no ill effects from her ordeal.

He looked into Edmund's room and wasn't surprised to see that his overnight bag was gone, though since Dixon hadn't returned to the house, he assumed Wallace was was still taking his surgery today.

He, Margaret and Bessy were playing in the nursery when the doorbell rang. John left them to it and arrived downstairs to see Jane ushering Wallace inside. His left eye was blackened and John felt a thrill course through him as he realised that he had done that.

"Mr. Thornton. I wonder if I might speak to you for a few moments."

John considered the man before him for a moment then finally nodded and directed him into the study. John stood before the desk, leaning on the edge as he waited for Wallace to speak.

"I have behaved in a most disgraceful manner and I want you to know that I am truly sorry." His eyes were downcast with shame.

John didn't answer.

"I realise that you will probably not want to retain my services but these people should not suffer because of my foolishness. I want to assure you that I have some friends who believe, as I do, that everyone deserves affordable health care and I shall ask one of them to contact you."

Still John didn't speak.

"Finally I would like you to extend my deepest apologies to Mrs. Thornton and I want to assure you that there was no impropriety on her part."

"I already knew that," John assured him. "But I shall tell Margaret what you've said."

"Thank you." Wallace nodded and turned away. "I am sorry to have taken up so much of your time. Good day, sir."

John stood where he was for several minutes until Margaret came down to find him. She could tell from his demeanour that he had seen Edmund.

"He's gone," John said. "His choice, I didn't ask him to leave."

Margaret nodded her understanding.

"I confess, I am relieved, though I also feel slightly cowardly for not facing him again."

"There is nothing cowardly about you, Margaret, and nothing to be gained from facing him. He wanted me to tell you that he's very sorry and hopes that you can forgive him."

Margaret didn't know how to respond to that so instead she tried to change the subject.

"You still haven't told me what happened at last night's dinner."

John smiled, recognising her ploy but going with it nevertheless. "There is talk of a new machine being patented in America, better and faster than our machinery, they say, but it's probably all bluff and bragging."

"And what of Fanny, did Watson have any news about her?"

"She is keeping well, spending his money as if it were going out of fashion."

"Oh dear, we had better hope this new speculation of his pays off then."

"The railroad is still strong, so he says, but with all the investment in building new lines, it could take years before they see a return."

"Then let us hope that it matures before Fanny bankrupts him," she teased.

"If it doesn't come good, I'm afraid it will bankrupt him."

"Does he have that much invested?" Margaret asked, for surely no one would gamble with money they could not afford to lose.

"He does," John confirmed. "He has invested three times now, and some of the other local business men have invested more than they should."

"But what if it fails?" she asked. "Surely he would not invest more than is prudent?"

"Not only has he invested his own money, he has borrowed so that he might invest more."

"Foolish man," Margaret said, shaking her head in consternation. "With sums like that invested, we must indeed pray that he is successful."

John was surprised to see Daniel Whitaker at his office the next afternoon and because of his uncomfortable countenance, John immediately wondered if his friend, Doctor Wallace, had told him of what had happened with Margaret. John couldn't and didn't hold Whitaker responsible for the actions of his acquaintance though, and greeted him warmly.

"I'm sorry to disturb you at work, Mr Thornton."

"Not at all." They shook hands. "Please, come in, sit down. If you came to see my mother, I'm afraid she is visiting Fanny this afternoon."

"Oh no, it is you I have come to see." Whitaker rather reminded John of a schoolboy who had been summoned to the headmaster's office. "Before I begin, I would just like to say that whilst I don't know what has happened with you and Dr. Wallace, if offence has been caused, I truly apologise for sending him your way."

"No apology necessary. The matter is history."

"Good." Whitaker smiled, though he still looked nervous.

"Was there something else?" John asked gently.

"Well, yes, actually." Though he didn't elaborate any further for a few moments. Finally he took a deep breath and began. "You must surely have noticed that your mother and I have formed a friendship of sorts over the past few years."

"I had." It was hard to miss since his mother dined with Whitaker and his sister at least once a week.

"Well, I find myself at something of a crossroad. I care a great deal for your mother and... well, I find that I would like to formalise our relationship and..."

To make things easy on him, John interrupted. "You've no need to ask my permission before you ask her to marry you."

"No, I realise that, but I should very much like your blessing all the same."

John steepled his fingers together as he considered the man before him.

"You have my blessing, of course, Mr Whitaker. Though I can't claim we are close friends, you are a good man and I believe you will be good to my mother."

"Thank you," he smiled slightly. "But I'm sensing some hesitation."

John couldn't deny it.

"My mother is a very strong woman; circumstances dictated that she had to be and although I believe that she cares for you, she is not given to displays of sentiment."

Whitaker nodded in agreement. He had discovered as much for himself.

"She has also been alone for nearly twenty years now and is, shall we say, set in her ways. While I have no wish to hurt you, I feel I must caution you that, despite her feelings for you, I think there is still a chance she may reject you."

"Believe me, I know." Whitaker nodded gravely. "And I realise that in declaring my feelings for her, there is a very real chance I may lose her forever, but I simply cannot remain silent any longer."

John understood how he felt. He got to his feet and held his hand out to the other man.

"You have my blessing, sir, and my sincerest wish that she will accept you."

"Thank you."

When he had left, John sat back down and turned his chair to look out of the window. His mother had always been a large part of his life and while he wanted her to be happy, the idea of her moving to live with Mr. Whitaker was discomforting.

220

He knew that he couldn't allow his needs to come before hers, especially since John had a family of his own now but still, she would be sorely missed if she did accept Whitaker's proposal.

Chapter Thirty One

Daniel Whitaker was usually a happy-go-lucky sort of chap, eager to try new experiences with scarcely a thought to the possible consequences. His time in the merchant navy had been fraught with danger but it had taught him to enjoy each day. It had also introduced him to new cultures, new ideas and new people. He had learned to trust his instincts, a trait that had served him well in his printing business.

When he had asked Beth, his first wife, to marry him, he had scarcely thought about it. Not only was he certain of his feelings for Beth, he was sure of her feelings for him. They had enjoyed many happy years together and he had never regretted his decision to ask her to become his wife.

Now he found himself in an unusual predicament because while he knew that he loved Hannah Thornton and he believed that she too cared for him, he was none too sure of her reaction to his proposal.

He had known that he loved her for a long time now but fear had always kept him from taking their relationship any further. Should Hannah reject him, things would become awkward between them and he would almost certainly lose her friendship, something that was almost unthinkable.

However he couldn't go on as he had been, content with the occasional meal and good conversation. He wanted more, needed more. And if she rejected him, then so be it.

With all these and more thoughts running through his head, Daniel made his way to Rose Cottage to await Hannah's return from her daughter's home.

Jane let him in and saw him to the parlour, where he proceeded to pace for the next hour, his fingers turning the ring box he had carried in his pocket for the past two month over and over. Finally he heard hoof beats outside and forced himself to be still.

It seemed to take her an eternity to reach the house but as she finally came into the room, he found that he was wholly unprepared.

"Daniel, what ever is the matter?" She asked him, looking concerned.

"Nothing," he said, swallowing hard. "No, that is not true, there is something." He was doing this all wrong. He mentally shook himself and stepped forward to take her hands. "Won't you sit down," he asked as he guided her forward, further into the room.

Still perturbed, Hannah took a seat and tried to look calm. She had a feeling that she knew what Daniel was about to say but he looked so troubled that she was worried something serious had happened. He took the seat beside her, though he kept hold of her hands.

"Hannah, we've been friends now for quite some time, and acquaintances for even longer. I hope you know that I have the utmost respect for you and that... that I love you very much and I would, I mean, I was wondering if you would do me the honour of becoming my wife."

"Oh, Daniel," she pulled one hand out of his grip and cupped his cheek. "I began to think you would never ask."

Daniel swallowed. Since she hadn't offered a simple yes or no, thanks to his tension it was taking him a while to process her words.

"Is that... is that a yes?"

"Of course it is, you foolish man."

"Oh," Daniel's carefree smile finally shone through. "Oh, that's wonderful news."

Though she was pleased, Hannah wondered how she would tell John. While he and Margaret knew about Daniel, they never asked about him and she never spoke of him, except to tell them when she was dining with him.

She hoped that John would be happy for her but it would be a big adjustment for both of them. Hannah could hardly remember a time before John, he had been such a large part of her life for so long. She was lucky that Margaret had so readily accepted her as well, since many a bride would want to keep their home and husband to themselves.

Still, as hard as it may be for all of them, Hannah had more than done her duty as a mother, now it was time that she thought about herself. After all, she wasn't getting any younger.

Dinner that evening was a slightly stilted affair. Hannah was trying to find the courage to tell John and Margaret that she was engaged to Daniel Whitaker; John was trying to keep his expression neutral and not ask what had happened while Margaret looked from mother to son, clearly sensing the tension in the room but unsure of its cause. Even Bessy seemed to realise something was different and actually ate her food for a change, rather than trying to play with it first.

They ate in silence, the only sound was the gentle scrape of knives and forks on the plates.

Margaret took a sip of water, wishing it was something slightly stronger.

"Mama, finish."

Grateful for the distraction, though also wary of breaking the silence, Margaret turned to her daughter and wiped her mouth with her napkin.

"Good girl, darling. We're having syrup sponge and custard for dessert today and as you've been such a good girl, you can have a little extra."

Bessy smiled her big, toothy grin, for syrup sponge was her favourite.

Hannah laid her knife and fork down and looked at John, who had also finished eating. Jane began clearing their plates.

"Shall I bring dessert now?" she asked the elder Mrs. Thornton, for in the servants' eyes she was still the head of the household, something else that was about to change.

"Give us a few minutes, thank you, Jane. I'll ring the bell when we're ready."

Jane nodded and left while Margaret and John looked expectantly at Hannah.

"There's something I have to tell you," she began. "Mr. Whitaker came to see me today to ask for my hand in marriage and I have accepted."

Margaret was stunned. While she knew that Hannah and Mr. Whitaker were friends, the friendship had lasted so long that Margaret had begun to think nothing more would ever come of it.

John smiled; clearly he had known something she hadn't because he didn't seem to find anything unusual in her statement.

"That's wonderful news, mother. As much as I will miss you, I am glad you've found someone worthy."

"Yes," Margaret agreed. "I am a little surprised by the news but he is a lovely fellow and I sincerely hope you will be happy together."

"Thank you both," Hannah smiled. "I know this will be a big change for all of us but we have settled on a date in April, so we will have a few months to adjust to our new circumstances."

Margaret suddenly realised that this would be their last Christmas together. Well, they may share Christmas dinner in the future but this would be the last Christmas where Hannah was a member of the household.

"I wonder if I should write to Aunt Shaw and postpone our visit in December," Margaret said. "I find that, if this is to be our last, I would rather spend it with my family."

"Mrs. Shaw is your family," Hannah said without malice, confused by her statement.

Margaret smiled but was not surprised to feel the sting of tears in her eyes. She reached across the table and grasped Hannah's hand.

"Technically perhaps, but family is about so much more than blood."

Hannah squeezed her hand and smiled, blinking back tears as she was also feeling slightly emotional.

"Come now," John said, swallowing down his own discomfort at the thought of losing his mother. "This is supposed to be happy news and the pair of you look on the verge of tears."

"It is happy news, John," Margaret smiled at him.

"But still, it is the end of an era," Hannah added.

John placed his hand on theirs.

"Aye, it is," he agreed, his voice thick with emotion. "But all I want is your happiness, Mother. I hope you know that."

"I do, John. I do."

"Mama," Bessy called, holding her hands out, clearly feeling left out.

Margaret smiled as she withdrew her hand, wiped her eyes and then picked her daughter up out of her chair, holding her tightly against her chest.

"Don't worry, sweetheart, we still love you too."

Bessy flashed her toothy grin and held her hands out to Hannah.

"Gram-ma," she said.

Margaret passed Bessy to her grandmother, who hugged her tightly and closed her eyes as she inhaled deeply.

Here was another person she would miss, possibly even more than John and Margaret but she knew she couldn't live her life for other people, it was time to forge her own future.

"Thank you, both," she said, smiling at John and Margaret. "I know I don't say it often enough, but I hope you both know how much you mean to me."

"We know," Margaret assured her.

"We do," John agreed, getting up and kissing his mother on the cheek.

Chapter Thirty Two

Edith was very sorry to hear that Margaret could no longer visit at Christmas, though Margaret wondered if it was because she truly missed Margaret or because she enjoyed the fireworks that might erupt should Margaret spend too much time in the company of her aunt.

For her part, Mrs. Shaw expressed her regret, though it seemed perfunctory rather than heartfelt. Margaret wouldn't have been in the least surprised to find that her aunt was actually relieved that her manufacturing relations were unable to attend. What would her London friends think of them!

Margaret found that she didn't much care who looked down on her and John, for they were surely not worth wasting her energy on.

She wrote back to them both, expressing her regret again and hoping that something could be arranged for the following year. Bessy would be three next summer and she hadn't yet met any of Margaret's side of the family.

Margaret's next letter was harder to write as it was to Frederick. She did so enjoy receiving his letters, though both reading and replying to them only served to remind her of the distance between them. She was far too young to think of retirement but in her idle moments, she did sometimes dream of taking an extended holiday, like the Maitlands, and spending quite a few of those months in Spain.

By that time, of course, they would both be very different people and she worried that their fraternal bond would somehow diminish with time. She put those thoughts aside and continued to update Fred on her news.

In his letter, he had told her that his third child had been born, his first girl, and he had named her Margarita, after Margaret. She was moved by the gesture. He had also enclosed a photograph of his young family. He and Dolores were seated with him holding the middle son, Jose, Dolores holding Margarita and Enrique, the eldest son, standing proudly in front of them.

Fred hadn't changed much but he looked even more tanned than she remembered and his hair looked slightly lighter, no doubt bleached by the Mediterranean sun. Dolores looked as beautiful as Margaret remembered her to be. Both looked happy and in love, though somewhat tired.

When she had finished her reply, which would be mailed

along with their Christmas gifts, she wrote her usual Christmas letter to Mr. Gilbert, a friend of Mr. Bell's from Oxford who had also known her father in his youth. Mr. Gilbert had written to her shortly after Mr Bell's death and they had been corresponding ever since, though they had yet to meet. Mr. Gilbert had informed her that they had met when she was a child but unfortunately Margaret had no recollection of it. She had invited him to stay with them many times, since he had often expressed an interest in her and John's endeavours but as yet he had not found the time to take her up on the offer.

With that letter finished, she put her stationery away and joined John on the sofa where he was reading the Sunday papers. Bill raised her head for a moment but lowered it again when she realised that neither food nor attention would be forthcoming.

"Anything interesting?" Margaret asked.

"There's still a lot of fallout from the collapse of the Royal British Bank. The jury found Scott Palin guilty of poisoning his wife."

"About time," Hannah said, looking up from her embroidery. "How long was the jury out? Five days?"

"Three," John informed her before continuing his round up of events. "Parliament has passed the new Police Act into law, and America has elected a new President, another democrat."

He handed her the sections of the paper he had finished with.

"I wonder if Milton's police will be affected by the act at all?" Margaret mused.

"I don't think so, unless they're given a greater area to cover."

Margaret was thankful that their little community was so tight knit that they had never once had to call the police out here. To be fair though, she knew that part of the reason was because the closest tavern was a three mile walk away and any troublemakers generally caused their havoc close to the tavern.

There was silence for a while then as each of the Thorntons happily engaged in their own activities for a while.

"Will we hold a Christmas party again this year?" Hannah asked. "Only with double the workers we had last year, it will cost a lot more."

Margaret looked at John. The party last year hadn't been particularly costly and the hands had made all the arrangements, they simply gave Higgins the budget to distribute as he saw fit.

"It wasn't so very expensive," Margaret said. "The workers made the food and drink themselves, we just paid for the ingredients. Besides, I think it's good for community spirit. If we hold it the Saturday before Christmas again, it won't affect work as they'll have the Sunday to recover."

"I agree," John said. "I'll speak to Higgins, see what he thinks the budget will need to be this year."

"While we're talking, we also need to decide what the bonus will be this year," Margaret said. "Last year it was fifty percent of their weekly wage. Profits look very healthy since we expanded so we might even be able to increase it a little this year, say to 55 or 60 percent."

John hadn't seen the latest figures since Margaret had only completed them the day before.

"Show me on Monday; we'll decide then."

John raised his paper again, only to have it pulled down moments later by his daughter, who seemed to think that her latest work of art was far more interesting than his dull old newspaper.

"Dada, look at ma pic-sur!"

John put his paper aside, took the picture and pulled his daughter onto his lap so they could look at it together.

"That's very good, sweetheart," he said, slightly hesitant to ask his next question but compelled to none the less. "What is it?"

"Dada's mill!" Bessy said proudly.

John squinted. He supposed if he had imbibed enough alcohol, he might have thought this looked very much like a mill. Whatever his daughter's talents, it was highly unlikely she would ever be an artist. "Oh, I see," he said, smiling at her. "And a very fine mill it is."

Bessy grinned at him.

"Pay," she said.

"Daddy can't play now, sweetheart, daddy wants to read the paper."

"Dada pay!"

Knowing that he couldn't resist her for long, John gave in gracefully and sat down on the floor to assemble a wooden brick tower with his daughter. Bill came to lie beside them, eager to see what the little human was up to.

Margaret and Hannah smiled at each other as they observed John and Bessy. Though used to the sight, it was still odd to see such an imposing man dominated by a tiny girl who had yet to fully master the English language.

The air was cold and Margaret's breath froze as it left her body. She pulled her coat tighter around her and quickened her pace, anxious to be inside once again. She knew she should probably enjoy the cold while she could, because for the rest of the night she was likely to be far too warm and would be longing to spend a few minutes outside again.

She could hear the music playing as she approached and could hear the sounds of merriment from within. Already there was a small crowd of people outside, enjoying the chill in the air. Margaret smiled and greeted them as she passed by them and went into the community centre.

Last year's party had been held in the main part of the community hall with no problems but this year it was much more crowded and even the smaller rooms had been opened up to accommodate everyone. Though still large enough for the school, Margaret knew they would have to do something soon. Perhaps if they built the school, its hall could be used for gatherings like this, and the community centre could become a permanent church.

Margaret shook her head and chided herself, this was supposed to be a party and here she was thinking about their plans for the village.

She pushed her way inside, hung her coat on a free coat hook and stood on her tiptoes to try and see John. Though Margaret wasn't very tall, thankfully John was and she soon spotted his head of dark hair and made her way over to him. The noise was much louder inside and Margaret had to touch his arm to get his attention. He turned to her and smiled. To her surprise, he had Bessy sitting on his left hip.

"She wouldn't go to bed," he told her.

Margaret's look asked him which one of them was supposed to be the adult. John shrugged, asking what he was supposed to do. Not that she particularly minded her daughter being here, but when she had asked John to head home and tuck Bessy in while she finished up some work, she didn't expect that he would give in to her pleading and bring her to the party.

She shook her head but was unable to stop the indulgent smile that formed on her lips.

"Did you at least leave Bill at home?"

"Oh yes." He smiled, pleased to have accomplished one of his tasks. "Though she was barking like a loon when I left."

"She'll soon settle down," Margaret assured him.

"Do you want a drink?" he asked.

"I'll get it," she yelled in order to be heard. She reached up and kissed his cheek, then disappeared back into the crowd to find the punch bowl. There were two bowls of punch, one slightly alcoholic, the other not. One or many people always ended up spiking at least one, often both of the bowls so Margaret was careful to sip her glass to make sure it wasn't too strong before drinking some. She couldn't taste any alcohol yet so it was safe to drink. Margaret had nothing against alcohol (in moderation) but it was cold out tonight and the walk back to the house would take ten minutes, plus they had Bessy with them so she preferred not to drink this evening. Besides, it would only make her hotter.

She made her way around the hall, speaking to various people she knew, enquiring about their lives and their families, all the while doing her best to avoid the occasional elbow or foot that might be sent her way from one of the dancers. And she used the word dancer in the loosest possible sense! Everyone seemed to be having fun though, and that was what counted.

She headed outside a few times to cool off, usually finding more people to chat with out there. On her last trip outside to cool down, John joined her. Unfortunately he had discovered the down side to keeping a child up past it's bed time since Bessy was no longer the cute girl he knew and loved but a downright grumpy little thing with a surprisingly loud cry.

"I've got to take her home," he said.

"I'll come with you."

"No, I brought her, you stay and enjoy the party."

"They'll enjoy it more without their bosses around," she smiled.

John handed Bessy to her while he fetched their coats. By the time he returned, Margaret had settled Bessy into her arms and she was sound asleep, her thumb resting in her mouth. John offered to take Bessy but her slumber was as yet too light to be moved much without waking, so he draped Margaret's coat over her shoulders instead.

"How do you do that?" he asked, looking down at his now angel-faced daughter while she slept peacefully as they walked home.

"Trade secret. If I told you that, then I'd have to kill you."

John considered her argument for a while then shrugged. "Eh, but what a way to go," he said, raising his eyebrows suggestively.

"Why do you think I was so keen to leave," Margaret asked, her countenance completely innocent.

John smiled. He could see Bessy was growing heavy so he held his arms out to take her. She was sound asleep now and wouldn't awaken for anything less than an earthquake, so Margaret gratefully handed her over.

The house was quiet when they arrived back since Hannah was dining with Mr. Whitaker and his sister. Jenny greeted them as she had volunteered to stay and look after the house and Bessy while the others had joined the party.

"Jenny, why didn't you go and join the others when John took Bessy?"

"I said I'd stay, Miss Margaret, so I did."

"But Dixon is over the stables if we need anything urgently, John should have told you you could have the night off."

"He did," Jenny assured her. "But Miss Dixon was coming over to have tea with me so I decided to stay here."

Margaret smiled, understanding her choice. Jenny was still only sixteen years old and though her family was not far away in Milton, Margaret had the feeling that they were grateful to have her out of the house as it was one less mouth to feed. Ever since she had started work, Dixon had taken the girl under her wing and Margaret felt that Jenny now viewed her as a cross between a mother figure and an older sibling.

"Shall I take the bairn?" she asked.

"No, Jenny, we'll put her to bed but if it's not too much trouble, would you mind bringing a pot of tea to our bedroom? It's awfully cold out there tonight."

"Course not. Kettle's not long boiled so it won't take long." Jenny smiled. It was no wonder everyone liked Mrs. T. Even though Jenny was paid to look after the baby, here she was putting the child to bed herself when she didn't have to and then asking if it would be 'too much trouble' to have some tea! As if Jenny would ever refuse Mrs. T anything!

232

"Thank you, Jenny."

Jenny watched as she and the master headed up the stairs to Bessy's room. She watched as Mrs. T took his arm and leaned into him as they climbed the stairs. They were such a sweet couple and Jenny wished with all her heart that one day she might find a man like the master. He didn't need wealth, just to look at Jenny as the master did to Mrs. T; that would be more than enough to make Jenny happy.

Christmas morning felt very poignant since Margaret, John and Hannah were aware that it would be their last as a family but Bessy helped to keep the mood light with her childish antics. Together they walked to the community centre to hear the Christmas morning service. This was still hard for Margaret since she had always attended her father's Christmas day service and she still felt his loss very keenly on Christmas morning.

In the afternoon Mr. Whitaker, his sister Mary, as well as Edward and Eleanor Maitland joined them for Christmas dinner which helped bolster the mood and keep spirits high.

The day before, Margaret and Bessy had decorated the tree with ribbons, baubles and candles. Bessy had been delighted when Margaret lifted her up so that she could place the fine porcelain angel atop the tree, where she still sat now, looking down over the festivities.

Over the past few weeks Margaret and Bessy (mainly Margaret with a little hindrance from Bessy) had also made garlands and ivy chains which now adorned the room and mantelpiece. The cook had made cinnamon stick bunches which gave the rooms a pleasing homely scent and Dixon had fashioned a number of wreaths made of pine, holly, ivy and holly berries, some of which she had given to Miss Margaret. The rest decorated the servants quarters and Dixon's rooms over the stable.

The staff would celebrate Christmas the next day, Boxing Day, although all those who weren't absolutely necessary had also been given today off. Dixon was to host the staff Christmas dinner in her rooms tomorrow and Margaret had offered to help her set up the tables in the morning. Cook would obviously take care of their food and the other servants would handle the clean up between them .

Food had been prepared for the Thorntons to eat cold

tomorrow. Usually at least one member of staff was kept on duty but this year Margaret had insisted that they all take the day off. The staff were a kind of family and Margaret felt it was wrong to ask some of them to work. Besides, Margaret had enough experience in the kitchen that she thought she would be able to handle their needs for one day.

Despite all this, Margaret fully expected to rise in the morning to find that Dixon had prepared the cold breakfast and seen to Bessy's needs, as she had done previous years. Dixon seemed almost incapable of not looking after her mistress and though Margaret valued that loyalty, she did sometimes wish that Dixon would think of herself and her own needs a little more.

Though she tried to hide it from them, Margaret knew that her joints were giving her more pain over recent months. Margaret hoped things would improve when the warmer weather arrived but there was nothing tangible she could do to help Dixon.

As well as receiving a Christmas bonus, with Dixon's help Margaret had brought each servant a small gift, something they wanted rather than something they needed. It seemed almost unimaginable to Margaret that the notion of celebrating Christmas hadn't been widespread until quite recently. Indeed at the turn of the century, many businesses didn't even consider Christmas Day to be a holiday. Most people seemed to think that it was Prince Albert bringing his German Christmas traditions traditions over, such as decorated trees, that made celebrating the birth of Christ fashionable again.

The idea of showing charitable spirit hadn't been common either and owed most of it's popularity to Charles Dickens's story, a Christmas Carol.

The snow held off until early January when the white flakes transformed the landscape into a breathtaking winter wonderland that lasted two weeks. The roads to Milton became blocked but the train still managed to run and despite the fact that only cargo trains stopped at the mill, for a few pence the villagers could bribe the driver and catch a ride into the town.

Most of the shops in the village and been rented now, though some shopkeepers shared their premises since there wasn't a large enough population to justify a whole shop. Still, it meant that life was much easier for the workers this year since they could buy most produce locally.

Aside from an occasional flurry, the snow only lasted two weeks but everyone seemed to make the most of it. Snowmen were frequent sights around the village and the children often had snowball fights through out the streets, vexing more than one adult who was caught in the crossfire.

The crocuses pushing through the soil in Margaret's garden in late February were the first sign that winter was on its way out, cemented by the arrival of daffodils a few weeks later, heralding the arrival of spring.

As much as Margaret loved spring and summer, she was slightly sad that the winter was over. Being just that bit further outside of Milton meant that they neither gave nor received as many invitations in the winter months and she was dreading the resumption of dinner parties and social gatherings with people she did not much care for.

Sometimes Margaret wondered if she was antisocial or if many people were genuinely as superficial and mean-spirited as she believed them to be.

As Margaret played with Bessy in the garden one afternoon, she mused on this point briefly as she stopped for a moment to admire the spring flowers. Later she would look back on this day as she tried to remember exactly when everything started to go wrong, because right now she had little idea of the strife that the coming years held for her and her family.

Chapter Thirty Three

The first inkling that there might be trouble ahead came at Hannah Thornton's annual dinner party, brought forward to early April since it was to be her last given under her son's roof. The evening was going well and, being seated beside her friend, Eleanor Maitland, Margaret was enjoying herself; then over dessert the conversation turned to America and the troubles they were facing. In light of the declining trade with Europe, the western states were beginning to feel the financial pinch and the western banks were declining many business loans.

"They've only themselves to blame; their prices are too high," Mr. Hamper said. "Their cotton, for example, is much more expensive than that from the Caribbean,"

"But much better quality," Slickson added.

"True," Hamper agreed. "But Egyptian cotton is getting better each year and Indian cotton is just as good though still cheaper."

"It's a storm in a tea cup." Dickinson chimed in. "Cotton is still a new industry, these things take time to find a balance."

"But it isn't just cotton," Mr. Latimer said. "The decline in demand seems to be across all industries."

"But the country won't go bankrupt, will it?" Watson asked rhetorically, seemingly amused by the notion. "They'll lower the prices soon enough and trade will pick up again. You mark my words."

John caught Margaret's eye and she could see his silent hope in them that Watson was right.

Most of the guests seemed to agree with Watson but Margaret knew they were the people who had invested in American speculations, like Watson. She wondered how much of their opinion was based in fact and how much was hope over experience.

The end of April saw Hannah Thornton's wedding, which like her son's ceremony, was a simple affair, held in the same small church that John and Margaret had used. Since this was a second marriage for them both, they opted to keep everything low key, seeming to think it tasteless to be too lavish.

Hannah's dress was deep blue with cream lace at the collar and cuffs and button detail on the bodice. Margaret had noticed that she was wearing more colour recently, though she generally went for darker shades. The deep blue suited her perfectly and, since she wasn't a maiden, Margaret agreed that wearing white probably wasn't a good idea.

Mr. Whitaker wore a morning suit with a waistcoat in a similar colour to Hannah's dress.

Margaret was the only bridesmaid and Daniel Whitaker's childhood friend, Mr. Hains was the only groomsman.

There were no flowers in the church, save for the ones Hannah carried in her bouquet and she had kept the guests to a minimum; friends and close family only.

The only real sign of lavishness was Fanny and her dress, the skirt of which had needed to be pushed into the church pew since it was so wide. Rather than the voluminous petticoats most women wore, Fanny was now opting for a crinoline cage, which was the height of fashion and able to support a much larger skirt than traditional petticoats could. Margaret and Hannah both thought she looked slightly ridiculous but both were smart enough to keep their opinions to themselves.

The wedding lunch was held in Mr. Whitaker's house and while the food was delicious, it was also a very low key affair.

Thankfully Mr. Whitaker's house was very large. It had needed to be considering that not only was his family raised here but his sister and her boys had lived here too. All of the children had left now, forging their own lives in their own homes, meaning that Hannah and Mary could easily share the house without stepping on each others' toes. Mary seemed genuinely enthused for her brother and happy to welcome Hannah into his life.

In keeping with the wedding, the honeymoon was simple as well, two weeks in the Scottish highlands. From what she had heard, the highlands were even bleaker than the weather in northern England and as such, Margaret wondered what they would find to do for two weeks. When she had said as much to John he had simply smiled until she blushed as she finally realised what activity they would most likely be engaging in.

Chapter Thirty Four

Margaret was preparing the monthly invoices when John stormed into her office and threw a copy of the Milton Times down on her desk. Roused from her sleep, Bill raised her head, eager to protect her mistress from any danger. Seeing the master come in though, she lowered her head again but kept a wary eye on them.

"Thomas, leave us for a moment would you?" John said gruffly to the young man, who eagerly left. He had rarely seen the master's temper but he had seen enough of it to know that he never wanted to see it again.

Puzzled, Margaret picked up the paper and began reading.

"Oh dear," she said, after she had read the first paragraph.

Content with how smoothly the business was running and therefore confident enough to expand again, they had broken ground on the third stage of housing only three days ago. Now it seemed that they were to face more problems again.

"Exactly," John agreed, slumping down into the chair opposite his desk. He looked tired. "There has been unrest in India for many months now but Bernard Lenox has repeatedly assured me that the troubles wouldn't amount to anything. Now we have a full blow rebellion," he sighed.

"But surely it can be quelled."

"Most of our soldiers out there are sepoys, natives, and they are the ones leading the rebellion. The unrest is spreading and nothing they've tried seems to be able to curb it. It will take time to get more British forces out there and even then, I fear they will still be outnumbered. The company employees that haven't fled are being murdered. Even the women and children aren't safe, they are literally massacring any Christians, even those Indians who have converted to our faith."

Margaret closed her eyes and quickly said a silent prayer, asking God to watch over and protect those in danger and welcome those who were killed into Heaven. Still, she was more than just a reverend's daughter now, she was a businesswoman and that was the head she needed to be thinking with right now.

"India is a big country, John; surely the troubles will not affect the cotton trade."

"That is the optimistic viewpoint but in business we must plan for every eventuality."

"All right. So, let's look at the worst case scenario. Say that trade is interrupted, how long will our reserves of cotton last?"

"Perhaps two months. Possibly a little longer depending on the orders in hand."

"Cotton isn't perishable if stored correctly, why can't we just order enough cotton to last for a year before the troubles get too bad?"

"Because even if they could supply it, we have not long given the go ahead on the next phase of building and we need our cash reserves to fund that."

"Then we'll sell another property."

"The market is in decline as a knock-on effect of the difficulties in India and America's financial troubles."

Margaret already knew what most of the answers to her questions would be but she preferred to think a problem though from every angle, even if it meant covering old ground.

"What about getting cotton from Africa or the Caribbean?"

"Our reputation is based on quality. If I start using substandard cotton, we will not be offered nearly so many orders to bid on. If we are going to expand again we need to increase orders, not reduce them."

"But isn't Egyptian cotton gaining a good reputation?"

"It's improving in quality but not yet of a standard I'd like to use. They have also been known to face trouble with filling the orders on time."

"Can we not pay a higher price for the American cotton?"

"Short term, perhaps, but it will substantially reduce our profit margin. I'm not sure how long we could sustain the business without putting our prices up, which will have the effect of losing us more bids."

Margaret thought for a few moments but she wasn't seeing a way out of this.

"We could always go into wool instead," she said, deadpan. "It sometimes feels like you can't move in the Darkshire countryside without hitting a sheep. And sheep are so much more attractive than cotton plants, after all."

"Tempting." John smiled. "And if the outlay on machinery wouldn't bankrupt us, I'd say go for it, even if you are only joking."

"Frederick's firm does much of its business with America. They didn't trade in cotton a few years ago but I can ask him to make enquiries on our behalf. Indeed if the unrest does continue in India, then his firm will have to find alternatives for many products. Perhaps this could even help bolster the American economy."

"That's a lot of 'ifs'," John noted. "But I suppose it can't hurt to ask. In the meantime I'll head into Milton; some of the other masters will be at the club by now and they might have a clearer picture of what's happening in the cotton markets."

"Well, if the worst happens, I suggest we consider importing Egyptian cotton until the American markets calm down. It's not perfect but it is surely better than nothing."

John nodded his agreement and stood up.

"I'll write to Frederick today," Margaret assured him.

Margaret returned to her work, though her mind still played out possible solutions while she laboured. Thankfully whatever happened, they had the resources to ride any problems out. In fact they could subsidise the mill for years if necessary, but she knew that would halt their plans to expand both the mill and the village.

She had entirely too much on her plate at the moment. All these years she had been content for Hannah to run the household but now that she had remarried, those duties fell to Margaret. She had some experience of running a household after her mother died but with such a small budget, only one servant (and a valued and trusted one at that) it had not required a lot of her time. Now she had to see about ordering the right amount of food in for cook, getting the supplies the other maids might require, deal with the wages and tax for them all and decide on things such as menus herself. Really, she had more important things to occupy her time than deciding what the family were to eat on a Monday evening, but alas there was no one else to do it now and so she had little choice.

John returned home that evening while she was determining the menus for next week, but the news he brought wasn't good and he told Margaret that there was little hope of the problems being sorted out in India before the new year. The American markets were still looking unstable but as yet nothing too serious had happened. Cotton prices were coming down very slightly, but not enough.

"Did you see Watson?" she asked.

"He hasn't been around a lot recently. He's not seeing much, if any return on his speculations and Dickinson says he's having problems meeting the mortgage on the mill."

"Oh dear. I wonder if I should visit Fanny this week and make certain she is all right."

"I doubt she'd appreciate it, she'll probably think you've come to gloat."

"I would never take pleasure in another's misfortune."

"Aye but she would, so she thinks others will."

John and Margaret called on his Mother the day after she arrived back from her honeymoon. Both seemed keen to find out how she was settling into her new house, even though she had only been resident there for one night! If patience truly is a virtue then neither John nor Margaret felt very virtuous that day.

It appears however, that absence really does make the heart grow fonder, for Hannah greeted them both with a kiss on the cheek. Her husband, Daniel followed suit and kissed Margaret's cheek, which was perhaps rather informal but in keeping with his (at times) cheeky character, though thankfully he opted simply to shake hands with John. Hannah showed them into the parlour and ordered tea to be brought to them.

Daniel made his excuses, saying that he still had much unpacking to do and would join them later but Margaret suspected he wanted to give them some time alone.

"How are you?" John asked her as soon as they were alone.

"You've no need to fret about me, John, I am quite happy."

"Mother, how can I not worry?"

"I understand," Hannah smiled, for she felt exactly the same about John. "But it is not as if I rushed into anything."

John smiled. No indeed, a more than three year courtship and six month engagement could hardly be called rushing in.

"I'm fine," she assured him.

"I believe you. In fact you look quite flushed with happiness."

Hannah blushed slightly so Margaret chose to move the conversation on.

"How were the highlands?" she asked.

"Oh, quite lovely and unspoiled. It's a very harsh climate up there but truly spectacular scenery."

They continued to chat amiably about the honeymoon, the house and Fanny until Daniel joined them about an hour later.

Unlike Hannah, Daniel had a few more funny stories, about

the kilts, or skirts as he called them, which the Scottish menfolk wore for special occasions and the rumours about what they did, or rather did not wear underneath. He also had a few things to say about the accent, likening it to being barked at by a rather large dog.

Hannah enjoyed his tales, as did John and Margaret, though he was surely embellishing greatly on the truth.

When they left, after having been persuaded to stay for supper, John felt much happier.

"I think she truly does love him," Margaret said on the carriage ride home.

"And he her," John agreed, though he didn't look happy.

Margaret understood how he felt. While he wanted the best for his mother, he would still miss her no matter how happy she was in her new life. Only time would heal the ache in his heart. Margaret reached out and took his hand. He smiled at her, though the rest of the journey home was made in silence.

Margaret had expected to have to wait for up to a month for a reply from Frederick but in the event she received a reply just fifteen days later, which Dixon brought up with her as she came to help Margaret get ready that morning.

"I knew you were waiting for this," she said, handing the letter over.

Margaret sat in front of her dressing table so Dixon could do her hair and opened the letter, which unusually was on the Barbour and Co. letterhead and forwent the usual preamble in favour of getting straight down to business.

Whilst Frederick's firm didn't trade in cotton, they did have contacts in Egypt and after making enquires on her behalf, he had managed to secure her a very good price on raw cotton from one of Egypt's best dealers. The only sign that this was a letter between siblings rather than business associates was the fact that Frederick had put a kiss after signing his name.

Much to Dixon's consternation since her hair was only half up, Margaret got up and went straight to the dining room where she found John reading the paper. She told him of the contents of her letter.

"That is a good price, not far off what we were paying three years ago," he agreed. "And you're sure the dealer is reputable?"

"It is someone called Mattheson, who only trades in Egypt's

best produce. Frederick deals with him regularly."

"I've heard of Mattheson. He doesn't trade much in cotton but he has a good reputation for fruit and vegetables."

"He hasn't said, but I get the feeling that Frederick has done everything he can to get us the lowest possible price and reduced the firm's shipping fees to a minimum."

"Then thank him for me," he said. "And write back today placing our first order."

Margaret nodded; she would reply as soon as she got into the office. She sat down at the table and laid her napkin on her lap, causing John to cock a quizzical eyebrow at her.

"What?" she asked.

John had half a mind not to tell her that her hair was only half done and that she had come downstairs in her night clothes; he thought he would enjoy her reaction when she realised but he couldn't be that cruel.

"I was just thinking what an interesting hairstyle that is. Are we too poor to afford a full head of hair clips?"

Margaret raised her hand to her hair and grinned as she realised what she had done.

"Perhaps I had better return to Dixon before sitting down to breakfast."

With all the poise and elegance of a lady dressed in the finest regalia, she got up from her chair and headed back upstairs. John chuckled to himself as he turned back to his paper. Only Margaret could look as regal as a princess while dressed in her night gown.

Chapter Thirty Five

When Elizabeth Hannah Thornton turned three years old, her parents threw her another birthday party on the Sunday after her birthday.

John and Margaret would much rather have celebrated on their own again but Hannah was so looking forward to seeing her grandchild that they felt compelled to hold a party for her, though they kept it small and asked for any presents to also be small. Bessy was indeed born blessed, but her parents didn't want her to become spoiled.

Invited to the party were Fanny, along with her husband and son; Hannah, Daniel and his sister Mary, who also brought her youngest grandchild who was just a month younger than Bessy. Mr. and Mrs. Maitland were also invited, though sadly Eleanor Maitland still had no grandchildren that she might have brought with her. Still, she seemed in good spirits and always enjoyed spending time with Bessy.

Fanny seemed just as she usually was but Margaret noticed that Watson looked thinner and slightly haggard.

The children played together and with Bill in the garden under Dixon and Jenny's watchful eyes while the parents seated themselves at the table that had been set out in the garden. Fanny was regaling the Maitlands with tales of the parties she had attended and the new dresses she had ordered from London. At points her husband looked quite unwell and Margaret surmised that he had told her nothing of his current financial difficulties.

After the children had played for a while they were brought to the table so that Bessy could open her presents. Thankfully everyone had kept their gifts relatively inexpensive. She received some hair ribbons in many different shades, a painting set (Margaret really wasn't looking forward to Bessy discovering how they worked!) a scarf and mitten set, two books and from the servants, some hand sewn clothes for her favourite doll.

Margaret thought them all lovely gifts and even the ones she was too young for would be welcomed before very much longer. Sometimes she could hardly believe her daughter was three years old. It seemed like only yesterday that she and John were discussing the possibility if having children while in Spain.

When Bessy had thanked everyone and Dixon had taken the

gifts away, the meal was served.

Fanny looked quite scandalised to think that the children would be eating with the adults.

"I've never heard the like in all my life!" she exclaimed.

Margaret looked at her son, Malcolm where he sat quietly beside his mother. Her heart ached for the boy to have to sit there and listen to his mother essentially say that she didn't want to be around him.

"I do not want to tell you what this dress cost!" Fanny continued. "What would happen if they spilled something on it? Who will pay for a new one?"

Margaret had heard enough and stood up.

"Mrs. Watson!"

John raised his eyebrows in surprise. Margaret usually only used someone's title if she was about to read them their fortune and right now he wouldn't wish himself in Fanny's shoes.

"You are at my daughters birthday party, or in other words, a celebration in honour of the birth of your niece. To suggest that she and her peers should not be present at her own celebration is just insulting and if you really dislike your own offspring so much, why don't you leave the poor boy here. I would be more than happy to show him the love and affection you seem to be so lacking in."

Fanny's jaw dropped open for a moment, then she gave a rather good impression of a fish for a few moments as she struggled to find her words.

"Watson, are you really going to let her speak to me like that?"

Watson looked as though he didn't have the energy for an argument but right at that moment he couldn't think of a way to avoid one.

"Mrs. Thornton, I'm afraid Fanny is right, that is hardly a ladylike manner of address."

"Who are you to tell me what is and is not ladylike?" Margaret asked, straightening her back even more and actually appearing to grow taller and more formidable. "I have met many people from the ruling classes and I have met many people from the working classes and I can tell you categorically that they all care for their children a great deal more than your wife appears to care for hers. Why even our country's monarch, Queen Victoria, who has just had her ninth child I might add, is said to adore her children so I can assure you, Mr. Watson, that the only unladylike behaviour here is your wife's."

Fanny stood up. "John!" she snapped, clearly looking for her brother to rush to her aid.

He simply shrugged since he agreed with Margaret.

"Well, I have never been so insulted in my life." Fanny stood up and, roughly grabbing her son's hand proceeded to drag him inside. "We are leaving! Watson, have the carriage prepared."

Margaret watched her leave and when she was out of sight, she closed her eyes and seemed to shrink.

"Oh dear," she said, sitting back down. "I did not handle that well at all."

Eleanor Maitland seemed to disagree as she began clapping. "Bravo!" she cried. "Perhaps that wasn't the most productive argument I have ever witnessed, but what you said was long overdue."

"Indeed," Mary Bristow agreed. "She has brought that poor boy to the house to see his grandmother on a few occasions now and I have never seen her speak a work to him that isn't a reprimand. And to be quite frank, a better behaved boy I have never seen. Why he does not even speak unless prompted."

Hannah Thornton looked upset by the whole display but she nodded at Margaret, letting her know that she bore no ill feeling towards her. Margaret suddenly wondered how she must feel about Malcolm. Margaret was just his aunt but Hannah was his grandmother.

"Perhaps we should return to the meal," John suggested. "Unless Margaret has anything else she would like to get off her chest?" He turned to her looking quizzical.

"Mind your tongue or you will be my next target," she teased, though her heart wasn't in it. She had just dressed Fanny down in public, which would surely do nothing to endear Malcolm to her. In fact she might even blame the boy for it, though Margaret knew she would receive the lion's share of Fanny's anger.

Still, she needed to try and mend bridges. When everyone left she resolved to write to Fanny and try to smooth over their troubled relationship.

Fanny Watson wasn't a stupid woman by any means but she had never had any real need of her intelligence and thus it had lain fallow ever since she was a girl.

She didn't remember much of the hardships her family had to endure when she was young but because both mother and son felt guilty that she had been deprived of the life and wealth she had been born to, as soon as money did become more plentiful, a good deal of it was spent on her.

Her dresses, her music lessons, her education (such as it was) had all been freely given. Her weekly allowance was higher than that of her peers and any tantrums she might have thrown were dealt with kindly since both her brother and mother could vividly remember her tears when as a small girl, she had cried because she was so hungry.

As such, with her almost every whim indulged, she had grown up selfish, foolish and with very little insight into herself. She believed that all she had to do was look pretty and act in a ladylike manner and the world would give her everything she wanted.

However, that didn't mean that she lacked any insight and Margaret's words had stung her so because they had hit home.

She remembered the years just after she had married Watson, when she had longed for a child but was never successful. She would dream about holding him in her arms and singing him to sleep. How very different that picture had been from reality. After nine months of discomfort and twelve hours of pain she was presented with a pink, wrinkled thing that cried almost constantly.

Fanny had been more than happy to leave him in the care of his wet nurse. She did try to love him in the beginning because she felt that she must, and so every day she would go to the nursery and look at him. She tried holding him, she tried singing to him, she tried reading to him, but Malcolm never did anything but cry.

Not long after giving birth, Fanny had come down with an assortment of illnesses and Dr. Donaldson had assigned strict bed rest. By then Fanny had so little energy that she didn't mind staying in her bed. In the end it had taken her three months to recover her health enough to leave her bedroom, and even longer for her to fully recover her strength, none of which had helped her to forge a bond with her son.

However, even though she didn't much care for him, Fanny wanted to do right by him and only the best would do for her boy. She hired the best nanny, bought him the best toys, the newest books and when he was old enough he was to attend the best boarding school money could buy. Unfortunately, none of this increased the affection she felt for him. As he grew older the nanny would bring him to see her but he didn't do anything. When he was old enough to speak he would babble something she couldn't understand when prompted to but that was hardly endearing. It sometimes seemed to Fanny that he didn't have a personality, he was so placid at times.

She knew that she should feel something for him, and at times she wished she did, but her overwhelming emotion when forced to spend time with him was irritation.

Watson wasn't much better but he did seem to have a bond with the boy, at least until recent months. Almost since Christmas he had been rather more withdrawn than usual, working longer hours and at times almost monosyllabic when he was home. He had even lost most of his interest in marital relations, which Fanny couldn't honestly say she was sorry about but it did strike her as odd.

Margaret Hale was like her own personal demon, sent to remind Fanny of everything she lacked. Whereas Fanny worked hard to appear ladylike and elegant, Margaret simply was those things. While Margaret had only a few friends, they were very close relationships, while Fanny had many friends but no one she could really confide in. Where Margaret clearly loved her daughter with all her heart, Fanny simply couldn't love her son, and whereas Watson wanted Fanny's body, it was clear from his every action that John truly adored his wife, mind, body and soul.

But that was where Fanny's insight stopped, at her own failings. She was unable to look deeper and wonder why she did not have those things. She wasn't able to look at her personality and wonder if perhaps she attracted the wrong sort of friends. While she sometimes wondered if she had made the right decision in marrying Watson, whether or not she loved him, or indeed if he loved her, were not things she considered.

The carriage ride home was largely silent. Fanny tried to provoke a reaction from Watson but he seemed too tired to argue with her. At times she had wondered if he was ill but when she questioned him, he pushed her concerns aside. If something ever should happen to him she knew that Malcolm would inherit everything. She was sure her brother would look after the mill for them until her son was of age so that she and

Malcolm could continue to live in comfort. As such, the idea of Watson dying didn't frighten her very much at all, though Fanny would sorely miss being a wife and having someone to accompany her about town.

As their carriage pulled up outside their townhouse, Fanny looked at her son where he sat opposite her, next to his father. Perhaps if she had been blessed with a daughter like Margaret, it would have been easier to love him, but she supposed that unless Watson wanted to resume marital relations, something she had no intention of pushing for, she would probably never know.

The tipping point for Watson came at the end of August that year. Although he was seeing very little, or more accurately, no return on his investment in the American railroad system, up until that point, he did still have a stake in the Lewis and Western Railroad.

In August though, to add to America's existing financial crisis, the Ohio Life and Trust company went under due to the fraudulent activities of its management. The knock-on effect was unavoidable and its failure threatened to cause a run on other banks. The incident also brought the poor financial status of the railroads to the public attention, further undermining their position.

On the 30th of August, the Lewis and Western Railroad Company declared bankruptcy.

Chapter Thirty Six

Every Friday, after Mary had finished serving the third lunch sitting, Margaret always shared a meal with the girl. Of course she was no longer a girl. Nearing her twenty second year now, she cut a fine figure of a woman. Higgins's rise to the position of overseer also meant that she was able to keep herself better and her clothes, though far from being as fine as Margaret's, were much nicer and better kept. She smiled as she saw Margaret enter and, pulling her house coat off, she came around the counter with two hot bowls of stew and fresh bread on a tray. True to form, there was also a small bowl of stew for Bill who, as usual, lay on the ground beside Margaret. Never having been allowed a pet of her own, Mary loved spoiling Bill whenever she saw the mutt.

Margaret poured them both a glass of water from the jug on the table and thanked Mary as she set the plates down.

"How are you keeping?" Margaret asked.

Strangely Mary looked a little coy. She had always been a shy and quiet girl but she had warmed up to Margaret over the years so to see her so nervous again was slightly disconcerting.

"Mary?"

"I have... well you see, there's this lad wot' works in t' mill. Sam."

Margaret smiled. Young love, of course!

"And you and Sam are courting?" she asked.

"Oh, no! Well, maybe." Mary frowned. "What I mean is, he's asked me to go t' harvest festival dance wiv 'im."

"Then even though this will be your first engagement, you are indeed being courted, Mary." she smiled. "So what is he like?"

Mary waxed lyrical on the boy for a good half an hour and it was clear to Margaret that although he had only just asked her out, Mary had probably 'been sweet on him' (as Mary might say) for some time.

Margaret left then, pleased that her offer to help Mary do her hair before the dance had been accepted. She also might have an old shawl or two that Mary might borrow so that she looked and felt her best, and Margaret resolved to have a look this evening.

She had just stepped out from the canteen, when she spotted Fanny being helped down from her carriage and entering the offices. Even from the distance of fifty or so meters, Margaret could clearly see that something had distressed her. Fanny did not seem to have noticed her.

She sighed deeply, for she had been reading the newspapers and there could be only one reason for her visit. As much as Fanny might irritate Margaret sometimes, she truly had no desire to see her hurt.

She headed back to the office, with Bill trailing behind her, and cornered Thomas, asking him to run to the house and ask that afternoon tea be prepared for Mr. Thornton and his sister. Then, knowing that Fanny probably would not want to see her right now, she wrote a hurried note and asked Alice to knock on Mr. Thonrton's door and hand him the note. Poor Alice was the newest recruit to the offices and easily the most frightened of the master, though since she was the only other person around right now, Margaret had no other options but to ask her.

Margaret retreated to her office and closed the door.

John watched as his sister sat down with as much dignity as she could muster under the circumstances.

John had never really liked nor disliked Watson. He could be amiable company at times, but he was also prone to use underhand methods which made John question his character but still, he was far from being a bad person. At least that's what John had always thought before now. As he watched his sister dab her tear-filled eyes, he hated Watson with an intensity he didn't know he had.

John had been expecting a visit like this of course; he just hadn't expected Watson to get his wife to do the dirty work.

As mean-spirited and selfish as his sister could sometimes be, John still didn't like to see her in distress. He went around the desk and pulled her into his arms. Fanny broke down then, losing all semblance of control as she sobbed on his shoulder.

John heard a gentle tap on the door and called for them to come in, though he didn't release Fanny and Alice, looking scared out of her wits, handed him a note and beat a hasty retreat. John opened the note and read it over Fanny's shoulder. It said that Margaret had arranged for tea at the house if he wanted to take Fanny somewhere more private.

He held Fanny for a few more minutes until her sobs began to subside, then he pulled away and looked down at her.

"Come back to the house," he said, handing her his handkerchief to wipe her eyes with. "We can talk there."

Fanny nodded. As yet she hadn't said a single word.

John helped Fanny outside and into her carriage and they rode in silence back to the house. He kept his arm about her shoulders until they arrived and once again he helped her down and then into the house. The maid was clever enough not to offer to take their coats but simply tell them that tea had been laid out in the parlour, before disappearing.

John guided Fanny into the room and sat her down, then prepared her a cup of sweet tea which he handed to her.

"Thank you," Fanny said, her voice so quiet it was almost inaudible. She look a long sip of tea, as though to fortify herself, then put her cup and saucer down and began her story, though she kept her eyes firmly focused on her tea cup. "I suppose you know why I am here?"

"I can guess," John said, "but why did Watson not come?"

"He felt that you would be more inclined to listen to me."

"You've only just learned of this, haven't you?" he asked kindly.

"He told me yesterday." She nodded.

"I'm sorry." John reached out and placed his hand over hers where it rested on her lap.

Fanny swallowed and for a moment it looked like she might cry again, but she managed to keep her composure.

"So what did he send you here for?" John asked gently. He wasn't being mean but Watson could want anything, like lodgings, a job or simply money. When she didn't answer, he gently squeezed her hand. "You can tell me."

Fanny glanced at his face briefly and though she looked away again, she must have been pleased by what she saw there because she continued.

"The bank has foreclosed on the house and the mill. We will lose everything, John."

"What can I do?"

"Watson..." Here she hesitated, possibly remembering that when John's business had been forced to close its doors, Watson had offered John no help at all. "Watson would like you to lend him some money."

"No." John said firmly. He and Margaret had discussed a few options last night after they had heard of the railroad going bankrupt. They hadn't reached many conclusions but they had agreed on not lending Watson money. "I have discussed this with Margaret-"

"Her!" She pulled her hand out of John's grip. "What does she have to do with this?"

"Everything. Margaret is my business partner and the money you are asking to borrow is in fact hers."

"No wonder she won't help, then."

"We want to help, Fanny, truly we do but it comes down to this. I will not lend money to someone who has already gambled with money he didn't have."

"But John, we will lose everything! How can you deny me, I'm your sister!" Her tears began to fall again, large, fat droplets formed on her lower lashes before cascading down her cheeks. She had always been good at eliciting guilt in him.

"I'm sorry, we will help in any other way we can but we can't just hand over cash."

"Why not; Margaret did to you? She gave you eighteen thousand pounds!"

"No, she invested eighteen thousand pounds in the mill because she trusted me not to fritter it away."

"Oh, John, why must you be so stubborn." Fanny wiped at her eyes. "We will be destitute. I'll be thrown out in the street and probably end up in the workhouse," she cried.

"Don't be so dramatic, of course you won't."

"But the bank is taking our house and the mill, our livelihood!"

"Fanny, Margaret and I don't have piles of cash lying around. The money we have is for this project and the profits we make we reinvest in the mill and village."

"You could help us if you wanted."

"Aye. I could also burn handfuls of cash; that would have the same result as giving it to Watson."

"But there is an investment that could solve all our problems."

"Another speculation?" he almost spat the last word, such was his distaste. "Has he learned nothing? And what about you, Fanny? Surely you realise that our father's speculations ruined our family when you were a child, now Watson has ruined himself the same way, and you want me to lend you money so that he might speculate again?"

"Please John!" she reached out and grabbed his hand. "Please! I don't know what will become of us if you don't help me."

Though it broke his heart to have to turn her down, he knew he must. "I will help, of course I will. I shall do everything in my power to find Watson a position and you can stay with us for as long as you'd like, but that's all I can do."

Fanny remained silent for a long while, a frown marring her features and John wondered what she was thinking.

"He lied to me," she said eventually. "He said this speculation was a sure thing and then when things did go wrong, he still lied to me. I kept asking what was wrong but he wouldn't tell me anything."

"I'm sorry."

"He's my husband. Isn't there some law or vow that says you mustn't lie to your wife?"

"Even if there were, you know it wouldn't be enforceable."

"I can't believe I married such a man. I was so foolish." She dabbed at her eyes again. "He doesn't love me, you know?"

"Do you love him?" John asked, surprising her. He knew exactly what she was angling for.

Fanny took a moment to consider which answer he would believe. "Not any more."

"Fanny, I will take you home now to collect your things, but you can't come and live here without Watson. He is your husband and you agreed to marry him, you can't back out of it now just because it's inconvenient. There might not be a vow that makes you promise to be honest, but I know there is one that says 'for richer or for poorer'."

Fanny pouted and began to sip her tea again. John could almost hear her thinking as she wondered what tactic to try next. Her usual arsenal of tears and guilt hadn't worked. If he'd been a betting man, John would have placed ten pounds on Fanny having a fainting spell next and sadly, he would have been right.

Fanny put her tea down. "I should be going." she said, getting to her feet.

"You don't have to," John assured her. "You can stay here for as long as you'd like."

"Well, we still have a home right now, so I suppose I should enjoy it for as long as I can."

John stood up to accompany her out but Fanny hadn't taken two paces when she swooned and fell back towards him. He knew she was pretending because her muscles were rigid. He would never forget the time when Margaret had fainted while she was pregnant, and he vividly remembered how lifeless she felt as he carried her inside. Fanny was all together too controlled to be unconscious.

Nevertheless, John gently lowered her body to the floor and knelt down beside her.

"Fanny?" he called gently.

Her eyelids fluttered theatrically for a moment before she opened her eyes.

"Oh!" she cried before sitting up. "Whatever happened."

"You collapsed," he said, choosing not to use the word faint.

"I fainted? Well, I suppose I am under a lot of strain, it's hardly surprising, given my delicate constitution."

"You didn't faint exactly. It looked more like you fell."

Fanny frowned. "And what exactly am I supposed to have fallen over?" she asked indignantly.

John shrugged and helped her to her feet.

"Do you think you can make it to mother's house in the carriage?" he asked her once she was standing again.

"Mother's? What makes you think I'm going to see Mother?"

"Because you want her to talk me into loaning Watson some money," he answered simply. "But even if you do get her to agree to try, the answer will still be no. Maybe you'd be best to go home and tell Watson to do his own dirty work next time."

Fanny looked outraged. Unable to think of a suitable reply, she stormed out of the room, slamming the door behind her.

Thankfully her carriage was still waiting in the driveway but as she went to climb in, she saw Margaret and her dog walking up the driveway towards the house. Fanny turned towards her.

"I suppose you're enjoying this?" she called out to the other woman.

Margaret waited until she was closer before responding since she didn't wish to start an argument in public.

"Fanny, I am very sorry about what has happened and I hope you will believe that it gives me no pleasure."

"Don't take me for some kind of simpleton. You might have John fooled but I see what you really are; you're a spiteful, mean old hag!" She turned to the carriage and climbed in.

"Fanny, please, I do not wish you any ill will and John and I will do everything we can to help you."

"Ha! That's not what John said. He told me that you are the reason he won't lend Watson money. You!"

"I don't believe you," Margaret answered; she knew Fanny was just lashing out in frustration. "We discussed the options together and he would never have said it was my decision because we both agreed on that point."

Fanny turned away as though Margaret was suddenly distasteful.

"Driver, drive on!" she called.

Margaret stood in the driveway and watched until the carriage was out of sight, her heart heavy. Finally she turned and went into the house. John was in the parlour and was pouring them both tea from a fresh pot he had asked for. Margaret slumped into the seat beside him and gratefully took the cup as Bill settled herself in her usual spot by the fire.

"Don't let her get to you," John said, sensing Margaret's bleak mood.

"Maybe we were wrong," Margaret looked at him. "She is family after all, so maybe we should loan Watson some money."

"And watch him fritter it away?"

"Maybe he won't, surely he has learned his lesson."

"Fanny said he wants the money for an investment that will restore his wealth."

"Oh no," Margaret sighed.

John reached out and took her hand.

"We have not yet considered the wider implications of the railroad going bankrupt," John said. "Watson invested the most but he was not the only one in Milton to do so."

"Are there others now in difficulty too?" Margaret asked, for she knew that many of the other investors were fellow mill owners and she was worried for the other mills.

"Hopefully they will not have over-extended themselves as Watson did, but it's too soon to tell what the long term effect on Milton will be."

Margaret sipped her tea and tried to ignore the feeling of foreboding that came over her at John's statement.

Chapter Thirty Seven

It took Watson a further two days before he felt pressured enough to approach John himself. Since it was a Sunday, Watson went straight to Rose Cottage and, hat in hand, knocked on the door.

John and Margaret were playing in the garden with Bessy and Bill when he arrived, enjoying one of the last days of summer while they could. As Jane came out to tell them of his arrival, Margaret offered to keep Bessy while he spoke with Watson.

"You should be there," John insisted. "Any decisions made will effect you, be it loaning them money or asking them to move in here."

Margaret nodded. Though she had no desire to see Mr. Watson at his lowest ebb, John was right and she should be involved in the decision-making process.

John picked Bessy up and handed her to Jane, asking the girl to take her to Dixon or Jenny while John and Margaret went to speak with Watson.

Watson was standing in the middle of the study-cum-library when they joined him. He looked surprised to see Margaret accompanying John but he didn't say anything. Their unusual marriage was well known and he thought that he might alienate John should he ask Margaret to leave.

"Thornton, Mrs. Thornton," he nodded at each of them. "It's good to see you both again."

John gestured to the sofa and chairs that were grouped around the fireplace. Watson sat in one of the armchairs while John and Margaret both sat on the sofa.

Margaret took the opportunity to look closely at Watson and found that he looked even worse than he had at Bessy's birthday party. His face was almost gaunt now and the circles under his eyes were so dark that they almost looked like bruises. Despite everything, Margaret felt a great deal of pity for him.

"What can we do for you?" John asked, somehow managing to keep a civil tongue in his head, in spite of Watson trying to use Fanny to get money out of him.

"I think you know why I'm here," he said.

"If you've come to ask for money, the answer is still no." John said since he didn't want to see the man beg.

"I know. Fanny told me that you were adamant but she also

said that you would help us."

"We will try."

"Thank you." He paused then and looked down at the hat he was still holding so tightly that his knuckles were turning white. "The mill closed yesterday. It will not reopen again tomorrow." That admission seemed to cause him some anguish. "I have also missed a few mortgage payments and as of tomorrow, the house will belong to the bank. We will be homeless."

"You and Fanny are welcome to come and stay with us," Margaret assured him.

"Thank you." Watson swallowed. "She also said something about helping me get a position."

"I'll do what I can," John promised. "I take it you have no other resources you can call on?"

"Just the house and mill which I used as security for the loans. The bank owns both now and they will be sold at a loss so that the bank can recoup some of its money."

"I'm sorry," Margaret said honestly. "I wish there were more we could do."

Watson looked for a moment as though he might say something foolish but he quickly thought better and looked away.

"What of the workers?" Margaret asked.

"What of them?" Watson answered.

"Well, I assume they are now unemployed but are their wages paid up? Are there jobs available at the other mills?"

"The workers will go down as another creditor," Watson said, sounding irritated. "Though there's little hope of them getting paid now."

His disinterest in the plight of his workers angered Margaret. It was his foolish actions which meant that they were now owed money and unemployed. For the sake of civility though, she held her tongue. If she was going to live with Fanny and Watson, it wouldn't do to have bad blood between them. Well, certainly no more than there already was.

She could see that John also wasn't pleased with Watson's answer but like her he kept quiet. The silence began to grow uncomfortable.

"When will you be moving in?" John asked.

"Well, tomorrow, if that's agreeable."

"It is." John stood up so Watson follow suit. The men shook

hands and after a rather curt goodbye from each, Watson left.

John sat back down and looked at Margaret.

"Is there no way we can expand early?" Margaret asked her husband. "Surely Watson's machines will be auctioned off cheaply. We could buy them and expand a little early."

"But the housing is far from ready for an expansion like that."

"I know," Margaret sighed. "The seven hundred houses that are currently being built won't be finished until the end of next year."

"That's a long time; the families can't last that long with no wages coming in."

"Well the machinery will surely only take up one floor, we could turn one of the other buildings into a dormitory for them," Margaret suggested.

"The mill wasn't built to house people and families," John said sensibly. "There are no facilities and with all those people crowded into one space, life would likely be no better than in the slums of Milton."

Margaret couldn't disagree with him.

"What if they were to walk here? I know it's a long walk but surely that's better than nothing. At least we can offer them the jobs and it's their choice to take it or not."

"When the alternative is starvation, that's not much of a choice." he said. "Plus, we don't have the orders to expand yet."

"Then we could take over Watson's unfilled orders."

That gave John an idea.

"Or we could buy the whole mill at auction," he suggested. "It would put a serious dent in our finances, but on the plus side it will increase our turnover."

"But that money is to expand our mill and the village."

The houses currently being built were the third stage of the project. The fourth, or final phase of building work was the largest planned at over a thousand houses, which would then take the population of the village up to around four thousand, quadruple what it was at present.

"Aye, and buying the mill would delay the final phase of building for at least five years, maybe longer."

"But we would still have the funds to complete the current phase?"

"We should do. It depends how much the mill goes for at

auction but in our favour, lots of people have been hit by this speculation; I don't think we'd have much competition to buy it."

"Oh, what a mess." Margaret sighed. "Whatever we do, there doesn't seem to be an ideal solution."

"Aye," he agreed sadly.

John put his arm around her shoulder and pulled her to him. Margaret settled against him and he kissed the top of her head. They sat like that for a while, each lost in their own thoughts. Eventually the door opened and Bessy came toddling in with Dixon in her wake.

"I'm sorry, Miss Margaret, Master, but she was adamant that she wanted to see you."

"Don't worry, Dixon." John said. "Why don't you have a rest until after dinner, we'll look after Bessy."

Dixon was about to argue but Margaret looked over at her and shook her head. Sensing that they were troubled, Dixon retreated to the nursery where she had a little darning put aside to do when she had a moment.

Margaret sat up as John reached down and scooped Bessy onto his lap, then she settled back against him.

"Daddy, why are you and Mummy sad?" Bessy asked. Her language skills had improved a lot over the past few months, though some of her pronunciation still required some work.

"Because your Aunt Fanny is in trouble," he tried to explain in terms she might understand.

"Was she naughty?" Bessy asked.

"No," John smiled at her simplistic view of the world. "Her husband lost some money, and it's causing a lot of problems."

"Have they looked for it?" she asked.

"They have," he assured her.

"Did they look under the bed? I lost my bear once and I was sad, but Dixon found him under the bed."

John and Margaret smiled at her.

"Yes, sweetheart, they looked under the bed."

Bessy frowned, considering the problem. "Maybe we can help them look," she suggested.

Margaret smiled. "We already have, darling, but it's no good. Tomorrow your aunt and uncle are coming to stay with us for a while and they're bringing Malcolm; won't that be lovely? You'll have a playmate."

"Can he stay in my room?" she asked.

Margaret sat up and looked at John, who shrugged.

"I suppose so, if you'd like him to. Now, it will be dinner time soon and if you're a very good girl and eat everything on your plate, we might just be able to talk Daddy into reading us another chapter of The Snow Queen."

"Will you, Daddy? Will you please?"

"Only if you're a good girl, as Mummy said."

"Yay!" Bessy cheered and waved her arms.

"That's not very ladylike," Margaret said, trying to hide her smile.

Bessy stopped immediately, folded her hands in her lap and sat completely still, offering the sweetest smile she could muster.

John and Margaret laughed.

"Come on, sweetheart," John put Bessy on the ground. "Go and wash up ready for dinner."

Margaret followed her out to make sure she did a good job and John could hear her chattering about the Snow Queen all the way along the hall.

Dinner was a fairly subdued affair but thankfully Bessy injected some life into the proceedings. Though she wasn't a demanding child, well no more than most, something about Bessy commanded their attention no matter what other troubles might be weighing on their minds.

At the moment Bessy was having a hard time learning to use her knife and fork properly and made sure that everyone knew it. Margaret assured her that all it would take was more practice, while John offered to buy her some chopsticks so she could eat like the Chinese. After he'd explained exactly what chopsticks were, Bessy thought that a laughable idea but stopped complaining so much about her English cutlery.

After dinner Margaret took Bessy upstairs and Dixon got her ready for bed. Once she was tucked under the covers, John and Margaret came in. Margaret sat on the floor beside the bed and held Bessy's hand while John, after kissing her goodnight in case she fell asleep on him, settled in the chair by her bed and opened the children's books he had brought up with him. Bill settled herself in the doorway, as though guarding the family moment from unwanted intruders.

"Right, where did we get to?" he asked Bessy, though the page was bookmarked.

"Gerda met the reindeer," she reminded him.

"Oh yes, that's right, and what did the reindeer tell her?"

"That he knows where Kai is because it's where he lives." She was getting impatient.

"And where does he live?" John prompted.

"Lapland, and before you ask that's in the north pole."

John smiled and began reading to his daughter.

Though she tried to stay awake as long as possible to hear if Gerda managed to rescue Kai, eventually Bessy could keep her eyes open no longer and drifted off to sleep. John put the book down and Margaret moved over by his feet, resting her head on his knee as they watched her sleep for a few moments.

With a gentle tap on her shoulder, John let her know that it was time to go and they silently left Bessy to sleep. Margaret went to their bedroom with Bill in tow while John headed downstairs; when he joined her a few minutes later he had the brandy decanter and two glasses with him.

Though it was still quite early, Margaret had changed into her night clothes so that she might feel more relaxed and John followed suit. They sat in the chairs by the fire and although it was still too early in the year for it to be very built up, it bathed them in a gentle warmth.

"So, any more thoughts?" Margaret asked as he handed her a glass of brandy. She didn't decline it.

John shook his head.

"So basically," Margaret began. "Our options are, either we buy Watson's equipment, expand the mill before the housing is built and let the workers walk here every day. That has the benefit that the housing project could still be finished according to plan, although it gives the new workers a ten mile round trip from the Princeton district ever day. The other option is to buy Watson's mill outright, meaning that the workers will have employment close to home, but still live in miserable conditions. Plus it has the downside that it will put our building plans back by many years."

"That about sums it up," he agreed.

"Is this a choice we can make?" she asked. "All these lives, do we really have the right to play God with them?"

"We aren't playing God," he assured her. "We're trying to improve their lot."

"I know, but maybe we should ask which option they might prefer?"

"Or we carry on with our existing plan to build the village, thereby lifting not only Watson's workers from poverty but others in Milton too. The final stage of our expansion will change the lives of well over a thousand people. Do we really have the right to delay that because some of the workers would have to walk to work for a year or more?"

He had a good point; by buying the mill, they would be relegating those final fifteen hundred or so employees to years more living in dismal conditions.

"Plus," John added. "If we do take over Watson's, you know that he will want to be reinstated as master."

"I would not mind that so much, as long as we made sure that he was fair with his workers," she admitted. "Although overall I think the better option is to expand our mill before the houses are finished. It will make life harder for the workers for a while but long term it will make things better for more people. And I can talk to Mr. Anderson and see if he can complete the current work any faster."

"Good idea," John said, reaching out for her hand and smiling warmly at her. "Are you sure you don't mind having Fanny here?"

"She is family, we cannot turn her away."

"I know," he sighed. "I just hope she keeps a civil tongue in her head and stops with her snide remarks."

"We will cope." She squeezed his hand. "And besides, if the worst come to the worst, our bedroom door locks!"

"Is that all you ever think about," he chided with a smile, though he would be prepared to bet that he thought about it a good deal more than she.

"Well, if you didn't make it so enjoyable, then I would probably be more virtuous."

"So your wantonness is my fault?"

"Oh yes, absolutely."

"And who am I to blame for the desire you ignite in me?"

"Well that, of course, is down to your male urges, it is nothing to do with me."

"Well then," John withdrew his hand from hers and rested his chin on it as though he was thinking. "Perhaps I had better visit Malmaison and engage the services of one of their young ladies."

Margaret got up and went to sit on his knee.

"You wouldn't dare," she taunted.

"Oh? Why not?"

Margaret turned serious and cupped his face in her hands.

"Because you love me too much to risk catching something and passing it on to me." She leaned down and kissed him softly, almost reverently.

John smiled. She was right, again.

"I that case, I believe that leaves only you who can sate my carnal urges."

Margaret smiled, moved her hands from his face to rest on his shoulders and leaned forward to kiss his neck.

"Only a wanton woman would know how to do that." John moaned with pleasure.

She paused momentarily in her ministrations.

"Well you taught me."

"Exactly," he agreed. Margaret could hear the smile in his voice.

Chapter Thirty Eight

Because of the bad feeling between Margaret and Fanny, John thought it better if Margaret stayed at the mill in the morning while he took care of Fanny and Watson as they settled in. A second bed was moved into Bessy's room which, though more than large enough for two beds, did require a toy trunk and a book case to be moved around. The largest spare bedroom, which had belonged to his mother, was then made up for Fanny and Watson.

The Watsons arrived at eleven that morning with trunk after trunk of belongings, and more was still to come, according to Watson. John thought that some of it might have to be stored at the mill if there was much more. Jane, who had always been Fanny's favourite servant when she lived at home thanks to their shared love of gossip, was asked to help with the unpacking. Since they didn't have a nanny with them, John took the opportunity to steal Bessy and Malcolm away and take them up to the mill. They were both too young to see inside the mill yet but John thought he could show Malcolm the offices and warehouses.

Margaret's face lit up as all three came into her office, each child holding one of John's hands

"Oh, my word, what have I done to deserve all these lovely visitors?" she asked, kissing each of the three in turn.

As expected, Malcolm didn't answer.

"We wanted to see you, Mummy," Bessy answered for them all.

Margaret smiled; no one could ever accuse Bessy of being shy.

"Well I'm very glad that you wanted to see me, darling, for it lights up my day to see your smiling face." She bent down so her face was close to Malcolm's. "And you, my dear. What a lovely surprise it is to see you. Are you looking forward to living with us?"

Malcolm nodded.

"I thought I'd give them a tour of the place," John explained.

"That sounds like a wonderful idea. May I join you?"

"It will be our pleasure," John smiled.

"Yes," Bessy seconded. "Our treasure!"

Margaret smiled and bent over to pick Malcolm up and place him on her hip. John did the same with Bessy and they headed out to the mill with Bill bringing up the rear.

As John pointed various things out to the children, Margaret held Malcolm tightly and although it took a few minutes, eventually he put his arms around her neck and clung on tightly. He stayed like that for a while so Margaret spent most of the tour with her back to John and Bessy so that Malcolm could see what John was talking about over her shoulder.

When they reached the raw cotton shed, Bessy wanted to get down and began jumping on the bales.

"Careful," Margaret admonished. "I don't want you to get hurt."

"Yes, Mummy."

Margaret put Malcolm down to see if he wanted to join in but he stayed where he was. John went up to Bessy and, taking her hands, he helped her to jump up and down. Margaret followed suit with Malcolm, though it took a fair deal longer for him to start jumping on his own. Eventually though he began to smile and put some effort into jumping.

They stayed in the shed for a long time because Margaret had never seen Malcolm so animated before and she wanted it to continue for as long as possible. It was Bessy who called a halt to things in the end by complaining that she was hungry, so they headed back to the house to share lunch with their new house guests.

Margaret was surprised to be greeted by Jenny rather than Jane but it soon became clear that Fanny had thrown most of the household into chaos. Though she wasn't usually one to gossip, Jenny felt she should give them some warning of what had been going on in their absence.

"I'm sorry to have to be the one to tell you this, but Mrs. Watson was insistent that she have her own room so Mr. Watson has been moved into the room next to yours. Dixon is in her rooms, quite put out over something that Mrs. Watson said to her, and though she will not tell me what was said, I think she was very hurt. Jane has been commandeered to help Mrs. Watson with anything she requires and the kitchen have been given special instructions for all the meals, which cook seems quite up in arms about."

"Thank you, Jenny, we will take care of it." John gave a weary sigh.

"I'll go and speak with Dixon," Margaret said. "Why don't you see what has cook so upset?"

John nodded and Jenny took the children as they both headed to their respective tasks.

In the kitchen John found the cook muttering under her breath as she worked.

"And what with people starving in the streets, it's just a waste of good food, that is. Nothing wrong with the lunch I made. Why I'd have been happy to serve that to Queen Victoria herself, I would-"

"Mrs. Baker?" He said from the kitchen doorway.

She turned to him, looking ready for a fight until she realised who had addressed her.

"Oh, Master. I'm sorry, it's been quite a morning around here."

"So I've heard. What seems to be the problem with you?"

"Oh, 'tis nothing, Master."

"Yes it is," he stepped further into the kitchen. "Tell me what Fanny has been doing?"

"It's the meals," cook admitted. "She says that she is very delicate at the moment and that she cannot eat dairy produce of any kind, so now I must throw what I was preparing for lunch away and I must not use it in any meals from now on. How am I supposed to cook without using butter, milk, cream or eggs?" she asked.

John nodded, that was a tall order indeed. "Well, the way I see it we have two choices. One, you can cook Fanny a separate meal from the rest of us without those ingredients. I'm betting one glance at the rest of us eating your amazing bechamel sauce would be enough to change her mind. Or the other option is to just ignore her. Use dairy products as you would normally but tell her you have made substitutions if she asks you."

"But that's hardly honest, master."

"No," he agreed with a smile. "But then I doubt there's any truth to Fanny's supposed allergy to dairy products. I lived with her for nineteen years and I never saw any ill effects."

"Aye, well happen Jane would tell her if we tried option two, so I'll just make Mrs. Watson her own meals. Sommat like Mrs. T had to eat while she were with child."

Remembering how much Margaret had hated that bland diet, John laughed.

"I think that sounds grand, Mrs. Baker." He turned to leave but stopped in the door and turned back. "And remember, I'm master of this house, not Fanny. If you have any more problems, come and see me."

"I will, Master. Lunch will be served in ten minutes."

John nodded and left. He knew his sister could be demanding but he hoped this was just a reaction to the embarrassment she had suffered and the changes she had been forced to endure. If so, he dearly hoped that she would calm down soon. A good servant was worth their weight in gold and John would be loathe to lose any of his current household staff.

"Very well, don't tell me," Margaret said. "I shan't force it out of you but know this, you are my lady's maid, Dixon, mine and no one else's. For the duration of Fanny's stay, you will answer only to me and Mr. Thornton, do you understand?"

Dixon smiled and nodded, knowing that although Margaret was giving her an order, she was only doing it to save Dixon having to obey Fanny's demands.

Margaret reached over and took Dixon's hand.

"Whatever it was she said, I'm truly sorry if she hurt you."

"Oh, it was nothing really," Dixon brushed her concerns aside, though Margaret could tell that Fanny's words had cut deeply.

"I hope that's true. Now, I have to return to the house and welcome our new house guests," she said with very little enthusiasm. "Why don't you stay out here this afternoon? I'll have Jenny bring a nice pot of tea for you to share and after lunch, you two can watch the children in here if you'd prefer. I'm sure Fanny would never deign to enter the servants quarters so you should manage a pleasant afternoon."

"Well, that sounds lovely, Miss Margaret. Thank you."

"No thanks necessary. You are a godsend, Dixon, and I will do everything in my power to make sure you are afforded the respect you deserve."

"Thank you." Dixon squeezed Margaret's hand as she blinked back tears. There had been many points in her life when she had wondered if she'd made the wrong choice in not having her own family so that she could stay on with the Hales. At times like this though, she knew she had made the right decision, for a more loyal family could not be found.

"Just one more thing before I go," Margaret said. "I would like to try and bring Malcolm out of his shell a little. We were playing on the cotton bales this morning and I swear that is the first time I have ever heard him laugh. I would like to hear more of it, if possible."

"I'm sure that between me and Jenny, we can devote some time to the lad without upsetting Miss Elizabeth." Dixon smiled.

"Thank you," Margaret smiled and then took her leave as, with a heavy heart, she headed back to her house.

She entered the dining room to find John already waiting and Jenny settling Bessy into her chair. Malcolm was on John's lap since he didn't have his own chair yet, though the boy looked very uncomfortable with the situation.

"Perhaps Malcolm would be more comfortable in Bessy's chair," Margaret suggested.

Bessy certainly liked that idea and began to wriggle until Jenny let her down. She ran to her father, eager to eat her lunch on his knee, while Jenny settled Malcolm into the recently vacated chair and pushed it up to the table.

"The gardener's already made a start on a second chair," Jenny informed them. "It's not too pretty, he says, but he hopes to have it sanded and varnished by the end of the week."

Their gardener happened to have a bit of a talent for woodworking, something he'd learned from his uncle as a boy. He had made Bessy's chair after Jenny explained the trouble she was having balancing Bessy on cushions so that she was at the right height to eat from the dining table. Though he claimed his work wasn't pretty, and perhaps it wasn't ornamental, it was functional and well finished, which was more than enough for Margaret.

Knowing that the Watsons would likely be with them for some time, she had asked him if he might be able to complete another chair for their new house guest and he had been thrilled by her request. Though he refused her offer of payment, Margaret intended to add a bonus to this week's pay packet for his trouble, especially since making the chair was in addition to his usual duties and he was doing it mostly in his own time.

"Thank you, Jenny. Why don't you take a pot of tea and some lunch out to share with Dixon. I'll bring the children over to you when we're finished here."

"Thank you."

Just then Fanny and Watson entered so Jenny bowed

and beat a hasty retreat.

"You have children at the dinner table?" Fanny asked, clearly outraged at the idea.

"We do." Margaret wasn't going to get into an argument with her and for once Fanny decided to hold her tongue and sit down.

Jane and Sally served the meals of cold game pie served with onion marmalade, fresh salad and bloomer bread. As per her request, Fanny was served the salad with only white bread.

"What's this?" Fanny asked.

"I'm sorry, Ma'am," Sally answered. "Cook didn't have time to prepare anything without dairy in. She'll have some steamed chicken ready for you by this evening though."

Fanny's expression turned sour but she didn't say anything else.

"So, how are you settling in?" Margaret asked.

"Very well," Watson answered, though his smile was a little tight.

"Things are much smaller here than at our house," Fanny explained. "There is not very much storage and your closets are tiny but I am slowly finding a home for everything."

"Good," Margaret smiled.

Cook had already cut the children's meals into manageable pieces and Margaret was glad that Bessy was using her knife and fork properly for once. She was also surprised to note that Malcolm's table manners were excellent; clearly his former nanny had been teaching him. Fanny cast an occasional wary eye in the direction of the children but didn't comment.

"I heard from a friend over in Marston this morning, Adam Longwood" John said. "He's just about to take on a second mill there and he's looking for an overseer for it. I know it's quite a distance away but I thought I'd mention it to you."

"Don't you have a position for him?" Fanny asked. "Everyone is always going on about you expanding the mill."

"I'm afraid not," John had hoped not to be this direct but Fanny left him little choice. "Our management styles are too different for it to work."

"Where is Marston?" Margaret asked

"About fifty miles north and a little more inland," John said.

"That is quite a distance," she agreed.

Watson hadn't said anything as yet but he looked thoughtful.

"Overseer or manager?" he asked finally.

"Overseer, but you'd be looking after the day to day running of the mill with no one above you but Longwood."

Watson glanced at his wife then turned thoughtful again.

"I suppose I could take lodgings in the town during the week," he suggested. "I'm sure there are landladies in Marston who would offer a room to a working man."

"Aye," John agreed. "And then you can wait for something a little closer to home to come along."

Margaret wasn't sure how she felt about Watson working away, presumably if he did come home it would only be for one day a week. Though having said that, his presence didn't seem to be doing anything to alleviate Fanny's more dramatic tenancies, so perhaps she would be easier to deal with if her husband wasn't around.

The rest of lunch was a somewhat stilted affair and both Margaret and John were glad to escape back to the mill.

Chapter Thirty Nine

Though he looked for work in Milton, Watson was unsuccessful. There was a lot of bad feeling towards him because of the failed speculation and even those who had positions weren't inclined to offer them to him. In the event, Watson also didn't take the job in Marston as the police arrived at Rose Cottage the day before he was due to meet with Longwood and removed Watson to a debtors prison.

Fanny wailed and screamed, working herself into a frenzy as she tried to stop them taking Watson away. Fearing that Mrs. Watson might be arrested for her behaviour, Jenny bid the gardener's lad to run to the mill and fetch the master as quickly as possible but by the time he arrived, Watson had gone and would be sent to the local gaol or worse, a debtors prison, until his debts were satisfied.

As soon as John got to the house, Fanny threw herself on him, wailing and begging him to help Watson. He tried to calm Fanny down but she was hysterical and it was beyond even his skills to calm her.

When Margaret arrived at the house a little later, having also been alerted by the gardener's lad, she quickly took in the situation and called for the gig to be readied. She then poured a large glass of brandy which she handed to Fanny, ordering her to drink. It made her cough but Margaret was insistent and kept her sipping the glass until it was gone.

She topped the glass up again just as Dixon entered.

"The carriage is ready," Dixon informed them.

Margaret handed Dixon the glass and asked her to do her best to get Fanny to drink it. John managed to detach himself from Fanny and they left, heading into Milton and to the Magistrates Court. Bill barked and scratched at the door for a long time after they had gone because she wasn't used to being without Margaret. Eventually though she curled up and lay on the mat in front of the door, waiting for her mistress to return.

"What do we do?" John asked Margaret as they journeyed towards Milton.

"As a Magistrate, can you do anything?" she asked.

"I can try but for the police to arrest him, it is likely that an order for payment has already been made by the Queen's Court and unless he pays, he will go to jail."

"As I understand it, if someone truly has no money to

satisfy the debt, they can petition to be released after two weeks, can they not?"

"Only if the creditors agree."

"Which they are not likely to if they have gone to the trouble of getting this order from the court." Margaret shook her head in frustration at the seemingly hopeless situation.

"Exactly. I think we have to face the fact that unless the debt is paid, he will go to prison."

"The debtors prisons are horrific places; I'm not sure Watson would survive in there." She sighed. "I don't think we have any choice but to settle the debt for him."

"We've just spent the last of our cash reserves on the housing project. If we are to pay off the debt, we will have to liquidate another property which will take time."

Margaret knew that he was right.

"Do we know the extent of his debts?" she asked. "Perhaps if they were not too high we could manage to get the money together?"

"He hasn't said how much he owes. I suppose we will find out shortly."

They arrived at the court and went to see the clerk, who would hold details of all local legal proceedings. Thanks to John's position as a magistrate, the clerk was happy to help them.

"The order was obtained by the Provincial Bank of London and two individuals, Mr. Miller and Mr. Laurie." The clerk explained.

"How much is owed?" Margaret asked.

The clerk duly told them how much was owed to the bank and to the the other gentlemen named.

"Who are they?" Margaret asked John.

"I don't know them well but they were friends of Watson's who run a woollen mill near Milton. I understand that not only had they loaned Watson money but they had also invested in the failed speculation themselves."

"I have their office address on the paperwork," the clerk offered. "It's not far from here, in fact."

"Then we must talk to them and see about settling the debt," John said. "Only if they withdraw their complaint can Watson be released."

"When you've sorted everything, Mr. Thornton, tell them to ask for Mr. Johnson; I'll have the paperwork

273

rushed through for you."

"That's very kind of you," John said, offering the clerk his hand.

Mr. Johnson was pleased to help. Not only was Mr. Thornton a fair magistrate and a good sort of fellow, Mr. Johnson's younger sister was married to Thomas, who worked with Mrs. Thornton at the mill. Both Thomas and his sister were forever going on about how kind the Thorntons were to them and the others who lived in the village.

Mr. Johnson wrote down the office address for them and they left after thanking him for his trouble.

Unusually the office of M&L Woollen mill was separate from the mill itself, which was located out of town. Mr. Thornton introduced himself to the receptionist and asked to see the owners. He correctly assumed they would know why he and Margaret were here and they were soon ushered into Mr. Laurie's office.

John explained that he would be willing to cover Watson's debt but that he would need time to gather the cash together. He thought that he could probably get three thousand together by the end of the week. With Thornton's I.O.U. in hand, signed and witnessed by the receptionist, they were happy to withdraw their complaint against Mr. Watson immediately.

Settling the bank loans would be much harder but they both had a good relationship with Mr. Latimer, who worked for the Provincial Bank of London. They settled in his office and after making sure they had tea, Mr. Latimer sat down and got straight to the point.

"I assume you're here about Mr. Watson? I'm terribly sorry," Mr. Latimer said. "It was not my decision to begin these proceedings; that was all handled by head office."

"I understand," John assured him. "But I'm hoping we can come to an amicable settlement."

"I hope so too. I don't suppose you have the cash to pay off the bank loans?" he asked

John shook his head. "We have the assets but not the cash. It would probably take us several weeks to sell one of our properties at a fair price."

"Forgive me for asking," Margaret began. "But the bank has taken ownership of Mr Watson's house and mill, is that correct?"

"You're wondering why we are pursuing the debt if we have

the properties to sell?" he surmised, to which Margaret nodded. "Well, it seems that the loans he was granted exceed the current market value of the properties."

Margaret looked shocked.

"Believe me, I was as upset as you when I discovered this. Mr Watson is not my client but he should never have been granted such sizeable loans."

Mr. Latimer rested his elbows on the desk and steepled his fingers as he thought the problem through.

"I wonder if it might be possible for you to take the loans over?" he mused. "You do all your banking with us, do you not?"

"Yes," John agreed.

"Well, you have always been good customers and I know you have the assets to settle the debt should anything untoward happen. Perhaps I can speak to head office and suggest that you buy the properties back from us, slightly above current market value to cover the loans, but the bank would then sign the deeds back over to you and when prices improve, you can sell them and redeem the loans. Would you be willing?"

John and Margaret looked at each other.

"What would the repayments on the loan be?" Margaret asked and Mr Latimer did some calculations and told them.

"That is the lowest interest rate I can offer you at the moment," he explained.

"We can afford the payments on the house," Margaret said to John. "And the mill should pay for itself."

"And it would be an asset," John said, trying to talk himself into something he didn't want. "And as Mr Latimer suggests, we could sell the mill on at a later date."

"It seems to be our only option," she agreed.

John turned to Mr. Latimer.

"If you can arrange it, you have a deal."

Mr. Latimer needed to send a telegram to the London office so John and Margaret left, agreeing to return at 4pm for an answer. With little else to do, and no desire to return home without news, they went to Mr. Whitaker's house, for surely John's mother would have heard the news by now and be worried.

Hannah had indeed heard the gossip and welcomed them. John told her of what Mr. Latimer was trying to arrange.

"And do you think it will work?" Hannah asked.

"I wish I knew, Mother. We can only hope."

"I have spoken to Daniel," Hannah said. "He has some money and is willing to help."

"Thank you," John smiled. "But that money is for his retirement and Watson owes thousands."

Despite her stoic nature, Hannah paled.

"We will get him out," Margaret assured her. "Even if we have to sell some property, we will settle the debt as soon as we can."

"Foolish, stupid man," Hannah muttered. "So if you are able to take over the loans, can you afford the repayments?"

"For a while," John assured her. His mill was doing well and could support the loans on the house and Watson's mill for a time, at least. "We will of course get the mill up and running as soon as possible and we will rent the house out as well. We think that the combined income from both should cover the repayments."

Hannah seemed reassured by his statements, though still not at all happy with the situation.

"And what will happen to Watson?" she asked.

"I have no idea. We will deal with that if, or rather, when he is released." John sounded as though he didn't much care what happened to Watson, and right now Hannah couldn't blame him.

They stayed with Hannah for another hour, talking mostly about inconsequential things while they waited to return to the bank. At half past three they left and walked back to the bank to find Mr. Latimer was waiting for them.

"I have good news and bad news," he told them, gesturing for them to take a seat.

John nodded for him to continue.

"The London office has agreed to sell you the properties for the value of the loans secured on them, plus any costs we have incurred. That will wipe out Mr. Watson's debt."

John sighed with relief. "And the bad news?"

"It will take at least a week to draw up the new deeds and the mortgage paperwork and I cannot have the debt complaint withdrawn until that is done."

"A week?" John checked.

"Possibly five days, but only possibly. I will do everything I can to get this transaction completed as soon as possible."

John looked at Margaret who nodded her agreement.

John stood up and reached out his hand. "You have a deal."

Mr. Latimer shook hands with them both and assured them he would contact them as soon as he had the necessary papers.

They returned to the courthouse, where they had left their horse and gig earlier, and ventured out of the town to Hillcrest Prison, where Watson would be held until he could be transferred to a debtors prison. They asked first to speak to the warden and, after bribing him with ten pounds, he assured them he would do everything he could to stop Watson from being transferred. Prison was not a place for ladies and as such John had to visit Watson alone. Margaret could have remained in the wardens office but his practice of taking bribes combined with the rumours she had heard about his treatment of inmates meant that she preferred to wait outside with the gig.

Watson was sitting on the bed (which was really little more than a wooden shelf) with his head in his hands. He looked up as John approached and smiled with relief. His smile soon faded when he noticed John's grim expression.

John explained what had happened and that Watson would have to remain in prison until the paperwork was completed. Watson looked terrified at the prospect, for everyone knew that jail was no place for a poor man. John gave him all the cash he had with him to use for bribes and told him that he would do everything he could to get him released as soon as possible.

Watson thanked him, though it was clear from his questions that he thought John could be doing more to secure his release.

John returned to the gig, pleased to get away from the prison and breathe fresh air again.

They then returned to Milton and called on John's mother again to keep her informed of what was happening. She was relieved, though worried about how Fanny would take the news. After speaking with her husband, she decided to return to Rose Cottage and stay with them for a few days until Fanny had calmed down or Watson was released, which ever came first.

While his mother packed, John went outside for a walk. He and Margaret had walked a lot today, needing the distraction and to expend some of their nervous energy. Now though, John just felt tired. Truth be told he didn't really care what happened to Watson, only the effect it would have first on his sister and on their finances. He was worried that by overextending themselves they had put their plans in danger but Margaret was right, they did have the resources to cover the loans so in the worst case scenario, they would simply have to delay the final stage of building at the village. Still, it seemed wrong that so many futures were now at risk because of one man's foolish gamble.

While he was gone, Margaret took the opportunity to make sure Hannah was all right about leaving her husband so soon after they were married. It was a difficult question to pose, since she didn't want to make her feel that she couldn't come and stay with them, but equally she didn't want Hannah to feel that she had to.

"Thank you for your concern," Hannah said, genuinely touched by her thoughtfulness. "In an ideal world we would all do only the things which we wanted to but the truth is we all have duties to perform."

"I believe your motherly duty now falls to Mr. Watson to fulfil. You have watched over and looked after this family for long enough and whilst I would never want to stop you or make you feel unwelcome in our home, I also don't want you to feel that you must return with us. You are entitled to your own happiness, Hannah."

To Margaret's surprise, Hannah took her hand.

"You are a fine young woman, Margaret Thornton, and I couldn't be prouder of you if you were my own daughter."

Margaret had no idea how to respond to that since it was completely unexpected.

"Thank you," she said, feeling foolish for such an inadequate response.

"Loving my son is thanks enough," she said, before turning brusque again, "Now, I must go and pack, I do not want to keep John waiting for too long."

Margaret and John lay in bed that night, facing each other and holding hands but too mentally exhausted to do anything more adventurous.

Fanny was still just as distressed when they arrived home and even Hannah was unable to calm her. Just the thought of Watson in prison, even for only a short while, seemed to distress her. Finally Cook offered the use of some laudanum (which her husband been given for pain after an accident earlier in the year) and after a strong dose, Fanny finally fell asleep.

Hannah had been settled into the only remaining bedroom and after a mostly silent dinner, everyone chose to retire early to bed.

Margaret and John lay mostly silent, lost in their own thoughts and only talking occasionally.

"We should do something for the staff," Margaret said. "They have had to deal with a lot today."

"Perhaps we can arrange some extra time off."

"Good idea."

They lapsed into silence again.

"Did we do the right thing?" Margaret broke the silence again.

"I don't know." John answered. "But I don't think that we had any alternative."

Finally their exhaustion began to outweigh their over-active minds and they drifted off to sleep.

Fanny seemed less hysterical the next day but she still cried for most of it. Hannah did her best to comfort her daughter but it seemed she could accept no comfort. Margaret thought her behaviour very odd considering that she didn't seem to care very much for Watson.

On the fourth day she seemed to grow weary, refusing to eat much and spending most of her time in her room, something that continued over the next few days.

"It won't do," John told his mother, after all their cajoling had failed to have any effect on her. "She can't spend the rest of her life in her bedroom."

"What else can we do?" his mother asked. "We've tried everything we can think of."

"I know," he agreed with a deep sigh.

Hannah reached out and patted his hand. "She will come out of it."

"I hope so, Mother."

"She went through something similar after Malcolm was born."

"Did she?" That came as a surprise to John, though he admitted that he hadn't tried to see more of Fanny than was absolutely necessary in recent years.

"Aye. About a week after the birth she began crying a lot, then coming down with one imagined ailment after another.

Dr. Donaldson came to see her a few times and he diagnosed melancholia and recommended complete rest."

"You think it might be the same thing?"

"I'm not even sure I believe in melancholia. I always thought it was something ladies in the south did to get a bit of attention."

John smiled slightly. His southern belle had certainly never suffered from melancholy, even after losing both her parents.

Chapter Forty

Margaret was quite worried for Fanny. She vividly remembered how her mother had been forced to keep to her bed while she was ill and that had looked like low spirits in the beginning. She prayed that Fanny was not ill also.

She also remembered how her mother loved to be read to and how she would sit with her for hours, reading letters and stories until her mother fell asleep. Though she was much busier now than in those days, she vowed to find an hour every day to visit Fanny and read to her.

After a trip into Milton, she managed to purchase a copy of The Tales of the Alhambra and every evening before John got home, she went into Fanny's room and read a little to her.

The first two days Fanny told her to go away, then she tried ignoring her, turning away and lying still until Margaret finished reading and left.

Watson finally returned eight days after he was taken. He looked very gaunt and unwell and Hannah was worried for his health. His return did nothing to cheer Fanny and eventually he stopped trying see her.

Margaret wondered if Fanny was embarrassed by him and if that was why she was upset, not because her husband had been taken, though she really did seem quite listless. Two days after Watson was released, Hannah returned home.

John reopened the Watson's mill a week after they completed the purchase, reinstating most of the workers who had lost their jobs. Though he still looked quite unwell, John had little option but to also install Watson as the manager since he didn't have the time to run it himself. Watson had no control over money matter though, and he, Hannah, Margaret, Higgins or one of the other overseers were always there as well to make sure that things ran smoothly, which is to say in keeping with Thornton's Mill, not the sometimes brutal practices of the other mills.

Watson argued that he was being undermined by being watched and not having a say in financial matters, to which John assured him that he was free to leave if he was unhappy. He chose to stay.

Margaret was forced to hire another person to help her with the accounts as she gave Thomas the majority of the additional work created by taking on the second mill. She also put in more hours herself but kept telling herself that it was not forever.

Still, every day she went into Fanny's room and read to her. Once the tales of the Alhambra was finished she moved onto Persuasion by Jane Austen.

Christmas that year was a sad occasion, with Watson getting drunk and falling asleep before the meal was served and Fanny refusing to leave her room.

As the new year rolled around, Margaret prayed that the coming year would bring a change in luck, not so much for them but for the other residents of Milton.

Dr. Wallace had been unable to find a suitable replacement to take over his Wednesday surgery but true to his word, each week one of his colleagues or friends would arrive to see to the villagers and their needs. It was far from ideal but it sufficed until the following February, when John returned from a quarterly magistrates session in Milton with some rare and very welcome good news.

Fanny still kept to her room and Watson preferred the study so that he might be alone. It was clear that he did not like relying on their charity and so he kept to his own company as much as possible.

"How was it?" Margaret asked, kissing John's cheek and handing him a glass of brandy. While he enjoyed his position as magistrate, he did find these sessions rather draining and fraught with arguments as they tried to decide on various local issues. As such, Margaret was always ready with a warm welcome for him. Tonight he was late returning home so she expected him to be even more curmudgeonly than usual.

"Quite productive," he said, surprising her with a smile. He took the offered drink and stole a playful kiss.

Margaret was momentarily speechless as she watched him walk to the sofa and sit himself down. He patted the seat beside him, asking her to join him, which she did, eager to hear what had bolstered his mood.

"I believe I have found us a new doctor," he said.

"Really? What happened?"

"You know Mr Townsend."

"The Magistrate who owns mines? Coal mines if I'm not mistaken."

"Aye, that's him, and very wealthy the business has made him and his family too. His eldest son is to inherit the business but his younger son, though he will receive a good income from the mines did not wish to pursue the same career. Townsend though it a good idea that the brothers were not in competition and supported his desire to become a doctor. He arrived back from Edinburgh Medical School just last month."

"Oh?"

"Yes. It appears that while there he was greatly influenced by the Scottish Enlightenment Movement, which believes in the ability of rational men to change society for the betterment of everyone."

Margaret smiled. "And he wishes to help our villagers?"

"Aye, and Milton as a whole. He's seeking donations to try and set up a free clinic for the poor and for a reasonable donation to his clinic, his father believes he might be inclined to treat our workers for little or no fee. Apparently he has already expressed interest in what we're trying to achieve here."

"Oh, but that's wonderful news. We must invite him to come and look around and share dinner with us."

"Already taken care of. I followed Townsend home and he introduced me to his son, Arthur. He has agreed to come out here tomorrow afternoon to take a tour of the village and dine with us in the evening."

Margaret leaned over and kissed his cheek.

"It will be so nice to have a regular doctor again, someone the workers can come to trust and open up to."

"Indeed. Would you mind giving him the tour?"

"Of course not, if you don't mind?" She was very aware of how badly things had ended with Dr. Wallace.

"Why should I? I suggested it."

Margaret didn't know if John was so relaxed because Arthur Townsend had his roots in working class northern stock, and therefore was not a threat to him or as she hoped, because he finally believed himself worthy of her love. Either way Margaret was pleased that John wasn't letting what happened with Wallace cloud his judgement. And he truly had nothing to fear from any other man because she would never willingly leave him.

Watson scoffed slightly over dinner as they discussed the doctor but he didn't say anything. He seemed to be declining and his consumption of alcohol had risen drastically in recent weeks. Whilst Margaret sympathised with his plight, she also knew that it was all of his own making and would not cosset him, as she felt slightly more inclined to do with Fanny.

The next day she and Bill were ready and waiting as John brought Townsend into her office. She warmly shook hands with him and when John excused himself, they left the office and she began showing him around the mill.

She started with the canteen, introducing him to Mary (who was far more taken with Bill's visit than this stranger) and the two other girls who now worked there, then she took him into the mill, explaining how the machinery worked and the safety procedures that they had in place to try and protect the workers. While they walked she explained about the savings book they had set up and about the school and childcare facilities they had in place for the children.

Next she took him to the community centre, which still housed the school and nursery. It was rather crowded now and Margaret told him that the next phase of building included a purpose built school as well a larger hall which could be used by the school and for other local events.

Next she took him around the village, showing him the decent housing, the sanitation and the small parks. She stopped and spoke with some of the ladies she saw going about their business as well as stopping in to see the shopkeepers. She introduced the doctor to everyone she spoke with and they all expressed how pleased they would be if he did join their community, albeit on a part time basis.

Albert insisted she call him by his Christian name since, to him at least, those who addressed Mr Townsend were addressing his father. Understanding how he felt, for even though John's mother was now Mrs Whitaker, she would always be the real Mrs Thornton in Margaret's mind, she in turn asked him to call her Margaret.

With the tour over they returned to the canteen where Mary happily made them some tea while they talked and tempted Bill to her side with some of today's casserole.

Albert told her of his time in Edinburgh, the wonders of the medical school there and the many clubs and societies that existed to encourage reason and broaden the mind. Margaret was fascinated, but she also knew that terms must be discussed at some point.

"So, what could we offer you that might tempt you to offer your services to the workers?" she asked.

"I confess, having seen the good work you are doing here, I

am already tempted, but alas I do have plans myself. Has your husband told you of my idea of opening a free clinic in Milton?"

"He did, and I think it is a wonderful idea."

"As do I. Unfortunately many others do not share our altruistic sentiments and I am finding it difficult to solicit donations."

"We would be more than happy to help you achieve your goal, within reason."

He smiled at her caveat and proposed an amount. Margaret quickly ran through the finances in her mind. They could afford the amount he proposed without it affecting their long term plans.

"Whilst I will have to discuss it with my husband before confirming anything, I believe that would be acceptable."

Albert raised his mug of tea. "Then here is to a long and fruitful partnership."

Though highly unusual to toast with mugs, Margaret nevertheless tapped her mug against his and smiled.

Leaving him in Mary's care, Margaret hastened back to the office to discuss the donation with John. He greeted her with a kiss and readily agreed with her assessment that they could afford the donation.

Dinner that night was a jovial affair, save for Watson's slightly inebriated presence. Albert tried in vain to engage him in conversation a few times but his answers were curt and to the point. Eventually the three of them decided to just ignore his presence and talked amongst themselves.

Margaret later discovered that Watson was more upset than usual because, when he had ordered a child beaten for lateness this morning, Higgins had forbade it, arguing with and overruling him in front of his workers. Watson had been told many times that the only punishment that would be tolerated was by way of fines, but he wouldn't listen.

"A stern beating never hurt anyone," he would argue. "It puts 'em right much faster than a fine, though they should still be docked for lateness."

So now he sulked, wondering how it was that he had gone from master to underling, and blaming everyone but himself for his misfortune.

When spring arrived the air lost its chill as the countryside exploded in a riot of colour. Margaret loved this time of year and as she walked to or from the mill with John, she frequently made him pause so that she could admire the rugged landscape. Sometimes she wished that she still had the time to draw like she used to in Helstone, for this was surely a landscape that needed capturing on canvas. Alas she didn't have the time but she didn't really mind. Perhaps when Bessy was old enough they could come out one Sunday and she could start to teach her to draw.

Right now she had to go and read to Fanny, though she was beginning to despair of ever reaching her. Today though, as Margaret sat down, Fanny turned to face Margaret instead of turning away from her.

Margaret ignored the change and began reading as usual. They had moved onto a new book now, Shirley by Charlotte Bronte and over the next few days, she though that Fanny might be showing an interest in the story. Finally on the Thursday she simply said, "Don't stop," as Margaret was about to close the book.

Though she had precious little time, Margaret read an extra chapter that day.

By the Monday, Fanny was sitting up, ready for Margaret's visit and she began asking questions about the story.

The next day Margaret finished the book and as she laid it down she asked, "What would you like to read next?"

"Can I ask you a question?" Fanny asked, her manner shy.

"Of course."

"Do you like me?"

Margaret considered her response for a moment before answering.

"I don't think that's the right question to ask."

"You don't like me." She looked away.

"I didn't say that, but what I think shouldn't matter to you. The only question of import is, do you like yourself?"

Fanny turned sharply to her but quickly looked away. Margaret reached out and took Fanny's hand. She knew she had to be careful with her next words, that in the next few moments she could either make herself a new friend or an new enemy.

"I know what people say about me, Fanny. Some think me haughty, arrogant and condescending. Others say I am forward, brusque and even unladylike. It seems that I cannot win, that some people will always find a reason to dislike me. It hurts sometimes, because I know that those people don't know the real me, for if they did I hope they would not think so ill of me. I can bear their scorn and ridicule, however, because I like myself. My parents gave me good principles to follow and as long as I am true to them and to myself, I find it hard to worry about what others think of me."

"You think that I don't like myself?" Fanny asked.

"I think you are adrift. Perhaps confused might be a better word. I don't think that you yet know who you are, or what kind of person you want to be."

Fanny was silent for a while until finally she asked, "Tell me about your parents?"

Margaret was happy to. She told Fanny of Helstone, of her parents and Frederick. She told her how excited she had been to go and stay with her cousin Edith in London, and how disappointed she had been once she arrived there, how lonely she had been and how she had longed for her parents. She told her about the lessons; the music lessons, the singing lessons, the dancing lessons and the deportment lessons. She told her of the rules; the many hundreds of rules that dictated how she must behave at all times and in all situations. Then she told her of her joy at returning home the first time for the summer and how over the years, the time she spent living with Aunt Shaw had helped her to appreciate her parents all the more.

"You must think me very shallow," Fanny said when Margaret had finished.

"It is not for me to pass judgement upon you, Fanny."

"I suppose being virtuous is easy for you; having a preacher for a father must have given you good values to follow since you were young."

Margaret laughed softly.

"Oh, if that is how you see me then you think far too highly of me, for I am as flawed as everyone else. I can be prejudiced and slow to change my mind. Why, I have said many hurtful things and sadly, a lot of those things I said to your brother before I really knew him. I am truly quite appalled when I think of how I behaved when I first came to Milton. I also have a shocking temper, which I believe you have had occasion to witness yourself." She smiled, trying to lighten the mood slightly but Fanny didn't smile back. "My father used to say that it is the journey that matters, not the destination, but it took me many years before I truly understood what he meant. The point I think he was trying to make is that we all fall short of the ideal at times, but the point is not to be perfect for we are all flawed in different ways. It is the attempt at perfection that matters. Failing to live up to our own expectations is to be expected, and it is allowable in God's eyes as long as we try again and do not stop trying."

"So you do not think me beyond redemption?" Fanny asked, her eyes shining with unshed tears.

"No, Fanny. I think that like the rest of us, you are struggling to make the best of your life and yourself; you are just a little lost at the moment."

"Thank you for talking with me."

"It was my pleasure." She squeezed Fanny's hand one last time them released it. "It will be dinner time soon, do you feel up to joining us?"

"Thank you but no, not tonight."

"Then I shall return tomorrow and perhaps we can choose a new book."

Fanny smiled and Margaret left. When John remarked on how long she had spent with Fanny today, Margaret found her eyes drifting to Watson. She chose not to let Watson know of Fanny's improvement, less he do something to upset the delicate equilibrium Fanny seemed to be regaining.

"I got involved in the book and lost track of time," Margaret said. She could see from John's expression that he knew she was hiding something, but he didn't say anything more until they were alone in their bedroom that night.

"So, do you want to tell me what really happened with you and Fanny today?"

"Of course," she said, curling herself into his side as she got into bed. "We talked, that's all. She asked me if I liked her, and from there she began asking me questions about my life."

"Jane said she has looked happier these last few days. Why did you not want Watson to know?"

"I am not certain to be honest. I believe she is recovering from whatever ailed her but she is still fragile. When she sees Watson, I would rather it be at her own behest."

"Good idea," John said, turning her onto her back and leaning down to kiss her. "But you have sorely neglected your husband today. Why, I do not think I have even seen you for two full hours!"

"Indeed I have not been a very good wife today, Mr Thornton." Margaret smiled. "Perhaps you will allow me to make it up to you?"

"Well, that depends. What did you have in mind?"

Margaret whispered in his ear. What he heard was obviously very pleasing as his smile widened and his eyes blazed with fiery passion.

"Why yes, Mrs Thornton," he said, his voice slightly hoarse. "I believe that would be acceptable."

As the the days grew warmer, Margaret and John found their workload increasing, not getting easier. Watson was frequently the worse for wear in the mornings now and prone to make mistakes at the mill so two people had to be sent to Milton with him each day. One would watch the mill itself while the other made sure the administration was done properly, something Watson had been able to handle alone until recently.

John and Margaret had discussed various options, including letting Watson take the mill over again as Master in the hopes it would boost his spirits but in the end it was just too big a risk and they couldn't justify it. John's mother was still happy to help them and increased her hours to four mornings a week, but even that didn't lessen their workload by a great deal. They also felt guilty for taking her away from her husband but there were few others who they could trust as they did Hannah and they would have been lost without her help.

Since they were both overworked and feeling the pressure, at times they were a little curt with each other, though they were usually quick to apologise. As well, more and more frequently of late they were both too tired to do anything other than sleep when they finally got a moment alone together, which was a sorry state of affairs for they both missed the closeness that they were used to.

Margaret tried to look on the bright side though. The new housing was coming along nicely and it would not be too long before the mill and village would be able to expand once again. Though there was a feeling of unrest among the mill hands in Milton, Margaret knew that a strike would not affect Thornton's mill, though it could still cause difficulties at Watson's Mill. Fanny was also slowly coming back to life. She read by herself for many hours a day now and had started coming to share dinner with them a few nights a week. She seemed wary of Watson in his inebriated state, but so far he had left her alone.

Finally, though Margaret was not seeing as much of Bessy as she might like, she was pleased that Bessy and Malcolm were getting along well and that Malcolm was looking a lot happier these days. She was also grateful that they had followed Frederick's attitude to raising children, for if the children didn't eat with them, Margaret was almost certain that she would hardly ever have the time to see them.

As she and Bill took the carriage into Milton with Watson and Higgins one morning at the end of June, she was feeling somewhat resentful of her situation and silently wished Watson's mill would just disappear so that she and John could get back to their lives and their plans.

She would come to regret those words later on, but at that moment in time she could have no idea of just how close she was to getting her wish.

Chapter Forty One

John was in his office the reviewing the mill's inventory when he heard a commotion outside but he decided to ignore it as he had a lot of work to get through today and his overseers could handle most problems without him. Soon though the clatter of horses hooves was joined by shouting and with his concentration broken he went to the window with every intention of giving the workers an ear full but the look he saw on the faces out there stopped him cold.

The horses had not belonged to the butcher dropping off today's meat for the canteen as he had initially thought, but rather they belonged to the police. The officer's expressions were grave and John ran outside to see what had happened but he was accosted by his workers before he could even make it outside.

"What's going on?" he asked.

One of the men in front of him was Frank Gunderson, one of the mill's overseers. Whilst not insensitive, he was usually a no-nonsense kind of man and the fact that he was now tongue-tied sent a chill up John's spine.

"The mill in Milton," he finally managed to say. "There's been a fire."

Those who were there would swear that they had never seen a man turn so pale as the master did at that moment.

"Margaret?" John somehow managed to ask, though his mouth was suddenly drier than the Sahara Desert.

"No news, Master. The constable came to get ya as soon as he realised what were happenin'. He left locals fightin' the flames."

With a roar and seemingly inhuman strength, John pushed those in his way aside and ran out to the courtyard. Those who were watching would later say that they were glad the younger constable offered the master his horse for, judging by the look on his face they were certain he would have taken it by force otherwise, and they did not even want to think what could have happened to the master then.

He jumped into the horse's saddle and without a backward glance, took off for Milton at a gallop.

He arrived outside the mill to be greeted with utter confusion. The smoke hung thick and heavy in the air and he could hardly see anything as he jumped from the horse's back and ran towards the mill.

"Margaret!" he called, ignoring the searing pain the smoke caused in his lungs and wiping at his eyes as the acrid smoke stung them, causing tears to stream down his face. He stumbled forward, calling for her with all the power he could muster. Higgins found him first, alerted to his presence by his cries. He grabbed his arm but John pulled away.

"Master. Master!"

Finally John registered his presence.

"She's alive," Higgins assured him, though his countenance was grave. "Follow me."

John did, and watched in horror as a breeze came in, blowing some of the smoke away for a moment so that he could see for himself that the mill would soon be little more than charcoal and ash. The smell was horrific, not just smoke and oil but also burned hair and things John didn't even want to consider.

Higgins led John around the wall of the mill and through to the road at the back, which is where the walking wounded had congregated since the wind was blowing the flames towards the front entrance of the mill and it had quickly been blocked by fire. Finally he spotted Margaret, sitting on the pavement at the side of the road, a blanket around her shoulders. She was arguing with someone who wanted her to remain still and wait for a doctor, while Margaret wanted to help treat the other survivors.

"Margaret," he called.

She turned to him then and in an instant all her strength vanished. Her face crumpled into an expression of horror and she ran at him, throwing herself into his arms and holding him tightly.

John held her tightly too as she cried on his shoulder and said soothing nonsense to her until she calmed down. Finally she let him go and stood away, wiping at her tears as she did so.

The blanket had fallen from her shoulders as she ran to him but she had moved so quickly that he had not had a chance to take her image in. Now that he did, he could see why the young woman was chiding Margaret to see a doctor, for her left arm was badly burned, the material of her dress had seemingly fused with her flesh. Her skirt was also badly burned on the left side and he would not be surprised if she had more burns on her legs.

"What happened?" he asked, taking her left hand and raising her arm to get a better look at her injury.

Margaret stared at her arm as though she had never seen it before, then for the second time in their marriage, she collapsed. Higgins was the one to catch her this time and he laid her gently out on the ground.

"Someone has gone for Dr. Townsend and there's another doctor around here doing what he can." Higgins told John. "I'll go and see if I can find 'em."

John took his jacket off, rolled it up and slipped it under her head as a pillow. Albert Townsend was the first doctor Higgins found and he was only too happy to treat Mrs Thornton, although she had not been his patient previously. He examined her there in the street, fearing that she couldn't wait until she got back to her home or to his free clinic. He looked at her arm first, then (decorum be damned) raised her skirt to see if the scorch marks on her skirt had made it through to her skin. He looked up at Thornton and Higgins.

"Listen closely," he said to them both. "She's in shock; that's why she passed out. She has relatively minor second-degree burns on her upper thigh that will wait to be treated but the burn on her arm is serious, third or possibly even deep enough to be a fourth degree burn. I need you to take her back to my father's house. Whatever you do, do not pull the material that is stuck to the wound off; cut around it if you have to but if you try and pull her clothing off, you will take her flesh with it. Douse the wound with strong alcohol like brandy and then soak a dressing in the same spirit and keep it over the wound until I get there. Have you got that?"

Higgins nodded.

"You're not coming?" John asked.

"I'll be there as soon as I can, or I'll send another doctor if I can't get away, but there are many here much more seriously wounded than your wife. Just remember, bathe the arm in alcohol and keep it covered until I or another doctor gets there."

Higgins once again nodded and made to pick Margaret up since she was still unconscious but John roughly pushed him aside and picked her up. Higgins collected the master's jacket, more out of habit than anything else. Part of him felt that he should stay with the workers, but another part of him knew that the master was in no fit state to take care of Miss

Margaret and that he needed to be there for her. She had been there for his beloved daughter, Bessy, god rest her soul, and now it was time he finally repaid that kindness.

Mr Townsend was surprised to see Thornton on his doorstep but when he saw Mrs Thornton cradled in his arms, he quickly surmised what had happened and stood back to let them in. Mrs Townsend guided John to the guest bedroom while Higgins asked if they had any alcohol to bath the wound with. He only had whisky but he was happy to see it used to treat Mrs Thornton if that was his son's say so.

He fetched dressings and bandages along with the alcohol and they headed upstairs. Higgins almost backed out of the room when he saw that Miss Margaret's dress had been removed and all she had protecting her modesty now was her petticoats, but then he remembered that there were more important things happening and that he had a job to do.

John sat next to Margaret on the bed by her injured side and was using Mrs Townsend's sewing shears to cut as much of the remaining material of her dress away from the burn as he could. Higgins handed him the bottle and dressings when he was done and John held a dressing to the neck of the whisky bottle, turning it upside down to douse the material.

The burn was on the outside of her arm and extended from about two thirds of the way down her forearm to three inches above her elbow. He carefully washed the wound with the spirit, using probably more than he needed to but he wouldn't take any risks with her. When he had throughly cleaned it, he tore her petticoat slightly above and below the burn hole in it, then bathed that burn also. He couldn't quite remember if the one on her thigh needed bathing but then again, better safe then sorry.

Finally he doused fresh dressings in whisky and draped them over the wounds, protecting them from the air. When he was finished he looked up. Higgins was keeping his eyes averted from Margaret's scantily clad form and Mr and Mrs Townsend had left the room.

With nothing else to do, John brushed her hair off her forehead and gently stroked her cheek, hoping to wake her.

"Master, I'd best go check on the mill."

"Aye," John agreed. "I should but-"

"Nay, you're where you should be. I'll be back as soon as I can."

"Thank you."

John stayed at Margaret's side, holding her hand and brushing her cheek. He knew that he should check on the mill with Higgins but he couldn't bring himself to leave her side. What if she were to awake and find no one there?

Higgins returned a while later, looking grave.

"What's happening?" John asked.

"Near as we can tell, fifty dead, another fifty or so injured and a few alive but not expected to make it."

John knew that mean that almost two hundred had escaped unharmed but that was small comfort right now. "And Watson?"

"Unaccounted for, assumed dead. The fire's out but the mill is still too hot to allow anyone inside yet, even then, identifying the bodies will be difficult."

John wondered how Fanny would take the news.

"What happened?" he asked Higgins.

"One of the piecers says... well she says she saw Watson with a cigar but she might be mistaken. The police are still questioning people though, makin' sure there was no foul play."

John gave a mirthless laugh.

"Of course!" The man he had been trying to help had burned the mill down. What irony!

"The constable said he'd come and speak to you when he knew more and wished Miss Margaret a speedy recovery."

"Thank you, Higgins." He looked up at the other man. "Perhaps we should get help from the village. Food, medical supplies, that kind of thing."

"Those that aren't workin' are already here," he said. "They brought supplies and are helpin' to carry the injured to the clinic or their homes."

John smiled, pleased that they were pulling together in this time of tragedy, though help was little compensation for lost loved ones.

Dr Townsend came by after a few hours, looking tired and dirty. Only his hands were clean and they contrasted almost comically with his ash and soot stained clothes and face. He checked the burn, bathed it with alcohol again then applied clean dressing over her arm and bandaged it.

"As soon as she awakes she can be taken home," he said. "For the next few days, the burn on her arm must be cleaned twice a day with with alcohol."

"No offence, Doctor, but why alcohol? I thought honey was used to treat burns."

"It's something I heard about in Edinburgh. There is much talk about how to halt the spread of infections these days and alcohol was something I had heard about. I and others have had reasonable success using it, though of course we wouldn't usually choose whisky. Before I come tomorrow I will try and buy some ethanol which is much stronger. Unfortunately I have used up my personal stocks."

John knew that Dr Donaldson recommended honey for burns and he wondered who he should trust. Should he leave his wife in the hands of this recently qualified young man who treated the poor, or should he ask for the services of the tried and tested Dr Donaldson? Causing offence really wasn't something he was concerned with.

"Whilst cleaning the wounds, any dead skin must be gently removed; don't pull it off," the doctor continued. "The burn on her arm will not hurt since the nerve endings are too damaged but she will soon feel considerable pain in the surrounding tissue. The burn on her thigh will also hurt. I'll give you some laudanum to help ease her pain and she is to take between one and two teaspoons as necessary, four times a day."

"Why isn't she waking?" John asked him.

"She has received a terrible shock, both from what she witnessed and her injuries. Her body has shut itself down for a while so that she can better deal with these traumas. She will awaken soon, I am sure."

John prayed that he was right.

Seeing how upset John was, Albert Townsend went up to him, put his hands his shoulders and turned John to face him.

"She will be fine," he said with confidence. "Her injury is bad, to be sure, but as long as we keep that wound clean she will be fine."

John looked into the other man's eyes and was reassured by the confidence he saw there. He nodded his understanding,

"Good." He released John and stepped away. "I must get back to the clinic. I will come and see Margaret tomorrow and make sure the wound is not becoming infected."

"Thank you, Doctor."

"No thanks necessary." He smiled wearily and left.

True to the doctor's predictions, Margaret did awaken a

while later, though she was crying with the pain. John gave her the laudanum as directed and Higgins called a carriage to take them home.

"How do you feel?" John asked her.

"I must help them." Margaret said, fighting against the wave of listlessness and euphoria the laudanum was making her feel.

"Everyone is being treated, there is nothing you can do."

Margaret decided not to argue and lay back. She was feeling very sleepy again and began to doze, a pattern she would repeat for the next few days. Since her clothes were ruined, Mrs. Townsend lent Margaret her heavy winter cloak which covered her from head to toe, protecting her modesty during the ride home.

The carriage ride felt as though it took an eternity and John hated every second of it as each jolt seemed to cause Margaret further pain. They both sighed with relief as they arrived home and as he gathered her into his arms again, Margaret drifted off to sleep once more.

As John carried Margaret into Rose Cottage and up to her bed, the house was abuzz with activity. It was clear that news had reached the staff here and they were all worried for their mistress. John's expression was grave and no one dared ask him what was happening but Higgins came in and updated them on the situation while Dixon and Fanny followed John upstairs.

John sat Margaret on the bed and took the cloak off her before laying her down over the covers. He explained to Dixon what had been done for her and what needed to be done over the next few days and she listened intently.

Fanny stayed silent and watched what was happening. In her heart she already knew the truth, for if Watson was all right, he would surely have returned with John. When John had finished explaining what Margaret needed, he turned to her and his serious expression became one of compassion as he saw Fanny's anguish.

Fanny no longer needed to hear the words but as her tears began to fall, John gathered her into his arms and told her anyway. He didn't tell her that the fire was probably Watson's fault, for that was a burden that she didn't need to carry.

She stayed in Margaret's room after that, watching as John and Dixon undressed her, washed her soot-stained body and changed her into a clean night gown before settling her under the covers. Margaret fought them since she just wanted to be left alone to sleep but they managed the task eventually.

Fanny's tears came and went at odd times but she did her best not to become hysterical.

When Margaret awoke in the early evening, she asked to see Bessy and Dixon went off to fetch her. Bessy came bustling into the room but halted when she saw the large bandage on her mothers arm. Margaret did her best to ignore the pain she felt and held her good arm out to the girl. John lifted her onto the bed and Fanny watched with fascination as Margaret wrapped her good arm around her daughter and closed her eyes.

She seemed to take a great comfort just from her presence, but that sensation was completely alien to Fanny and it fascinated her.

"Mama?"

Fanny turned to see her son Malcolm standing in the bedroom doorway, looking worried. He had clearly picked up on the tension in the house but didn't know what had caused it. As she looked at the small boy, for the first time she was able to see Watson in his features. Then she remembered that Watson was never coming home and her son would never know his father. She wondered how she could tell him such devastating news. Was he even old enough to know what she meant if she said his father was dead?

Tears stung her eyes as she thought about all that this small boy had lost and she held her arms open to him. Hesitantly, Malcolm walked into her embrace and as her tears began to fall in earnest, she tightened her arms around him and held him tightly against her.

For the first time since Malcolm had been born, Fanny finally felt like a mother.

Chapter Forty Two

Margaret was confined to her bed for the next two days, though she argued against it and disliked taking the laudanum since it made her feel so tired. Fanny noticed that she often turned her head to the fireplace, probably seeking Bill's comforting presence but like so many on that fateful day, Bill had been another casualty of the fire. Margaret had stated that she owed her life to the dog but then, confused and disorientated by the smoke, Bill had soon been overcome and the flames had claimed her body, as the smoke had claimed her life.

Fanny had never had a pet but she knew the great affection Margaret harboured for the animal. Why, Margaret was rarely seen without her large black mongrel trailing in her wake and although she couldn't understand her affection for the mutt, she did feel for her.

Fanny watched as the house around her operated like a well oiled machine, everyone knew their duty and they set to it with vigour. Fanny felt like a spare part. She desperately wanted something to occupy her and take her mind off the awful events but she had nothing, and when she asked John or the staff if she could help, they simply assured her that everything was under control.

So Fanny finally decided to find her own task and when John left for the mill after breakfast, she picked up his paper and took it up to Margaret. Margaret was dozing, having been almost force-fed more laudanum, so Fanny pulled a chair up beside the bed and began to read aloud from the newspaper. Personally Fanny had never had much time for newspapers, she preferred gossip, but she knew that Margaret liked to read them. To her surprise she even found a few articles that were of interest to her, like the awful events in India, the visits Queen Victoria and Prince Albert were making and the trial of a local man accused of swindling his business partner.

Margaret awoke and listened to Fanny but she was unable to remain conscious for long. Fanny continued to read whether she was awake or asleep, hoping that just by being there she was offering some small comfort to Margaret, just as she had been comforted by Margaret's regular presence when she was feeling low.

When the Doctor came in to clean and redress the wound, Fanny was about to leave but Margaret asked her to stay and keep reading. The dressing obviously hurt as it was removed and the wound cleaned, but Margaret gritted her teeth and forced herself to focus on Fanny's words.

When he was finished, she asked how long the wound would take to heal and when she could get back to work. Dr. Townsend told her that the wound would probably be mostly healed in six weeks and completely healed in three months, but he warned her that she would have extensive scarring and probably some restriction of movement in the arm. He wanted her to rest for at least two days but after that she could possibly do some light work, but she wasn't to do anything that might aggravate her wound. He also explained about the importance of cleaning it with the ethanol he had brought with him and of keeping the area clean, dry and protected at all times.

She asked if she needed to keep taking the laudanum which Dixon kept trying to pour down her throat (only a slight exaggeration) and the doctor told her no; she could take it for pain if necessary but she wasn't obliged to. He suggested she try only one spoonful which would take the edge off her pain without impairing her functions too much.

He left then and Margaret got herself out of bed and went to sit in one of the chairs by the fire. Fanny rang down and got some tea for them to share and they sat in silence for a while, still slightly awkward in each others company.

"I'm sorry about Watson," Margaret finally said. Perhaps it wasn't the most tactful conversation starter but it had to be said.

"Thank you. And I'm sorry that you're injured and that Bill..."

"Oh, Bill was only an old stray," Margaret pushed her condolences aside.

"To me, maybe, but you cared for that creature. It was clear for all to see."

Margaret couldn't deny that and she blinked furiously as her emotions finally threatened to overwhelm her. It was to no avail though as fat tears began to run over her cheeks. She didn't just cry for Bill, she cried for those workers who had perished; she cried for Watson and Fanny, she cried for the pain she was enduring and she cried mostly because the whole miserable, sorry situation could have been avoided.

Fanny reached out and took Margaret's hand in a show of

solidarity as her own tears started to fall again. Margaret offered her a faint smile through her tears, which continued to fall unabashed.

When finally her tears dried, she felt a little easier. The situation was still horrific but Margaret felt that she could bear it a little better.

John returned at lunch time, looking tired and haggard.

"What happened?" she asked, knowing that he had spent the morning in Milton.

Fanny excused herself so that they might talk in private.

John sat in the chair Fanny had vacated and ran a hand over his face.

"The police have concluded that it was an accidental fire caused by Watson."

"Watson?"

"Three of the workers saw him with a lit cigar near the sorting room where the fire started."

"On no," Margaret sighed. She couldn't help but wonder if perhaps it hadn't been an accidental fire, for Watson was surely aware of the substantial danger fire posed to the mill. "What of the workers?" she asked.

"Sixty two now dead, another forty or so with injuries ranging from serious to mild and around two hundred uninjured but unemployed. We were lucky, really. If it hadn't been for the fire drills we ran last week, I'm certain many more would have perished."

The fire bell and the drills, a practice run of what the workers were to do if the fire bell was ever rung, had been Higgins's idea. They had arranged a fire drill every year at the new mill but it had been harder at Watson's mill since there weren't as many exits, nor anywhere that readily leant itself to housing the fire bell. Only last week had the bell been installed in the courtyard and the workers put through their first practice of what they were to do upon hearing the bell.

Margaret said a silent prayer of thanks, for surely the fortuitous timing was more providence than coincidence.

"What of the mill?" she asked.

"Completely destroyed," he answered. "The only glimmer of good news is that our insurance is up to date. It will probably take a while to be paid but it will cover the loan on the mill and then some, so our plans to expand the village should be safe."

That was indeed a glimmer of hope, for once the new housing was finished, the workers could be rehired and rehomed out here. It wouldn't make up for the loss of life or income but it was better than nothing.

"We must make sure they're taken care of until the houses are finished," Margaret said.

"I have given a large donation to Albert for their care, and the villagers are sending meals into town for them."

Margaret nodded. She would try and make some more permanent arrangements when she was allowed back to work.

Fanny was downstairs when to her surprise, Jane came in and announced that Dr Townsend was back. She went out into the hallway to see him, concerned that something was wrong.

"Doctor, can I help you with something?"

"Oh, no, nothing is wrong," he assured her, noting her worried expression. "I went to see Mrs Dawson who was injured in the fire but is staying with her daughter in Thornton village, then I remembered that I had forgotten to leave the ethanol for Mrs Thornton." He reached into his pocked and withdrew a bottle of the spirit, which he handed to Fanny,

Fanny noticed how tired he looked.

"Are you sure you're all right, doctor?"

He gave her a weary smile. "I'm fine, Mrs Watson, but thank you for your concern."

"Have you eaten at all today?"

"Well-"

"I didn't think so. You'll be no good to your patients if you're not fit and healthy yourself. Let me have the kitchen make something quick for you." When he looked hesitant she pressed the point. Fanny was after all a skilled manipulator, only this time she was using her skills for someone else's benefit. "Please, as a thank you for all you have done for Margaret and the others."

He smiled. "Thank you. Far be it for me to refuse a..." he had been about to say 'grieving widow' but thought perhaps it was better not to remind her. "Thank you."

She ushered him into the parlour and had Jane bring up tea, bread, butter, jam, a slice of cold game pie and some salad. As he tucked into the food, he realised how hungry he was and that he had skipped lunch and dinner yesterday and only had the quickest of breakfasts this morning.

While he ate, Fanny asked him about his other patients and he explained to her all about the free clinic and how he was treating those who were unable to afford a doctor.

"I am surprised you are treating Margaret then, for she is quite one of the wealthiest women in the county."

Albert thought that was overstating things a little, but she wasn't wrong in principle. "I was the first doctor to happen across her at the mill and, no offence to her regular doctor, I care about what happens to her. Not only are she and her husband helping me financially with my clinic, what they are trying to achieve here with Thornton Village is incredible. Wealthy or not, she is someone special and I simply want to make sure that she is cared for."

"Oh, believe me, Margaret is never short of someone to care for her," she said, unable to keep some of the bitterness from leeching into her voice.

"No," Albert smiled at her obvious jealousy. "Good people rarely are."

He wasn't sure if his words would make an impact on her of if she truly was as superficial as she appeared to be, but when she blushed and looked away, he knew that he had shamed her.

Having said that, he thought she really was quite an interesting young lady since, for all her apparent bitterness to her sister in law it seemed clear that she envied her, though from her earlier behaviour when he had cleaned Margaret's wound, she evidently also had some level of care for the other woman.

He was intrigued by her and hoped that sometime in the not too distant future, he might have an opportunity to get to know her a little better.

The next week Lloyd's of London sent out a loss adjuster to investigate the claim and assess the damage. He spent two days in Milton, first going over the mill site, talking to the police and the survivors, then going over the mill's inventory and costs with John. He returned at the end of the second day satisfied that there had been no foul play and assured John that a cheque would be issued as soon as the paperwork had been completed.

The atmosphere around the town of Milton was gloomy, not just because of the mill fire but also because many businessmen were feeling the pinch of the failed speculation, the financial difficulties in America and the problems in India. Indeed the atrocities being reported in the papers about the attacks being carried out by the natives against good Christian men, women and children in India were shocking to even the most cynical of people.

Margaret was also in fairly low spirits herself. She tried to put a brave face on things but as well as the other tragedies, she was in constant pain which was wearing her spirit down. Although she understood why her wound must be cleaned and scraped every day, she grew to hate it and the pain it caused her. Not that she was prepared to admit that she was bad tempered.

She buried herself in her work and the preparations to expand the mill once again, seeing it as her penance for the mill fire, even though logically she knew that those deaths were not her fault.

John begged her to take more laudanum but she refused because she simply could not bear the way it made her feel. The only time she did take some was at night time so that she might get a good nights rest.

John felt for certain that when the new housing was completed (thanks to an extra push from the builders, they would be finished before Christmas) and the mill expanded, Margaret would cheer up, for she loved the community that they were creating here.

She disliked herself for allowing her injury to affect her moods so much, for there were many others who were much more severely injured than she, but still she could do little to change how she felt. Even Bessy's presence could not cheer her to the same extent and John began to grow fearful for her.

He had just made up his mind to call Doctor Townsend out to see her again when she became violently ill after dinner one evening. Fearing that she could have caught an infection, John rode to Milton that night and fetched the doctor back with him.

Margaret seemed recovered by the time they got back and to his surprise, Fanny was sitting in her bedroom with her, keeping her company until he returned. Given Margaret's fearful moods recently, he would usually expect Fanny to have made herself scarce, but she often seemed to be hovering around, making sure Margaret was all right. It puzzled him, but he had more important things on his mind at the moment.

When Margaret saw that John had dragged Albert all the

way out there she snapped at John that he shouldn't fuss over her so, but since he had come all this way, she nevertheless allowed Albert to examine her.

He checked her wound first, which showed no sign of infection, then he took her pulse and asked her a lot of questions, most of which didn't make any sense to Margaret but she answered them dutifully since she was too tired to argue.

"Well," Albert sat back, smiling. "I don't think you have anything to worry about, Margaret."

"Are you sure?" John asked, stepping closer. "Surely being that ill cannot be normal."

"It can be if one is with child."

"But..." John's face turned ashen. "But I thought morning sickness occurred in the morning?"

"Often but not always. I also believe that her condition is responsible for her lethargy and possibly her recent mood swings."

Margaret frowned as she listened to the Doctor, unsure of how she felt about being pregnant. As she thought about it, she realised that her monthly friend hadn't visited for about seven weeks now, but in the recent commotion with the mill fire and associated chaos, she had completely forgotten about it.

"With child?" she said slowly, as though sounding the words out for the first time.

"Yes," Albert smiled, though it faded when he realised that Margaret looked just as concerned as her husband. "Is there something you aren't telling me?" he asked, looking from Margaret to Fanny to John.

"When Margaret had Bessy," John explained. "She was very sick for the last few weeks, headaches, nose bleeds, she even collapsed at one point. Dr. Donaldson feared she would go on to develop seizures which could kill her."

"That sounds as if he was worried about something called eclampsia," Albert said. "It's a condition some women suffer while pregnant and is often fatal, but the good news is that it very rarely happens with a second child so you have every reason to be hopeful."

John certainly didn't feel hopeful.

"I understand that you are worried," Albert said. "But please try to relax. The chances are that Margaret will come through this without any difficulties at all, but getting overly anxious will not help either mother or child."

John wished he could believe him.

"Thank you, Doctor," Margaret smiled then looked from him to Fanny. "I think John and I need some time alone, if you wouldn't mind."

"Of course." Albert agreed, but he had some further advice to impart before he left. "I recommend you stop taking the laudanum, or take as little as possible. I realise you must be in a lot of pain but-"

"It's fine," Margaret assured him. "I haven't been using much because I don't like how it makes me feel."

"Good," he smiled, then sat down beside Margaret and took her hand. "I truly believe you have every reason to be hopeful, Margaret, but if there should be any problems at all or even if you just need some reassurance, don't hesitate to come and get me."

"Thank you."

Albert stood up and, after shaking hands with John, left the room with Fanny.

Both John and Margaret stayed silent for a long time. Neither of them were sure what to say because they hadn't really had time to digest the news yet.

Margaret had always wanted more children but they hadn't discussed it because she wanted time to watch Bessy grow up a little before having a second baby. Well Bessy had not long turned four, which she supposed was a decent gap.

John was wondering how he had let this happen. He was so careful when they made love because he feared he would lose her if she ever did become pregnant again. Of course he knew that no method of preventing pregnancy was completely effective, but he still felt that this was his fault. He dashed a hand through his hair and finally turned to look at Margaret. To his surprise she had a small smile on her lips. As though she knew that he was looking at her, her smile faded and she turned to him.

"You don't want this baby, do you?" she asked.

John sighed and sat down beside her, taking her hand.

"Margaret, I would love more children, truly I would, but if it's a choice between another child and you, I choose you every time."

"We cannot change what has happened," she said simply. "It is done. I am concerned that there might be ill effects but until I see signs of them, I am going to choose to be happy about this."

"I wish I could shut my emotions down so easily," he said.

Margaret smiled. "Actually, I feel relieved. I have been so emotional lately, melancholy one moment and angry the next. It is a relief to know that there is an explanation and that I am not losing my mind."

"Your moods didn't shift this drastically when you were pregnant with Bessy," he said.

"No, but understandably I have more to be upset about this time. I can't claim that the timing is good, or that we shouldn't have talked about this, or even that everything will be all right. All I can say is that I would like another child, and I hope you will find a way to overcome your fears and look forward to having another baby."

"How can you be so cavalier with your life?"

"I'm not being cavalier, darling. I promise that I will do everything in my power to get through this safely, but since I cannot change the situation, I must make the best of it."

John briefly considered the idea of an abortion but quickly discounted it. Not only would Margaret's faith probably make her reject the idea, he knew that it could be even riskier than proceeding with the pregnancy. He really had no choice but to try and make the best of this, and pray that Margaret would suffer no ill effects this time. He leaned forward and kissed her gently.

"I love you."

"Good." Margaret smiled. "Because I'm going to be around for a long time."

"Is tomorrow not your day to work in the village?" Fanny asked Albert as she accompanied him downstairs.

"It is," he smiled at her. "I shall check on Margaret while I'm here, just to make sure they have no major concerns."

"Well, I hardly think that is likely," she said with a smile. Knowing her brother he would fret for the next seven months regardless of what the doctor said. "But I was thinking more of offering you a room for the night. It seems a shame for you to ride back to Milton just to turn around and come back tomorrow."

"Thank you but I didn't come prepared to stay. I need clothes and medicines that I haven't brought with me." He smiled. "I do however, find myself short of a nurse for tomorrow as my usual assistant is still caring for her brother who was injured in the fire. I wondered if perhaps you might like to assist me tomorrow?"

"Me!" Fanny looked shocked. "Why, I... I... That is, I know nothing of medical matters, I really am not sure how much help I could be."

At least she hadn't said no outright, which he took as an encouraging sign.

"You would not be required to do anything medical. I may ask you to hand me instruments, find the medicines for patients and perhaps write instructions for them. Really, no training is required."

"Well... I..." Fanny considered his offer and found that the idea was appealing. She didn't much like the idea of tending to the workers but Dr. Townsend interested her and she found that she enjoyed his company. She might also enjoy helping him. "Yes, I would be happy to help you, Doctor." She smiled.

"Wonderful! I shall come to the house and collect you on my way to the village, say nine tomorrow morning?"

"I will be ready," she smiled as he walked to the door.

As he opened the door he turned back and gave her a broad smile. Fanny felt as if she had butterflies in her stomach, which was actually a rather pleasant sensation.

"I'll see you tomorrow." He said,

"Yes." She returned his smile. "Good evening, Dr. Townsend."

"Call me Albert, please. We are practically colleagues now, after all," he teased, and with a final bow, he placed his hat back on his head and turned away.

Fanny closed the door behind him and leaned against it. She didn't really understand how she felt, but she knew that she liked it very much.

Chapter Forty Three

Margaret awoke the next morning in John's arms. She could tell just by the light streaming through the curtains that she had slept late once again. What did surprise her was that John was also late rising. She lifted her head off his chest and supported it with her right hand under her chin as she looked at him. As expected he was wide awake.

"Please tell me you aren't going to start wrapping me in cotton wool already?" she asked. "I cannot be more than seven weeks pregnant and if I am forced to endure being coddled for another seven months, I will most likely do serious bodily harm to someone." She was only half teasing.

John smiled slightly.

"I had no wish to coddle you," he said. "Only to show you that I love you. Last night we discovered that we are to have another child and so far I have done nothing but fret. When I awoke this morning I realised that if something did happen, I did not want our last months to be a torrent of work and arguments."

Margaret smiled, pleased by his words.

"So I have resolved to get some help in the management of the mill. After all, we will soon be doubling the workforce, yet we have only taken on one new man in the office. So, I intend to make Higgins the Mill Foreman, he will be second only to me. And you, obviously."

Margaret tried not to laugh at his slip. "Go on."

"Thomas is already your second in command on the accounts but I think we should formalise that and give him more responsibility. You already have one new clerk but I think we should take on a second who can help out with general administration as well as the accounts, who can help out wherever he's needed."

"Or she."

"Aye," he grinned. "Or she."

"I think that's a marvellous idea. I feel as though we have been slowly growing apart for most of this year, and not because we are unhappy, just because circumstances seem to be conspiring against us, but I have missed you and Bessy."

"What have you missed?" he asked, interested to gather ideas.

"Our walks over the fields, with and without Bessy. Our impromptu picnics. Our late nights on a Saturday and our long lie-ins on a Sunday. Our dinners with Nicholas and the Maitlands. Going to a concert in town."

John realised that so much of their life had slowly been eroded, not just by the events of this past year but ever since they had moved the mill out here and begun expanding. How easily he had crept back into the role of master, how readily he had given up his home-life, albeit in tiny increments. As he looked into his wife's face, he vowed not to make that mistake again, for as he looked back over the past few years, all the high points had revolved around Margaret, not the mill and right now, the mill could go hang for all he cared.

"How do you feel?" he asked, and watched as her happy expression faded. "I meant your arm," he clarified with a chuckle, for every morning since the fire he would ask how she felt.

"Oh," she blushed. "It is a little better every day. I am so glad that it doesn't have to be cleaned twice daily now, for it is almost unbearable and once is more than enough."

"Well, let's get dressed for the day, then after putting in a few hours at the mill, I am taking you for afternoon tea at the Mitre Hotel."

"Oh, I am honoured. What have I done to deserve this?"

"I do this for every handsome girl I meet," he teased.

Margaret glared playfully at him. "Then I shall have to buy you some blinkers."

He laughed and Margaret found her gaze drawn to his lower lip and she found herself leaning forward to kiss it gently.

John caught the change in mood and his laughter faded.

"Margaret?" he asked, for they had not made love since the mill fire, both because they were too busy and because Margaret had been in too much pain.

"I want this," she assured him, knowing that he would take every care not to hurt her injured arm.

John gently rolled her over onto her back and looked down at her. Her dark hair was splayed out across the pillow and she looked quite enticing as she smiled up at him. She really was a marvel, he mused, and by some miracle, she was his.

As Dixon did her hair, Margaret was quite surprised to hear from her that Fanny had already left the house to help Dr. Townsend with the surgery. She had noticed an improvement in Fanny's attitude lately, but even that did not extend to helping the poor.

Though certainly very improper since her husband had not been dead many weeks, Margaret was forced to wondered if perhaps Fanny was a little sweet on Albert.

She realised of course, that Fanny had never loved Watson, and she knew that ever since the disastrous speculation, their marriage had been in serious trouble. In fact ever since they had come to live at Rose Cottage, Margaret doubted they had spent even a total of twenty hours alone in each others' company.

Of course Fanny would be subject to censure if she did show interest in another man before observing a proper mourning period but Margaret had a lot of time for Albert and if indeed something was brewing between them, she had little doubt that Albert would make sure that Fanny was not compromised in any way. In fact she felt that Albert could be very good for Fanny and found herself hoping that her suspicions were right.

Albert stopped into the office later that morning and Margaret went into John's private office so that he might check and clean her wound in without an audience. Thankfully John was in the mill at present, for he always hated seeing the pain she suffered when her dressings were changed.

"So," she said as Albert began ministering to her. "I hear you had a new nurse today?"

"Ah, I see that gossip still travels fast," he smiled.

"Not so fast, but then it only had to travel from the ground floor to my bedroom."

"True," he chuckled. "And yes, I did have a new nurse."

"Did she enjoy it?" Margaret asked, hissing with pain a moment later as he gently pulled the dressing off and began swabbing the burn with ethanol.

"To be honest, I am not sure." Though he noted her discomfort, he knew that she liked to be kept distracted. "At times she looked rather green around the gills but overall, yes I would say she enjoyed the experience. At least, she has volunteered to help again next week."

Margaret smiled, though it was somewhat tight.

"I fear that she has been rather unfairly maligned," he continued. "For while she does have some very obvious faults, she does not seem anywhere near so bad as gossip had led me to believe. And, of course, who among us does not have a fault or two."

"I believe you are correct and that, at heart, Fanny is a good person."

Albert caught her eye and smiled.

"You like her?" Margaret ventured.

"It is too soon to say," he looked away, back to the bandage he was now wrapping around her arm. "I find her interesting, and I certainly enjoy spending time with her, and I must confess, she is most handsome..."

"But," Margaret prompted.

"But her husband has only just died and I would be foolish to read too much into these interactions yet. I'm sure she is lonely and still quite upset. She may well simply see me as a friend and it would be unkind to pressure her for anything else until she is recovered from her grief."

"Indeed," Margaret smiled. "But many a good relationship is built on the solid foundation of friendship."

"Aye," he said as a wry smile turned the edges of his lips up. "There, all done."

"Thank you." Margaret breathed a sigh of relief.

"It won't be many more weeks now until it starts to scar, I think it's time you strapped your arm up at night."

"It's always bandaged overnight," she said, confused.

"No, I mean like this." He demonstrated by touching his left hand to his left shoulder. "The scar tissue that forms won't be elastic like skin is and if you don't stretch the joint as the scar tissue is forming, you will have reduced mobility and pain for a long time."

He explained that she was to bandage the burn very loosely at night, then showed her how to bandage the arm so that it was kept bent while she slept.

Margaret gave a long suffering sigh, though she agreed to do it.

Later that day as they took tea in the town, she told John of the possible blossoming romance between Fanny and Albert. Although he too had been surprised to hear of Fanny's offer to help Albert, he hadn't considered that his sister might have feelings for the doctor. Like Margaret though, he found the idea pleasing once he became used to it. She could do a lot worse for herself than Albert Townsend.

"And have you noticed how much time she has been spending with Malcolm?" he asked.

Margaret nodded, feeling a pang of guilt. Ever since the fire she had been spending less time with her own daughter, as well as failing to praise Fanny for her new found affection towards her son. She said as much to John, who felt bad when he saw the tears shining in her eyes.

"You must not fret," he said. "You are an excellent mother and Bessy loves you dearly. I explained to her that you were in a lot of pain and that you found it difficult to be friendly for too long and she said that she remembered how she had cried when she fell over the week before, and that she thought her Mama was very brave."

Margaret's tears increased at his words, for her behaviour over the past few weeks should not have won her any sympathy.

"Oh dear," she said, taking the handkerchief John offered. "I fear this pregnancy will turn me into an emotional basket case before long. One minute I am angry, the next in love and the next crying."

"You have nothing to apologise for." John smiled and took her hand. "You have been through an ordeal, and I don't just mean with your wound. It will take you time to come to terms with what happened that day and I'm certain that a heart as good as yours has earned the right to fire off a few tetchy remarks."

"I wasn't aware that I was in credit," Margaret laughed. "Perhaps while I have the excuse of being emotional I might tell a few other Milton men their fortunes," she teased as she spied Mr Slickson across the dining hall.

John followed her gaze but his smile faded as he saw the other master.

"What?" Margaret asked.

"There is more talk of a strike," John confessed. "Two of the mills have cut the wages again and there are fears that the others may have to follow suit. The men are not happy."

"But surely that won't affect us, being that we are out of town?" she asked.

"No, I don't believe so."

"Then why do you look so grave?"

"Because I am being blamed for the strike."

"What!" her surprised utterance came out louder than expected, drawing the gaze of surrounding patrons. "What?" she asked again in a slightly more reasonable tone.

"They say that what we are trying to achieve is undermining their position. The working conditions the good wages, the housing, everything. They are being compared most unfavourably to us."

"But surely there is no reason they cannot do what we have done, short of providing the housing, that is, though I know for a fact that two of the mill masters are richer than we are and could afford it if they wanted."

"Aye, but they don't see it that way. With the problems sourcing cotton, we had your brother's resources to call upon but many have opted to buy more expensive cotton rather than look into other markets, and many were also hit by Watson's speculation, meaning they don't have the reserves they did a year ago. Some are worse than others, obviously, but the picture is pretty bleak throughout Milton. And don't forget, the rent money we earn from the houses means that we don't have to make as large a profit on our orders, so we have been undercutting the local mills."

"But we just lost a mill, a brother in law and sixty two workers!"

"Aye, and all they see is the insurance cheque. They care about the bottom line, not people."

Margaret thought it was awfully unfair of them to blame her husband just because he wanted to give his workers a decent life.

"They should be ashamed of themselves," she said.

"Aye, but something tells me I shan't be invited to many more Masters' dinners."

"I'm sorry," she sympathised.

"Don't be. All things considered, it's no great loss."

"Another strike won't be good for Milton," she mused, sipping her tea. "People have been brought so low already that if the masters don't give in quickly, this could be very dangerous for the mill hands."

"And here I thought that spending thousands on a mill outside of Milton meant that you wouldn't have to worry about strikes any more," he teased.

Margaret found a smile for him but in reality she was worried. Milton had suffered so much recently, what would become of the workers if the strike lasted, as it had the last time? How many would starve or resort to thievery and violence?

John watched her, easily reading her expression and knowing how upset the talk of a strike had made her. He loved her for her big heart but he also cursed her for it, for what was the point in caring about something if you could do nothing to change the outcome?

Even with everything he and Margaret were doing at Thornton Mill, they were still only helping a fraction of the people who needed help. What of the others? They were surely unable to employ everyone who needed decent living conditions, so what were they supposed to do? Simply turn their backs and ignore their plight?

Though he had always deeply resented their intrusions into his business practices, for perhaps the first time John Thornton thought of parliament in a helpful light, for surely they were the only ones with the power to improve conditions among working men.

By the time Margaret had finished preparing for bed that evening, John was already in bed, reading The Ugly Duckling.

"I've heard of light reading but children's books?" she teased.

"I thought I might read this to the children next," he answered simply.

For a moment Margaret thought he was getting carried away, since they had only known of her pregnancy for one day, but then she realised he meant Bessy and Malcolm. He always liked to read the books before he read aloud to the children each evening, so that he might enjoy them also. Margaret rather suspected it was because, like the children, he wanted to find out what was going to happen and unless he had already read the book, he would find it hard to stop after only one chapter.

Even in these busy times of late, John had stuck to his story time with Bessy, though regretfully, Margaret had been somewhat lax about joining him. She vowed to change that. It was family time, and she did so love to hear his deep, baritone voice as he read. He also had a talent for bringing the stories to life and injecting the words with the relevant emotion.

Margaret slipped her dressing gown and nightdress off and climbed into bed beside him. She took the book from his hands and reached across him to lay it on the night stand, then gestured for him to slide down the bed, which he did. Then she proceeded to position his left arm against the pillows and curl into him, resting her injured left arm across his waist.

He smiled as she positioned him. It had started because she had been in so much pain with her arm that he had feared hurting her. In frustration she had simply moved him where she wanted him and he had been so enamoured of her simple, direct action, even though it was a sign of her frustration with him, that he had allowed her to position him every night since. Indeed he purposefully stayed where he was so that she would have to position him.

Once she was settled, he brought his left arm up and around her shoulders; tracing light patterns with his fingertips on her skin.

"I had a lovely day today," she said, kissing his chest. "Thank you."

"And your arm?" he asked.

"Bearable. I do miss the laudanum to help me sleep though." Last night she had been very restless indeed.

"I know," he said with a smile in his voice.

"I didn't keep you awake, did I?"

"I'm afraid that when you use me as your pillow, I cannot help but be kept awake by your restlessness."

"I'm sorry," she raised her head and looked at him, her expression contrite. She had tried her best to keep still but evidently it hadn't been enough.

"Think no more of it," he said, using his left hand to gently press her head back onto his chest.

They lay there in silence for a while until Margaret finally voiced her thoughts.

"John, do you ever wonder what will become of us when we are old and grey and too feeble to work any more?"

"You, my dear, will never be feeble." He craned his neck forward to kiss the top of her head but as she looked up at him, he clumsily kissed her forehead instead. They laughed and and tried again, this time their aim was true as they found each others lips.

"Seriously though, do you give much thought to the future?"

"Honestly? No. I don't mind what the future holds for us as long as you are a part of it."

She smiled, though it was a pale reflection of her usual smile.

"What troubles you?" he asked.

Margaret looked down at his chest, playing with the smattering of hair she found there.

"Margaret," he gently prompted.

"Ever since the mill fire, I can't seem to stop myself thinking 'what if'. What if I had died that day? How would you and Bessy cope? What if something happened to you, for I know that I couldn't cope without you. Then I keep replaying the events of that day over and over in my mind, like an endless play that just starts again once it has finished. I keep thinking what I could have done differently, what I should have done differently."

"I don't know much about trauma but I am sure that what you are experiencing is perfectly normal," he tried to reassure her. "I know that you don't like to talk about what happened that day, but perhaps it would be good for you to finally tell someone. I would be happy to hear every detail.

Margaret's eyes flashed to his then she quickly looked away. She could never tell him of what she had witnessed that day, the horror, the Bill's cries and the workers screams, the futile attempt to rescue those who were beyond hope. The only reason she hadn't died in that fire was because Bill had snarled at her, blocking her path back into the mill and Higgins dragged her away, but some of the things she saw would haunt her until the day she died, she was sure of it. Though she believed that she could bear it, she couldn't share those images with John, for she couldn't in all good conscience burden him with such horrific things, especially given his tendency   to blame himself for her misfortunes.

John sensed her hesitation.

"Or maybe you could write them down. Start a diary perhaps," he suggested, then a better idea occurred to him. "Or write a letter to your father, telling him about it. Wherever he is, I am certain that he watches over you if he can and probably witnessed all that happened that day."

He saw Margaret's brow furrow as she considered that idea.

"Perhaps I will try that." She smiled as she thought about it, almost able to hear her father's voice in her head already, answering her questions in his quiet and intelligent way.

As she lay her head back on his chest, she felt lighter already at just the idea of writing to her father, as though his spirit was already shouldering some of the burden she felt.

317

"Thank you," she said softly. "I don't deserve you."

"Nonsense," he said gently. He licked his fingers and reached over to snuff the candle out, leaving them with just the moonlight that seeped through the curtains to see by.

"I love you," she said, and John felt her warm tears hit his chest and roll away.

"Hey," he sat up and pulled her to him, cradling her in his arms as she cried. He disliked seeing her in this much pain, both emotionally as well as physically, but he hoped that by releasing her emotions she could start to heal. He stroked her soft hair and waited patiently until her tears abated before leaving her there while he fetched a handkerchief for her.

"Thank you," she said, wiping her eyes and smiling almost shyly at him.

"I hope you know that you never have to be ashamed of your emotions, Margaret. I believe they are where your indomitable spirit comes from and I value them more highly than anything. Even your negative emotions."

She laughed at his kind words and set the handkerchief aside.

"Are you ready to sleep now?" he asked.

Margaret nodded, so they lay back down and though it took a while, they eventually drifted off into a sound sleep.

Margaret sat at her writing desk, looking down at the half-finished letter to her father, unsure if she could continue.

On sudden impulse, she knew she couldn't. Tomorrow she would resume the letter but today she had already relived too many traumas. She slipped the letter into her desk drawer and locked it, then headed off to find Bessy. Tomorrow she would include Malcolm in their activities but today she needed to bond with her daughter again.

Though her work was not finished, she had left the mill at lunchtime today so that she might start on this letter and still have time to spend with her daughter. John was still hard at work and as she and Bessy walked out into the countryside around Milton, she suddenly had an urge to see his handsome, smiling face, so she turned and they headed towards the mill instead.

Bessy loved visiting the mill because everyone around there adored her and she was the centre of attention. Bessy did so love being adored, but then what child didn't?

As they entered the mill yard they were accosted. Most people just said a cheerful "'Ello" to "Miss Elizabeth" to which she would smile and say hello back. Some would stop and talk for a moment, which she liked even more. Finally they made their way into the offices and headed for John's door, only to find his office empty. Margaret turned back to the hallway.

"Oh, Thomas," she called as her assistant came out of their office.

"Afternoon Mrs Thornton. Didn't expect you back this soon,"

"No indeed," she smiled. "Have you seen my husband?"

"He went into Milton about half an hour ago."

"Oh, nothing serious, I hope?"

"I think he'd been planning on the visit, so nothing out of the ordinary, I'd say."

"Thank you," she smiled and went back into John's office, closing the door behind her.

This morning he had categorically told her he was at the mill all day. In fact he had been complaining because he still hadn't finished the inventory and wanted to get that job out of the way for another year.

Margaret went to his date book, opened it to today's date and there it was, staring back at her.

1.30 ET

Who was ET, she wondered. All his other appointments had names and sometimes places. Like the entry on Friday had the time, *'11am'*, the name, *'Mr H Bowden'*, the place, *'TM'* (Thornton Mill) and the subject, *'shop lease?'* meaning Mr Bowden might want to lease a shop in the village.

The more she thought about it, the more suspicious this ET entry became. Was John even in Milton, as Thomas thought, or had he gone somewhere else? He surely didn't expect to see her until the end of the day, around 8pm this evening. That gave him a lot of time for whatever this ET wanted.

She slammed the diary closed, ashamed of her thoughts, and left to take Bessy for the walk she had originally intended. She did her best to put the incident out of her mind for it was making her short tempered and this was supposed to be a nice afternoon spent with her daughter, not another round of her struggling to hold in her temper.

She did a good job of pushing it from her mind until they

returned home and Jenny took Bessy away for her bath. Alone once more, she began to replay the possible implications of that entry over in her mind.

Until last night, they had not lain with each other since the fire. That was a long time for a young, virile man to go without relief. Perhaps seeking not to burden her with his desires, he had found another way to discreetly relieve them. Perhaps he had twisted things in his mind until he truly believed that he was actually doing her a kindness.

She was tempted to return to the mill and see how many other entries there were that mentioned ET. Was this a regular occurrence or a more recent event?

Was John even capable of what she was suspecting? John was a moral man, a good man and a just man. She truly believed he would never want to hurt her. Had he simply thought that she would never find out?

No, ET must be one of their business contacts or friends. She wracked her brain trying to think of anyone they knew with the initials ET, other than Bessy of course, because she was certain that he wasn't with her. She even got their address book out but could find no one with the correct initials.

Whoever this ET was, he or she was a new acquaintance.

She knew she would drive herself slightly insane if she did not find something to occupy her until her husband returned, so she decided to go visiting. She packed a basket with various treats that the mill workers would not usually have access to, and headed out to visit some friends. They no longer viewed her gifts as charity for she explained that in the south, when you visited the home of another, it was polite to bring a gift to thank your hosts, which wasn't untrue, exactly but perhaps not the whole truth. Nevertheless, it had quietened their arguments about not taking charity.

She called first on Mrs Webber, whose oldest daughter, Sarah was getting married in a few weeks. Margaret thought that she would enjoy hearing about their wedding plans.

Chapter Forty Four

Margaret arrived home to find Fanny in the back sitting room working on her embroidery. She really didn't feel she was up to enduring company at the moment and was about to turn and quietly leave when Fanny noticed her.

"Oh, Margaret, how lovely to see you. How was your day?"

Margaret smiled politely and sat down.

"Oh, nothing out of the ordinary. What about you?"

"Oh, this and that, you know."

Not really, Margaret thought.

"I heard you helped Albert out at the surgery yesterday. How did you find it?"

"Oh, most interesting. Some things made me feel quite queasy, as when he lanced a boil on young Peter Braithwait," she shuddered at the memory. "But overall I found it very rewarding."

"I'm glad." She tried to sound enthusiastic but failed miserably.

"Yes, I have offered to help out every week."

"Really?"

"Yes, it is quite unlike me, I know, but Albert is such a wonderful man, doing all he does for the poor, that I feel it is my duty to help where I can. Do you know what most doctors charge for a visit?" she sounded outraged.

Unlike Fanny, Margaret knew exactly how much a consultation with Dr Donaldson cost, but Fanny wasn't looking for a reply.

"I couldn't believe it! No wonder so few working class people can afford it."

"I'm glad you've found a new interest," Margaret stood up. "Now if you'll excuse me, I really would like to go and see Bessy for a while."

"Oh, of course. I'll see you at dinner, I expect."

"Yes, I expect so." Margaret turned and left before she could be drawn into any further discussion.

She headed upstairs and collected Bessy from the nursery, taking her into her bedroom. They both lay on the bed and Bessy told her mother all about the picture Jenny had helped her draw after they got home today. Margaret listened to the girl's chatter, letting it soothe her raw nerves. She heard John arrive home but chose to stay where she was and after a few minutes he came to find her.

"Daddy!" Bessy smiled, jumping from the bed and launching herself at her father, who swept her up into his arms.

Margaret got off the bed and went and sat at her dressing table to remove her jewellery.

After greeting her, John set Bessy back down on her feet, telling her to go and wash up ready for dinner. Bessy ran off, eager to please her father.

"And how was your day?" John asked, coming up behind his wife and kissing her shoulder.

"Fine," she tried to smile but it looked cold and brittle.

"Something wrong?" he asked.

"No, nothing's wrong. How was your day?"

"Tiring." He turned away and removed his coat.

"Nothing unusual?" she asked.

"Not especially. Why do you ask?"

"I just wondered what had made you tired, that's all."

"Just inventory. You know how much I dislike that task."

"I suppose it took you all day to finish?"

"Yes," he gave a weary sigh and Margaret closed her eyes. Despite her anger earlier, now she only felt pain and though she tried her best to keep calm, tears began to leak from beneath her closed eyelids.

"Margaret?" John said, noticing that she was bowed over. "What's wrong?" he asked, coming closer.

"Nothing," she managed to say in a reasonably steady voice.

"It's not nothing. Tell me what troubles you? Please."

His warm words did nothing to quell her pain but they did reignite her anger and she lifted her head and stared at him in the mirror.

"You're upset," he said, noticing her tears.

"It would seem that I have an aversion to being lied to," she said, her eyes flashing with anger.

"What-"

"Bessy and I thought we would surprise you this afternoon with a visit, only to discover that you weren't there and had some clandestine meeting arranged with someone who's initials are ET."

"I'm sorry, I didn't mean to lie to you." John looked contrite.

"I'm sure you didn't. I'm certain that you hoped your deception would never be discovered."

"Margaret, it's not like that-"

She raised her hand to cut him off.

"I don't want to hear it. If you don't mind, I've had a long day and my arm is hurting quite a lot so I think I would like to have an early night."

"Margaret-"

"Fanny's downstairs, I'm sure she'll enjoy having dinner with you."

Seeing that she wasn't going to hear him out, John turned and left the room, leaving the door slightly open in his wake.

As soon as he was out of sight, Margaret put her elbows on the dressing table and rested her face in her hands. She had thought she would feel better after having confronted him but she didn't feel any different, and so with a weary sigh, she rose to get changed for bed. It was only just gone eight but she could read for a while, she supposed. She was tempted to sleep in one of the spare rooms but before she could think any further about that, a small yip directed her attention to the door, through which a tiny black and tan dog was making its way to her.

Margaret smiled as she bent to retrieve the puppy from the floor.

"Where did you come from?" she asked.

"Margaret," she looked up to see John leaning against the door frame, looking amused. "I'd like you to meet ET, otherwise known as an English Terrier."

Margaret cringed with mortification.

"I made enquiries a while ago, after the fire but she was too young to leave her mother. She turned three months old today so I went to collect her. I am assured she is already house-trained and though she'll be a small dog, the breed is very loyal and brave. I was planning on giving her to you after Bessy had gone to sleep but since you decided not to join us for dinner..."

"Oh, John," she cried. "I'm so sorry." She was absolutely certain that at one time she would have listened reasonably and rationally to his explanation. "What must you think of me?"

"Is it very wrong of me to enjoy the fact that you were jealous?" he asked, seemingly taking pleasure in her discomfort.

"Probably," she agreed, walking up to him, the puppy still

323

clutched in her arms. "I just... I feel so irritable all the time."

John put his arms around her and drew her to him. She wrapped her injured arm gently around him for her right arm still held the puppy.

"You are in pain, it is only to be expected, love. Albert thinks you will be healed in another six to eight weeks, so try to focus on that."

"Can you bear me for that much longer?"

"I can," he assured her, kissing the top of her head before pulling away. "So, I take it we are keeping her?" he asked.

Margaret was already so taken by the puppy that there was no way she could give her up.

"I'm surprised I'm allowed to after exhibiting such childish behaviour," she said.

"Margaret, please, stop being so hard on yourself. I did lie and you were justified in being hurt until you found out the reason. Had I realised I would be discovered or how much it would hurt you, I would never have done it; it was thoughtless of me and I apologise."

Margaret smiled warmly at him.

"How is it that I can make a total fool of myself and yet you end up apologising to me?"

"I guess I'm just a fool in love." He bent down to kiss her lips. "Now, we will talk no more of it; agreed?"

"Yes," she smiled. "Thank you, both for such a thoughtful gift and for being so-"

"Shh!" he put a finger over her lips. "We agreed, no more," he reminded her before removing his finger and stealing a kiss. "Now, did you want to stay up here or will you come down to dinner and show off your new puppy?"

"I will come down."

"Good, because I have also been ordering some paraphernalia for the mutt which I collected from mother's house today."

Margaret placed the puppy into his arms so that she could wrap her good arm around him and stretch up on her toes for a kiss.

"I love you," she said, her eyes begging him to believe her.

"I know. And I love you, moods and all."

Their romantic moment was somewhat spoiled when a tiny tongue began licking Margaret's chin.

"Oh," she pulled out of reach. "You scamp!" she gently

chided with a smile. "Let's go and see what your Daddy has brought you, shall we?"

"I am father to no dog," John assured her, though his stern words were somewhat spoiled by his smile.

Despite his assurance that the dog was no child to him, he had certainly seen fit to spoil her with gifts. He had bought a number of round cushions that he explained could be set in front of the fires and in Margaret's office as beds. He had bought her a handful of collars in various shades with matching leads, many more than the dog could have worn out in one lifetime. He had also ordered a number of small toys which he thought the puppy might like to play with, as well as pigs ears as treats for her.

Even Fanny seemed rather taken with the creature, though she had despised Bill, probably because she wasn't what one might call an attractive dog, at least not in her looks.

Upon hearing the commotion and cooing over the puppy, Bessy managed to break away from Jenny and since Jenny couldn't leave Malcolm alone, both children and their nanny were soon introduced to the dog. Bessy soon lost interest when she realised that this dog didn't know the same commands as Bill had and therefore wouldn't do what she was told.

To everyones' surprise though, after dinner, Malcolm sat with the puppy cradled in his lap until it was time for bed. He seemed reluctant to leave the animal but dutifully followed Jenny up to the nursery.

The pup made it's way along the sofa until it butted up against the next warm body, which happened to be Fanny's, and then promptly settled on her lap.

"Oh, what an adorable little thing," she said stroking it's head. "Malcolm certainly seemed taken with it, didn't he?" she asked.

"He did." Margaret answered, pleased that she was paying her son more attention these days and noticing things she would once have missed or ignored.

"I wonder if he might like a puppy of his own," she mused. "It would be good for him to learn to care for something."

"I believe the breeder still has some of the litter left, would you like me make enquiries for you?" John asked.

"Would you? That would be wonderful, John. Thank you."

"My pleasure," he smiled at his sister, keen to encourage any concern or consideration she showed to Malcolm.

Margaret was tempted to say he could have this puppy since he was so taken with it, and she get another, but it had been a gift from John and she could not bring herself to give it away.

"Perhaps if John would give us the details of the breeder, we might take the children into town tomorrow and Malcolm could pick his own puppy."

"The breeder's not in Milton," he said. "He's over in Penton, about an hour away by coach, but I'm sure he'd be glad to see you. He's had three litters of English Terriers quite close so he's having some trouble finding homes for this latest litter."

"Then I shall leave the office early tomorrow," Margaret said. "If we leave here about eleven, we should be back in Milton just in time to have a spot of lunch together,"

"Oh, wonderful." Fanny grinned. Since losing Watson she had often bemoaned the fact that because she was forced to observe a period of mourning, she had not socialised at all out of respect for her husband, though in reality her invitations had dried up around the time that his speculation failed. Although she was still forced to wear black, Fanny was very much looking forward to rejoining society, even if only in a limited fashion with her sister in law.

That evening Margaret settled the pup on one of its bed cushions by the fire in their room, where she seemed quite content to sleep since it was nice and warm.

When Margaret had finished her toilette, John was still sitting by the fire, finishing his nightcap so she came and sat with him.

"We must think of a name for her," John said.

"How about if we let Bessy decide again?"

"Oh no, she'll probably want to call her Peter or something equally ridiculous."

Margaret laughed. The fact that a female dog had been called Bill had greatly irked him.

"I promise to confine her to girls names," she promised.

"You realise we will be paying for Malcolm's animal, don't you? Watson's estate is actually in debt, not credit."

"I know. I also think it is probably a good idea if we start giving Fanny some housekeeping money."

"You want us to give Fanny money?"

"Well Watson can't any longer and although we have no legal obligation, she is our moral responsibility, John."

"She is not. I raised her, paid for her education, paid for her lodgings, her keep, her wardrobe and I paid for her wedding. We have done more than enough since Watson's speculation failed to help her and her family."

"You know that she has no means of supporting herself, John; would you see her on the street?"

"Of course not," he snapped.

"Well, if she is ever to find another husband, she will need to regain her standing in society, for which she will need an allowance so that she might call carriages, take tea with other ladies and when she is out of her mourning clothes, buy herself some new dresses."

John sighed in defeat, for he knew she was right. As much as he appreciated Fanny's improvement in attitude recently, she still seemed just as useless as ever in his eyes. He knew he was being harsh and that most ladies of means, and gentlemen for that matter, didn't work but the women in his life, namely his mother and his wife, had both insisted on helping him with the family business. Fanny couldn't even be relied on for entertainment since her singing voice lacked the required melodious quality to be enjoyable and her piano skills were somewhat rudimentary, despite the many pounds he had spent on lessons over the years.

He thought back to their visit to see Frederick in Spain. Oh, how he had envied Fred and Margaret their relationship, they were so easy and open with each other, they understood each other almost instinctively, despite spending much of their childhood apart since Margaret had spent many months of the year in London as companion to her cousin. He had watched them one night as they had walked home from the opera, arm in arm, chatting and laughing easily. Truly John would have loved to take a turn around town with his sister, only he knew that they had so little in common that both would end up resenting the other's company.

Still, she was his only sister and he vowed to try harder. Perhaps it wasn't too late for them.

The next morning at breakfast, Bessy was given the grand job of naming Rose Cottage's newest resident and she chose Rosie. Margaret thought it very fitting, if not particularly imaginative.

After putting in a few hours in the mill office, Margaret

returned to the house to collect Fanny and the children. Jimmy had already set the horse to the carriage and once they had climbed in, he drove them to the breeder. As they approached, Margaret thought that it was a good thing that Jimmy had been here just the day before, for she would probably never have found this farmhouse on her own, tucked away in the countryside as it was.

The breeder was pleased to see them and happy for them to see the pups and the parents. To Margaret's surprise he led them into the farmhouse kitchen, where the puppies and their mother were sleeping in a large basket by the Aga.

"They're the wife's thing," he said. "I do t' farm, she does t' livestock."

"Livestock," his wife laughed, coming over to shake their hand. "We only 'ave dogs. We breed collies for t'shepherds and the terriers for ratting."

"They're adorable," Margaret said spying the five pups. "I'm surprised you have so many left."

"Aye, we've 'ad some big litters. Maisy there, she had nine! I could hardly believe it myself, she's such a wee thing, and the one a'for her, Daisy, she had seven."

Malcolm had already sat down on the floor beside the basket and was talking softly to the puppies. Three of the puppies remained sleeping but the other two were interested in their new visitor and came to the edge of the basket to see him. Maisy, the mother, raised her head to look at the new person, but soon lowered it again, seemingly worn out from her mothering duties.

"I'm surprised you keep them in the house," Margaret remarked.

"Wouldn't normally but Maisy were looking a wee bit sickly just after she had t' pups, so I'd rather 'ave her where I can keep me eye on her. She's a grand dog, she is, best ratter I ever seen and I'd hate to lose 'er."

One of the puppies had clambered out of the basket and was trying to climb Malcolm's chest to lick his face.

"I think he's chosen," Margaret remarked to Fanny, who turned to see. The other puppies had awoken now and realising that a stranger was in attendance who might give them attention, another two of them made their way over to Malcolm. The fifth puppy however, moved away and hovered in the corner. He was the smallest, probably

328

the runt of the litter.

"Have you picked one?" Fanny asked her son, crouching over him to see the dog he held.

Malcolm nodded and pointed to the smallest dog in the corner of the basket.

"That one?" Fanny asked, sounding surprised.

Malcolm nodded.

In a low voice, Margaret asked if she could speak with the housewife and was duly ushered out into the hallway.

"No offence, but is that little one the runt of the litter?"

"Aye. We didnae think he would make it but he's stronger than he looks."

"I just want to make sure the puppy will be okay. Malcolm is very shy at the best of times and he's only recently lost his father. If something were to happen to the puppy as well-"

"Trust me." The wife patted Margaret's arm. "It were touch and go, but at three months he's perfectly healthy, just a little small."

"Why is he so shy?"

"The others tend to bully 'im 'cos he's weaker. I'm glad of your takin' him really, cos I do hate to see the others being mean to 'im. I always have a bit of a soft spot for the wee ones."

Margaret smiled, sensing a kindred spirit.

They returned to the kitchen and Margaret paid her for the puppy, then a few minutes later, they were all in the carriage heading back towards Milton.

They stopped at the White Horse Hotel's restaurant but they were too late for lunch so they opted for afternoon tea instead, enjoying a selection of sandwiches, cheese and biscuits, scones with jam or cream and cakes. The hotel was reluctant to let the children in at first, until Margaret asked to see the manager and explained that the children were very well behaved. The manager knew who Mrs Thornton was (who in Milton didn't?) and he did not want to upset someone of her wealth, though he cautioned her that if the children did misbehave, they would all be asked to leave.

Jimmy looked after the puppy while they went inside and seemed quite as taken with the little dog as Malcolm was.

Fanny saw many of her old friends and acquaintances there and said hello to them all. They all offered their sympathies for the loss of her husband and, to Margaret's eye at least, seemed to be warming to her again. Perhaps they thought that Watson's death counteracted his bad financial advice and were now more willing to forgive his wife.

They were asked to join Mrs Jones and Mrs Small, which they did. The ladies seemed to find it immensely interesting that the children had been allowed in and Margaret took the blame for that act since she didn't want Fanny's friends to think ill of her sister in law.

They ate their fill, chatted for a long while and Fanny caught the ladies up on all the recent happenings in her life, though she left out any more unpleasant events. Many people stopped by the table to talk to them and Fanny received invitations to call upon many different women that day.

Some asked how Margaret's injuries were healing, though thankfully a lot forgot to ask. The bandages were hidden by her long sleeve and from the outside there was no visible sign that she had ever been hurt.

By the time they left, Margaret was getting tired of all the small talk and false pleasantries that were being exchanged and was glad to return to the village before she lost her temper again.

On the way home, Malcolm decided to call his puppy Scone, after the treat he had enjoyed so much at lunch. Fanny tried to talk him out of the name but Margaret rather liked it.

Margaret had thought that much of the new puppy's care and training would fall to her, but Malcolm proved to be devoted to his new friend. Under Jimmy's tutelage who, though his main experience was with horses also proved to be good with dogs, Malcolm learned how to train Scone to obey simple commands, like sit, and more complex ones, like fetch.

Scone would always prove to be a shy dog, unlike Rosie who always got her point across, but over the next few months Scone came out of his shell a little, as did his master, Malcolm. Margaret watched their progress with great joy as the dog finally taught this quiet little boy how to play.

Chapter Forty Five

As autumn approached that year, things had greatly improved for Margaret. Her burn had finally scarred over and while the scar tissue still looked red and angry, it didn't hurt very much at all now. Dixon had found a balm recipe containing aloe, avodaco and apricot oil, powdered willow bark and opium which when applied twice a day and the area then covered in bandages, helped to sooth the pain caused by the tight scar tissue and relieve some of her discomfort. She still had to strap her arm up every evening but thanks to the balm, she was even handling that discomfort with much more grace recently, especially since her moods seemed to have levelled off.

Indeed she was feeling much more like her old self again.

She also enjoyed the fact that at four and a half months pregnant, she was beginning to show. She loved looking down and thinking about the child they were going to have.

Albert had done a lot more reading on eclampsia since she discovered she was with child and had finally managed to set John's mind at ease, having been unable to locate a single case among his colleagues in Edinburgh where a woman had suffered the same symptoms in a second pregnancy.

Though things were looking brighter for the couple, things began to look even bleaker in Milton when the workers finally went out on strike over their lowered wages. Even though Thornton Mill was spared the strike action, it broke Margaret's heart to think of all the families going hungry. If she could have, she would have taken them all on but alas, even after the final expansion, they still would not be able to employ them all. Plus, that expansion was at the very least, three years away.

Her hopes for a quick end to the strike proved futile and by the first week in November she was having sleepless nights.

John worried about her but she did her best to assure him that she was just upset and this was nothing to do with her pregnancy. To give him his due, John was also concerned, though he was better able to manage his emotions having grown up in Milton and become more accustomed to the strife.

"I just wish there was something I could do," Margaret sighed as John comforted her in their bed. "I cannot even take a basket there now because as your wife, it would only be seen as us supporting the strikers and create more problems between you and the other masters."

John raised himself up onto his side and propped his head on his hand.

"What?" Margaret asked, knowing he had had an idea.

He frowned but didn't answer her for a few moments.

"Well," he began when had thought things through. "You can't take a basket, but Nicholas told me some of the workers have been."

"Of course!" Margaret sat upright. "I can't be seen to be involved, but I could see if the workers wanted to get organised and all donate a little. I could also donate supplies, anonymously of course."

John yawned. Though it was almost one in the morning, he knew he wasn't going to get much sleep tonight. Thankfully tomorrow was Sunday and they could sleep as late as they wished.

Margaret got out of bed, pulled on a robe and collected a pencil from her writing desk, a sheet of paper and a book to lean on before returning to sit beside John.

Rosie raised her head as her mistress moved but soon settled back upon her bed when she realised that neither food nor attention would be forthcoming.

Margaret set the pencil to the paper and began writing a list.

"I can ask Reverend Hall to make a plea in church tomorrow for the villagers to all donate a little something. We used to do something similar at the Harvest Festival in Helstone, all give a little from the harvest or what we could spare from our pantries to be donated to the poor.

John watched her as she began scribbling.

"And the weather is turning cold, so I am sure coal and peat would be welcomed."

"And blankets," John added.

"Right. Clothes of any kind might be welcomed actually."

John looked to the frost on the window, then to the fire in their bedroom that while not very built up any longer, still warmed the room nicely. The workers couldn't have picked a worse time to strike, really, with the harsh Milton winter coming on. They truly must have been desperate.

He'd donate some coal from the factory, he decided. Anonymously, of course and he supposed they could spare some money.

When Margaret finally got done with her list, she settled

back down and this time quickly drifted off to sleep but when he awoke the next morning, he was surprised to find Margaret already up and doing her own hair.

"Isn't that what you have Dixon for?" he asked.

She turned and smiled at him.

"I don't have time today, I have so much to organise."

"Margaret," John sighed and got out of bed. "Much as I understand your desire to help, you can't be seen to have anything to do with this."

Margaret frowned. She knew he was right, but she had become something of a perfectionist and she wanted this done properly.

"Go and speak to Higgins," John said. "He's an ex-union man, he'll know what to do and how to organise it. And get a hundred pounds from the safe to start the collection."

"A hundred pounds?" she turned to him, shocked.

"Aye. We don't know how much longer this will go on for, do we. And Christmas is but a few weeks away now."

Margaret felt tears prick her eyes at his generosity, for one hundred pounds was no small gesture.

"I think A Christmas Carol is rubbing off on you," she said, wrapping her hands around his waist and hugging him tightly. John was reading it to the children again since it was one of Bessy's favourites.

It wasn't the book, of course, it was the man. A man she loved with every fibre of her being.

"More like you rubbing off on me," he answered, hugging her back.

"Nonsense, you always had a good heart."

"Aye, maybe, but it was you that breathed life into it." He kissed the top of her head. "Come back to bed. You hardly got any sleep last night and the Reverend won't be here to take the service until midday. You'll still have plenty of time to see Nicholas first."

Margaret looked up at him. "But I'm not tired any more," she said, fluttering her eyelashes at him.

"And I suppose you want me to tire you out?" John smirked.

"Only if it's not too much trouble."

John answered by sweeping her off her feet and into his arms, carrying her over to the bed.

"You are a temptress," he said as he laid her down on her

back and hovered over her.

"Am I?" she asked, innocently.

"Oh yes."

Margaret spun them around until she was on top.

"Well then, let me tempt you," she said, lowering her lips to his neck to begin her delicious assault on him.

The collection to help the Milton mill workers went very well indeed. So well that Higgins had to hire a cart and make multiple trips into town with all the food and clothes that the villagers had donated.

He gave the items and money to the union leaders who were managing the strike, since they would know who had most need. The goods and money were gratefully received but the men were still angry that the workers of Thornton Mill wouldn't join them in the strike.

"It's right good of you to give us charity," Sean Middleton, one of the union leaders said, his voice dripping with sarcasm. "Just a shame your master couldn't see fit to help."

Having endured comments like that for the past three days as he delivered goods, Nicholas finally snapped. He grabbed Middleton by his collar and slammed him into the wall.

"All you see is your plight, isn't it? You don't look at the bigger picture, don't stand back and see the damage you're doing to good, working men!"

"What, men like you?" he scoffed.

"NO! Men like John Boucher, God rest his soul. We drove that man mad with the last strike and left his kiddies with no one in the world, but I learned my lesson. There's two sides to every story and often a lot that you don't know about."

"Like what?"

Nicholas wanted nothing more than to hit this man but he wouldn't reduce himself to that level. Taking a deep breath, he released him and stepped away.

"Like my master, Thornton. Because of his position, he can't be seen to help you, to sympathise with your plight, but this whole thing was his wife's idea, collecting and organising all this stuff. She wanted to do it herself but knew she couldn't. And that money you and your pals were so pleased to receive the other day? Hundred pound of it were Thornton's, given to me by the man himself!"

Higgins regretted those words the moment he had spoken

them. He looked around the three union leaders as he spoke.

"You repeat that to anyone, and not only will I deny it, I'll swing for ya myself. You got that?"

Another union leader, Billy Ruskin came forward and shook Higgins's hand.

"You have my word it won't leave this room. And tell your master and your friends, we appreciate the help. I don't know how much longer this strike is going to go on for, but things are gettin' desperate."

"Aye," Higgins agreed. "We'll do what we can for ya."

"Thank you." Billy walked Higgins out into the street and they stood there for a moment, watching the misery around them.

"Some Christmas this is going to be," Billy said with a resigned sigh.

"Aye." Higgins agreed. "You don't think masters'll yield before then?"

Billy took a deep breath and let it out as a long sigh while he considered the question.

"Doubt it."

"Is there no way you can go back?"

"We can go back," Billy said. "But masters have said we'll have to take lower wages still. We couldn't live on t' last pay cut, children are dying and we need to put a stop to it. A fair wage for a fair day's work. Do you know that if we do go back, now we won't even get sixty percent of what your Thornton pays."

Higgins knew that, of course, he just didn't want it to be true.

"Aye. Best of luck to you."

They shook hands and Higgins left.

In early December the third phase of housing was completed and Thornton's Mill was able to expand again hiring a further seven hundred workers. Unfortunately this didn't help matters and only increased the disquiet that those still working in the Milton mills felt.

Christmas was a subdued affair for most people that year as even those who could afford to celebrate were unwilling to show extravagance in light of so much suffering. Many hoped that the new year would bring happy news but things only got worse as an outbreak of cholera began to sweep through Milton.

Albert was rushed off his feet, trying to help people but as he explained to anyone who would listen, the outbreak was likely due to polluted water and until Milton had decent sanitation, cholera outbreaks would continue.

Children were the worst affected with most of those who caught it, dying. The population grew even angrier and on the fourth day of the outbreak, when yet another young child had perished, the mill hands had reached breaking point and rioting broke out.

It would later be estimated that approximately three to four hundred men took part in the riots and the police were severely outnumbered. Though the violence only lasted for one day, more than enough destruction was caused in that short time. Private homes of the wealthy and powerful were ransacked and looted while factories, mills and official buildings were badly damaged before the local regiment of soldiers was finally able to quell the rioters. When the dust finally settled, Milton was a broken town.

The only good thing about the riot was that the well, which Albert believed to be responsible for the outbreak, had it's pump so badly damaged that it was unusable. New cases of the disease grew fewer every day, but the damage had already been done. Between them, the rioting and the cholera outbreak claimed over two hundred lives in the space of a week and a further fifty men were arrested and put on trial for their actions during the riot.

Silently, and with typical northern stoicism, the town set about restoring itself. The mills that were able to, reopened and the hands returned to work, their spirits well and truly broken. Those mills that weren't able to reopen set about filing insurance claims and replacing their damaged machinery.

The whole town swept, scrubbed, brushed, painted, washed and repaired until a month later the only real signs of the horrific events that had occurred was the mourning dress and black arm bands worn by so many who had lost loved ones.

The residents of Thornton Village looked on in shock and horror at what had occurred. They were angry at the authorities that wouldn't look beyond the actions of the rioters to see the troubles that were brewing beneath. A petition was started and over seven thousand people from Milton and the surrounding villages signed it. Some of the convicts had their sentences commuted to prison or transportation but two, those deemed to be the ring leaders, were hanged in a public execution outside the gaol.

At the end of January, Edward and Eleanor Maitland were invited to dinner with the Thorntons and Albert at Rose Cottage. Over dinner Edward announced that he had finally been moved by the riots to take action.

"As you know, there is a by-election coming up in Milton and I have decided to run for parliament," he said once they had retired to the drawing room.

Against the usual social etiquette, the women had not split off to go to the sitting room.

"I've had enough of Londoners thinking they know what's best for us and as much as I dislike government, I have come to the conclusion that the only way to change things is from the inside."

"I think it's a marvellous idea," Margaret said. She she knew him to be a good man and that he had been striving for something worthwhile to occupy him since he retired. "You shall have our vote, sir."

"Thank you."

"Which party will you run for?" Margaret asked.

"I thought the Whigs. They have done much good in recent years with abolishing slavery and trying to redistribute power away from the aristocracy, plus they seem to have a better understanding of both industry and country life," Edward explained. Knowing his friend's distaste for parliament, Edward looked to John to see what he though of this madcap scheme.

John considered his old friend for a long moment before he finally smiled. "Aye, I think that's a grand idea."

"Well, one thing is for certain," Eleanor joked. "He certainly can't be any worse for Milton than our last MP."

They raised their glasses in a toast and John vowed to do what he could to help his friend.

Albert had many questions and suggestions for Edward, who after five minutes held his hand up in defeat.

"Let me get elected first, lad," he laughed.

"I'm sorry." Albert looked abashed and smiled sheepishly. "I just see so many wrongs in this world that need righting."

"Then perhaps you should run," Edward suggested.

"I'm needed on the ground," he said, though he sounded

regretful. "Still, perhaps if you do manage to drive through some social reforms, I can find the time to run."

"Albert works entirely too hard," Fanny said. She hardly ever spoke when conversation turned to news or politics so everyone was surprised to hear from her. "You should see him, always running about helping this person or that person. Why, during the cholera outbreak and the riots I though he would work himself into an early grave!"

John smiled at his sister's loyalty.

"Indeed," Edward agreed. "I have heard many good things about our young doctor here."

"Mr and Mrs Maitland are among my rather few donors," Albert explained to Fanny.

"Well in that case, I will vote for you too," Fanny told Edward, leaving the others looking at each other, wondering if Fanny even realised that she did not have her own vote.

Margaret took a sip of her wine to try and hide her smile, for really, Fanny was making such an effort to improve herself that it was rather mean to laugh at her.

Chapter Forty Six

"Margaret, how lovely it is to see you," Fanny said, bustling into the sitting room and placing a quick kiss on her sister-in-law's cheek. She rushed to Malcolm and kissed his cheek, then patted Bessy on the head. "You must excuse my excitement but I have had a marvellous idea, although I shall need your help with it."

Margaret gestured for Fanny to take a seat as she replied. "Of course."

"Wonderful!" Fanny's smile was radiant. "I told Albert you would help."

Jenny decided that now would probably be a good time for Scone and the children to have their afternoon walk and said as much, offering to take Rosie with them. While she liked walking her dog, Margaret sensed that she might be here quite some time so handed the pup over to Jenny.

"Perhaps you would be kind enough to ask the kitchen for some tea on your way out," Margaret asked Jenny.

"Of course, Mrs. T." Jenny smiled and left the room with the children and dogs in tow.

Margaret turned her attention back to her sister in law.

"I will be happy to help you, Fanny, but perhaps you might like to tell me what this idea is and how I might be of service?" There was no malice in her words, indeed she took pleasure in seeing Fanny so jovial.

"Oh! Of course, I am sorry. I am quite too excited to keep a thought in my head today."

Jane entered then with the tea tray and Margaret poured while Fanny began her tale.

"Well, last week I was having tea with Mrs. Mercheston and she was saying how she and Mrs. Richardson had been reminiscing about the grand balls that used to be given in Milton and how the modern occasions are not a patch on those from their heydays. Though to be fair, if everything I hear about Mrs. Richardson's joints is true, there is no way she could be fit for dancing. She suffers from terrible gout, or so I've been told. But that is beside the point."

Margaret smiled. Despite all the improvements in her character of late, Fanny still loved gossip and probably always would. For some reason Margaret now found it endearing rather than intrusive as she once had.

"The conversation got me thinking," Fanny continued.

"Albert is always looking for new ways to raise money for his clinic and it occurred to me that I might organise a ball and sell tickets to it."

"A charity ball?"

"Exactly."

"I should be very happy to help you organise it." Margaret smiled.

"Oh, no!" Fanny cried, as though the idea was ludicrous.

Margaret tried not to take offence at that.

"What I mean, is that I am looking forward to organising it."

"Then how can I be of assistance?"

"Well, truth be told I am a little wary that people will not come. It is only two months after the riots and Milton is not exactly known for its philanthropy. I am worried that the concept might offend some people."

"Given how low an opinion most Milton manufacturers have of me, I hardly see how including me will help your cause."

"Well, this is what I was thinking. You have spent many years in London and must surely know all sorts of grand people. I hope that if we can get someone rich or famous to come, then that will tempt more of Milton society to attend."

"Oh, Fanny, it has been many years since I kept any company in London besides my family."

"But you must know someone," she cried.

Margaret bit into a ginger biscuit as she thought, a frown line marring her smooth forehead.

"I suppose I could ask Mr Gilbert," she mused. "He is well known."

"Mr Gilbert?"

"Robert Gilbert," Margaret clarified. "He is a writer."

"You don't mean R.H. Gilbert, do you?"

"Yes. He was a friend of Mr Bell's from Oxford, and to a lesser extent, my father. I haven't seen him for many years now and we really only exchange letters at Christmas time, but he is intrigued with the village we have built here and has mentioned coming to visit a few times now. Perhaps I could persuade him to coincide a visit with your ball."

"Oh, that would be marvellous!" Fanny said. "Although I suppose I ought to try reading some of his books before I meet him."

"Yes, that might be a good idea." Margaret laughed that Fanny clearly held him in high esteem even though she had never read his work for herself. "So, when did you plan on having this ball?" she asked.

"Oh, I had not given much thought to dates yet. I suppose I will need time or organise everything, then sell tickets. Perhaps in April? Two months should be enough time, don't you think?"

"Probably, but the baby is due in April, so if you require my help for anything other then tempting someone famous, I won't be much help to you by then."

"Oh yes." Fanny bit her lower lip as she considered the dilemma. "Well let's us have it in May then. You will be recovered by then, I hope?" Her tone implied that she had better be.

"Yes, I expect so," Margaret said, trying to suppress her grin. She supposed that Fanny could find worse ways to occupy her time and she wanted to be supportive.

"It is such a shame I will still have to wear black," Fanny sighed, looking down at her black dress. "I know mother wore black for years but it really doesn't suit me."

"Well, you will surely be in half mourning by then, perhaps you could wear something in lavender?"

"That is a very good point," Fanny grinned though it faded after a moment or two. "Though I shall still not be allowed to dance."

"But as hostess your duty is to look after your guests anyway, so perhaps that is not such a big disappointment."

"Of course. We threw many parties while Watson was alive and I am an excellent hostess."

"I don't doubt it." Margaret's smile grew tight as she remembered how few of these parties she and John had been invited to.

"Oh, this will be fabulous! I am very much looking forward to it."

"Well, I hope it works well for you. I shall write to Mr Gilbert once you have decided on a date and see if he would like to come."

Unfortunately Fanny's organisational skills, while good from a hostess's perspective, were atrocious from a businessman's (or woman's) perspective. She had simply gone about booking places and services without taking into account the costs. The first Margaret knew of this was when she visited her mother-in-law one weekday afternoon. Hannah had been helping Fanny but only yesterday had she been allowed access to the paperwork. Once Hannah had calculated the costs involved it showed that Fanny would be making a substantial loss!

"But is she not asking for discounts from the vendors?" Margaret asked, shocked that Fanny had not considered the implications of cost.

"No. For someone who is trying to organise a charity ball, she seems remarkably unwilling to accept what she calls charity!"

Margaret rolled her eyes. "We can't let her lose money. Either Albert's clinic will be forced to pay, which he can ill afford, or John will be lumbered with the bill."

"Exactly," Hannah agreed. "Which is why I have compiled a list of suppliers we must visit. I have divided it into two in the hope that you might share the task with me."

"Of course," Margaret agreed.

"Thank you. Today though, I think that we should go to the Mitre Hotel together. The hire of the ballroom is the single biggest expense and we will be better placed to negotiate a lower price if he thinks he will be upsetting the wives of two rich, local businessmen."

Margaret smiled, impressed by her devious line of thought.

"Then let us go and see him now. I got to know the manager a little when I first returned to Milton and we have been friendly ever since."

Hannah offered her arm to Margaret and together, with Rosie trotting behind, they set off at a brisk walk to the Mitre Hotel, where they proceeded to flatter, cajole and browbeat a hotel manager into letting his ballroom for free!

"Margaret," Hannah smiled as they left. "I had no idea you had such feminine wiles at your disposal," she teased.

"Well I confess, I only use them in aid of a good cause."

Over the next two weeks they visited every supplier to Fanny's event, from the caterers to the florist to the band and many others. Those that would not be beaten down on price were promptly fired, with Hannah spinning Fanny a tall tale or two about them being difficult and needing to be let go.

Slowly things began to come together.

Margaret insisted Fanny wait until she had conformation

from Mr Gilbert before she announced his attendance to the world, and in true Margaret style, she confessed everything to him in her original letter requesting his presence. Though he had a few questions in his return letter which Margaret happily answered, he finally agreed to come and visit her and attend her sister in laws 'infernal party' as he called it.

He was to stay for two weeks though because he also wanted to speak with the locals and understand what exactly had happened during the riots, for although he was a fiction writer, his books often dealt with social reform and the issues facing the working classes and the poor.

In March, Edward Maitland won the by-election for Milton and took his seat in parliament.

That same month, Margaret and John gave the go ahead for the final stage of building to begin in the village. It was a long project this time, taking at least three years to complete, possibly longer if there were any setbacks. It really was too early to be liquidating more assets, especially after the damage the previous year had done to the financial markets, but given how long the development would take to finish, they thought it possible to take a risk. Besides, they both wanted to be doing something tangible to help Milton and offering more decent jobs and homes was the only thing within their power.

Aside from her morning sickness lasting rather a long while this time, Margaret's pregnancy proceeded with relative ease and in April, she went into labour.

Albert attended the birth, but more because John was so anxious than because Margaret needed him and at six thirty three on the Monday evening, Margaret gave birth to a handsome baby boy.

While Dixon took him to be washed, Margaret took the opportunity to do the same, then enjoy a nice cup of tea in bed with her husband. By the time Dixon returned with the boy, Margaret was growing tired but she roused herself enough to give him his first feed, shielding her modesty with a shawl.

Finally Bessy was allowed to see her mother and, caring nought for her mother's recent ordeal, ran in and jumped up on the bed, eager to see her new brother.

"He's very pink, Mummy," she declared.

"He will get less pink as he ages," she assured Bessy.

Bessy, having been denied access to her mother all day, and finally recognising the tiredness in her mother's eyes, laid herself down beside her Margaret and gave her a cuddle, much as her mother did for Bessy when she was tired.

Propped up on pillows, with her husband sitting to her right, Margaret finally succumbed to sleep, her head resting on John's shoulder. The baby was clutched firmly to her breast, his head resting on her shoulder and, having had a large meal, not to mention a rather tough day himself, he too was sound asleep. Laid out beside Margaret, Bessy had her head buried in Margaret's stomach while her father, the only one who seemed to be awake, gazed in adoration at his family. Even Rosie had gotten in on the action and lay curled at her mistress's feet, sound asleep. John didn't have the heart to send her off the bed.

Dixon turned and took in the scene before her, nudging Jenny to look as well. They shared a smile, for such a scene of domestic bliss was rare, even between those as in love as the Thorntons. They didn't have the heart to remove the baby from his mother, nor even to chastise the dog for this overly familiar behaviour.

Though John sent them away so that he might enjoy this moment with his family, they stayed close in case they were needed.

Margaret awoke about an hour later to find herself surrounded by love, literally. Bessy and the baby still slept soundly, though John smiled warmly when she turned to him.

"You must be sore," she whispered. "Sitting so long in one position."

John placed a feather-light kiss on her lips. "Not in the slightest. How could I move and disturb such a beautiful scene?"

Margaret smiled at him. "I suppose we must decide on a name soon."

They had discussed many possibilities for both girls and boys, but no formal decisions had been made.

"Do you have a preference?" he asked.

Margaret thought for a moment, considering all the boys names she could remember.

"I think Alexander was my favourite," she confessed.

"Why?" he asked.

"Because Alexander the Great built a mighty empire, and like his father, I want our son to build himself an empire based on your legacy."

"Our legacy," he corrected her. "But how could I argue with reasoning like that. Alexander it is."

They spent the rest of the evening in their room, eating dinner up there with Bessy, until fatigue once again caught up with Margaret. Dixon removed Alexander to the nursery while Jenny readied Bessy for bed and Margaret fell into a deep and refreshing sleep.

She recovered much more quickly from this birth than she had from the first, though she stayed at home for two days before returning to work. She kept her work hours light for the first week, simply wanting to make sure that everything had been done and that there were no problems.

She was amazed at the progress Thomas had made since he was first taken on, soon after she returned to Milton. He had matured into a fine young man who was quite at home in his role as accountant and not afraid to argue his point if need be. Margaret had complete confidence that he could cope in her absence, but she still liked to check, just in case! Thomas understood her perfectionist tendencies and liked her company, so he didn't feel undermined by her checking up.

Thanks to increasing the staff at the end of the previous year, John was also able to spend a great deal more time at home than he would usually, enjoying his new son, though they were both of them were very careful not to make Bessy feel neglected.

Chapter Forty Seven

Thanks to her morning sickness, Margaret hadn't gained as much weight with this pregnancy and as she took to walking the hills and fields with baby Alex and Bessy as soon as she was able, it soon fell off so that by the time Robert Gilbert arrived, to be greeted by Margaret with Alex clutched in her arms, he was hard pressed to believe that Margaret had given birth just three weeks ago.

Margaret laughed as he said as much.

"Ah, thankfully the ladies of the north are a good deal hardier than those from the south," she smiled. "Which I must say is very liberating." She kissed his cheek in welcome then showed him up to his room.

"I'll leave you to unpack. Come and find me in the back sitting room when you're finished and I shall have tea ready and waiting to refresh you after your journey."

Robert considered himself to be a man of the world but the sight of this genteel southern lady walking around with her child on her hip like any common washer woman, was enough to surprise even him. He could tell that she kept her child with her out of love rather than necessity though, and he found that endearing. Though childless himself, his sister had practically left her children to be raised by the servants.

When he joined Margaret half an hour later, she was cradling the baby in her arms, talking nonsense to him, though she rang the bell when he appeared and had the nanny take the boy away for a while.

"So, how was your journey?" she asked as she poured him a cup of tea.

"Most satisfactory. I was able to take the train most of the way, which is so much smoother than a horse and carriage over long distances."

"Yes indeed. Though generally maligned, I find that industry is doing much to improve our country," she agreed. "And before I forget, I want to thank you personally for agreeing to attend this charity ball. My sister Fanny is somewhat flighty but the cause is a good one and I should very much like for this event to be a success."

"Think nothing of it, my dear. You are not the only well known do-gooders in Milton, for Albert Townsend and his free clinic are also making quite a name for themselves."

"I am glad of it," Margaret smiled. "As a matter of fact, he is running his clinic in the village today. Perhaps when you are refreshed we might walk into the village and I could introduce you."

"A wonderful idea," he agreed.

Over dinner that evening, Robert proved to be just as entertaining a story teller in person as he was in his literature, regaling Margaret, John, Fanny and Albert with stories from his travels, his work, his family and his acquaintances. Margaret suspected that some tales were embellished, but it did not lessen her enjoyment of them.

"So how do you and Margaret come to know each other?" Albert asked over dessert.

"Ah, well I met Margaret when she was just a girl and when I heard that she was an orphan, I felt compelled to reach out to her again."

"Come now, Mr Gilbert," Margaret chided. "I think we both know that isn't quite true."

Unexpectedly, Robert smiled. "Mr Bell was right, my dear, you are as sharp as a tack."

"Excuse me?" Fanny asked, clearly confused.

"I believe Mr Bell asked Mr Gilbert to keep a discreet eye on me after he passed away," Margaret explained.

"So he did. I had thought that you were none the wiser, though."

"Please," Margaret smiled. "A man I have only met once, and that more than ten years previously, suddenly wants to become my new pen friend?"

"And here I thought I was being very cunning and clever." Robert shrugged cheerfully. "It must be difficult to get away with anything when one has such an intelligent wife, hey Thornton?"

"Oh, I don't know," John smirked at Margaret. "She still hasn't guessed what I have bought her for her birthday."

"No," she admitted, trying to glare forbiddingly at him but only succeeding in looking amused. "And he is driving me slightly insane with all his teasing."

"But her birthday is not for another three weeks, almost," Fanny said, shocked that her brother should care enough to buy something so early. Watson had never shown that kind of affection towards her. Or she to him, if she was being honest. She looked over at Albert and wondered when his birthday was.

"Let's just say, her gift will take some time to be prepared," John said, enjoying the exasperated look his wife was wearing.

"At this rate I shall no longer care by the time my birthday arrives."

"Oh, I think you will."

A part of Margaret wanted to wipe his smug look off his face but the other half, the stronger half, wanted to kiss him for this delightful torture he made her endure every year. Were she a weaker woman, she might already have searched the house in search of his gift but she couldn't deny him the pleasure of seeing her face when she finally received her present.

Mr Gilbert watched the couple with interest, for he had rarely seen two people quite so in love, nor two people of standing who were so in love that they were quite so willing to thumb their nose at convention. It pleased him immensely to witness it for though he had never experienced true love himself, he knew how important it was and frequently wrote about it.

Over the next few days John showed Mr Gilbert around the mill, the village, introduced him to some of the workers who might be willing to share their experiences with him and then left him to his own devices, content to see him at dinner every evening.

Nicholas took him into Milton on the Sunday and introduced him to the one surviving union leader who had not been arrested or hanged, and over the next week he went into Milton most days to speak with the locals, the police and the militia about the riot.

By the following weekend his pocketbook was crammed with notes, facts and material which gave him many ideas for his his books and stories. So much so that he found as the Saturday of the charity ball arrived, he did not begrudge attending in the least. He was due to return to Oxford on the Wednesday and his head was brimming with new stories that were just itching to be told. Attending one ball seemed like a small price to pay.

He and Mr Thornton had also got along surprisingly well considering that one was an educated gentleman while the other was a rough-hewn manufacturer. Each found the other to be most open minded, with Mr Gilbert as keen to learn about matters of business as Mr Thornton was to discuss the classics or literature late into the night.

Margaret found that she was rather less happy about attending the ball than Mr Gilbert, but she knew that she should support Fanny. She didn't so much mind socialising, she was used to that and could manage one evening. What she wasn't looking forward to was wearing her evening gown.

Modern fashions for evening wear had ladies in short sleeves and Margaret was horribly aware of the disfiguring scar on her arm. Though now completely healed, the tissue was mottled with light and dark patches and the flesh sadly lacking on that part of her arm, as though a chunk had been cut away. She didn't so much mind people seeing it, but she would mind the disgust that the 'ladies' present would show at such a grievous wound.

She had managed to pair one of her evening gowns with a similar shade shawl, but she could not find a way to keep her scar covered by it. She and Dixon had even tried sewing a wrist band and attaching the shawl to it, but as soon as she raised her arm to dance, the shawl had fallen off her shoulders and the scar had been visible.

But there was little else for it. Dixon had some white lead power which they were going to try and use to help cover it, but Margaret wasn't hopeful of achieving brilliant results.

Dixon was just styling her hair when John came in to the bedroom. She smiled at him in the mirror, knowing how upset Dixon would be if she moved from her current position.

"I like your hair like that," John said, coming to stand beside them. Dixon was pinning each curl to the crown on Margaret's head, leaving a few well places tendrils of course, and placing tiny light green roses through out. "Though I do think that the colour of those roses will have to be rethought."

"They match Miss Margaret's dress," Dixon said stiffly, feeling slightly insulted at the implication.

"I think these will do much better," he said, withdrawing a box from his coat pocket and opening it to reveal a number of small, pale blue satin roses.

Dixon huffed so Margaret turned to look.

"They are beautiful but they are completely the wrong shade for my dress," Margaret smiled at him, hoping he wasn't upset.

"Are you sure," he asked.

"Positive," she assured him.

John frowned. "Where is this dress?"

Margaret turned back to the mirror so that Dixon could continue. "It is the one in the large closet, in the white garment cover."

John went into the closet and emerged with the dress, currently obscured by it's protective covering which John began to remove.

"This dress?" he asked, showing it to her.

"No, not that one." Margaret looked into the mirror, getting a little frustrated with this inane conversation. "Excuse me, Dixon."

She got up and went into the closet herself, but he appeared to have taken the correct hanger out.

"That is most odd," Margaret said. "I know I put the dress back here after I looked at it."

"Maybe you will like this one better," John said.

Margaret stilled and rolled her eyes at her stupidity, her frustration evaporating in an instant. This was one of John's games.

"What have you done with my dress?" she asked, emerging with a playful smile on her face.

"It's gone. This is the only garment you will need tonight," he said, holding the dress out towards her.

Margaret accepted the garment and held the hanger up to better see it.

It was a pale blue silk with a fitted bodice and no sleeves. It was very pretty but not vastly different from her original dress.

"What are these?" Margaret asked, fingering two tubes of material that were also attached to the hanger.

John took one from the hanger and, holding Margaret's arm out, ran the tube of material along the arm until it was a few inches below her shoulder. He then fastened it using a small lace which tied at the back. The end at her wrist was wide and bell shaped, hanging elegantly down as she raised her arm.

"Happy birthday," he said, kissing her cheek.

Margaret had told him nothing of her discomfort about revealing the scar in public yet somehow he had known.

"Oh, John, this is so thoughtful."

He smiled, delighted with her praise.

"How on earth did you manage this?" she asked.

"Simple, I paid a visit to Mrs Dawson and told her of your

dilemma. She suggested the detachable sleeves and already had your measurements on file, though the corset is laced since she thought your measurements might be slightly different after having just given birth.

She stopped wondering when he had found the time to do all this and simply turned to him and wrapped him in a loving embrace.

"I love it," she said.

She could happily have spent the rest of the evening in his embrace but Dixon's polite cough reminded her that she had better get ready. She kissed him then stepped out of his arms.

"Thank you," she said again.

"My pleasure." He left Dixon to replace the roses in Margaret's hair, taking his own suit into the dressing room to change before going down to wait with Mr Gilbert for Margaret to finish getting ready.

When she finally came into the parlour, she looked radiant. The dress complimented her complexion and the sleeves hid her disfigurement. Indeed, anyone looking at her now would think she lived a life of indulgence at the Royal Court, not that she spent her days toiling in a Darkshire cotton mill.

John and Mr Gilbert both stood up as she entered and admired her for a moment, before John stepped forward.

"You look enchanting," he said.

"Indeed," Mr Gilbert agreed. "You will be quite the belle of the ball, I am sure."

Margaret blushed at their praise and allowed John to help her into her summer cloak. He then offered her his arm and they headed out to the carriage.

"You must save me a dance," John said as they journeyed into Milton.

"Don't be silly, I shall have more than enough space on my dance card for all of you."

"I fear your husband is right," Mr Gilbert added. "Once those gentlemen get a look at you, you shall be hard pressed to find space for us."

Margaret smiled politely but she knew better. Even supposing she was considered handsome, her reputation as an independent woman was enough to make her distasteful to most men in Milton society.

Before going into the ballroom, John delivered Margaret to the ladies room so that she might remove her cloak and collect her dance card while he and Mr Gilbert headed to the gentlemen's dressing room to remove their coats and, on this occasion, pay for their tickets.

John had expected to pay for Mr Gilbert's ticket since he was their guest but while they waited for Margaret earlier he had stated that he should like to buy his own ticket. John now saw why, for when he asked another gentleman how much the tickets were, and was told they were ten pounds, with a dramatic eye roll and a sigh, Mr Gilbert looked shocked.

"Ten pounds? Is that all?" he demanded, handing forty over instead. "This is for charity, ten pounds hardly salves my Christian conscience!"

Not wanting to look bad in the eyes of this respected author, all the other men present began handing over extra money. John smiled to himself as he left. Mr. Gilbert was a canny old man!

He waited outside the ladies dressing room for Margaret and was soon joined by Mr. Gilbert, with whom he shared a knowing smile. When Margaret finally joined them, both John and Mr. Gilbert escorted her into the ballroom, one gentleman on each arm.

Fanny was waiting just inside the ballroom and was greeting everyone as they entered and making introductions.

"How is the attendance?" Margaret asked.

"Oh, very good. I did hear a few people turn their noses up at the idea of paying for a ball but when they heard that Mr Gilbert was to attend, they soon changed their minds."

"Good," Margaret smiled. "Is Albert here yet?"

"Oh yes, he is in the ballroom talking with some of the gentlemen. He believes some of the guests might be interested in making a donation to his clinic, so he is eager to make himself amenable."

"Indeed. And might I say, you look wonderful, Fanny. Lilac is a lovely shade on you."

"Oh! Thank you." She looked behind Margaret to see Mr and Mrs Slickson entering. Margaret knew from Fanny's expression that she had been dismissed. She saw that John was talking with Mr Hamper so she rejoined Mr Gilbert who was waiting for her a few paces away and together they made their way around the ballroom.

As they mingled, Margaret received dance invitations from Edward Maitland, Mr Whitaker and of course, Mr Gilbert.

When she opened her dance card, she saw that John had already filled his name into the first set. Unfortunately etiquette determined that she wouldn't be allowed to dance any other sets with him, though part of her wished that he had filled his name in for every dance.

Margaret could see that many of the women present would have liked to dance with John, but when they met up after half an hour, he had only asked for dances with his mother, Eleanor Maitland and two wives of the other Mill masters, both of whom were old enough to be his mother.

Poor Mr Gilbert had hardly received a moment's peace since they entered the ballroom and though Margaret knew that he could be curmudgeonly at times, he was the very epitome of charm this evening, saving his few snide comments to whisper to her once his companions had departed. He asked a fair few ladies to dance, all of them young enough to be his daughters but no one refused him.

When the first set of dances began, John took Margaret's hand and led her to the dance floor. She had been right, no one outside of their group of friends had asked her to dance, which he found most odd. He thought that even if he had been a stranger who had been told all about her reputation, once he saw her he felt that there was no force on earth that would have prevented him from asking her to dance.

Thankfully Margaret didn't appear to feel slighted by her lack of invitations but welcomed the respite from dancing so that she might talk with her friends. Once the second set had finished, they made their way to the tables for supper. Thanks in no small part to Hannah Thornton managing the seating chart, their table was with The Maitlands and the Whitakers, Mr Whitaker's sister, Mary and Mr Gilbert making up the eight.

Margaret asked Hannah where Fanny was, concerned that she would be on her own.

"I seated her and Albert with the Nicholsons, the Smithsons and the Reynolds."

Margaret smiled, knowing full well that those three were the richest families in the room. Dinner was a most enjoyable affair since they were among friends but eventually it had to end and the dancing resume. Margaret took a turn with Mr Whitaker and Mr Gilbert but after that was content to return to her table and watch the festivities with Hannah.

It might not have been very polite but one of Margaret's favourite pastimes was people watching. Their interactions, their body language, their often exaggerated expressions fascinated her, and it was an interest she had been delighted to find that her mother-in-law shared.

At ten o'clock they decided to leave since it was never good form to stay too late at a ball. Two gentlemen stood by the exit with collection boxes, which once again Mr Gilbert made a grand show of donating to.

"You really didn't have to do that," Margaret said as they climbed into the carriage.

"Nonsense, the cause is a good one. I may as well donate publicly and hope others follow suit than do so behind closed doors."

"You are very kind," Margaret smiled at him.

"It is you two who have been most kind and generous to me. I believe I have been living the middle class life for too long. I have forgotten what true struggle is and you two have allowed me to rediscover something dear to my heart, as well as my charitable spirit."

"I hardly think we can take credit for your charity," John smiled.

"Of course you can. Your enterprise here has shown me that not only that it is possible to make a real difference in peoples' lives but that all the poor and downtrodden really want is an opportunity, not a handout. I am most impressed with your endeavours and should you ever have any difficulties, I hope you will come to me so that I can assist you in whatever way is necessary."

Impulsively, Margaret leaned over and kissed him on the cheek.

"You know, in all the time we have been doing this, I don't believe anyone has summed up our endeavours quite as succinctly as you just did." She smiled as she sat back down next to her husband.

"Well, I am a writer," he smiled.

Mr Gilbert removed a hip flask from his coat and detached three silver shot cups that sat atop the lid. He poured a generous measure of whisky into each and handed one to Margaret and one to John.

John raised his cup. "Here's to succinct southerners!" he teased.

Mr Gilbert raised his glass. "Here's to northern enterprise!"

Margaret raised her glass as her free hand sought John's and squeezed gently. "Here's to being given an opportunity."

They clinked glasses and quickly drank the spirit down.

The End

About the Author

Cat Winchester was born in East Anglia. After her wanderlust finally abated, she settled in Edinburgh with her family and three dogs.

Other Books by Catherine Winchester

Hope for Tomorrow
What You Wish For

<u>Past Series</u>
Past Due
Half Past
Past Life

Printed in Great Britain
by Amazon

52148641R00203